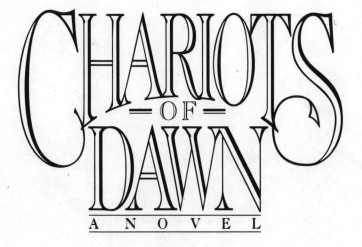

CHARIOTS OF DAWN

A NOVEL

KAY STEWART

Thomas Nelson
Nashville

Copyright © 1991 by Kay Stewart.

Published in Nashville, Tennessee, by Thomas
Nelson, Inc., and distributed in Canada by Lawson
Falle, Ltd., Cambridge, Ontario.

Library of Congress Cataloging-in-Publication Data

Stewart, Kay L.
    Chariots of dawn / Kay Stewart.
        p.   cm.
    ISBN 0-8407-3343-7
    1. Church history—Primitive and early church, ca. 30-600-
-Fiction. I. Title.
PS3569.T465254C48   1991
813'.54—dc20   91–26229
                                                            CIP

Printed in the United States of America
    2 3 4 5 6 7—96 95 94 93 92

To E. J. and Mabel Stewart—earth knows no finer love than theirs—and to their son, Don, my husband, whose loving support made this book possible

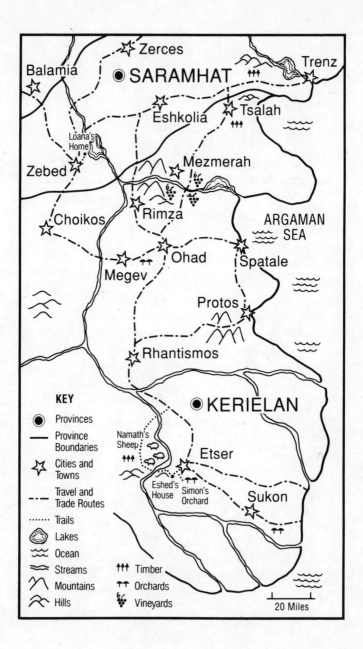

Zerces
Balamia
SARAMHAT
Trenz
Eshkolia
Tsalah
Loana's Home
Mezmerah
Zebed
ARGAMAN SEA
Choikos
Rimza
Ohad
Spatale
Megev
Protos
Rhantismos
KERIELAN

KEY

◉ Provinces
— Province Boundaries
✫ Cities and Towns
–·–· Travel and Trade Routes
······ Trails
🌀 Lakes
〰 Ocean
〜 Streams
⋀ Mountains
⌒ Hills

Namath's Sheep
Etser
Eshed's House   Simon's Orchard
Sukon

††† Timber
†† Orchards
🍇 Vineyards

20 Miles

PROLOGUE

Sun seeped gold onto the low rim of black hills across the bay and spilled belated warmth into the icy water that separated the shores of a rock-bound cove. Blackened, water-soaked shafts of wood stuck in the sand, forming a jagged lacework against the sky. A moan came from beneath the splinters, and a matted head with mud-encrusted locks reared painfully to squint at the sun's first rays.

Eshed shivered. His clothes had been all but torn from his back during the splintery ride to shore. Bruised to the bone, he stirred. All of his limbs worked. He pulled himself painfully to his feet and viewed the glassy surface of the water for signs of life . . . *so still* . . . all of the turbulence of the previous night swept clean.

Slowly he picked his way through mud and over rocks, poking under wood piles, hugging his frame against a cold morning wind. He was alone. There was no question. *Alone.* His mind pushed the thought away, but it returned as surely as the cold wind that wrapped his body and spun grit into his eyes. Fear of the elements clutched his throat. A tear traveled down his blood-stained face. Everything he saw suggested wild, uninhabited country. Where would he go? He would have to find shelter from the chill winter wind soon . . . and food . . . to strengthen him for thinking. The sticky open wound in his head throbbed beneath his testing fingertips. Sand stung his cuts, whipped by the wind that cloaked him. After ten years of living, his body was all that was left to him.

The boy's legs wobbled and threatened to give way as he climbed a sandy knoll. He paused to reestablish his footing. He plunged on and, topping the crest at last, sought a pathway through the small scrub oaks and scant tree cover that separated him from an unknown countryside. Minutes collected into an hour of confusion and stumbling before he spotted a small building through the growth. Feeling a surge of hope, he rubbed his hands on cold arms and moved closer, looking for signs of life. He found a narrow path leading to a gate post and leaned against it to catch his breath. His palm struck an indentation and he pulled away to discover something etched in stone. A fish shape stood in relief with a single word chiseled alongside: *Checed*. The name of the occupant of the small house? Shakily he found the door and pulled a cord of bells that hung to one side. He heard a shuffling within and his head swam with the waiting. Foggily he watched a robust man swing open the door. Eshed tumbled across the sill and the floor met him.

"Pala!" The man knelt beside him. A woman tending a fire in the rear of the room hurried to his side. "There was a shipwreck in the bay. . . . This must be a survivor."

Eshed's eyes blinked wide and he struggled to sit up. The man helped him, and Pala brought a quilt, wrapped him in it, and urged him to the fire.

"I . . . I am Eshed," he stuttered gratefully. "I am the survivor . . . only me." He shivered violently and tears filled his eyes. The big man gathered young Eshed in his arms.

"I am Checed . . . the stone mason, and this is my wife, Pala."

The woman, tall and sturdy, smiled and took Eshed's hand, warming it between her own. "You may stay with us as long as you like," she said.

It was this sequence, as later Eshed looked back, that gave him the understanding that he had been pulled from the water's icy grip for a special purpose. This would be a story much like any other except for another singular event in A.D. 33.

Throughout time there have been those who have responded to the call of God. Eshed is such a one. This, then, is the story of a son of God and his response to the power of Christ's purpose . . . after the Resurrection.

PART 1
CANDLES IN
THE WIND

I will search Jerusalem with lamps . . .
Zephaniah 1:12

CHAPTER 1

"Ho, there."

A commanding figure in a golden, wheel-spiked chariot flung one halting arm in front of Eshed, nearly toppling him from his horse. *Circans.*

He was making good time toward his appointment in Saramhat. This was no time for military gymnastics. A swift appraisal told him the centurion was not alone. Banked in shadow, another chariot moved slightly and three horse soldiers rested near their mounts in the midday sunshine.

Saramhat was not held by Circans. Why were they here blocking his way?

Eshed leaned toward Zerubabel's head as if to dismount and whispered a command in the horse's ear. Swiftly they were away, leaving the centurion open-mouthed. As he sped through the leafy glade, Eshed could hear swords being drawn and the commotion of soldiers mounting horses.

A thickly grown trail presented itself, and Eshed cut from the main road. "Head down," he commanded Zerubabel, clinging to his neck. Haste was important, but so were their eyes. The trail slowed them, and he heard the chariots enter the path behind him. He could hear the centurion swear as he encountered the brambly growth. Chariots were swift on an open plain but cumbersome in such foliage. Eshed could hear the slashing of the swords and the shrill nickering of the double-harnessed horses. He smiled.

Reins, harness, and spiked wheels would soon be helplessly mired in bramble.

Not daring to rest in thought, Eshed sped on. The horse soldiers would soon follow. He came to an open space and used it to advantage. If caught, he could be detained for days—or worse. Glancing back, he saw the horse soldiers invade the same pathway.

Circans! Known to be brutal and erratic, they were everywhere these days. Eshed felt no urge to parlay with them. Especially not now, not today!

The soldiers' horses were chosen from the swiftest and hardiest in the known world. Most were boated in to Protos from Amargania, a distant land whose horse breed was superior. Eshed's hope for outrunning them was bleak. *Steady, Zerubabel, steady . . . every step counts!* The horse was breathing heavily.

His heart pounding in his throat, Eshed seized upon an idea. He circled around behind the horsemen and took a little known trail. Steep and rocky, it took a mountainous route to Saramhat. Zerubabel was not as swift as he was nimble, and Eshed counted on the latter for advantage. As loose rocks kicked out from beneath them, he banked all hope on his faithful mount. Never had he asked more of him.

The incline was even worse than he remembered. But today it would serve. It had to!

The Circans' confusion at losing him so close in chase gave him the start he needed. But soon, too soon, they were pounding up the trail behind him. It would be a fight to the finish. But he would prevail. Someone was waiting for him in Saramhat.

Five whispering, tittering girls gaped at him from the

doorway as Eshed tugged a grimy tunic over his dark, thick, curly head of hair.

"Come in!" He gestured with a free hand, revealing a tanned set of muscular shoulders.

Clutching the brass handles of copper basins of hot water, they sidled past him, grinning to one another. It was obvious they thought him a well-favored young man with a fine profile and dark twinkling eye! He ducked behind a cloth-draped brass rod, forsaking their glances. He shook the dust from his muslin travel coat and placed it in a tall cedarwood closet. Tapping a few crusts of mud from his thonged sandals, he dropped them to the closet floor. *Five Circan soldiers, five maidens.* Danger had camped on his trail today. He grinned wryly. *Why are life's most precious, private moments invaded by strangers?*

The scent of roses and hyacinths wafted through the portal from the garden below. Steam rose from the bath being poured in the marble basin and with it the clean, sharp smell of herbs. Legs apart and arms crossed, Eshed gazed reflectively through the aperture. The face of his beloved came before his thoughtful eyes, and Eshed's spine tingled with anticipation. His hand stroked his jaw, the fingers trembling.

A clatter of sandals and a buzz of whispers took the girls from the room. He wrenched his girdle from about him, flung it on the floor beside his unwound turban, and eased into the massive, sunken tub.

Gratefully he basked in the silken water, soothing muscles knotted from the rigors of the road. He dipped his head back in the water and rested a moment. Slinging water from his hair, he blinked streams from his hazel eyes and felt the claws of tension release their hold. His head rested on two-winged gold seraphim that crowned the tub.

A clash of trays and tongues in the garden below jarred his musings. In a strange language, a servant was ordering the arrangement of trays of food in the garden portico. Huge flasks of winter wine were being prepared for his guests.

Visually he prepared his part in the day's festivities. The rehearsal of soft stringed music, pleasing in meter and tone, lulled him. Slowly he gathered himself from the tub, and as the water fell away from his body, he reached for a hefty gold-embroidered towel. He draped his lean body with the creped softness of a white, toga-style robe. A metal mirror on the closet wall reflected his effort to pull an ivory comb through thick, wet hair strands. The shoes prepared for him were a soft creamy leather, supportive at the sole but with many airy crevices on top. Never before had he seen any like them and probably would not again. After all, today was a singular day . . . his wedding day.

"Hold still, mistress!" Proustia's fingers pulled a wide silver wrap tight about Loana's slim waist, tying it in a disappearing knot behind her.

"We should have bound your hair first. I see that now!" The tiny sharp-featured servant pulled a wisp of dark, shining hair from the knot and draped it over Loana's shoulder. Her sea-blue eyes sparkled against the pale cream of her skin as the servant fluttered about her. Proustia flicked the crisping pin from Loana's hair and with sure fingers began layering the inky silk into a natural crown.

"Hurry, Proustia—I cannot be late! Father won't like it and neither will . . . Eshed." Her lips curved softly as she pronounced his name. How much did she really know about her groom? Too little really, but his impatience with scattered forces and late entrances were well known among his cohorts. Proustia had announced Eshed's breathless arrival on horseback a scant hour ago. Loana wondered if he was ready yet.

Eshed chose a hallway strutted with columns and moved silently across the dustless floor in search of an exit. It was a strange household to him, the priestly house of Jarad in Saramhat province, which adjoined his home province, Kerielan. As priest of Kerielan, he could not boast of a home as richly endowed as this one, but his dwelling had as its reputation the faithful rendering of the tenets of his God.

His eyes swept the veranda. Somewhere nearby, his bride was in preparation.

"Eshed!" He turned and saw a smiling Loana waving from an upper balcony, her dark hair cascading over the stone handrail. The deep dimple caressing her jaw was obvious even from afar. His hand gave a greeting as she was whisked back inside by Proustia, who was struggling to finish binding her hair. *Impulsive Loana*. Her whereabouts were supposed to remain secret and she was not to see him until the ceremony! A bride was a gift to be cherished and lingered over till the time came to reveal her. Anticipation hammered his ribs.

The first stairway he found led into the garden. His host had already entered the portico, and Eshed hurried to him.

"Eshed, my son," Jarad called to him. "Good timing. The guests are coming into the garden!" Jarad flashed an appreciative smile and clasped Eshed's shoulder. Turning, Jarad conferred with a servant who struggled under a large platter of delicacies.

Eyeing the colorful platter teetering on the young man's shoulder, Eshed plucked an olive and put it in his mouth. "So much food!" He spit the pit. "My purse is heavy. Do I contribute to this feast?"

"No, no. This is my pleasure. When a man has only one daughter and no sons, he must do it all!" he winked.

"But—"

"Eshed, you will have the expense of Loana from now on. Let me celebrate being rid of it!" Jarad chuckled, an elbow to Eshed's ribs. Eshed joined in laughter at Jarad's bit of bravado, for Loana had been his heart and sole purpose for so many years.

"Have a fig cake!" Jarad presented one from the platter.

"No . . . thank you . . . I'm much too excited to eat!"

Then Eshed spotted someone he knew. "Excuse me, Father Jarad. Simonus! Tamar!" He rushed to greet his good friends from Kerielan.

The two men embraced and tiny Tamar stood on tiptoe to receive Eshed's kiss. "Ah, isn't this a remarkable day? And you are here to share it with me!"

"Eshed! You could have any girl's heart today . . . look at you!" Tamar stroked his vestment and stood back to take in the full effect. She was rewarded with a throaty laugh from the groom. The couple were dressed in their finest muslins, and Simonus had carefully combed his ruddy beard. Tamar's hair glinted rich brown in the sunlight and swung loosely over her shoulders in contrast to the bride's hair, which would be tightly bound today to signify Loana's commitment to Eshed and a new life. Eshed decided to forgo mentioning the Circan chase for now. A jarring amid the pleasantries. But sometime this evening he must warn Simonus to be watchful when returning to Kerielan.

"I am sorry to ask, but if I do not, someone will—" Simonus spoke in confidence. "Is this a marriage or an alliance of priestly households? If an alliance, you rise in it." His hand took in the richness of the scene. Imported tapestries and satin pillows lined the portico. Abundant food of great variety filled the tables. Gardens pressed greenly as far as the eye could see. Balconies exposed a view of vineyards passing down the hillside to a lake of considerable proportion.

Eshed studied his strange shoes carefully (a gift from Jarad along with his bridal vestment) and in like tone murmured, "When you see the bride, you'll question no further." The conspirators smiled. "Even a priest is permitted *some* personal choice, you know." Eshed rocked on his toes, hands clasped behind him.

Tamar stroked his arm, and he was grateful for the silence that followed. There had been jealous murmurings against his marrying outside his home province.

Several marriageable young women from Kerielan had been advanced by the council as candidates to become the mistress of his household, but from the time Loana had accompanied her father to the yearly conclave of priests the spring prior, Eshed's eyes could not comfortably take in another.

Jessia, who had once taken his eye but never his heart, had been a council choice. Long-limbed, full-breasted, and agile, with hair the color of rain-soaked ripened wheat, she had a fine carriage and industrious nature. From a large family herself, she would likely produce many strong sons.

Then there had been Sheila, a council favorite, due, he suspected, to her father's generous bequests to the temple from his grain production. Sheila's mother had trained her in all the womanly arts save one. She could not bridle her tongue, which Eshed considered a *must* for his spouse. Her kinky hair framed a pleasant face, but he was greatly relieved when, just as the council put her name forth, Laban asked for her hand. Her father, unaware of the council's interest, gave Laban his promise.

Beryth, the village flirt, was hardly worth mentioning. She had unashamedly pursued him at every function, sharing her food with him, rolling her large, cowlike eyes at him, and trying to get him alone. Such obvious devotion should be rewarded, two of the single councilmen thought, but Eshed suspected that these fellows, Daman and Zerach, really wanted to be rid of her themselves. Daman had rebuffed her aggressive behavior on more than one occasion, and she had once fallen right into Zerach's lap on the pretense of stumbling over a rock at a picnic. She had stroked his neck and yanked his beard playfully before he managed to eject her from his knees.

Eshed felt fortunate in gaining the council's approval for his marriage to Loana, a veritable princess compared to the nubile choices in Etser. They had found Jarad most agreeable to the proposal, and since he was part of their jurisdiction of priests, no one put forth a formal objection. Whispered exchanges and finger tapping told the real story. Eshed heard their words, not their silence.

"You are from Kerielan, I believe?" Nebow, a swarthy, richly ornamented friend of Jarad's pushed in upon Eshed.

"Nebow . . . am I correct? So many new names . . . but your face rings true." Eshed grasped his hand, glancing impatiently over his shoulder as the time for his bride to appear approached. Fresh flowers festooned the doorway, awaiting her arrival, and two trumpeters, horns slung by their sides, framed the opening, prepared to match tones at her entry. The sun's last rays glistened on the special weaving of their ceremonial garb and caught the golden cords that held the horns.

"Allow me to present my nephew, Telles." Nebow's guttural voice yanked him from his musings. At his shoulder stood a darkly handsome, somewhat effeminate young man. Eshed took his hand. Telles smiled, but his eyes glinted sullenly. "I'm afraid he once had designs on your Loana himself," Nebow confided with a wink.

"Please, Uncle . . . we are old friends—nothing more," Telles grimaced.

Eshed nodded. Nothing could shake his confidence today. Loana was to be his!

"Not the marrying type," Nebow whispered hoarsely in Eshed's ear.

Jarad wove his way through the crowd, chatting with friends along the way, and took his place at the altar. Its marble bore gold leaf designs down each side. Eshed knew what the symbols meant, but in his excitement he was unable to concentrate his attention on a single one of them. Jarad signaled him forward and whispered some last-minute instructions in his ear. The first trill of the trumpets spurred Eshed to his assigned place before the altar, his foot brushing against two gold cushions on which he and Loana would soon kneel to seal their vows.

According to custom, the groom's eyes were to remain on the priest during the bride's entrance. Jarad stood tall in his white toga cowled with deep grey inserts, buckled at the waist with a heavy gold clasp. The buckle gleamed softly in the fading daylight, and the outline of a figure in relief caught Eshed's eye. It was the form of a man with his hands flung upward. There was a round, blazing object with jagged edges in his hands, and his hair came to the same frazzled conclusion. Surely Jarad would not be wearing the ancient symbol of the sun-god! Jarad received the golden breastplate from a servant and fastened it in place with the traditional blue ribbon, covering the offensive buckle. With so many thoughts vying for his immediate attention, Eshed pushed Jarad's unpriestly attire from his mind. He fastened his eyes on Jarad's face. The elder priest's hair hung in dark rivulets against his furrowed brow, which contrasted the softness of his eye as he watched Loana approach the altar.

The bride's hair was caught in a circle about her head,

laced with a silver cord that pulled an attached train of late spring flowers. Its long oval spilled softly over white, gossamer-gowned shoulders onto the floor behind her. Her waist was tightly bound to signify the new binding of her time and energy to their union. The trail of flowers made a full circle, a symbol that their coming together was to be eternal and fruitful.

Perfume from Loana's flower train stirred him, and as the trumpet tones dwindled away, he turned and offered his hand, signaling acceptance of his bride. She settled gently at his side. Her blue eyes, like the sea at noontide, washed over his face in expectancy and love.

Eshed watched like one in a dream while her lovely lips formed the vows. It was not his priestly tone that responded but a softer, slightly hesitant voicing of the vow: "and my home will be your home . . . and my people, your people." There was no hesitation in his eyes, however, as he faced her with his pronouncement, a blaze of love emanating from his face. They knelt upon the pillows and were sprinkled with hyacinths and rose petals, damp with spring water, a symbolic merging of priestly households.

Jarad lifted long arms and intoned a benediction. In that moment, Loana became mistress of the priestly house of Kerielan.

That transaction completed according to Saramhat custom, the customs of Kerielan now prevailed. Taking Loana by the hand, Eshed raised her to stand before him. Removing the veil of flowers and laying it to one side, the groom pulled the crisping pin from her hair and the dark mass tumbled forth. Kissing her eyelids and fingertips, he led her forth to the festivities which would continue for a week. That night ten maidens with lighted lamps would see them to the bridal chamber.

CHAPTER 2

Loana drowsed against Eshed's shoulder. It was hard to keep her eyes open in the predawn light. They had crept away from the house like refugees, she reflected. Something about avoiding the sun's heat. As happy as she was to be with Eshed, she would have enjoyed it much more with another hour's sleep! She rocked on Zerubabel, with Eshed's arms about her and the little white donkey pulling a cart of her belongings behind them.

Eshed strained his eyes against the darkness, watchful for the gleam of peaked hats in the emerging light. With Loana along, he wanted no repeat of his earlier journey, and he hoped the dim light would provide the cover they needed, for a time at least. They were slowed somewhat by Lily, the white donkey, who refused to pull the cart with anything resembling speed. An uneven sound from the cart wheels caused Eshed to look behind. Something dark appeared to be tumbling from the cart . . . No! Someone was mounting the cart from behind.

"You there!" Eshed called, causing Loana to bolt upright and nearly lose her balance. Eshed stopped Zerubabel and was off in a flash. The donkey cart hit a road rock, and a splintering sound announced the flying of a wheel. Eshed sprang upon the figure in the cart, and the entire assemblage toppled toward the ditch.

"Eshed!" Loana screamed.

With that, two more men, swathed about the head and face, sprang from the ditch to assist the first with knives. One pulled Loana from Zerubabel's back and flicked her gold necklace from her throat with the knife blade. Her screams roused Eshed from struggling with the cart climber and sent him toward her, the third man jumping for his back.

Eshed grabbed the man with the necklace just as the other mounted his back. Around they went as Eshed tried to swing the man from his back, his fist full of unwinding turban from Loana's attacker. The cart climber was rifling through the disabled cart. Loana surged forward and grabbed a cooking pot from his hand, toppling him backward into the ditch. With swiftness and determination born of terror, she swung the pot at the man on Eshed's back and connected with his head. Yelping with pain, he let go, seeing stars as he fell.

Eshed seized that moment to separate Loana's attacker from his knife and pull the turban tight around his throat. Loana scooped up the fallen knives, brandishing them in front of her, as the cart climber emerged from the ditch, screaming at the others, his head bleeding, his clothes in tatters.

"Vasculla! Emiton nas!" He spoke a strange language. The man choking in his own turban understood and signaled surrender, his hands thrown high. Eshed released him. Pulling their pot-swooned friend by his feet, they disappeared as they had come.

Loana's eyes were fixed on the knives gleaming in the sunrise. She sank back into the dust, weak and trembling.

"My love, are you all right?" Eshed stooped to pick her up.

She looked at him uncomprehendingly and began to laugh. Puzzled, he raised her up to see her eyes and check her throat, nicked by the knife. He dabbed at the spot with a clean cloth from his tunic. She continued to laugh. Suddenly he knew. Hysteria.

He looked at his brown palm, the blood-tainted cloth dangling from his fingers. He couldn't. But he had to! Slapping her resoundingly on the face, he gathered her in his arms as her shrill laughter turned to tears.

"My love, you were such a clever, brave one. Please, we're all right now. I didn't want to have to strike you!" How he hated himself at this moment. Trying to dodge the Circans, he had put her in jeopardy from robbers. Everyone knew they operated in this area by night. In his haste to avoid the obvious, he had forgotten the night people, who lay in wait in ditches for their prey.

Soon Loana gained control. She hardly wanted to, it felt so good in his arms. But they had a wagon to repair and belongings to check. To their joy, they found that nothing was gone.

"They clearly wanted only gold . . . something immediately tradable," he said as she shuffled through the bolts of cloth and cooking pans.

"If they had found my hammered copper trays here in the bottom, they would have taken them." Loana poured some provisions from a large mesh bag, broke flat loaves for serving, and portioned out some curds from a skin.

Eshed, who had repaired the broken cart wheel, dusted his hands on his tunic front and took the food. There was no stream nearby for washing. Their first meal out of doors was not the picnic they had anticipated.

"I'm sorry about your necklace. Your father gave it to you for a wedding present?"

Loana felt at her throat as if suddenly remembering the loss.

"Oh! Yes, he did." A tear came to her eye. "I was so frightened for you that I forgot."

"Loana," he said as he pulled her to him, "I was afraid for

you, too! I wonder if either of us would have resisted so otherwise. For all they wanted were things—things can be replaced." He examined her tear-stained face and ran his finger down the bridge of her nose, thoughtfully. "We certainly put them to flight, didn't we?"

Early summer had been chosen for the nuptials because of the heavy ritual demands of winter and spring. Since the elders of Kerielan could minister in his absence, this allowed an extended summer honeymoon for Eshed and his bride. Not the year allotted most couples, in the care of the groom's family, for Eshed had none. But summer stretched invitingly before him. It was much more than he had expected under the circumstances. The ritual demands of the fall were heavy and his alone to bear. It was the custom, however, to allow priests generous time to put their households in order.

Eshed and Loana were provided summer lodgings, an unused vineyard overseer's cottage in a tree-coved spot by a stream, on the large estate of Namath, one of the Kerielan elders. Eshed's remembrance would be of sun streaming through partially shuttered windows and birds chattering them into wakefulness. To awaken languorously in a similar embrace to the one in which they fell asleep seemed a true luxury to Eshed, exceeding his fantasies. After a protracted period of small talk and caresses, Loana slipped into a sturdy muslin apron, and, with hair still loose about her shoulders, kindled a small charcoal fire to heat the baking oven.

He propped his head and shoulders with a mound of Namath's sheepshearings and watched while she wound her long hair atop her head and restrained it with a cord. She splashed her face with chill spring water in a stone basin, bringing the color up in her cheeks. She then fell absorbedly to grinding the wheat burrs into soft flour that soon became a flat bread, quickly baked for breakfast over the charcoal fire. Grapes fresh from the vine and goat's milk from the dairy was their usual fare.

"Tell me if you like the taste of this." She offered him a little cake stuffed with dates and honey, hot from the oven, as he rolled from the mat one morning. "Ah—ah—ah . . . you must wash first." Loana pulled the cake from his lips and wagged her slender finger under his nose. He made a playful grab for her, and she sprang away, upturning the milk pitcher. Eshed's eyes crinkled. Laughter escaped his lips at the sight of her dampened skirt. A furrow in her brow was replaced by the deep dimple in her cheek as she began to giggle. "How is it that you always get the better of me?" She stamped her foot in mock exasperation.

Towering over her, he reached out and stroked the dimple he loved so much, his eyes penetrating hers. With her off guard, it took only a swift movement to rescue his cake from her grasp.

"Vulture!" she shrieked, cracking him playfully on the skull with a wooden spoon.

Often Eshed and Loana picnicked by the stream at midday or roasted meat for their supper on a pit under the stars. On such star-filled nights, they took a quilt from the cottage and snuggled under the protection of a large tree. Intoxicated by the clear summer night and cooled by occasional breezes, they found their lovemaking sensitive and lush.

"Eshed," she whispered one evening as they lay in the grass watching the smoldering of a thousand luminaries against indigo heavens.

"Yes, love?" His fingers stroked the softness of her hair.

He twined a curl about his finger and rubbed the scent of it against his face.

"Did you ever expect—I mean . . . did you know it would be like this . . . for us?" She nuzzled his cheek with her eyelash.

"No . . . I only hoped . . . we would be content with one another. I never thought it could be so . . . *good*."

"Just *good* . . . is that all you can say?" she probed, teasing him and running her finger over his bare chest.

"You always have *words* for things . . . the things I really *want* to say . . ." He gave up the struggle and, trailing his hand along her waist and flank, pulled her under his eager loins once more, his tender lips tasting the flesh of her neck and breasts as she murmured dreamily against him.

When they were satisfied, they lay trembling at the power of their love, still embracing.

"I wish . . ." she sighed.

"Yes . . . ?" Sleep was overcoming him.

"That we could just stay here . . . like this. Forget about Kerielan . . . or Saramhat . . . or anything . . . and just live."

"Um . . . hum." Eshed's hand sought hers. He folded their hands together over her soft, round breasts. "But . . . I have a priest's vestment to wear, and you must be what you are." He smiled into her eyes, his face glowing with contentment. "My wife . . . in Kerielan."

The stars burned down through the inky summer coolness. Eshed slept. Loana lay drinking in the crescent moon for a long time, her thoughts returning to a sunny afternoon when, barely out of childhood, she had played hide and seek among the trees with her cousins. Drusilla, slightly older than she, turned to her as they sat plaiting their hair, waiting to be "found."

"Loana," she hissed, giving her braid a yank.

"Ouch!" Loana turned and slapped Drusilla.

"Shhh!" the older girl admonished. "Let's get out of here . . . and not tell the others where we went!"

Loana nodded, her eyes shining impishly, cheeks flushed from running. "Where shall we go?" the little one asked.

"I know—let's get our fortunes read!" Drusilla was always full of splendid ideas.

"Where? How?" Loana pressed, unwinding her hair again.

"An astrologer in Saramhat—some sort of priestess—she knows everything!"

Loose hair flowing out behind her in the wind, Loana presented herself at the astrologer's tent. Drusilla thrust her forward. "You go first! I will stand guard . . . in case we were followed."

"But why would that matter?" Loana asked, her eyes round.

"Er . . . well . . . we don't want those babies hanging about . . . when we are doing important stuff like this. They might listen!"

Loana nodded. Drusilla pressed a few kodrantes into her hand from the little leather pouch that swung from her sash and pushed her through the opening.

The astrologer, in a cone-shaped hat and layered robes of crimson, much gold about her throat, observed the young customer with interest and not a little surprise.

"Well, my beauty . . . what can I do for you?" she crooned.

Loana flushed. No one had ever called her "my beauty" before. In the fresh beginnings of young womanhood, her fledgling breasts, round hips, and skin as fresh as a rose at dawn made her a sight to behold.

Wordlessly, the child proffered the coin. The personality

before her was awe-inspiring. The astrologer indicated a cushion for her to sit on. Taking the kodrantes, the woman made three passes over the tapestry chart on the ground with cupped hands, then rested them in her lap, coins clinking against the hush of the tent.

"And what is the date of your birth?" she inquired, one eyebrow raised. While Loana whispered the answer self-consciously, the woman placed coins in specific locations about the wheel.

"Your father . . ." Her eyes were on the bottom of the wheel. ". . . he is in some high order . . . a priest, perhaps?"

Loana nodded, her eyes big.

"And you . . ." Her long finger pointed across the colorful wheel with its animal hieroglyphics. "You help him."

"Yes . . . my mother . . ." Loana offered.

"*Morte* . . . that is . . . she is dead." She pointed to the auspicious house. She rambled on, her interpretations like a strange language to Loana's ears. Then the astrologer paused for a moment, pursing her lips.

Loana leaned forward, straining to see what *she* saw on the chart. The woman sat back, took a deep breath, and said, "You will lead an exciting life . . . it is all tied to this man . . . here!"

"My father . . . ?" Loana couldn't think who she might mean.

"No . . . your father shows in other places in your chart, like . . . your house of money.

"Your loves of the moment will be men of intrigue . . . mystery . . . challenge." She paused. "Are you in love now?"

"Oh—no!" Loana flushed, hardly daring to think of such things, much less speak of them.

"Never mind. You soon will be . . . and many times you will fall in love . . . before you meet *this* man." Her hand rested on the house of partners. "He, however, will be different from them, for he shows in a separate house, a stronger one for you because of where your moon rests . . . in that same house. Here . . ." She pointed to another wedged portion, "are your lovers . . . and your impulse rests on them. That house is ruled by Neptune—illusion! Do not trust them!" Her eyes grew dark. "They will fool you and misuse you!" The bracelets jangled a warning note.

Loana's fingers flew to her hot cheek. What was she saying?

"If you dally with these wastrels, you could miss him!" She flicked a coin squarely into position over Loana's moon. "And he, the love of your life, is worth a hundred of them . . . easily!" She licked her lips.

Loana fell into the game. "But . . . how can I miss him if I am meant to marry him?"

"Impulse . . . and desire—strong forces for you—could cause you not to recognize him when he comes."

Loana bit her lower lip. "Will he not be handsome then?" He sounded so sturdy.

"Oh yes!" she assured her, grasping her hand across the chart. "Very! Here he is . . . a Venus partner . . . a partner worthy of your heart! But he will be busy and in a responsible position, for your ruling house of partners is the Goat . . . and here . . . in your house of Others where he makes his living . . . you show Saturn . . . his rule over you. In that house with the fish in residency, he may be a priest as well!"

"Which means . . . ?" Loana still did not see her part in the scheme.

"He will be on important business when you meet him. You will not notice him if you are busy playing . . . as you are wont to do!"

Her little brows beetled over sea-blue eyes. "But . . . I am only a child . . . yet . . ."

The astrologer laughed, patting her hand. "Ah, yes . . . Loana . . . but in your case, age really has nothing to do with it. You will always be at play . . . in one way . . ." She winked. ". . . or another."

Loana snuggled closer to Eshed. Well . . . she had proven that old witch wrong! The images fled before her sleepy eyes. She hadn't been playing when she met Eshed . . . well, not much . . . she had noticed him right off . . . and he her! The old woman had been right about one thing, though. He was certainly handsome. She stroked his muscled shoulders. And good—worth at least a hundred Daminens, Josephs, Telleses, Cyruses, Justuses, Percivals, Octaviuses . . . Cassiuses . . . Davids . . . Byrons . . . Larnans. She wondered what Eshed would think if he knew she had been told to "wait for him" by the astrologer.

The summer sped glowingly and rapidly by. They climbed the hillsides and fished the stream near the cottage. They made their own summer wine from grapes outside the door, mirthfully pelting one another with grapes and streams of juice as they worked the fruit with their hands, elbow deep in wooden casks. The juice flowed into tall earthen bottles which they chilled in the stream after an acceptable time of mellowing and shared with the few persons who interrupted their island of new beginning.

One morning the light fell softly and belatedly through the shutter, and Eshed perceived the scent of new air mingling with the crackling bread crusts on their morning fire.

"Loana."

"Yes?"

"You must help me pack today."

With a swift intake of breath, she returned to buttering the broken loaves. "Yes, Eshed."

Now her duties as mistress of Kerielan would begin in earnest.

CHAPTER 3

A day's journey lay between the cottage and their home in Etser, for they were slowed somewhat by a donkey cart of gifts and Loana's personal belongings.

"Balky beast!" Eshed admonished the white donkey, pulling at her rope collar.

"Lily doesn't know your handling yet!" Loana chuckled.

"She will!" He gave the donkey's flank a slap.

Each time they stopped for food or rest, the little white donkey from Jarad's stall had to be encouraged with switches to resume the journey. Frequently, both of them had to apply leafy licks to her heels. When she began moving reluctantly forward, they remounted Eshed's horse quickly, before the beast changed her mind.

Leaping up first and pulling Loana to sit sideways in front of him, Eshed sought ways to make his bride comfortable. Once he thought to simplify things by arranging a place for Loana in the cart among soft pillows and sleeping mats, but the donkey merely lowered her haunches and brayed mercilessly in response to the added burden.

Eshed's warm cheek found Loana's as the horse plodded through sandy soil and small brush near his home outside Etser. As they topped a slope in the final road bend, he pointed to a small brown house he had fashioned with his own hands.

"There, love! We will soon be home." He urged Zerubabel with a well-placed kick of the heel, and Loana strained forward to get a better look through the brush along the roadside.

"Oh . . . Eshed." Loana felt a heavy pulsing in her throat. "What if your people don't *like* me? What if . . . ?"

"What are you saying? *You* are the mistress of Kerielan. *I* love you . . . which means they are bound to at least *like* you." His encircling arm squeezed her tightly to him.

A welcome of banquet proportions greeted their arrival. The little brown house was bursting with people of Etser and farmers from the surrounding area. The lure of music and an array of basketry, home-fired pots, and provincial tapestries lined the crowded hallway of their home. Pipings and strummings of village youth were accompanied by winks and much laughter as the couple expressed surprise and pleasure over each gift and giver.

Loana's delicacy and warmth were noted, and the women clucked their approval in Eshed's ear as their men stood respectfully by, some shifting their feet and eyes uncomfortably.

"Thank you . . . thank you!" He moved among them, accepting their congratulations, detecting in brief eye contact a certain strain.

"Namath . . . thank you again for the use of the cottage! Ah ha! You must have been the one who told everyone we were coming." He clasped Namath's shoulder.

"Blame Serena!" Namath gestured to his wife who was chatting with Loana. "She sent me to Etser yesterday when one of my sheepherders saw you packing that incorrigible donkey! We thought you would never get here!" Namath laughed, but Eshed caught in the amiable gentleman's eye some reserve as he watched Loana. He hoped Namath had not been pressured by the jealousy of others in his absence. Namath's influence on the council was well-known. Whisperings were bound to go on in the community, no matter what one did, but he did not like those closest to him being badgered because of his choice.

Continuing to mingle, he grasped the hands of well-wishers and tried to ignore the knowing glances cast Loana's way. Eshed felt any resistance would be carried away like a straw in the wind, once people knew Loana.

A big bear hug from behind restored his sense of security, and he turned to greet Simonus. Tamar squeezed through the crowd and took Eshed's arm, standing on tiptoe to kiss his cheek lightly.

Eshed presented a mock scowl. "I might have known you'd do something like this, Tamar."

"What have I done to displease you?" Tamar pouted prettily.

"This gathering . . . I know you are the one behind it. Don't deny!" Eshed held up his hand to silence her objection.

Tamar turned her head first to one side, then another, contemplating an appropriate response. Her lips curved in an enigmatic smile. She caught sight of Loana. "Loana!" she called, ignoring the men. "Welcome home!" Hand aloft, she wriggled through the doorway to the other room and gave the bride a hug. Appreciating Tamar's warmth, Loana sparkled.

"Thank you, my brother." Eshed beamed at Simonus. "And thank Tamar for me, too . . ."

"Tamar has been thanked already, Eshed," Simonus responded. "She loves it when you tease her!"

After they had enjoyed a generous meal, sporting the best-loved dishes of neighboring cooks, glasses were passed, and Simonus proposed a toast of wine to the new couple.

"And may their days together be many . . . and filled with

song . . . and their nights be precious . . . and bring them sons to wear the priestly vestment . . . and daughters to rock the cradles of many grandchildren!"

Eyes misted by the heartfelt pronouncement, Eshed raised his glass with the others. A tender look passed between him and Loana, standing half a room away in a swirl of women. Music resumed, and the men locked arms in a high kicking dance of antiquity reserved for wedding celebrations.

The women scurried about, restoring furnishings to their proper place and picking up trays of soiled crockery. The crowd swept away, leaving an orderly house and a burgeoning pot of greens, along with flatbreads and meats for the next several days' provision.

Eshed drew aside the heavy purple curtains of the bedchamber and brought Loana's personal belongings from the cart in large knotted totes of fabric and small cap-topped baskets. He stacked them in the tile entry so that she might prepare for the night's rest. As she busied herself with preparations, Eshed excused himself to go into the garden to pray.

"Can I do anything to help you before I leave?" he wanted to know, tying the phylactery about his forehead.

"Thank you, darling. It has been such a heartwarming evening . . . my only need is for rest." She placed both hands on his chest and her forehead to his chin. Eshed cradled her in his arms for a long moment, rocking her gently from side to side, then kissed her forehead and departed.

A redolent golden moon dipped in cloud milk lit his way. Except for a light rustling of moving air in the olive trees, the garden was hushed and autumnal in feeling. Eshed felt suddenly depleted after the push of the journey and the jostle of the welcoming party. He moved with weariness to the large flat prayer stone that shone in the moonlight. Clasping his hands before his eyes, he leaned against the stone with more than his usual weight.

It took time for his whirling brain to settle into a mode. When it did, Eshed found himself asking to be guided as never before. After all, he had a new responsibility now, one for which he had no experience. To be a good husband to Loana was his duty and sincere desire. He was only recently beginning to feel some confidence about his calling to the priesthood. Well liked and honored by his people, he had many things yet to learn about being a *good* priest, and he wanted exceedingly to be what Kerielan needed.

In many ways, it was a difficult time to pursue his vocation because old forms were changing. Definition of worship practice was pivotal. Portions of the worship ritual pulled at his brain as he prayed, "*El Shaddai* . . . we honor you and lift our voices to you . . . hear our supplication . . . be merciful to us, for we are lowly and stumbling . . . make us walk uprightly . . . make your face to shine upon us. Abba . . . hear us."

He had prayed for several moments when he sensed something on his left shoulder. Thinking he had shifted into a tree snag, he pulled away, but the sensation of pressure remained. He opened his eyes and made out the form of a man's hand. Startled, he turned his back to the prayer stone, fully facing the intruder. He was in the presence of a very splendid being. Moonlight glowed brightly on the man, who was arrayed in a white tunic with gold at the throat and wrists. His feet were sandaled, and he looked for all the world like a priest from some realm of heaven.

"Come." He took both Eshed's arms in his hands and led him to the arbor. They sat within, surrounded by drying leaves and a cool autumn breeze. Yet Eshed felt strangely warm. In the deep night of the arbor, the man's face still glowed. Eshed's own

hands and raiment gave no such indication of lingering moon-light. Still speechless, he managed with difficulty to raise his eyes to the glowing face again. Penetrating eyes . . . Other-World eyes, *Eshed thought with a little shiver. The long hair was wavy and red-brown. The man smiled at Eshed as if he had known him forever, and when he spoke, the timbre of his voice took Eshed's breath away.*

"You are a priest."

"Yes." Eshed could hear his own voice, usually deep and strong, wavering.

The man's expression spoke of a very special acceptance and understanding of Eshed, a camaraderie of sorts. In a flash, Eshed's brain grasped the phrase from the temple scrolls . . . "Great High Priest!"

As minds are apt to do in unusual circumstances, Eshed's grasped half of the message without gleaning the import of the visitation. He found himself staring at his visitor, open-mouthed, waiting for the man to declare himself. For an instant, he wondered if he had fallen asleep at his prayer stone and begun dreaming. But he had never seen this man before, not even in a dream. Who could he be?

Great High Priest . . . Melchizedek . . . Lord of Lords.

"The Christ!" Eshed's whisper seemed to echo out of the small chamber, and the hum resounded through the trees. He sank slowly to his knees, never taking his eyes off the majestic countenance.

"Eshed . . . you have committed your priesthood to my cause." Eshed's heart beat very fast. For the first time . . . the first time—*he sensed what that meant.*

"I . . . I have . . ." Eshed stammered.

"If you are now ready to commit your life to me, personally . . . I have greater work for you to do."

Eshed's heart was clattering against his rib cage. His throat

*tightened. He couldn't take his eyes from the man's face. He felt
secure, yet some part of him wanted out! "And that is?" he managed at last. "What do you want of me?"*

*"You must trust me completely to work out the details of your
assignment. Can you do that?"*

*"Yes, I think so, if you help me." Eshed felt as he had when as
a young lad he was first handed a sack of counting stones.*
Could *he do it?*

*"I will help you even before you ask." The Lord grasped
his shoulder. "But you still must ask, as you have been doing
at your prayer stone. And one more thing . . ." His eyes struck
a warming response in Eshed. "Remember, Eshed . . . I
love you . . . wherever you go, whatever you do . . . remember!" Even the radiance of his smile conveyed a note of authority.*

*He stood and stepped back, receding into the dark fo-
liage.*

Eshed watched him go and sank slowly back against the
lattice. He was silent for what seemed like a very long time.
His eyes roamed the garden. It looked the same as
always—the vegetable plot in the corner, the prayer stone
ringed by olive trees, the fig tree under which he had studied the prescribed rituals in the scrolls as a novice priest
some three years earlier, the arbor with its trailing vines and
sweet scented blossoms now drying at season's end. Yet
within, Eshed knew that *nothing* was the same . . . *nor ever
would be* the same again, nor was he the same man who had
ridden through the gate, bearing his bride, only hours earlier. Eshed thought of Loana and knew he must get back to
the house. Still, he moved slowly, reluctantly, toward the
rim of light that grew from within the outer door at the back
of the house. He would keep silence on the matter, for certainly he had no words tonight!

Customarily bustling in his gait, he entered the house

softly and leaned, trembling, on the doorsill, holding the curtain aside with his body. Loana was piling covers atop the mat as he watched. She saw him from the corner of her eye and turned. "Oh, love . . . there you are. Do we have any more quilts?" She hesitated, scanning his face, sensing something that had not been there earlier. He was so boyishly handsome, and there was a depth to his dark hazel eyes . . . but it was not that . . . there was a deep peace—or was it *excitement* that she was reading?—that had erased all his weariness. Pursing her lips in a question, she hesitated, then dismissed his posture as something belonging to the prayer life of a priest. She watched him unlace his phylactery and remove the scripture from the tie to replace it with a new one on the dawn.

"I believe you have found *all* the quilts. Tell me, is it winter already?" Eshed's lip curved into a little smile, and he wagged his head at the mound of covers she had accumulated.

Loana shivered, "It seems very cold to me." She pulled the top quilt from its odd angle and squared it with the others.

"Ah, yes . . . our land is closer to the ocean than Saramhat, and our evening breeze *is* sometimes damp." Eshed let down the heavy ties at the bedchamber window to keep out the air. "You will become accustomed to it. Until then . . ." He held his arms open, and Loana sprang into his embrace. Laughing, they tumbled onto the cushion together.

Soon he heard Loana's even breathing. She had rolled from his embrace and was fast asleep on her side of the sleeping mat. Eshed arranged the coverlet around her shoulders and lay back on his pillow, watching the threads of moonlight sifting through an open skylight. He locked his hands together behind his curly thatch of hair and wondered if sleep would come for him that night. His mind ran through the entire sequence with the Christ. He would have doubted that it had happened to *him* but for the reality of the scene. It was more real than anything he had ever experienced before. Everything else was shadow compared to that moment.

CHAPTER 4

After a brief but restful night, Eshed arose, washed, drank in a crisp invigorating sunrise from the prayer stone in the garden, and pulled on a fresh tunic before arranging floor pillows for the first breakfast they would share in their new home together. Simonus and Tamar had supplied the morning's milk, and Loana poured it from a large earthen jug into two translucent blue bowls. Eshed watched the hot wheat groats bob to the top of the liquid.

"The bowls . . . they are remarkable . . . they are from . . . ?" Eshed searched for a name. Loana's eyes twinkled as he groped for the identity of the giver.

"Father," she offered, laughing. Eshed's ruddy face flushed under his travel-browned skin. So much had transpired in a short period that he had lost track of such details.

Loana's slim fingers offered him a large spoon from his own larder, and he received it eagerly, grateful for its austere familiarity.

He offered the first blessing in their new home and they ate, almost shyly at first, punctuating the meal with many plans for the day. They finished with pears from a large basket of fruit.

"These are from Simonus' orchard," Eshed offered between bites.

"Ummm." Loana wiped juice from her chin with an

apron corner. "They are so juicy. I must make a drink from them soon."

Following breakfast, Eshed toted in the remainder of their packings from the cart and placed them in the areas where they would be used. He unpacked the heavy floor covers and mats and left the pots, utensils, and small carvings for Loana to arrange. Holding her narrow shoulders in a one-armed embrace, he bestowed a lingering kiss, and departed quickly to speak to the elders regarding the current needs of his flock.

"Do not expect me before sunset," he called as Loana waved from the doorway, acknowledging his message with a smile and a flick of the dust cloth.

Eshed turned the scroll over in his hands. The seal and parchment bore Nebak's insignia.

The priest had been concerned about Nebak, the new priest in Ohad, whom Eshed would soon ordain. Nebak had a difficult job ahead of him for so young a priest, Eshed told himself, forgetting all the obstacles he himself had overcome in administrating the congregation at Etser.

Unrolling the scroll, he stepped from the tree shadows and quickly scanned a message in Nebak's remarkable script. Addressed to the council in general and Eshed in particular, it was a record of details untended by the former priest. Nebak needed specific answers to many things before he moved ahead.

"Ah, I knew it!" Eshed sighed, speaking to Simonus, who had just walked up through the pear trees. Eshed had been concerned about Ohad for many months now. Elidad, the former priest, had been slipping for some time. When Eshed had been deployed to help him, the elder priest had lashed out in denial as his competence and finally, his very life, slipped from him. The challenge of Ohad had passed to Nebak.

"The council feels that you should make another trip there . . . soon." Simonus' words reflected Eshed's thinking. "I know you have just arrived home. When you get things in order here and Loana settled, maybe then."

Simonus turned his attention once more to the trees in his orchard as Eshed re-rolled the scroll and put it in his tunic, securing it under the girdle.

"The pears Tamar left were some of the best your orchard has produced! Loana is already talking about what she will do with the ones that are too soft to eat . . . if there *are* any," he chuckled.

"Ah . . . good . . . good . . . take one now. For when the sun is high, you will be thirsty then." Simonus' husky voice rang through the trees as he clipped dead branches and piled them for fire. He reached for one with a fine blush and handed it to Eshed, who pocketed it.

"We will meet tomorrow night and discuss the administering of fall ritual," Eshed suggested, throwing a leg over Zerubabel's front quarter. "I am off to notify other council members . . . come to my house at sundown. We will break bread together. I go to see Martseah now!"

"Greet him for me as well!" Simonus polished a pear on his vest and bit into it.

A kick of Eshed's sandaled foot prompted a brisk trot and then a canter from his mount. They entered a stand of sycamores. The breeze within cooled them as the sun climbed toward its zenith. Brown lacings of shadow flowed across the horse's head and soothed Eshed's eyes from the glare of the sun. He slowed Zerubabel to take advantage of the coolness. The cloister of leaves inspired reflection, and Eshed relived events of the past day. *Returning home . . . always a cherished experience but this time with my very love, Loana.* Remembrance of their wedding trip brought little shivers to his spine. Being alone for so long, the blessed-

ness of union with such a woman was indescribably precious. He wondered if anyone could appreciate what it
meant to him. *Only those who have known a great deal of
loneliness as I have would understand.* Then the
gathering . . . his friends sharing his happiness. *It was all
too, too good.* And to be followed by a meeting with the
Christ . . . Jesus . . . new Lord of his life . . . what could he
say? Such a thing had been granted to few men. What remained was such a lightness of spirit that he had the sensation of flying when he was standing still. The leaves that
brushed against his shoulder looked different. The sky was
bluer . . . the air fresher . . . even the horse's ears, as he
viewed the path between them, had a certain beauty. His
eyes took in the texture of fine hairs that poked from within
the ears and the tawniness of the mane as it flicked in the
breeze . . . a beautiful animal . . . totally dedicated in serving him, obedient to every tug of rope and poke of toe. The
Lord had spoken of his commitment, as a whole person, to
his cause. Was this what he meant? Could it be that Eshed
could be measured against his horse and found wanting?
He pondered the extent of his commitment. In time, it
would come clear.

As one who wakes from a dream, Eshed blinked back
the sun after his leafy solitude. Two bends in the road from
Etser.

"MARTSEAH . . . leather fittings," read the sign in front
of a familiar stall. Eshed slid off Zerubabel's flank and
lashed his mount to a tree, leaving him to rest in cool
shadows.

"Good brother, how goes it?" Martseah's blonde head
bobbed at Eshed through the doorway. "Jacel! Fetch a jar of
water for Eshed's horse when you have finished delivering
those goods. He should be cool enough to drink by then."

His young apprentice, a tousle-haired boy of ten or so, scrambled off with an arm load of pelts. Eshed greeted Martseah, then nodded to Jacel. Seeing his industry reminded him of his own apprenticeship at the same age under Checed. He had learned stone masonry in this very village, where Checed had come to build a home shortly after the shipwreck.

"Come . . . refresh yourself." Martseah waved Eshed through the doorway and indicated a jar of clear, cool water and a gourd dipper next to the pallet. Eshed crossed his legs and sat down on the cushion. The sharp aroma of leather drew Eshed's admiring gaze to offerings lining the shelves and hanging from the walls. Born from several generations of leather artisans, Martseah had worked pelts since he was old enough to hold a tool.

"Whew!" Martseah exhaled as he dropped down in front of Eshed and took a sip of water from the shared gourd. "This shop has been crawling with women this morning, telling us of your Loana. Her beauty and friendliness are on every tongue. The older women are wondering how you will get your work done with her in the house, and the girls are making a goddess out of her," Martseah confided in his rapid delivery. "Beryth came in and wanted me to make a wide leather belt so she can cinch herself into a small waistline. How am I to make a belt for that toad shaped little creature, I ask you . . . and what difference will it make if I do?" He snickered. "I heard her tell Naveh that Loana has a waist like a wasp . . . Naveh really did not care to hear that right now!" Martseah handed the water gourd to Eshed. "I am sorry I did not come to your welcoming party last evening." His eyes grew serious. "It was because of Naveh—her time has almost come."

"Ummm," Eshed murmured, swallowing, his face sparkling with amusement. "I understand—I thought perhaps I would already be engaged for the blessing of another tow-headed leather artisan!" He yanked playfully at a long lock of straight yellow hair falling over Martseah's chamois vest protecting his pale blue muslin tunic. His turquoise eyes twinkled, and the paleness of his skin showed a crimson blush.

"Oh, but I did not forget your homecoming!" He sprang up and brought down two nodahs from their resting place on wall pegs. They were beautifully crafted. Face shining, he placed them into Eshed's lap. They were identical in size, and each had a leather carrying strap to be slung over one shoulder, the bottle resting on the opposite hip. One was marked with a large monogram "L," and one with an "E." Eshed stood and looped his over his head, arranging the flat portion against his hip. He gave it a resounding "thump" with his hand. Eshed was awed. Martseah and he had grown to manhood together, but this was the sort of gift one gives a brother.

"The fit is perfect. Did you have my exact height? They are most handsome," Eshed smiled broadly. He could hardly wait for Loana to see hers.

"I fitted them on Naveh and myself . . . and hoped our sizes would correspond well enough."

It was true that Eshed and Martseah were similar in height. Eshed was slightly more stocky and muscled, while Martseah was of a lanky, wiry frame. Naveh was tiny, like Loana.

"I am eager to meet your Loana and see for myself if what they say is true!" Martseah could be considered a good judge of such things. Naveh had been the most favored maiden in the village, and many were astonished that Martseah, coming from a righteous but rather humble background, had won her. Naveh, whose parents were Namath and Serena, came from a background of substance. Namath had much land and many sheep.

"Eshed!" A female voice caused both men to turn toward

the parted drape that separated the living quarters from the shop. It was Naveh, moving laboriously, with one protective hand on her burdened abdomen.

"I thought you were still in the marketplace, buying vegetables." Martseah strode to her side and put a protective arm about her shoulders. She smiled at him, her auburn hair resting in waves against his tunic.

"You are looking well, Naveh. Martseah tells me it will be soon."

"Yes . . . I do not know about the ones after, but it is very hard to wait for the first baby. However, the way it is today . . . we may not have long to wait." She smiled a tired smile and leaned more heavily on her husband.

"Come, my love, you must rest now." Martseah turned toward a curtained area, supporting her back with his arm.

"Bring Loana by soon!" Naveh admonished.

"I will . . . and Martseah . . . we meet tomorrow night at my house for supper. Thank you for the nodahs!" Holding them aloft in one hand, Eshed bade them good-bye.

Leading Zerubabel a few paces to the temple, Eshed retied him. Pulling a sack from Zerubabel's back, Eshed slung it over his belt and hurried inside, pausing to touch the doorpost reverently. The familiar temple stone set mosaic cast colored reflections on him as he passed the door.

"Haman!" he called.

He was answered by the quick, shuffling steps of a stooped little man. Elfin-faced with eyebrows continually arched in surprise, Haman was the temple key-keeper and orderly. Squinting through the dim light, he hissed a garlicky, "The priest—oh, welcome home, sir." He offered Eshed the key to his inner chamber with a quick bow of acknowledgment.

"The temple looks well kept, Haman. Thank you for taking such good care of things for me." Eshed spoke louder than usual as Haman could not hear well. He squeezed Haman's shoulder, drew a brass cup from his bag, and pressed it into Haman's hand. "For you . . . from Saramhat!" Eshed explained.

Haman turned the cup over in his gnarled hands, looking very closely at the scroll designs. It was not an elegant brass cup by brass smith's standards, but it was substantial. He held it reverently, with unexpected pleasure. A tear filled his eye, and he tried to stammer out his thanks. Eshed patted his shoulder, saying, "You are a good and faithful servant of the temple."

Eshed's sandals clattered over the old stone floor. Everything looked much as he had left it—the altar rail, heavy dark draperies, tapestry-lined seating area. He was in charge again. It felt good. The scratchy old key turned painfully in the lock.

Inside the study chamber, he pushed the creaky shutter open to let in some air. Musty . . . probably not opened all summer. Haman had a way of forgetting about this little chamber, but as long as the main temple was well ordered, Eshed forgave him this oversight. Sweeping aside some tattered scrolls on the table, he drew a pair of brass candle lamps from his sack. Boat-shaped, they were for his study chamber, a gift from Jarad. Holding them to the light of the window, he regarded the intricacy of their rendering. Turning the overlaid leaf design into the light, he perceived a small flaw near the base. It could probably be polished out, he reflected. He took a goatskin flask from the wall peg and filled the lamps with olive oil through the wick holder at the top. Making a place on the shelf for them, he resolved to read by them on his next day in Etser.

Brushing aside a narrow curtain, he pulled from the small closet his breastplate, its symbolically rendered stones glistening on the golden surface, and the ephod, a brightly embroidered linen garment with deep blue tunic that kept the cold cut of metal from his flesh. He ran his fingers over the brilliant blue, green, scarlet, and purple stones. *After months of release from its burdensome implications, it will feel good to don the priestly vestment again.*

CHAPTER 5

Plucking a striped napkin from his pocket, Eshed rolled and knotted it securely to keep the streams of moisture from his eyes. With the flat of his palm, he brushed sweat from the horse's neck where it was beginning to collect.

"Hey, little one, take your ease. We are having a warm welcome today," he confided.

As if in agreement, Zerubabel began to plod doggedly into the shade of the first of three groups of cedars through which they would pass. Namath's holdings were large indeed.

A soft breeze cooled Eshed's neck. He angled his head upward, admiring the huge timbers so valued for building home interiors. His own floor of cedar, shared by Namath, was a substantial addition to his humble dwelling. Eshed drank in the familiar aroma, darkly rich to the senses. The flowerings of nasturtiums and daisies appeared, along with mossy rock and fern . . . that meant water was nearby. Soon he found the crystal relief of a blue pool coved within a bulk of softly sighing trees.

Kneeling, he bent his face and shoulders into the water and came up sputtering to find he was not alone at the water hole. Where his hand pressed the bank, a lizard struggled to release its tail. He chuckled as it scampered away, a colorful streak with an iridescent diamond shape on its head, leaving its tail behind.

Zerubabel snuffled in the cool water and drank deeply, and Eshed searched for the pool's source. It appeared to have sprung from the rocks above. The sound of a waterfall beckoned, and, roping his mount securely to a branch, Eshed climbed toward the musical sound of rushing water. Running his fingers through the dampness of his hair, he pressed deeper into the ever greening world. Not knowing exactly where he was going or why, he climbed on, feeling strangely drawn.

Securing his feet on the rocks as he climbed, he folded dew-pearled leaves away from his body and pushed into a moist, sun-spun grotto that he did not remember. The waterfall, banked in rainbow, broke through the green. Eshed could hear the high trill of distant birds and the nearer warbling of nesting wrens.

Quietly, unwilling to disturb the scene surrounding him, he sat on a flat rock near the singing water. A peacock fanned tall on the path before him and strutted silently into the nearby leaves, his feathers brushing Eshed's hand and leaving a trail of majestic color. Eshed rested his head against the tree behind him. He felt a new calmness and a greater sense of the majesty of God's nature.

He heard the clear strain of some marvelous instrument, and the scent of bread wafted through the still air. He saw a flower-woven basket filled with a strange fruit he longed to taste. The colors of the peacock's feathers still surrounded him and became a rich robe around his shoulders. On his feet he wore sandals of gold, and gold webbing circled his head.

A white-robed figure holding a large napkin filled with warm, fragrant loaves approached. As he drew nearer, Eshed said, "My Lord." For the moment Eshed forgot all else but the joy of knowing him and of being with him again. He waved Eshed onto a large rock that seated them both. They ate in silence. In such rare and splendid company, no words seemed adequate.

The environment echoed the transcendent quality which poured from the Christ—a depth of Being that had no sounding point, a harbor with a snug and warming shore on an ocean with no floor. The cooling sheets of water falling had a depth and sheen he had never observed in the clearest of mountain streams. The trees were fragrantly alive, and the bands of rainbow a brilliance that could be felt as well as seen. It was a place of wholeness and healing and joy that defied description. He chewed the bread and marveled at the warm interplay of softness and crust that formed its substance and the chilling sweetness of the burgundy and pale yellow fruit they shared. Eshed felt no need of any kind . . . a strange departure for him. Cradled in the still rapture of the moment, his eyes sought the Lord's.

Something new was in his Lord's eyes. He had a plan. As he revealed this plan, involving many people and many lands, vivid images appeared at his shoulder. The pictures were of sheep, his sheep, he said. They appeared to have no leader and were ambling about aimlessly, seeking food and shelter from the gathering storm. The little lambs were bleating loudly in search of their mothers who were calling frantically for them in the confusion. The wool of many sheep was stained with blood, and their eyes were glazed in pain. Wolf packs could be seen on the perimeter, ready to close in. Some of the animals had lain down in despair a stone's throw from a secluded cave that could be guarded amply by one good ram with horns. The cave was high enough from the plain where they languished to provide warning of an enemy's approach. Some were simply running, panic-stricken and purposeless.

The picture dissolved into nothingness. The fruit and bread had been disposed of. Eshed rested back against a tree trunk, deep in thought. His hand found a pocket in the peacock coat, and he drew from it a hard object. A round, flat stone with a word chiseled on its surface.

The Lord's lips formed the word on the stone, and in that moment Eshed understood that he had been chosen to minister to the lost sheep. He felt he should protest his inadequacy, but the words wouldn't form on his lips. He looked down at the stone. The Master's hand rested on his shoulder, and he looked into the ageless eyes.

"You are Eshed . . . an outpouring."

The Lord placed three strands of crystal blue stones about Eshed's neck and replaced the gold webbing on his head. It was a symbol of his yoking to the Lord through his Holy Spirit and a token that Eshed would continue to grow and yield fruit at the Spirit's instruction.

He knelt before the Lord, and hot tears of unexpected blessing washed his face.

Shaking dust from the striped blanket, Eshed hung it in the stall and looped the rope over it. His head swam with the events of the day. *The Lord has lit a fire in me that nothing can quench!* Perhaps tonight he could share some of his vision with Loana. He must surely share it soon, for it could hardly be contained!

He stamped noisily across the entry porch, placing his hand on the door lintel and whispering to himself the sacred words that blessed his home and insured a peaceful entry. He opened his eyes to towels and a basin of water that Loana had prepared for his return. Sitting on the stone step, he stared at the clay scarab that fastened his leather thongs and pushed it aside, releasing his feet from the sandals. Removing the coarse woven travel coat, he dipped his face and arms in the cool water, then watched his toes disappear under the water's crust in the basin. The evening was developing a chill as the sun made its final bow behind a crest of trees. After washing hastily, he shook the water droplets from his limp hair and dried his feet and legs, pouring water into the roots of a young terebinth tree beside the porch. Slinging the towel over his shoulder, he pushed the socketed door and padded barefoot across the tiled entry, his damp feet leaving a serpentine trail on the dark stones he had polished and squared by hand.

"Loana." His deep voice produced a little echo in the hallway chamber.

She was working at the sideboard, chopping roots and greens from the garden. The top layer of her skirt was hitched up on each side and tucked into her apron sash. Her legs were brown and feet bare, her hair swathed in a blue cloth. He locked his hands and dropped them over her head, like a net, coming to rest on her waist. She wriggled around and greeted him, hugging his muscled back. Noting a little mud fleck on her cheek, he rubbed it away tenderly with his square, brown hand.

He looked at his hand thoughtfully, still holding her close. Hard work had provided this parcel of land on which he built his house, and more hard labor had raised its walls. Eshed took a certain joy in arduous tasks.

"Ah . . . look . . . my callouses from handling tools and stones have softened. I am so glad. I would not want to scratch your face."

Loana nuzzled his palm and kissed it. Putting his hand around her waist again, he drank in her lips.

Finally, drawing back from him, she asked, "How did your visits go?" She sensed his great peace. His face lit up as he recounted his day. She stirred a fragrant pot that was bubbling on the fire and threw in fresh vegetables. When he reached the part about Martseah, he excused himself, took a lighted oil cephel from the shelf by the door, flapped into his sandals, and went back to the shed where the nodahs hung over the horse's rope.

He swung proudly into the house with the nodahs slung over one shoulder, like a young lad with his first string of fish.

Turning, Loana saw him enter, smiling mysteriously.

"Do you have a free shoulder?" His eyes twinkled as he placed the candle on the shelf inside the door.

"I think so. Why?" She dried her hands on her apron. As he approached her with the strap, she held out her arm and he dropped the nodah into place. She lifted the bottle to admire the "L" tooled into the side. He held his nodah up for her inspection.

"Eshed, they're lovely! Where did you get them?"

"Martseah, my childhood friend, made them. He is a fine leather smith in Etser. You approve, then?"

"Oh, yes!" Loana's eyes sparkled. "We have a little of our summer wine left to fill them too."

"Martseah will be very pleased. He is anxious to meet you!" Eshed responded.

Loana fingered the smoothness of the leather and adjusted the strap to her hip.

"And when will that be?" she asked.

"Tomorrow night. I have invited the elders here for a meeting. We will have dinner together." He smiled blandly.

Loana's jaw dropped. What could Eshed be thinking of? She blanched and took a little step away from him.

"I cannot do that!" she said in measured tones.

"But why not?" he asked softly, his dark eyes riveted on her face.

"I am still unpacking and settling the house. Such a meal would take two days' preparation." She was incredulous that he would propose such a thing.

"Surely, you had such preparations to make as mistress of Jarad's household. Did he never bring elders home for you to feed?"

"Of course . . . frequently. But he gave me notice—and I had servants to help!" Exasperation was showing on her face, making lines he had never seen on her flawless skin.

"You will have the women's council to help you with such matters soon!" Eshed waved his palm.

"*Soon* is *not tomorrow!*" Loana's voice was shaking now. With a flick of her skirt, she turned her back on him.

Eshed's mind raced for a solution.

"What of all the food left by the women at our welcoming?" He stroked his beardless chin and gestured impatiently.

Loana's arms were across her bosom now, and her little waist sucked in with the next breath. "*There is not enough, Eshed.* The house is not ready—and—and . . ." Her jaw was set, her back stiff. "*No self-respecting mistress of Saramhat would allow others to plan and supervise such a meal for her!*" There! It was out! Her pride was involved.

Eshed composed himself, suddenly assuming his role as master of his house. Wasn't Loana supposed to obey him in all things?

"It seems a very simple thing to me," Eshed replied somewhat condescendingly, his brow furrowed.

Loana's face was as white with anger as Eshed's was flushed with his inability to overcome her objections.

"You put me at a disadvantage with your people, Eshed." Her voice shook slightly. Calmer now, she looked out the window. "We could lose face." Glancing sidewise, she saw the color drain from his face and knew that his manly pride was on the line. He was finally listening, and his emotions were doing a slow burn.

His head went down, and he shifted uneasily. He wanted desperately to keep Loana from knowing about the objections raised to his marrying someone from Saramhat. Still, if she did not obey him in this, he *would* lose face with the elders. How could he approach them now and tell them his bride was not ready to receive them?

A pear with a leaf still on its stem protruded from the top

of a dark grapewood basket on the chopping board. Shakily, he picked it up and rubbed it against his tunic, watching the sheen come up. Simonus . . . *Simonus!* A plan formed quickly in his mind as he replaced the fruit. Looking up, he saw her move back, once again, to the chopping board.

"Had I known it was too soon, I could have asked to have it at Simonus' house. Tamar has helped me on many such occasions," he mumbled uncertainly.

Loana was crying now, wiping her nose and eyes with the tip of her apron. The exquisite nodah, forgotten for the moment, swung emptily on her hip as she stirred the pot one last time and ladled the hot broth and vegetables into the wooden bowl pulled from the larder.

"No, no . . . it is *my* responsibility. I will do it somehow," she sniffled.

A mixture of relief and apprehension swept over the young husband as he hung his nodah on a peg by the door and sat upon the floor cushion to await his dinner. He was once again master of his house . . . *but at what price?* He had grown very close to Loana and had no wish to displease her. Still, they would have to make sacrifices . . . both of them. He bowed his head and placed his hands together, prayer style, resting them thoughtfully against his lips for a moment. Straightening and dropping his hands, he glanced furtively into her face as she placed the steaming bowl in front of him. She hung her nodah on the same peg, blew her nose on a clean corner of the soiled apron, and took it off, flinging it aside. Depositing herself across from him, she regarded him coolly.

Eshed returned the blessing. They ate in silence.

Against the backdrop of spoons scraping on wooden bowl bottoms, he cleared his throat and tried again.

"Would you be willing for Tamar to assist you tomorrow

if she is available? She is close by, and I could ride over early in the morning and ask her . . ."

"Does she not have her own home duties to perform tomorrow? What of her family?" Loana offered, hesitantly. After all, she barely knew Tamar. It seemed a lot to ask.

"There is only Simonus. They have no children, as yet. He will be one of those eating with us, so she would really be preparing for him as well." His eyes sought her face, eager for her pleasure.

"It would please me to have her help." Loana looked relieved, her lips curving agreeably. Dipping a large flat cracker in the soup broth, she handed it to her husband. Eshed took it with one hand and, seizing her hand with the other, pulled her to him, briefly, and kissed the side of her neck. Peace was restored.

The young priest sighed audibly. With such trifling matters to settle, would it ever be possible to tell her of his new identity and subsequent commissioning granted by the Lord? He longed to share it with her. Eshed nibbled at the cracker, brooding inwardly, a faint placating smile creasing his lips.

CHAPTER 6

Arrangements with Tamar were easily made the next morning. After Eshed loaded her donkey with a sling carrying a crock of fresh curds and a skin filled with morning honeycakes to take to Loana, he went to invite the remaining elders.

"Greetings!" Loana waved at Tamar as she rode the packed donkey through the gate. Struggling with her apron full of choice garden vegetables, she made her way to Tamar's side.

"Simonus will bring today's ripened pears when he comes for supper." Tamar's little-girl voice made the pears sound already ripe.

"Aren't these fine?" Loana rolled her apron open, displaying a fine assortment of yellow, green, and orange squashes and a large cucumber, dew-flecked and deep green. "I am told that you tended my garden so I could come home to this!"

"We watered and weeded a little . . . the sun and the rain did the rest." Tamar wrinkled her nose and shook her curls.

Re-rolling the apron, Loana held out her free hand for the curds. Tamar handed them down and then swung down herself. She disappeared into the shed with the donkey. After he was tied up, she joined Loana with the goatskin filled with honeycakes and a squat, rust-red jar of her own design crammed with thistle blossoms.

"You have already done most of the preparation and we

have only started!" Loana exclaimed to her lugubrious assistant.

"Nonsense! Most of the work is yours . . . it is at your house!" Tamar replied.

Dumping the vegetables on the chopping board, Loana doused them with water from a pitcher and scrubbed them with bound straw hung to dry near the board. "I am happy that this is a meatless meal," she confided. "Half the night I lay awake wondering how we could secure enough prepared meat to serve. This morning Eshed told me that according to the church calendar, we could not serve it anyway." She giggled, stowing the curds in a cool corner of the room, away from the sunlight. Meat, with its ritualistic handling, would have taken two days!

"There are no flowers just now, but aren't these thistle blossoms lovely?" Tamar was arranging the gentian blooms she'd brought in assorted wedding gift vases. Her chunky little fingers pulled at the stems, staggering the sizes of the heads with the larger, fresher blooms at the top of each bouquet. A select number remained in the rust pot she had sculpted for a housewarming gift to her neighbor.

"Yes . . . yes . . . they are!" As she filled the brass slipper-shaped candle lamps with olive oil from a crock, Loana flashed an appreciative smile Tamar's way. "Oh . . . oh . . . the oil just ran out. Where does Eshed keep the oil supply?"

Tamar crooked her finger and flitted out the doorway toward the shed. Loana followed. They took a gourd dipper down from the wall and filled the skin, as the kad Eshed stored it in was too large to lift. A large, stacked, wooden cask dripped in the corner, and the aroma of fermenting grapes met Loana's nostrils as she passed. "Wine!" She gulped. "I almost forgot the wine! What can we put it in?"

Standing on her toes, Tamar pulled a wineskin from a shelf over the casks. The top cask served as a press for the fruit in the bottom cask by resting on top of a loose lid and settling as the grapes fermented, forcing the liquid through a hollow reed into an earthenware jug. "Hold the kad at an angle. It is not full, and he will not want us dipping into it. We will have to fill the wineskin together," Tamar instructed.

"How is this?" Loana pushed her hair over her shoulder and supported the kad against her other shoulder, squatting in the dust. "Does he have a mellowing kad in the earth somewhere?"

"Lean it just a little more toward me . . . ah . . . that is it." Tamar caught the clear ruby stream in the skin, licking her fingers where it splashed onto her hand. "This *is* the mellowing kad." She met Loana's questioning eyes.

"The best wines mellow in the earth . . . like a child waiting to be born. That is what my cousin Drusilla told me, and she should know," Loana said smugly. "People come for miles to trade for her father's vintage. It is served at every important occasion and in the best homes of Saramhat. You drank it at our wedding!" Loana's eyes shone with the memory of it.

"It was certainly delicious. I remember that!" Tamar agreed, latching the wineskin. Hanging the cord over her shoulder, she untied a small bag from her girdle and poured a mound of dry leaves into her palm. Crushing them finely between her hands, she removed the reed from the hole at the cask bottom where the kad had been pushed under it to catch the stream. The reed fit neatly into a hole near the top of the barrel. Filling one end of it with the crushed herbs, she inserted it in the hole and, placing her lips against the opposite end of the reed, blew into the barrel.

"What is that for?" Loana asked, feeling a twinge of jealousy that some other woman knew her way around Eshed's house better than his bride.

"An old family secret!" Tamar winked. "Wait till you taste *this* wine! I have been putting herbs in both casks all summer. You will be happy you served it," she assured her.

Loana selected a taper, lit it from the fire beneath the cooking pot, and moved from candle to candle, setting the small room in a blaze of light. The meal was coming together with remarkable smoothness, considering her original misgivings.

Tamar half filled a water pitcher from the kad of well water and topped it with wine from the wineskin. It was an honor to help with the elders' meal. Only women of good repute whose husbands had standing in the religious community were asked to assist the priest's wife. Before Loana came, she had thought of it only as a necessity. Now her work had new meaning. She moved lightly from one task to another.

The door swung open, and Eshed was greeted by the softness of a candle-lit board spread with condiments, a proliferation of cushions and fresh flowers, and a mingling of rich aromas from the spicy vegetable dishes on the fire. Tamar was preparing washing basins by the door for the elders and handed him a towel as he entered. Unlatching his sandals, he looked up as Loana swept in, quite breathless, carrying finger bowls with flower petals crushed into the water and placing them near the cushions. She was hardly recognizable as the teary-eyed bride he had left in the morning. Her long hair flowed about her shoulders and was banded on the forehead by a purple cloth that matched the sheer opulence of her flowing Eshkolian-made gown. Centered on her forehead was an image he could not quite decipher, a dark greenish-black diamond. Eshed tried to remember where he had seen that emblem and recalled suddenly the little lizard who had left his tail in the garden where Eshed had been commissioned. He smiled, watching Loana scamper about, and mentally compared her to that tiny creature.

"Oh, Eshed!" She greeted him with a quick kiss. "Is everything all right?" Her hand swept the contents of the room, alive with her touch and a muted air of celebration.

"Quite beyond expectation, my love! The two of you have worked very hard, I can see."

Loana was grateful that the disorder she felt from stuffing belongings back into baskets and hiding unwashed furnishings with screens did not show. It was not the way she had hoped to entertain the first time, but it would have to do. Tamar, in a deep green muslin that set off her chestnut hair and rich coloring, hastened about, dishing up bowls of bulgur and preparing a separate set of hot dishes for the two women, who would dine together.

Simonus bustled in next, carrying the basket of promised pears, and close on his heels came the others. Tamar took the pears and placed a dozen or so on a hammered copper platter from Saramhat, while Loana joined Eshed at the door to greet their guests.

Martseah came in with Namath, the sheepherder, who was his father-in-law. Namath, stocky, swarthy, and barely taller than his daughter Naveh, extended a hand sporting a large jeweled ring for Eshed's grasp. Loana expressed her gratitude to Martseah for the nodahs, and he rewarded her with a big smile, perusing her face with the interest of an older brother intent on the prize carried home by his sibling. Dimpling, she turned her attention to the older man.

"Tell me, are you now a grandfather?" she asked.

Her husband smiled his approval. It was good that she was honoring Namath with this question as Martseah was his son-in-law and should defer to him in a gathering. She had an instinct for such things, young though she was.

"Alas . . . the midwife has been so long at Martseah's house, I believe she will learn leather craft before she will get to employ *her* skills." The gathering laughed. Namath could be depended upon to lighten any tense situation. "Should a messenger arrive this evening while we're at table, I expect Martseah to leave without *me* . . . or his horse!"

Martseah's lips fluttered a nervous half-grin as the group laughed again. He rubbed his scanty chin whiskers with his forefinger and shook his head. Simonus' robust laughter rang above the others, and Namath's black beard bounced off his barrel chest in rhythmic guffaws.

Containing himself, Simonus peered past the light of the oil lamp on the porch. "I believe it is Kamar approaching. Will Zerach and Daman be joining us tonight?" The question was addressed to Namath.

"Regrettably, they are away putting my flocks to new pasture just now." Namath had had a prosperous year, and his sheep had disposed of the available grasses and were being fed on the summer grass in the hills, which would soon be gathering frost. Daman and Zerach, two brothers, tended his flocks and lived on his lands with their parents. Now that Kamar the innkeeper had arrived, they were the only elders not present.

Eshed moved to assist Kamar with his wraps and hand him a basin. When all had completed their ablutions, Eshed called Loana, who was arranging the trays of crusty flat loaves, hot from the courtyard oven, on the tapestries that centered the cushions.

"Loana, our innkeeper in Etser . . . Kamar."

Kamar was the most traveled and worldly of the lot and always operated with a flourish, especially with the ladies. As his eyes came up, he rested them for several seconds on the pearl-cream quality of Loana's throat and neck. And he continued to hold her hand. A covert smile revealed her pleasure at this attention.

"My husband and I welcome you." At least her reply was proper.

Eshed clamped his fingers over Kamar's arm and somewhat abruptly assisted him to his place, next to himself. He hoped that no one but he had witnessed the unseemly exchange between his young bride and the widower.

When all were seated, Eshed returned the blessing. Loana and Tamar poured the wine as the men began dipping the bread crusts into the curds and filling their plates with vegetables. Loana was very pleased that she had thought to bring a little coffee from Saramhat. In Kerielan, it was considered a rich man's drink, and she would serve it with the honeycakes at the close of the meal. As she concluded her serving, she sat between Eshed and Kamar. Her perfume, a scent that had been the rage of Saramhat, met Kamar's nostrils, and he glanced at her appreciatively. Eshed's ears turned bright pink. He hoped they were not evident in the softness of the candles. Didn't she see her place? To correct her in front of these men would shame them both. He wished fervently that she would join Tamar.

"Simonus has suggested that the temple offerings be placed in consideration for the building of new candle racks. Namath, what have we in the purse?" Eshed began with the more trifling business. Difficult issues would be taken up after the meal. He shifted uneasily as one man after another glanced at Loana oddly. Only Kamar seemed pleased by the arrangement. *Kamar!* Eshed's nostrils flared as he caught Kamar ogling Loana openly. Eshed did not wish to make a scene. Where was Tamar?

Just then, Tamar entered the bedroom doorway from the inside and beckoned Loana to join her. Silently, Loana got to her feet and followed. As she walked away from the group, Kamar's eyes took in the effect of her slim but rounded form under the flowing gown.

Near the window, Tamar had placed dishes of food and condiments on a tapestry for the two of them and had been waiting for Loana to join her.

From the sleeping room, they could hear Namath's gravelly voice reciting figures to the group. Loana leaned into the cushion and picked up a bread crust to begin the meal.

"Eshed must have forgotten to tell you . . . we do not eat with the men, except our husbands. It is not our custom. Only in temple circles are we permitted to eat at the same time. Other women must wait until the meal is finished." The little-girl quality of Tamar's voice was noticeably soft against the backdrop of men's voices in the next room, and Loana leaned forward to catch her words, which only made Tamar more uncomfortable at having to instruct her in this matter.

Loana flushed to her hair roots. "I did not know. In Saramhat, I always sat at my father's elbow when the elders came . . . I cannot think why we shouldn't." Loana sounded petulant. It was no fun, eating in a corner like a pet cat! Still, she hoped she hadn't embarrassed Eshed too much.

Tamar gave a little shrug and smiled reassuringly at her hostess. Like her husband, Simonus, Tamar had a great sense of humor and had soon put the incident behind by eliciting laughter from Loana with her comments on life in Kerielan.

Nevertheless, Loana thought she detected some lifted eyebrows when she returned to serve the coffee, and she could not be sure whether it had to do with her previous behavior or the aromatic brew. They drank it gustily, but she knew that except for Namath and Kamar, it was alien to their lifestyle and could be viewed as an insult to the modest homes of most of Kerielan's residents. They had profusely complimented Tamar's honeycakes and Simonus' pears, and she felt a sting of self-pity that no one had seen fit to compliment her choice of coffee.

"Loana . . . for a bride you brew an excellent coffee. Tell me—is this blend Sukon or Eshkolian?" Kamar rescued her pride as she poured the second round of cups.

"It is called Rasatni . . . it is Eshkolian, I believe." She spoke a little breathlessly at this obvious attention.

Kamar inclined his balding head and his smoldering eyes, clearly his best feature, in her direction. "I must secure some for the travelers to my inn," he said. "They come expecting new things." His lips curved over the cup rim in a surreptitious smile for Eshed's bride.

The hour was late when the plans for the fall rituals and festivals were completed. The men began filing out into the darkness, one by one. Loana, who had spent the evening becoming better acquainted with her closest neighbor, stood at her husband's side to bid the elders good evening. Simonus and Tamar, the last to leave, loaded Tamar's empty vessels onto their mounts and returned to thank the hosts.

Tamar spoke first. "I will return to help you put things to order in the morning, Loana. Leave it all now, and get some rest."

"But you have done so much already."

"I will not hear of your washing a *single* pot without me. You have enough to do these days, and it has been a full evening!"

Loana was fascinated by the chopped cadence and tonality of Tamar's voice, so different from the flowing fullness of her own. "Thank you so much," she responded. "I *do* enjoy your company . . . and your help!"

The men stood by, beaming at one another, and Simonus winked. It was evident that a new friendship had been born this night. Eshed felt a surge of love. Simonus and Tamar had always been special to him. Now they would be special to Loana as well.

CHAPTER 7

Choikos . . . a dust bowl.

Through the haze Eshed made out the outline of ancient stone buildings, rising like mirages from the desert floor. Wind came and fanned a fine, powdery grit into his eyes, causing him to cough and his eyes to run.

Wiping his wet lids on his tunic sleeve, he thought of Barak, the man he must find here. A scribe in the synagogue of Mezmerah, Barak had left his teaching post there to work on duplicating the old scrolls. He was even now reported to be on his way to the timberlands of Tsalah to lead a group of scribes for that very purpose. Word was that he would first settle some business of a family nature in Choikos, and then proceed. Keeper of a fraying copy of the administration of the Festival of Booths, Barak could supply the information Eshed needed. The Etser copy had wandered off in Eshed's absence, and the council had sent him in search of a replacement as the Festival was due to be celebrated in the Spring.

The rectangular marketplace of the village was a cacophony of ware-hawking. Jumbles of pots, baskets, and coarsely woven cloth vied for space as hollow-eyed dwellers beseeched passers-by to purchase, scrawny hands and arms tugging at tunics of likely purchasers in the heat and grime.

Eshed, still on horseback, took the napkin from around his head and shook the dust from it, setting off a jangling in his muslin tunic, which had large inner pockets on each side below the sash. One pocket held coins and the other smooth stones. The coinage provided by Namath, who traded here occasionally, was of this province. The previous night, while he slept pillowed in a small shrub beneath a tree, Eshed had lain on the stones and put a few in his pocket. They were good skipping stones for spinning across water, a boyhood practice he still enjoyed. But he had encountered precious little water on this trip. The coins, at least, would surely come in handy in this place. Stones they had in abundance!

Eshed could not ask about Barak at the synagogue; Choikos had none. The square stone deity he passed just outside the village gave a partial explanation. These people were of a superstitious nature and had clung to the square, uncut stone as their deity against all odds. It could be said that the true word of God had only been able to pass through Choikos in the hands of such as Barak. No penetration had occurred. No ground had been supplied for its flourishing. If converts were here, they were quiet about it.

Weaving his way through a crush of villagers and dusty pack animals, Eshed wondered why anyone would bother packing an animal to this place to exchange such simple belongings. An old woman crossed his path, carrying a pack on her back. From it, she emptied onto the ground a small selection of pots and, when they had sold for a trifle, took the few coins to the nearby stalls, which sold a questionable looking fruit, full of blisters and bruises. Placing three of them in a loosely woven, shabby basket, she relinquished her coin and toddled away.

"Runzan! Runzan! Vednyzarot le suqut!"

"Bara bara vew soglan relu tar!"

"Runzan! Cara runzan!"

Eshed passed a dusty knot of hagglers. Several men were arguing, as best he could decipher, over the worth of a bony pack animal. Only the creature remained calm. Rowing his long ears to keep ahead of the flies, he gazed neither to the right nor the left, regarding the gesticulating men as a nuisance to be borne calmly, much like the flies.

Suddenly, in disgust, his owner caught hold of the rope and led the donkey away, leaving the hagglers to their empty invectives.

"Char! Char! Bruna stoka sclum! Porta! Porta!" Their fists beat the air.

Refilling his empty nodah at the watering hole, Eshed's eyes skimmed the crowd. Zerubabel drank from a common trough provided for the animals of those packing through. Men and animals, intent on the watering hole, jostled Eshed as he picked a path and followed it in search of Barak. The language barrier wasn't going to make it any easier, he reflected.

Before Eshed had gone very far, a commotion on the square caused him to change direction. Villagers were quitting their homes and shops and thronging an opening near the watering hole. Curiosity and the crush of the crowd impelled his return.

Everyone was jabbering and pointing to a man who was being lashed to a post. His eyes were wide with fear. A young and timid sort of man, he gave no resistance to the rough handling he was receiving at the hands of the local clutch of enforcers. Dark, tousled hair fell to his shoulders, rope-like, and his brown chest was bare. They began to lash him with an instrument composed of a stick and leather thongs. Eshed flinched, horror-struck. What could his offense be, to be so treated? He explored the faces of bystanders for some clue.

"Poor wretch . . . if he complains, they will add spikes to the ends of those thongs."

The remark, in Eshed's own language, was directed to

him. He tore his eyes from the man on the post to the stranger beside him. The man who spoke was leading a horse much like his own and attired in colorful clothing, obviously a merchant passing through.

"What is the man's offense? Do you know?" Eshed was grateful to be conversing with a kindred soul.

"I understand a little of what they are saying. Apparently, he was commissioned to do some work for an official of Choikos, and something was stolen while he was there. He is being blamed for the theft."

"Did he do it, then?" Eshed was hurting for the man, whose yells were ripping the air. There was a pause as the instrument of punishment was adjusted.

"Is there no way to get him released?" Eshed could not bear the thought of the spikes they were preparing.

"If I recall their form of justice here, he will only be released without further harm if someone pays for the offense."

"And how much is that?" Eshed asked.

The man turned to a native on his right and asked a faltering question. "Sera . . . vez . . . runtala . . . vor sen daz . . . parve?"

"Un bara et sentun couf vor runtala," the native replied.

"He says fifteen baskets or one burro," the man offered in a crackly voice, coughing from the dust the crowd had stirred.

Eshed looked up just as the heavy arm of the henchman began to swing the lash. The first pass came dangerously close to the weakened man's eyes. He clenched them shut and tried to avert his head, his knuckles white under the knot of ropes, his chest heaving in fear.

Suddenly, Eshed mounted and rode, parting the crowd. The brute with the quick arm drew back for another swing as Eshed appeared, dark-eyed and imposing. Taking the intruder for an official, he caught the thong in midair. Arrogantly, he held his stance, shifting his feet, whip dangling by his side.

Eshed's horse trotted briskly into the square. Then, peering into the dusty upturned face, Eshed realized he had no language for this moment. He reached into his tunic pocket. At this, the tormenter leaped backward. What if this stranger was a friend of the prisoner and carried a knife? Instead, two large coins bit into the dust. The stocky henchman bent over and retrieved them. After wiping them on his vest, he turned the coins over carefully, checking their value. A moan came from the post. The lashed man peered painfully through the dust. Why had the stinging blows ceased? What could he expect now? Fearing the worst, his head swam from shock and loss of blood. He closed his eyes, his chin sagging to his chest.

Squinting, the henchman challenged Eshed. "Stempa . . . stempa . . . tren . . ."

Eshed never took his eyes from the man's face. He was not about to be bluffed out of this move.

"Tren! Tren!" The man had a quarrelsome disposition.

Eshed did not avert his eyes, even though the moans coming from the post were weakening.

In desperation, the man held up three fingers. "Tren!" he reiterated.

The young priest had no way of knowing what the foreign coins were worth. More to the point, they *were* being considered fair exchange for the whipped man's release. Without hesitation, he threw down a third of the same denomination. An underling scrambled for it and tossed it to the brute, then hurried over and released the victim, who crumpled into the dust.

Trotting his horse to the man's side, Eshed slid off. He tried to hoist the bleeding body onto Zerubabel, but the man could not stand. Sweat beads on his forehead, Eshed perused the crowd for someone who knew the poor soul. Suddenly two women, one older, and a man surged through the crowd and picked him up. Without so much as a glance at Eshed, they hurried away. The crowd stood for some moments, murmuring and watching Eshed. The hench-man cast a dark look his direction and, motioning to his helper, took leave, glancing over his shoulder at the priest as he pocketed the money. Who was this stranger, anyway? Some troublemaker from another province, doubtless. Most knew how to keep their place in Choikos, but no, not this one.

Leading his horse, Eshed made his way back through the press of bodies. His eyes pierced the crowd, hoping to find the man who had spoken to him. If he could read door-posts and talk to natives, he might help Eshed find Barak.

He was gone.

The afternoon shadows were deepening. If Eshed was to find a decent place of rest in Choikos, he must begin now. His horse trailing behind him, he investigated the inns on the square, finally choosing one that was at least clean, though austere. He was shown a small cubicle with one tiny window up high to provide light and air, a mat on the floor atop some clean straw, and a small shelf on the wall for belongings. An oil cephel, aflame, cast a pool of light against the bosky walls from its perch on the shelf. The evening meal served to guests in a common room was rice cakes and vegetables, washed down by goat's milk. It was a far cry from Loana's artful turn of the ladle, but adequate under the circumstances.

Leaving Zerubabel tethered in front of the inn, Eshed took an evening stroll. The merchants' stalls were closed tight, as everyone repaired to their homes for the night. The only buildings alight were the sort a priest would not enter, places where strong drink and lusts of the flesh were offered. Music from crude stringed instruments poured from the openings. It would have been unseemly for Eshed to look in the direction of such things, and he did not. Had he done so, he might have been aware of two pairs of eyes on him. The girl lolled against a post in a doorway. Her filmy caftan fell away from her shoulder, and a long, turret-shaped earring hung from one ear. She caught the hand of the man who stroked her shoulders and, pinching his face between her fingers, turned his head as Eshed walked by. The man's eyes glinted in recognition of the man he'd seen in the square.

Eshed ambled in silence, his mind on the fellow who had suffered the brutal whipping. He wondered if the man could possibly be resting with any comfort tonight. His thoughts went also to Barak. Certainly he could not expect to find him among the few souls who wandered the plaza this evening. As he watched the faces flowing past him in the torchlight of the inns, he knew most were abroad for improper purposes.

Just then, as he passed a dark alley between two buildings, he heard quick footsteps coming his way. He was grabbed from behind and dragged into the darkness! He was jostled about in the scuffle, and the blackness became total.

The next sensation Eshed knew was that of being carried. Two men put him to rest on a mat. He pressed hard against his eyeballs, forcing them open from the dusky hammock of his helplessness. The older man brought an oil cephel and checked his head. The fumes of the olive oil in the lamp did strange things to his insides. Tenderly, the man bent over him and fingered the wound, removing the blood-soaked twist of muslin he wore.

"Brusta . . . vor liqu . . . raufla . . . stul!" he instructed softly, and the boy who was with him brought a basin of water and some clean cloths.

Eshed recognized them as the innkeeper and his son. He smiled his gratitude, weakly. He wished he could speak to them in their language. Feeling a little stronger, he tried to sit up. The oil cephel tilted oddly, and the floor came up to meet him again. The innkeeper clamped firm fingers on his shoulders and lowered him back on the mat. Damp cloths were applied to the cut on his head, where a blunt object had left a knot and an abrasion. Parting the woolliness of Eshed's hair, he dabbed the dirt away in the dim light of the candle. The young priest made a face but was silent. As his eyes began to focus again, he noted the gleam of a metal object around the innkeeper's neck. Swinging in and out of the coarse folds of his tunic was a cross . . . Christ's own symbol. Binding his head securely in a clean turban wrap, the man clasped his shoulders, reassuringly.

"Thank you," Eshed murmured, resting back against the straw. His color was returning.

The innkeeper nodded and smiled, motioning his son outside. Extinguishing the candle, the two left him to sleep.

Morning's light sifted through the small, high window as Eshed groggily formed an estimate of his condition. His head ached, and his eyes were still prone to jump about in his skull. It was a strange sensation. The point where the blow fell ached unmercifully.

A warm and inviting aroma met his nostrils, and he saw a board of hot brown bread, a crock of butter, and a bowl of warm gruel with a pitcher of milk and a dish of honey waiting for him in the corner of the small room. By sitting up and leaning against the wall, he managed to feed himself, slowly. The first few bites tasted good; then nausea set in.

He was forced to sit very quietly for some minutes before continuing. Finally, everything settled down, and he was once again able to eat. Satisfied, he felt much better and stood up to change his clothes. He had to be about temple business today . . . he was getting nowhere this way! Unexpectedly, his well-muscled legs buckled, and he found himself sitting dizzily on the mat again. When he awoke, the shadows in the room spoke of a later hour, probably high sun. He felt refreshed and much stronger. Carrying a clean towel, he made his way through the hallway to an opening where the well in the courtyard offered water for washing. He drew some cool water in a kad and splashed it on his face and hands. When he leaned forward to wash, his head spun a little, but cleared as soon as he stood up. His thinking was much sharper now. His horse! Zerubabel must need tending. Drying as quickly as his sore head would permit, he hurried to the tree where Zerubabel was tied in front of the inn. Munching contentedly on some grain in a basin, he took time out to curl a lip in greeting on seeing his master. He had been watered and brushed. Eshed fingered the gleam of his coat in the sun. The animal lifted his head and sniffed Eshed's face and then his bandaged head, nickering softly. The creature seemed to understand something of what had gone on last night.

Eshed was still putting the pieces together. He was wearing the same tunic as the night before, and it occurred to him that he had not checked the pockets. Slapping the pocket with the coins, he heard a reassuring jingle. The one with the stones still felt heavy. He pulled the coins from his pocket and counted them. They were all there! The innkeeper must have interrupted his attacker—certainly robbery had to be the motive for the blow on the head. After yesterday's encounter, the entire village knew he carried local coinage with him.

Finding himself at the innkeeper's stall, he rang the brass bell that hung overhead. A smiling face appeared. Eshed clasped the innkeeper's hand warmly in a gesture of thanks, and when he paid his lodging fee, he tossed in two extra coins. The big man pressed the two coins in Eshed's hand.

"But why?" Eshed queried, pointing to his bandage and having no words for the situation.

The innkeeper's face lit up as he made a prayerful gesture with his hands. Ah, that was it. He had ascertained that Eshed was a priest and, as a follower of the Lord himself, had wished to be of service.

The search for Barak uppermost in his mind, Eshed used sign language for several moments to describe the man with the parchment to the Festival of Booths. The innkeeper, however, was unable to comprehend his meaning. Clasping the man's hand in gratitude, Eshed smiled and departed.

Bewildered as to his purpose in Choikos, he led his horse up and down the small paths between buildings. Everyone seemed to be in the village this morning, on some errand or other. It made him feel suddenly very useless.

The cubicles he was passing were obviously private dwellings. The only sign of religious commitment he had encountered was with the innkeeper, and he could offer nothing of Barak or his whereabouts. In fact, there was no way of knowing whether Barak was still here. *It does not seem a profitable place to tarry for long,* Eshed thought, with a wry smile.

As he passed one cubicle, Eshed detected that, unlike all the others, it was occupied. A slight humming sound came from the doorway, and just inside sat a man whose age he could not determine, weaving a basket of river reeds. He suspected that the reeds had come in on pack animals as there was certainly no sign of rivers nearby. Available streams had long since dried up, and wells were few, making water a valued commodity.

The man sang a song of unknown origin as he twisted and wove the reeds, dipping the drying ends into a pot of water to keep them pliable. He sat cross-legged with a loin cloth about him, and his bare chest and shoulders were very brown. Blue-black hair with aborigine shadings fell, tousled, to his shoulders. Hollow-eyed and somber, he seemed incapable of smiling. Eshed observed familiar looking marks on his shoulders and back . . . *lash marks!* The poor man raised his eyes and studied his visitor wordlessly.

He held the partially finished basket aloft, anticipating a sale.

"Vorsey . . . luk . . . mas tuk?" He perused Eshed's features and the colorful stripe of his coat again. Suddenly, the remembrance of this man burst through like sun from behind a cloud bank, and a smile lit his face from ear to ear.

Sensing, rather than knowing, what the next move should be, Eshed pulled from his coat pocket a series of coins into which, unwittingly, he had mixed a stone. The aborigine dropped the basket and, ignoring the coins, reached slowly for the stone. He took it in his hand and rubbed it between his palms. He turned the stone over in his hand; it seemed to represent something he had been waiting for. He stood with a gurgle of disbelief and indicated, by signing, that he would go with Eshed. Puzzled, Eshed followed him.

No one was about. He led Eshed and his horse through a back path that took them immediately out of the village. Eshed could not guess the significance of the smooth stone, but the man understood the immediacy of it and took no pause to tell anyone where he was going. Unless . . . but no! Eshed's own experience in the garden was so recent, he could not fathom that this mission had sprung from that awareness. After all, he was really on temple business, and in search of a scribe, not this reed weaver!

Cold sweat beads lined the aborigine's forehead as he climbed onto Zerubabel behind Eshed. His lips and throat were dry with fear. *Will I get away this time?* He had confidence in his protector. *Did he not help me before? Who is he, anyway?* In his mind, he could see the threatening visage of his father. As a lad, he had been given over to servitude by his father to repay an old family debt. He had long since lost contact with his family. Each time he tried to find out if the debt had been satisfied, his "surrogate family" quarreled with him, bringing suddenly to recollection some amount not previously discussed. By law, they had him dead to rights, and by circumstance, he could prove nothing!

The smooth stone felt reassuring in his palm. *Prayers are answered, after all!* Hopeless for so long, he knew that now, whatever happened, he was on his way to a better life. At least he would be free!

The innkeeper had befriended him when he was there to deliver baskets. He told him that there is a great God who came to earth as a man and hears the prayers of all who believe. When he had lain on the rooftop at night, cooling from the dry heat and labor of the day, he had looked up at the stars and known it must be true. He gazed at the constellation Chesil (Orion) and knew that the same God who spun the stars in a gauzy lacework across the sky showing the figure of a man holding a club and a lion's pelt must be deliverer God. And some part of him believed it even before he knew the innkeeper.

They had traveled only a short distance together in thoughtful silence when Eshed felt something on his sleeve. They could hear the angry screams of pursuers behind them and turned to view some villagers moving smartly on burros. Eshed sought to brush away a brown twig on his sleeve and found it stuck fast in the cloth. Just then his companion gave a little yelp of pain. When he turned to him, Eshed saw that the aborigine's back was dotted with horrid darts!

The man turned and raised his arms, entreating them to allow him to go. Then the darts hit his chest. He began to crumple toward the ground in pain and shock. Eshed grabbed him to keep him from toppling off the horse and held him securely. Their destination was just over the small incline, and he prayed for the strength to get them both into the trees.

As they entered the green rim, it looked different from the path he had traveled going to Choikos. Eshed sensed that an extraordinary appointment of the type he had so recently experienced with the Lord had been provided for him and his new companion. They would be safe here, he knew surely, for no one entered the green rim whom the Master had not specifically invited! When at last they had sunk into the comfort of the moss and fern, the fugitive watched Eshed with great, dark eyes, and the young priest knew that despite severe pain of body and spirit, the man was grateful.

Water gurgling nearby beckoned Eshed. It had been provided for their wounds. After a short rest, he urged his companion into the water, and as he did, he saw that the many darts that had hit his own tunic were gone. Somehow, the tunic had protected him from the tiny, frazzled weapons and left him free to minister to the injured man. As the aborigine came up out of the water, he took hold of Eshed's arm for support. His back was full of little prick marks, in addition to the lash marks . . . but the darts were gone!

Eshed reached for his tunic, and the stroke of his finger detected a change in texture. *As he pulled the peacock coat over his shoulder, his companion turned to view the gold-laced hat with awe. He poked at it with his finger and stroked the peacock blue of his lapel, smiling and murmuring to himself. Eshed stepped from the muddy edge of the bank, and as he did, he felt the cushioned inside of the gold slippers and knew he had left the leather thongs behind. He was ready to see the King!*

They pressed deeper into the vines and trees. His companion paused to stroke the leaves and extravagantly colored blossoms, tugging at Eshed's sleeve and smiling with each new discovery. The young priest had never seen so many overdue smiles on a face at one time. It was working a kind of transformation in him. His face was assuming a rounder, ruddier look, and his eyes sparkled. There was something else. Eshed's ankle brushed his as they passed through a narrow space in the trees, and he saw a blur of silver by his foot. It was the aborigine's foot, now clad in a slipper of silver. He raised his arm to reach a new variety of milky white blossoms, and an amber satin sleeve was framed by inky green leaves. His webbed hat was peaked, like Eshed's, and of silver with green stones inset.

Adjusting the hat to meet his friend's forehead and so restrain the wildness of his hair, he thought, idly, how even his hair would change in time. The man touched the softness of the robe in mute wonder, and Eshed knew he had probably never seen such a thing, much less worn one.

When the trees parted, revealing the clearing with its rainbows and waterfall, the Lord sat alone in the arbor. The aborigine slid from the horse and broke into a joyful run, flinging himself, laughing and crying, at the Master's feet. Eshed chided himself for not seeing to it that he addressed the King respectfully, as was his due. A great burst of holy laughter issued from the arbor, and he realized, with awe, that the Lord was as pleased with his friend's exuberance as he had been with Eshed's reticence. His companion sat as close to the Lord as the stump would allow. Eshed paused where he was, reining his horse aside, that they might confer privately. After a brief time, the Lord motioned him inside. Dropping the reins and dismounting, Eshed shared the special bread and fruit with them, feeling both relieved and joyful that his companion was there.

The Lord rested his hand on the man's head and said, "You are Iysh, which means he who serves." His eyes rested on Eshed. "You could not have known that Iysh has been greatly oppressed all of his life. He served well in his village, but there was none who said 'Thank you' or, more importantly, none who truly loved him. He had been in great bondage of body, soul, and spirit until you came and showed him my love. You have fulfilled your name and calling well, Eshed."

The Lord received the stone that Iysh had carried with him from Choikos and upon which was written a message that only the two of them shared. Eshed did not know, nor would ever know, the message that hastened Iysh to the Lord.

The Lord regarded the stone silently for a moment and returned it into the palm of Iysh.

CHAPTER 8

Rounding the final curve the next evening, he was warmed by the sight of the candle lamps Loana had placed in the window to herald his arrival. Home looked so good to him! After his harrowing experiences, he longed for the comfort of hearth and wife. *I am glad I did not take her with me as I had planned,* he thought to himself. *It is clear these assignments are not for a woman. She is alone here, it is true . . . but with Simonus and Tamar close by, I know she will be looked after.* He fingered the blue hyacinth he had plucked along the way for her. *Constancy.* That was the connotation of the blue petals that had been sprinkled at their wedding.

Eshed approached the stall to tie his horse. He clambered down and led Zerubabel to his accustomed place only to discover that it was filled by another animal. *Who has come to visit at this hour?* Lashing his horse to an olive tree nearby, he tossed a blanket over him, resolving not to leave him in the cool evening air for long after his exercise. Eshed hastened to the house, uncomfortable with the thought of a stranger in his home under cover of night.

Eschewing his usual custom of washing and removing his shoes, Eshed strode quickly into the house. Comfortably seated on the dining pillows with cups of coffee and a platter of figs and dates, were Loana and Kamar! Surprise and civility were the masks they wore to greet him.

Loana, captivating in a deep rose tunic she had donned

for his return, hair glinting richly in the firelight, rose hastily and threw herself at Eshed, almost upsetting the coffee urn.

Eshed, conflicting emotions within his breast, held her briefly, then took her arms from around his neck. The displeasure in his eye was only thinly veiled as he turned to speak to the visitor.

"Kamar! To what do we owe your visit? Is there some news you carry?" Eshed's tone was businesslike. For the moment, he had decided to ignore the impropriety of the situation.

Kamar stood, clasped Eshed's hand in greeting averting his eyes. The elder cleared his throat, "I was just telling Loah—the mistress of Kerielan about the plight of the widow Sernas. There has been an extensive fire in her home and many of their belongs were lost. The mistress . . ." There was a glint in his eye as he nodded at Loana. ". . . has been very generous in her sharing." His palm indicated a tote of clothing and household articles she had prepared for him to take.

"I see. . . ." Eshed smiled down at Loana, somewhat relieved by the news. "Tell me, what else does the widow need?"

"Nothing, it seems, at the moment. My inn has supplied food and some of the townsmen have offered to rebuild the part of the house that burned." Kamar shifted from one foot to the other, his firm wiry frame bearing a rich tunic.

Pulling the knot from his belt, Eshed removed his travel tunic, which Loana dutifully hung on a peg by the door, retrieving the hyacinth that tumbled from the pocket. "What of yourself, Kamar? Wouldn't this be a good time to take her as a wife?" Eshed couldn't resist this suggestion. The elders had approved the match some time ago, but Kamar, for some unknown reason, was reluctant.

Kamar looked down and self-consciously toyed with the fringed sash of his robe. The gilt braid edging his dark turban accentuated his smoldering eyes. "I suppose . . . but business has been rather slow. And when we marry I would like to take her on a little trip—perhaps to Trenz."

"How lovely!" Loana enthused, snuggling under Eshed's arm. Encircling his back with one arm, she held the wilting flower to her face with the free hand, sniffing its fragrance.

Kamar was both lying and trying to impress Loana with his sense of culture, Eshed concluded. The elder had to be watched. He had fallen into some questionable habits, following the death of his wife, and only the concerted efforts of the council kept him in good standing. Sin was slowly and surely eroding his personal life. A speedy marriage could strengthen his position as elder, especially marriage with the widow Sernas, whose late husband was well respected in the community. Also, she had two nearly grown sons who needed a man's guidance as they prepared to take their place in the adult community. But Kamar seemed to have his eye on the younger women of late and anyone new to the village had his immediate attention.

"Undoubtedly, the widow Sernas *would* enjoy Trenz . . . the bazaars are reputed to be the best in the world. Also the inns are quite comfortable . . . but I'm sure Kamar would know more about that," Eshed offered.

Kamar stiffened at Eshed's tart attempt to defer to the older man. Wearied by the turn of conversation, Kamar excused himself, and made his way into the night. Eshed followed and stabled and fed his horse, brushing him down as he ate. It was a good release for both, as Eshed had words for Loana and he wanted them to be the right ones. Caring for Zerubabel gave him time for rehearsal and relieved his tension.

Entering the house, he washed and prepared for rest. He

found Loana busily arranging the multitude of covers. A little charcoal brazier sat nearby, warming the room before they retired. He took her in his arms and held her for a long moment, stroking her hair. She felt him trembling slightly.

Finally, he spoke.

"Darling, I know you intended nothing improper in having Kamar here so late, but it really is not right, you know?"

Loana pulled back from him, gasping a little. "But Eshed—I was only filling in in your absence. The widow Sernas . . ." Her eyes met his, guilelessly.

"That matter had been sufficiently handled for today. It could have waited for tomorrow's light. Why was he here so late?" Eshed could not conceal his annoyance.

"I don't know," Loana sounded like a child to Eshed. "I thought it was *important*. Also . . ." She looked suddenly uncomfortable.

"Also *what?*" Eshed tossed his head impatiently and pulled his hands from around her.

Loana dropped her eyes. "Kamar had some personal concerns he wished to discuss with someone . . . and you were not here." Scarlet was beginning to infuse her neck.

Gripping her arm with one hand, he gestured with the other, palm open, fingers gouging air. "Loana! That is not *your* place. You do not advise the elders! You are a woman, after all. . . . You advise only the women. Surely it could have waited for my return. *Kamar,* of *all* people, should know better, if *you* do not." He dropped his hand from her arm and began pacing about agitatedly. His eyes blazed and his nostrils flared. *It is like herding a bunch of children, this job of priest. . . I can't be everywhere at once!*

Loana stood uncertainly, arms leaden at her sides. His anger was new to her, and she could not decide how best to deal with it. Affection seemed out . . . for the moment. Her defensive strategy had failed. She could see nothing wrong with what she had done. *Am I supposed to be like a doll on the shelf? . . . only coming to life when Eshed is home? What are my responsibilities to him and his people?* She was clearly puzzled and not a little hurt. She chewed her lower lip, clasping her hands tightly at her waist. Her eyes followed his pacing.

Kamar! Eshed thought with disgust. Up to his old tricks—using a woman's sympathetic ear to gain her favor . . . and in many cases her heart. It was his downfall as men viewed it, and his charm as women viewed it. *I can't tell Loana how wily he is. She would only laugh. No point in blaming her. It's an old story. Still, she must learn to respect my position. I am her priest and his priest. . . .* Eshed turned and smiled at her slightly, his brow furrowed.

He can be such an enigma, Loana thought.

"Come to rest . . . enough for one day," she entreated softly, extending her hands.

Slowly and silently he undressed and flung himself on the mat, much like the "children" he was bewailing.

Loana extinguished the brazier and blew out the candle wick in the cephel. As it flickered out, she saw an after image of the grouted design on the dish shaped vessel. It was a lotus flower, but in her agitated state it resembled a claw reaching upward!

Sweeping her long hair to one side under her neck, she lay on one hip with her back to her husband as he struggled into sleep. Some hours later, wearied by his wrestling, Loana woke him, softly caressing his cheek with her hand. He reached up, groggily, and took her hand in his. She moved closer to him, under the covers. Responding swiftly, he seized her lips with his and hungrily claimed her, releasing them both to the opiate sleep of lovers.

Morning's light found Eshed rested and at his prayer stone. The air moving about him brushed the nighttime chill into his tunic, but the sun was pouring warmth into his bones in response. Or was it the remembrance of Loana's arms about him, forgiving and being forgiven as only love could do? He felt ready to take on the world this morning! As he rose from the stone, he heard a horse approach. He hurried to the front stoop. A tall man in the flowing tunic of a priest was tying his mount to a tree. As he pivoted, the morning sun caught a familiar profile.

"Jarad!" Eshed was more than a little surprised. He strode briskly to his father-in-law's side. The two men embraced.

"You honor us—we did not know you were coming!"

Jarad flashed the brilliant smile that he had bequeathed to Loana.

"My province has given me a little time to seek an assistant. I saw no reason why I could not visit the priestly house of Kerielan! Tell me, how is 'little Loana?'" He still used the term of endearment from her childhood.

"Father!" Loana squealed from the doorway, her arm around the kad. She quickly looped her fingers through the handle and set it aside, running to meet him.

As the two walked into the house in a partial embrace, Eshed shouldered the kad and walked around the bend and over the hill a little to the well that they shared with Simonus and three other farmers in the area. Letting the kad down by the rope, he thought how fortuitous it was that Jarad had come now. Another journey loomed, and now Loana would have company while he was away. Hearing the sound that signalled a full jar, he lifted it with the rope slung over the well's rim. As the jar surfaced, he pulled the rope through the worn groove in the stone lip and gripping the kad, loosened the knot from the handle. Water sloshed over the mouth of the jar, dampening his tunic, as he hefted it onto strong shoulders to carry home. Loana would be pleased. She could only manage a partially filled kad, which meant more trips to the well. The village women always carried a full jar but they had been trained to it from birth. Loana had had servants to do such tasks.

"Blea-ah . . . ble-ah-ah-ah!" The milk goats in Simonus' pasture were anxious to be milked and turned to morning grass. A young one poked a soft nose through the jigsaw fence railing as Eshed passed. He put down the water jar and stooped to pet the baby. The kid nibbled the bark on the log fence rail. Simonus' goats supplied milk for several farms, including Eshed's. With a sniff of Eshed's hand, the kid's curiosity was aroused, and it began tugging at his sash. Stroking its flank firmly, he indicated that the meeting was at an end just as the kid began chewing the colorful fringes at the sash end.

Eshed was eager to see Jarad, but slowed his steps down the hill. It was Jared's first visit with his daughter since the wedding and Eshed knew they would have much to share. His thoughts went suddenly to his commissioning and how he might divulge that to Jarad. It would be satisfying to include the elder priest in his new found joy in the Lord! Still . . . he had not been able to tell Loana yet. Loana had all she could do to understand her own responsibilities—as last night had displayed! Perhaps he and Jarad could make a journey together if the Lord willed. Eshed lifted the latch to the gate, cheered by the thought of sharing his special experience with someone.

Placing the kad inside the entry to the courtyard, he heard their voices bouncing off the stone walls of the open air vestibule, sharing the news from Saramhat. When he entered, the conversation stopped.

"Please . . . do not stop talking. . . . Feel free!" Eshed beamed at them as he gulped fresh cold water from a gourd and filled his nodah for the day's journey to Etser.

"And when will my cousin's wedding take place?" Loana

asked Jarad, plumping a round of dough and flicking it into the hot courtyard oven, powdery grains dusting her apron like soot.

Eshed carried a basin of water from the newly drawn supply to Jarad, seated on a bench against the courtyard wall. Removing his tunic and loosening Jarad's sandal straps, he began to wash the older man's feet. Drying them with a towel he'd slung over his shoulder, he noted how long and slender the priest's feet were. Jarad was a larger, male-shaped version of Loana. They were so very much alike, Eshed reflected, listening to Jarad's waves of merriment as he shared with her. He wondered what Loana's mother had been like.

"Artemis' bride is a fiery little thing. . . . She is the daughter of a brass merchant . . . related distantly to Nebow, I understand," Jarad responded, waving a flying insect from his face.

"And Drusilla . . . is she well?" Loana wanted to know.

"She has just given birth to a girl!" Jarad bent and looked at his newly washed feet, smiling his thanks to Eshed as he removed the towel and basin.

"Her name?" Loana scooped the hot tsuwl from the oven with alacrity, avoiding fresh burns on her fingertips. She sighed, mounding the hot loaves in a basket, pleased that she was learning to handle hot things at last.

"Let me see." Her father laced his fingertips together in a thoughtful pose. "Gena? . . No . . . Dorilla? . . . Um . . . No."

"Oh, Father!" she laughed, helplessly.

"Cheselia! That's it. It is *Cheselia.* I'm sure of it!" Jarad beamed, his ego salvaged.

Eshed was feeling very isolated by their conversation when suddenly Loana began recounting the dinner with the elders and the clever way she had concealed the unpacked vessels. Her story of the white donkey's antics on the trip elicited Eshed's sonorous laughter as well as Jarad's rippling cachinnation. Her hand flew to her throat when she told about the robbers. Jarad sobered and promised a new gold necklace to replace the stolen one.

"Will you be taking the white donkey back with you?" Eshed asked as the two men removed themselves indoors where Loana had spread a breakfast board in the main room.

"I think not . . . she will be useful here. In truth . . . she may refuse to go!" Jarad pulled himself together, red-faced from laughing, wiping his eyes with a corner of his tunic.

"How is it that you are traveling about, inquiring for an assistant. Is there no one in Saramhat, then?" Eshed changed the subject, easing himself onto the cushion, his eyes earnest.

The room was filled with the aroma of breakfast. Loana ladled hot spiced fruit into the blue wedding bowls Jarad had given them as he seated himself across from Eshed.

"Alas, Saramhat is becoming overrun with infidels, I fear. The commerce has attracted many low types." Jarad's face darkened, suddenly.

Loana placed the crusty bread before them, along with a dish of curds and a piping hot brew made from pomegranate bark. As she retied the pouch of cardamom seeds and cinnamon sticks Jarad had given her to lace the syrupy fruit, Eshed was painfully aware of the difference between the Kerielanian lifestyle and the one Loana had enjoyed in her father's household. His eyes swept the simple furnishings, certain that Jarad had taken note of it.

"We have many issues to contend with," Jarad confided, "and it is *time* that I train a successor."

The platter of bread passed from Loana to Eshed for the blessing. "But, Father, you are not old enough to think of that!" she admonished him, her deep eyes flashing.

"Ah, some days no . . . some days, yes . . ." He patted her hand. He did look weary, Eshed reflected.

Tearing the bread in three parts, Eshed lifted his eyes, intoning, "For the grain of the earth, the fish of the sea, the rain on the mountaintops, the fruit of the vine, and the honey of the comb, we give thanks to thee, Adonai, God of all that is. . . . Amen!"

Placing the tsuwl in Jarad's palm, Eshed asked, "Where are you inquiring for an assistant?"

Jarad let the warm brew glide down his throat. "I thought some of the larger provinces might have young priests who could be spared. Perhaps in the timberlands of Tsalah or the vineyards of Mezmerah," he responded. "So far I have only inquired in Megev."

"And?" Eshed lifted his brows.

"They are principally unlettered farmers and would require more time in training than I have. . . . I need someone partially trained—at least familiar with the rituals," the old man confessed. He rested against the wall, chewing the fresh bread.

"More tea, Father?" Loana lifted a polished brass urn she had brought from Saramhat, and Jarad lifted his cup. The hot pomegranate brew spewed forth in a froth of steam.

"Yes, and some more of that tsuwl." Jarad indicated another round like the one Eshed had divided. "It is excellent, my dear." Deftly he dipped it into the honey cephel and placed it on his platter, breaking off little morsels and popping them into his mouth. "Ah, my child . . . I almost forgot. I have brought you something." He dipped his fingers in the water bowl, swishing them through the floating bits of rosemary. Drying them on his tunic front, Jarad reached for a parcel which he placed next to Loana. He unfastened the heavy twine around the chamois parcel wrap. Loana eyed the bundle eagerly, barely able to keep from thrusting the wrap aside. But she did not want to spoil the moment for Jarad. He lifted from it an exquisite white gown with a mezach of opalescent stones in a scroll design. The fiery gems of the girdle caught the morning light and Loana sighed.

"From the loom of Nebow . . . your wedding gift." Jarad held it out to her, his eyes twinkling.

Loana jumped to her feet and held the floor length dress to her, hugging the mezach to her waistline. She was certain none of the women of Kerielan had ever seen such a thing, much less worn one. *They live such simple lives in their shapeless garments,* she reflected. Loana scampered away to put the dress on. The two men's lips curved in pleasure, as if watching a child at play.

"Sir." Eshed returned the conversation to more important matters. "What of Zabdiy, the carpenter? I have heard many good things of him. He has studied the rituals under the priest of Tsalah."

Jarad stroked his chin thoughtfully.

"That is a possibility. . . . But there is another . . . closer at hand." Smiling, he leaned forward as if to impart a secret.

"You are thinking of . . ." Eshed groped for the name of another candidate.

"*You,* Son . . . *you!*" Slapping his knee with his hand, Jarad rocked happily in his cross-legged position on the floor.

Stuck for a response, Eshed was still reeling from this suggestion when Loana swept in, replete with her new trappings. Her hair was arranged off her face with a few elaborately decorated combs and when Eshed saw the fit of the dress, it was his turn to gasp. Her arms were bare, and the mezach glittered unconventionally just below her bosom which was displayed amply by an inadequate crossing of the pieces of fabric that draped her well-formed shoulders. A slit on the side of the skirt also revealed a portion of her leg. She would not be permitted to wear it as the wife of Kerielan's priest! Her father rose, murmuring his admiration, and placed a tsamid on the upper part of her arm. The bracelet was hammered gold with a blue-black diamond shape on it. The same emblem had been on the headband she had worn the night of the elder's dinner, Eshed recalled.

"From the Nebow family as well." Jarad smiled.

"Oh, Father! These are truly glorious! Thank them for me!" Loana twirled in place, enjoying the seductive movement of the garment. "Eshed! Isn't it remarkable?" she simpered.

Her husband's face was aflame and his throat was dry.

"Yes," he managed at last, "it surely is." This was no time to voice the strong disapproval he felt, especially in the light of her father's obvious approval.

Jarad drew still another item from the parcel.

"Eshed . . . for you . . . from the Nebow family." It was a leather binding of soft parchment sheets, a diary or record of sorts, something indeed useful to the life of a priest. He turned it over in his hands. It was a beautifully rendered cephar and had been inscribed with gold letters . . . *Kerielan*. It was the gold lettering that brought him back suddenly to the reality of his task. He knew also that it would be a hard thing to explain to Loana, who was very close to her father and accustomed to having her own way.

Running his fingers over the leather binding of the parchment, he nodded and smiled his thanks to his father-in-law, hoping that the elder priest would not choose this moment to reveal his idea to Loana but in the next moment that hope was smashed.

"I have just asked Eshed to be my assistant in training for the priesthood for Saramhat," Jarad chortled. He was a loving, generous man but greatly lacking in discretion at times, Eshed reflected.

Loana placed her body next to Eshed's, sitting as close to him as possible. "Oh, wouldn't that be just perfect? . . . What do you think?"

"I think—" Eshed swallowed perceptibly, "that it is a very fine offer. . . but one entirely out of my hands." He laid the cephar to one side.

Loana's face fell. "But why? Is it not *your* decision to make?"

"Such a move would depend on a vote of the council. They would never permit it during the heavy ritual season, if at all. And if they did, I would have to pray about it alone as well, to have the answer. I am commissioned by Yahweh *and* man. My life is not my own, Loana."

Loana looked down. She pretended interest in the bracelet and took it from her arm, testing the design with her fingertips.

Jarad cleared his throat, trying to rearrange the silence in which they struggled.

"Perhaps something could be arranged . . . in time," he murmured.

Eshed sipped his hot brew. For the moment, he could not trust himself to answer graciously. They were treating him as if he had no life of his own before they entered the picture. His commissioning by the Lord would certainly prevent his accepting Jarad's offer, even if the council did not. To have to explain such a thing to his father-in-law, a priest at that, was inconceivable. He owed him deference but it was going to be hard to show it. Eshed suddenly felt terribly alone and misunderstood.

Setting his cup down, he squared his shoulders, sat tall,

and broke the silence. "Would you come with me on my rounds today?" he asked Jarad.

Cheese and olives were stuffed into rounds of tsuwl and tucked into their inner tunic pockets. "These should get you through the day," Loana said, kissing each man's cheek. Knotting her long sleeves out of the way, she returned to grinding a large mound of wheat burrs.

"You have much grinding today, Little Loana." Jarad fondled her cheek and tucked her under his arm for a farewell hug.

"It is *my* turn to prepare the twelve loaves for the table of shewbread this Sabbath!" she announced. Jarad was tempted to chuckle at her industry but sensing her pride in her task, replied, "They will be the best loaves that table has carried! I only wish I could be here the following Sabbath when the loaves are exchanged and *your* loaves are broken with wine by the priestly family!" He winked, watching her crush the burrs into a soft meal between the stones.

"Father . . . must you leave so soon?" Loana puffed a stray lock from her eyes with her lips and Eshed saw a little pout starting.

"We will see, my dear. . . . We will see," her father replied.

Ariel. House of Martseah. Born 7th day of Elul. Rites of Purification 21st day of Tishri.

Eshed recorded the rite just performed. A proud moment, Jarad had shared in the officiation. After that, Eshed had students to instruct and villagers to call on in regard to special offerings. It was a full day and the two men enjoyed their time together immensely, despite the threatening cloud over the breakfast conversation. It was a unique sharing that priests rarely encountered. For the most part, their occupations were lonely. They entered the simple dwelling that evening, ruddy from the crisp air, verbose and amused.

"Child," Jarad called to Loana as the two men washed for supper. He could see the blue of her skirt as she skittered by, a big bowl on her arm. "You should have seen the kid that got loose today." At this, Eshed joined him in laughter. "It was racing through the stalls while the nanny bleated after it. Baskets and bolts of cloth were tumbling everywhere. It ran between the legs of a man pulling a cartful of cedar spikes."

Jarad stopped for breath, and Eshed chimed in, "and the load of spikes rolled all over the ground . . . knocking people off their feet. In the confusion, the she-goat ran into Martseah's stall, but in a split second she was headed back out with Naveh, wielding a broom, right behind." It was Eshed's turn to gasp.

"But your husband, my dear . . . he is the one . . . yes . . . *he* is the one!"

Loana broke into a smile that showed her dimple. Tapping a wooden spoon rhythmically on the cutting board, she asked, *"What is it? . . . What has he done now?"* Her hand rested on the curve of her hip.

"No one could catch the little rascal," Jarad confided. "So Eshed grabbed a cloth from one of the stalls and dropped it over the kid's eyes as it flew by. It slowed a little, and he was on its back, plucking it up like a round of sheep shearings and returning it to the caravan stabled at Kamar's inn. The mother followed along fussing enormously . . . and everyone watching *cheered!*"

They shared the day's events with Loana over supper. She murmured happily as she tended the meal, careful to see that each man's preferences were met. It would be such a pleasure to look after them both every day in Saramhat, she thought as she poured the wine, watching the two beloved faces in the candle glow, especially with servants to help her! How she missed Proustia, who had mended her clothing and made new garments for her in the latest designs of the East! Proustia was also a fine herbalist and had compounded refreshing unguents of aloes, spikenard, and myrrh that kept Loana's skin glowing. She touched her face in remembrance. It seemed to be coarse already from the lack of these treatments.

Before extinguishing the final lamp that evening, Loana made another try at influencing her bridegroom. She braved the coolness of the air by wrapping her body in a filmy deep blue caftan. As her husband undressed, she slipped up behind him and put her arms around him.

"Eshed," she spoke softly, running her fingers gently through the hair on his chest.

"Yes, my love," he placed his hands over hers and viewed the top of her head over his shoulder.

"Will you consider Father's offer? It would mean so much to him."

The day with Jarad had been pleasant. Eshed was sorely tempted to comply or, at least, soften considerably toward the idea. The three of them *did* get on well together. Jarad was certainly a lovable man. Still . . . it flashed before Eshed's eyes as he prepared to speak . . . the scene with one young student today. He had a rather simple question that was well covered by temple doctrine. Jarad had answered it for him while Eshed was busy with another student. Still in earshot, Eshed realized that Jarad had winked theologically at a ruling that Eshed considered paramount to the faith. He would now have to find a tactful way to correct the boy's misunderstanding. It might have been overlooked in a novice, but for Jarad there was simply no excuse, his age and experience forbade such a reply.

Eshed took her hands down and turned to face her, resting his hands on her shoulders.

"Loana . . . you must understand. I have my responsibilities to Kerielan as well as this household. I do not wish to disappoint your father—or you—but I must do what is right."

"But how could it not be right if it would make us all happy?" Loana placed her slim fingers under his arm and pulled him to her.

He folded his arms over her shoulders and stroked her back as he spoke. "There are things you do not understand about the mantle of the priesthood. One of them is that I am the head of this household and of the community and you must not question my decisions. You must trust me to handle this one fairly and prayerfully. Can you do that?" He lifted her chin with his forefinger and looked into her eyes.

"I will try." She shivered a little. The cold was penetrating her thin garment. "But it seems so very hard to me . . . when everything could be so *easy*."

Eshed, sensitive to her chill, said, "Loana . . . why are you wearing that *useless* outfit? . . . Put something on your shoulders. Don't you have a *muslin* caftan?" he asked.

"Yes," she pouted, "but I thought you would like *this* one better. I guess I was wrong!" She turned suddenly from him, her voice tense.

He caught her hand, "I am partial to the blue cloth," he said, stroking the back of her neck. Levity might avert misunderstanding. "I just do not want your body to match it. Now under the covers!" Gentle, he slapped her hip and she slipped under the quilts, feeling cold all the way through.

Eshed quaffed the lamp. The household was at rest. Father Jarad could be heard snoring in the next room. It had been quite a day. . . !

PART 2
TAPESTRIES OF GOLD

CHAPTER 9

Passage through the thick brush was laborious. Zerubabel's belly was dripping moisture, and Eshed was soaked from the knees down as he approached the seaside village of Ohad. A fine mist shrouded the seaport this chilly morning and he would welcome a fire.

The white dome of the temple was discernible through the haze. *Nebak will be expecting me*, Eshed thought, but he felt no sense of elation on completing this long awaited journey. In its place was a strange leadenness. *Why can't I leave the situation with Loana and Jarad behind me? Every hour she spends with her father will make my stand on Saramhat more loathsome in her eyes. . . . Yet what else could I do?*

Nestling his head into the coarse wrap of cloth that warmed it and surrounded his throat, he wished fervently for a cuff of wool from Namath's dwelling. Flax-woven linen for ceremonial garments and muslin for everyday wear were the priestly garb, and in Kerielan that was adequate, but traveling into higher country should merit some privileges for such as he, Eshed reflected irritably.

Stabling Zerubabel in a stall provided behind the Temple, Eshed chided himself for his vanity. The heavy outer curtain of the temple showed much wear, as did the lintels. There was considerable work to be done here, and his thoughts were on personal garments!

In the dark foyer, he yanked the face wrapping back, exposing charcoal hair strands to a shaft of light from an upper window.

"Peace, my brother Eshed. It *is* you!" A cheery voice came at him from the darkness. Slowly, his eyes refocused on the form of Nebak.

Flickering light from the altar lamp profiled Ohad's new priest. Distant kinship had impelled him to service in the Ohad temple following the death of Elidad. Though related, they had never met. After the vote of the council, Eshed had met the young priest in Etser as he journeyed to Ohad and had given his personal approval. Eloquent of speech and mellow of temperament, Nebak had been in lifelong preparation for the priesthood. In writing and speaking, he had no peer, but whether he was fitted to restore this temple and exhort the dwindling group of followers would soon be evident. Eshed, by seniority and predisposition, was singularly qualified to help him.

As they embraced in greeting, though young in their relationship, Eshed had a presentment of destiny with his sturdy charge that ranged beyond these walls. Cherubic and fair in appearance, Nebak reminded Eshed of the creatures floating about the design of the faded temple tapestries.

"And how was your journey?" Nebak wanted to know.

"Wet!" the senior priest chuckled, shaking out his travel coat near the heat of the altar.

"Abahlia!" Nebak called.

"Right here!" a young woman's voice answered, and a head poked around the altar corner, where she had been busily polishing the brass.

"This is Abahlia who assists me here. She is related to Siddar of our council through Jeremiah, her father."

"It is good to meet you!" Eshed replied to her acknowledgment.

"Will you bring a quilt for Eshed and something hot to drink?" Nebak requested.

"Surely!" With a radiant smile for Nebak, she gathered her implements and left.

Nebak waved Eshed to a set of cushions in the bright corner he used as a study. They talked first of the particulars of the ordination ceremony. He had just introduced the need to refurbish the temple when Abahlia returned with a quilt over her shoulder and a tray yielding a pitcher of steaming goat's milk and thin slabs of wheat loaves.

"Some of the wood needs replacing." Nebak stated a fact that had not escaped Eshed's attention from the moment of his arrival. "And," Nebak added catching Eshed's eye on the tapestries as he wrapped himself in the quilt, "I am afraid I do not know how to go about restoring the tapestries. Some carpenters have agreed to give us a little time, however."

"We will find a way." Eshed inhaled the steam as he drank the hot milk. He was beginning to warm up, grateful to have Ohad's problems claiming his thoughts rather than his own.

Streaks of pink and amber were displayed on the lacquer surface of the water as the sun set behind returning fishing vessels. Eshed breathed in the salt air. *Invigorating*. If only Loana were here to share this sunset!

"Our timing is good," Nebak offered as they sauntered among the stalls teaming with villagers hurrying to finish their tasks before sundown. He pointed to the fishing boats, full-sailed in the evening breeze. "We can purchase some fresh fish for our dinner."

Eyeing the full-muscled men who hauled their nets laden with the day's catch to the stalls, Eshed felt good to be here. Knowing the people laid to Nebak's charge increased his usefulness. Colorful sails of ecru, rust, salmon, and grass green were being pulled down, one after the other, as the boats docked.

A young girl pushed past them with a tray of dried fruit on her head. Eshed's eyes were drawn to her. Brass discs dangled from the tray's edge and circles of them adorned her ankles and wrists. Flashing intermittently in the softened light, they attracted as much attention to the wide-set eyes as the fruit tray itself. She glanced sideways at the two men. *A heathen.* It was the only explanation for her demeanor. Eshed struggled to keep his eyes on Nebak whose attention remained, dutifully, on his sandals, hands clasped behind his back as he strolled. *It will be necessary to find a suitable mate for Nebak soon,* Eshed resolved. *Ohad thrives with temptation for a vital young man.*

They stopped at a fish stall where wetly shimmering samples of the day's catch were displayed on strings hanging from the roof post.

Stepping up to the "counter" where purchases were recorded, Eshed inadvertently jostled a woman with baskets suspended from a rod on her shoulders. Brown and red legumes spilled on the ground and he stooped quickly to pick them up. He trickled them into the basket. When he looked up, he saw Abahlia. She smiled her recognition.

"Ah, you are recovering tomorrow's meal," Nebak laughed, slapping Eshed on the shoulder as he straightened up.

Abahlia also was on her knees, and as she stood, the baskets swung unevenly on her shoulder and she transferred some greens to the opposite side for balance. "I thought you might enjoy fresh fish for supper this evening." She pushed the rod in place with strong fingers and stood tall, shrugging the rod to the most comfortable position.

"These look tempting, don't you think?" Nebak indicated two of the new catch to Eshed. Their pearlescent undersides were all that Eshed could see from his vantage point. He concurred and turned to Abahlia, who was watching Nebak. Her almond-shaped eyes lit up when Nebak placed the fish in the baskets. A large twist of cloth held her brown hair in a wound and knotted fashion behind her shoulder, a slight wisp showing at the neckline.

A shrill, raspy voice called their attention on the other side of the stall. A woman was haggling with a tradesman over his fish price. He raised his voice to be heard above hers. Suddenly, she flung the string of fish she was holding onto the counter, spraying blood and liquid on the tradesman, and stomped out.

She pushed past Abahlia's "Good day, Sarakabel," without a word.

Abahlia studied her feet, looking sorrowful.

"Who is she?" Eshed inquired softly.

"My kinswoman, Sarakabel of the house of Arag. She is . . . a . . . most . . . unhappy person."

"You are so gentle and soft-spoken, it is hard to believe you are related," Eshed said. As they walked back to the Temple, Abahlia poured out Sarakabel's story.

"She is related to me on my mother's side. Our part of the family are believers. Her part is not. They are weavers by tradition. She works at it still, offering her tapestries in the marketplace."

"Has she no husband?" Nebak was curious because she was not a young woman but was approaching her middle years.

"Yes. She is married to Ardon, the fisherman. . . . He is away for long periods, fishing, mending his nets, and selling her wares at other ports."

"Why doesn't he sell them here?" Eshed wanted to know.

The baskets swung gently at her side as she walked. "He

is a clever man with trade," she replied, "and he claims he gets a better price on the northern coast. Also they are childless . . . so he has only Sarakabel to come home to. . . . He is home once or twice a season."

Coming home to Sarakabel *was* a dismal prospect, Eshed thought ruefully. *Ah, but that was judgmental. . . . There is always a reason for these things if one is permitted to know what it is.*

"Is it the childlessness that has caused their unhappiness?" Eshed was moved to ask. After all, it was the ambition of every home to rear many sons.

"Yes, but that is not all. When Sarakabel was young she was very much in love with a young man of our village named Aridatha. He was tall, strikingly handsome, and sun-bronzed and was developing a good trade as a carpenter. They were betrothed. Ohad fell under attack by the Circans from up north. He went out from the village with a band of men to defend us. He never returned. She has not been the same since."

"What of Ardon, her husband?" Nebak asked.

"He was bound by an old custom to take her to wife in his brother's place. Ardon was away fishing at the time of the uprising and was spared. It is a sad match they have made, I fear. I understand that both of them tried very hard in the beginning." She bit her lip. Excusing herself, she hurried into the temple to finish preparing the evening meal.

Nebak lit the oil cephels and foraged in a back corner for the ceremonial vestments he would use at his ordination. Retrieving them from a dustladen shelf, he placed them in Eshed's hands.

"These have been so long in storage, I doubt they can be used." Eshed pointed to where the cloth had rotted in several places adjoining the embroidered hem.

Abahlia arrived with a steaming fish platter. Nebak's broad hands turned the garment this way and that, showing her the spots where the light peeked through. If there was one thing that must be unsullied, it was the priestly garment, and there was simply not time to make another.

"Sarakabel," she said. "Sarakabel is as quick with a needle—"

"As she is with her tongue?" the impish Nebak suggested. "I am sorry—that was ungracious." He blushed deeply.

". . . as she is with a shuttle." Abahlia's smile told him she agreed with his observation though it was not what she meant to say.

It was arranged. Abahlia would ask Sarakabel to accompany her to speak with the priests about the vestment repair at the next dawn. Recognizing the figure of her brother, Thaddeus, in the temple doorway, she withdrew. He had come to escort her home through Ohad's dark streets.

The purple cloth was taut in Sarakabel's expert fingers. A slight pull at the seam was all that was necessary to produce a fresh tear.

"Ach!" She disapproved of the priestly garment. "The weave has rotted. We should make another." She sat cross-legged on the floor mat as if she were already at the loom. Her dark tumble of silver-tinted hair obscured the sharp concentration of her features as she bent over the garment, turning the flaw to the light to examine it. Her figure was wiry and slightly bent from years at the loom.

"We are committed to a time for the ordination. There is much to be done while I am in Ohad . . .," Eshed ventured, receiving his portion of breakfast from a tray offered by Abahlia.

There was a long, scowl-filled pause as Sarakabel considered his words. "There is only one way." She wagged her head. "It must be rewoven in places. A common needle will add nothing." All of her movements were quick. The one thing she shared in common with her younger cousin were the hands, Nebak noted—they were incredibly strong and capable.

"Will you do it, then? We would be very grateful," Nebak enjoined. The young priest smiled ingratiatingly. He had a wonderful way with people, especially women, Eshed noted, in contrast to his own businesslike demeanor. They made a good working team. Eshed, the *Arakna,* the order maker, and Nebak, the poet.

Sarakabel squinted at the cherubic face before her. Her head wrap was askew and her hair fell in little frizzles on her brow, accenting deeply lined green eyes. A curt nod was the weaver's answer. She would return with the garment for the following day's ceremony.

Elders arrayed in their finest tunics were assembling. With a nod to one another and a reverential tap on the doorpost, they entered the temple for Nebak's ordination. There was a lightness about them. Though none had voiced it in his hearing, Eshed sensed that Nebak was a welcome tonic after the dryness of Elidad's final days as priest.

A woman's face appeared hesitantly at the door. It was Sarakabel. Eshed, in his white linen vestment with the blue ribband mantle, met her and received the garment. They stepped to one side of the doorway and he held the cloth to the light, searching diligently with his eyes and fingers.

"Incredible! I know where the holes were, but I cannot find the mend! You have done a remarkable job, Sarakabel." His fingertips brushed the fabric. Even the gold fringes had been restored.

Sarakabel looked down at her dusty sandals. Eshed thought he could detect the slightest trace of a smile on her face. Clasping and unclasping her hands in front of her, she turned to go, anxious to be on some errand, or perhaps just away from the temple.

Eshed put a restraining hand on her shoulder, "Wait. Could you . . . could you do some weaving for us?" he implored, cocking his head to confront her visually.

She turned sideways in the doorway and, hand on her hip, regarded Eshed over her shoulder, which was expertly draped with a rich tapestry scarf of her own design. Calculating eyes roamed the cloth hangings of the room, appraising each. She got right to the point. "What would it pay?" She gestured with an outstretched palm. "I am the only weaver in Ohad." Her fingers fluttered greedily.

Stymied by this obvious challenge from a woman, he searched for a figure, but none would come. *I have no idea what to offer from this run-down arrangement,* he thought, as it was still unclear what materials and labors were being donated. "It would be several month's work. . . . You would have to bring your loom here to insure that the original tapestries were reproduced. I am sure we can agree on a price." Eshed could not understand his bravado, considering the paltry offerings from which they were forced to work, but she agreed to return later and discuss the matter further. *A good businesswoman,* he thought, *she refuses to settle too quickly. It will require a little bargaining!*

Nebak refreshed himself in the ceremonial laver. Eshed laid out his priestly garments within reach and excused himself. The golden lampstands flared into life at the touch of the taper, and soon the polished incense pots were also smoking as tradition required. Eshed laid aside the taper and strapped the metal ephod over his linen vestment. The candle lamp's beam caught a glisten of stones as he knelt at the altar and, clasping his hands, prayed silently for some moments. He asked a blessing on the priesthood of Nebak that he might be worthy of his calling in every respect. Eshed had come to love Nebak, and his heart stirred with filial affection as he lifted his arms in supplication to signal the beginning of the ceremony. The elders gathered at the altar, and forming a circle, laid hands upon Nebak, and prayed for him. Facing the group, Eshed read from the holy liturgy, speaking the traditional words that made Nebak a priest in charge of his own congregation.

Still, it was not strictly a traditional ceremony. Worship practices were changing and would continue to change due to the rending of the temple veil on the day of the cross. Eshed had been only a priest in training and had not taken his vows, but the priests who had witnessed that turning point had been profoundly altered in their belief. In this congregation things would be different from what Nebak had learned alone with the scrolls on the hillside of Tsalah, his home, or in the synagogue school there. Already Eshed had ordered the stone deities removed from the garden along with a statue venerating the ruling prelate. Honor was to be reserved for the one true God and him only. There had been dissension among the elders over this which he planned to report to the jurisdictional council. He didn't wish to see Nebak pressured into a reinstallation as soon as his back was turned.

Nebak stepped forward in acceptance of his calling and sang the benediction. The tassels on his long sleeves caught the lamplight from behind and jiggled when his tenor voice spun a high note to the lofty ceiling. It was the most meaningful moment in any ordination ceremony, and Eshed's eyes misted as he watched Nebak.

Women were not permitted attendance at the priestly ordination but Abahlia had remembered Nebak's moment with a tray of sweet cakes and a hot, pungent brew that the elders and Eshed shared with him.

Ceremony and refreshments over, the elders shook his hand before filing into the busy village street to continue their pursuits. Eshed was the last to give Nebak the right hand of fellowship.

"You will be a worthy priest," he intoned, looking deeply into Nebak's roguish eyes. "Elohim has made this known to me." The tease left Nebak's eyes, replaced by a somber reflection. Nebak flushed and hung his head briefly, then grasped Eshed's neck and embraced him heartily, their two metal ephods grating unceremoniously.

An amassing of talent took place in the next few days. Workmen moved Sarakabel's loom into place accompanied by much fussing and fingerwagging on her part. Carpenters and gardeners were crackling about the premises, arguing and laboring new surfaces and greenery into being. Abahlia was making several trips a day to the marketplace to secure enough food to feed everyone. Eshed and Nebak spent their days answering questions and giving one another verbal support with the workmen and keeping contact through hand gestures when conversation became impossible.

"Do you have everything you need. Is the light adequate?" Eshed inquired of Sarakabel, who sat unperturbed amidst the confusion, lifting the shuttle of the standing loom, fitting the horizontal woolen threads against the vertical flax.

Actually, Sarakabel was very pleased with the location of her loom, though she would never say so. Through the vertical cords she could see everything that went on and still remain aloof from it. As she wove her way through ensuing days, she caught sight frequently of her kinswoman carrying little portions of honeycake, freshly baked, or hot drinks to Nebak as he went about his duties. She clucked her tongue and shook her head to herself. *What is the girl thinking of? Aunt Rachel's offspring always were hopeless dreamers, after all, but a priest? Really!*

"Sarakabel . . . you *must* eat something!" Abahlia scolded. She could not get her cousin to leave the loom and eat with her. Frequently, she had been forced to leave Sarakabel's portion by the loom and found it, hours later, untouched and stone cold.

Annoyed by her cousin's solicitude, Sarakabel shrugged her away.

"This soup is made of endive greens. You may have eaten it at my house when you were little. . . . Mother always said it would curl straight hair and give her girls good breasts for nursing babies." Abahlia's hand flew to her face when she realized what she had said. She had only meant to tease Sarakabel into eating something!

"What is that to me? I ask you!" Sarakabel's lip curled sarcastically. "Go on, now . . . make moon eyes at your priest, but do not say I did not warn you. You are asking for trouble, you are. He may be a priest, but he is only a man, after all!" she hissed.

"Sarakabel! What are you saying?" Abahlia was appalled. The soup began to slosh from the bowl in her trembling hands.

"I am not blind, child . . . and I never have been stupid!" Sarakabel yanked the bowl from her hand. "I will eat this, if you promise not to spill it on my flax." She took a big gulp, made a face, and wiping her mouth with the back of her hand, returned to lacing.

Abahlia *was* clearly in love. Even Eshed, immersed in his own pursuits, was certain of it. And Nebak was clearly confused. Eshed spied them conferring on a new wooden bench in the garden one morning. Such meetings were becoming more frequent. Of course there are many things to ask Nebak about these days, Eshed reasoned. But each one seemed to have a special urgency!

Eshed drew back into the shadow of a pillar. He did not wish to spy on them . . . and yet, in fact, he was! He peered around it discreetly. Abahlia wore the rapt look of a young girl who sees destiny eating honeycakes before her eyes, and Nebak's expressive face reminded Eshed of someone breaking in a new donkey, enjoying the ride but dreading the blisters! The timing of her attention was awkward to say the least, as Nebak viewed it. His poetic soul had in mind a lengthy, sentimental attachment. Perhaps some men selected a bride like a piece of livestock, but that was not his plan. He wished he didn't have to see her every day. The tilt of her head as she spoke to him and the smooth duskiness of her skin were very arresting. A little lift at the end of her nose complemented the unusual shape of her eyes. Eshed smiled as if reading his thoughts. *She is not beautiful in the classic sense that Loana is beautiful,* he reflected. *Still, a more interesting looking girl could not be found. Probably there is a rare mix in her background, somewhere. . . . She is very striking. . . . That is it. . . . She is unique.* That she would make a suitable mate for Nebak, he had no question.

The pageantry of the temple restoration moved ahead with determination if not speed. The days settled into a quiet blend of construction and routine parish tasks. One morning, a young couple brought their newborn for the ritual cleansing and blessing. The young mother, hair wet about her shoulders from her own morning ablution, held the six-week-old to Eshed for cleansing in the laver. As Eshed took the baby in his arms, the wrapping pulled askew, and he saw that it was a girl. He smiled at the young couple and handed the infant to Nebak. It would be his first blessing as their new priest. Nebak clutched the child nervously. The baby began to fuss and toss her head in the blankets. Nebak looked at Eshed imploringly. Eshed merely nodded.

"What name do you give the child?" Nebak remembered to ask, little beads of perspiration breaking out on his forehead.

"Ria." The father spoke, clearing his throat. "Ria, of the house of Simon." The young couple moved closer together, gazing happily at one another.

The senior priest moved to help Nebak with the purification of the squirming child. He lifted the heavy lid of the laver and offered to hold the infant while Nebak performed the ablution. They knelt before the laver, and after a brief prayer, Nebak began pouring a little water over the child to prepare her for immersion. As she wriggled in Eshed's firm hand, he moved his finger aside on her head where it was cupped in his hand and as they placed her tiny body in the water, he noticed an angry red mark on the side of her face and neck—a birthmark, not visible while she was swaddled. He felt a sinking sensation in the pit of his stomach. Not one to go along with old wives' tales of tragic early death for those who were marked in the face, he still regretted that a small girl, so perfect in every way, should have to bear this stigma.

As she came up out of the water, screaming, Nebak saw it too and the priests exchanged knowing glances.

"Simon . . . Marissa . . . you have a fine daughter." Nebak handed the baby, loose in her wrappings, to the mother. As soon as she received her, the baby blinked her big eyes and stopped crying.

"Thank you, Nebak." Marissa rewrapped Ria, carefully obscuring the mark with the blanket. Simon averted his eyes at that moment. They were obviously self-conscious about the mark, but neither mentioned it.

"Eshed?" Nebak gestured toward the child, deferring to him as the elder priest for the final blessing.

"Ria, of the house of Simon, may God's blessing go with you all your days . . . in the name of the Father . . . the Son . . . and the Holy Spirit . . . Amen," Eshed intoned, his hand on the infant's head. They departed noiselessly. Ria was asleep.

CHAPTER 10

Morning's light was the best time for loom work, so Sarakabel scoured, carded, and spun the wool by oil lamp at night. She was experimenting with several dyes so as to replicate the old tapestries. It was exciting to see the purples, golds, and greens emerge in the weftage. The warp thread or background was always a solid color, usually dark to make the fringes stand out. As each figure emerged, she built that section carefully, getting up and checking the other side of the loom frequently to see the finished side of the picture. Tapestries were woven from the wrong side. She became so absorbed in building the pattern that only the most wrenching events could draw her attention from the work.

Sarakabel was a painstaking craftswoman. She pulled the shorter thread of the emblem tight in her hands, dipping her fingers in oil. She only resorted to the wooden bobbin for the continuous thread that traversed the width of the frame, separating the design dramas. As she pulled the dark threads from the long wooden shaft of the hand spindle, she viewed with pleasure the golden cherubs that had just been formed in the weave and appeared to leap from the surface.

Abahlia, banging among the pots in the kitchen, was singing an old song from her childhood. Polishing a brass pot, she caught her reflection in the bottom. The image smiled back at her, widening as she thought of Nebak performing his first infant blessing that morning. *Perhaps, in time . . . it will be our child he blesses,* she thought. She placed the pot on the hook over the fire and poured well water into it. Dropping a few bones in it for soup stock, she began chopping fresh herbs to add later.

"If you meet me by the well . . . I will not tell . . . I will not tell," she sang happily. She danced lightly about the room, incorporating the herb chopping with her movements and sweeping the pieces onto a tray with one grand movement. Her light foot and sense of drama appealed to Nebak's sensitive nature. Her brothers, on the other hand, were much like Sarakabel. They only thought her silly and impractical, building their own judgments of life around worldly aims . . . money, acquisitions . . . and in their case, pleasant companions with which to hang about the bazaars. But Abahlia was intensely practical . . . as time would attest.

The weaver hummed the tune with Abahlia in spite of herself. There was an old taboo about singing at a loom. Yet here in the temple it seemed appropriate. She held the gold threads in place with a wooden comb as her other hand introduced the dark thread bobbin in a horizontal looping against it. Her mind went to the old legend of the warp and the weft.

"The warp . . . God," she whispered, stroking the vertical thread that was the backdrop and sustaining form.

"The weft . . . man." The activity of man was both stabilized and accessed as the horizontal thread interwove the warp.

Sarakabel cocked her head. It made an arresting story, but it had hardly been true for her, she mused. Her life seemed only a maze of disconnected threads with no real meaning behind. Oh, she had been cared for and protected, after a fashion. She had not been put aside or forced to support herself, but on the emotional level, life had little color. Weaving had been the central joy in her life. Only there did she find sustenance and form. There she could control what happened and make it beautiful. She hummed softly as she worked. It was probably the closest thing she had ever known to worship.

"Nebak! Nebak!" The voice of a young woman called from the temple entry. "My baby . . . my baby!"

Nebak and Eshed, poring over old records, hurried from the study toward the sound of her voice. Marissa was running toward them, holding Ria to her breast.

"What is it? What is wrong?" It was impossible to read her mood at his distance, and Nebak hurried forward and encircled the mother and child with his arms.

Tears were streaming down her face, but a smile was discernible beneath. She was laughing and crying in such a mix that he could not understand a single word she said. Just then, Eshed pressed at their sides and thrust the blanket from the infant for a closer look at the child. Marissa pointed wordlessly to the side of the infant's head. The birthmark . . . it was gone!

Sarakabel rose tentatively and crept closer for a look. Abahlia joined her from the kitchen.

Nebak gaped, open-mouthed. Catching the incredulous look on Eshed's face, he broke into wholehearted laughter.

"Thank you . . . thank you," Marissa managed at last.

Nebak embraced her with some appropriate words about the blessings of Yahweh and sent her on her way.

"What was wrong with the baby? She looked all right to me," Abahlia offered, after Marissa had left the building.

"That's just it," Nebak chortled. "When Eshed blessed her, she had a scarlet birthmark—now it is gone!"

All eyes were on Eshed. But he didn't notice them staring. His eyes were fixed upon his hands, palms up and trembling. Finally, his disbelieving gaze was drawn to the trio who mirrored his awe.

It appeared that Yahweh had removed the child's stigma through his touch!

Sarakabel's thoughts were tumbling over one another. *The priest . . . the baby . . . the birthmark—what does it all mean?* She remembered stories of early times when miraculous things were supposed to have happened, a wooden staff turning into a serpent, the sea parting so that her ancestors could escape their captors, fresh water running red as if infused with blood, things like that. But such things had not happened in her lifetime . . . not in Ohad. She did recall Ardon mentioning the hanging of some prophet whose followers had insisted he walked among them after three days . . . but that was far away and unprovable. What strange magic was in this temple?

Ardon. As she pulled the oil-darkened thread through the warp and tapped it into place with the comb, her mind went suddenly to her husband among his nets, and with that came a rush of practical things, things she understood. She could see him in her mind's eye, returning with a sack of coins from the sale of her sprang hair coverings. Lace bonnets of knitted horse hair, they were greatly favored by the women of the North, and she had difficulty supplying the demand. She had discovered their popularity, inadvertently, by packing a few inside the wall tapestries Ardon carried routinely to other ports. Her tapestries did well there too. The murals she designed based on the old legends were much admired. She had a keen sense of color and texture, which gave her a real edge in the marketplace. Even now, she was experimenting with other colors and textures for her sprang bonnets, and Ardon knew how to sell them. He would return soon for more of her work.

Sarakabel's fingers flew faster as she thought of his displeasure at her current project. It would bring no coin for months, only her daily food and the validation of being appointed to a special task. *I must knit some bonnets by the oil lamp and have them ready*, she thought.

Woolly-headed and burly, Ardon was a fine-figured man whose industrious nature would have been sufficient for many women. But Sarakabel wanted more . . . she wanted what she was promised the first time . . . attention and gentleness. Covertly, she watched the attitude of Nebak and Eshed toward Abahlia and herself. The cousins were, after all, only servants of the temple, yet they were treated with a tender regard. In the world of bazaars and trade boats, this was unknown to her. Most of her contacts with Ardon spoke more of a business venture than a loving partnership. She supposed it was good that they had this link since there was no binding of children, but it was so impersonal. Ardon, once reasonable and pleasant, had grown gruff with the years.

"I can hear them singing!" Eshed startled her from her thoughts. He reached out and touched a corner of the tapestry. Aureate cherubim gleamed against the scarlet thread of the background. "How were you able to duplicate the colors so perfectly?"

"Ah . . . I cannot explain . . . it is something that you develop an eye for in time."

"I only know what I have seen . . . and that is many tapestries that were supposed to be matched in color, but the yarns were very uneven in depth. At one time I was a stonemason and had the opportunity to work in wealthy homes and poor."

Silent for an interval, he watched her push and pull meaning into the fabric with her fingertips.

"Your husband must be very proud of your accomplishment," he ventured, with a two-fingered stroke of his chin.

"He is much too busy with trade to think much of what I do . . . except when I fail to do it!" She shrugged her shoulders and squinted at the work before her.

"Men fail to express themselves about important things like your work. I, too, have been guilty of forgetting to speak my pleasure at the good meals Loana cooks and her clever way of arranging and tending our simple dwelling." A stab of remorse went through Eshed as he spoke these words. "I am sure your husband . . . ah." He put a finger to his temple.

"Ardon," she supplied.

"I feel certain that *Ardon* appreciates it nevertheless."

The little flicker of a smile that was so typical of Sarakabel crossed her face. Given half a chance, Eshed reflected, it would break out and take over her mouth. She had restrained herself well, and the lines of her face betrayed the conflict.

Thoughtfully, Eshed took his leave and returned to the garden to supervise the plantings that were taking the place of the old stone deities.

Light rays were slanting at an odd angle from the opposite side of the room through louvered openings in the wall. It was late. Clutching the tapestry bag that identified her vocation, Sarakabel stood and began assembling materials to head for home. As she reached for the spindle, her head seemed to be imitating its twirling movements. The spindle was at rest. *Why does my head feel so funny?* she wondered, grasping the wall for support. Fatigue had won the day.

"Sarakabel! What is it? Are you all right?" Abahlia's voice was phasing in and out behind her. Her cousin reached out an arm to steady her.

"Ah . . . it is nothing . . . I am only a little tired," she responded, irritably. Turning to pick up the bag she'd dropped, she stumbled against Abahlia.

"You rest, Sarakabel. You have no reason to rush home this evening. Why not stay here? I can make a pallet for you." Still holding her arm, Abahlia strained to look her full in the face.

The weaver regarded Abahlia, whose eyes were softened with concern. She had never stayed from home at night, but she *was* feeling peculiar. She felt very safe in the temple.

"I will stay with you," Abahlia offered, seeing her indecision.

"No . . . I will stay. You go home to your family. I will be comfortable here, thank you." The gentleness of her answer was very pleasing. This was a new facet of her cousin. Abahlia felt privileged to witness it.

The young temple servant arranged a pallet with quilts in the corner and left Sarakabel a hot broth for supper. "Drink this . . . and go right to sleep," she admonished. Sarakabel agreed, shakily. She was not in command of herself, that was sure. After Abahlia had covered her with a quilt and tiptoed out, Sarakabel shoved the cover aside and pulled her tapestry shawl about her body. Drowsing into its fleecy folds, she felt reassured.

She slept comfortably for some time, but in the middle of the night, she wakened. Lying quite still for several moments, she considered how she had come to be in the temple by night. Then she remembered. She felt rested. It came to her that she might light the oil lamp nearby and knot some sprang work.

A candle burned continuously at the altar. If only she could make it to the light without stumbling, she might brighten this corner and continue working. Perhaps some weaving would be possible. She hitched up her skirt and tucked one leg under her. Her knee brushed the cup holding the remains of her broth supper. She finished it off. Cold and greasy but good tasting, it seemed to clear her head even more. Sarakabel braced herself with her other foot, the strong wiry calf exposed in the soft light. Glistening on her ankle was a delicate gold chain. Three golden leaves interspersed the chain links. She saw it each time she bathed or dressed. Her fingers brushed its surface and memories, like the black night, engulfed her.

They were to have been married in the fall. The leaves were a symbol of that eagerly awaited moment. *Aridatha* had given them to her as a betrothal present. Slim, wavy-haired and full of dreams, she had moved into his parents' home to await the wedding. He had swept her to him on the day he left to fight—with scarcely time for a farewell— had kissed her lips and left her trembling with desire and rage that he should leave her. Then word came. He was gone . . . no return. Her arms ached for months to hold him once again . . . and feel the beating of his heart against her tender ribs. Then in winter, Ardon had taken her in his brother's place. For her, it had been winter ever since.

She placed her feet firmly beneath her and sought to rise, but she sat back quickly. The loom . . . it looked odd. Why was she able to see it in the dark? A muted glow was behind it. Silently, squinting her eyes, she watched . It was not the altar candle at the other end of the room. The glow increased in spite of her narrowed eyelids. The light appeared to pass through the loom and form a shaft in front of her eyes. *Am I dreaming?* she thought. It seemed the only possible explanation. Warmth began to fill her corner as though a fire were newly built. Such a warmth did not come from her dreams!

"Sarakabel!" A figure stood before her. She started at the sound of his voice.

"Do not be frightened! I am the one who has brought you here."

Sarakabel's hands flew to her mouth. Her eyes opened wide.

Sitting beside her, he began to speak of her craft. He was the Master whose loom was the hearts of mankind. Love and concern from his heart and lips wrapped her like a warm shawl. Placing her oil-tainted hands in his, she gave her heart into his keeping. She began to weep, overcome by her own insensitivity to the gift of life that was hers.

"My Lord . . . I have been a hard, demanding woman. It is because of me that Ardon is so gruff and greedy. I see it now. I see it clearly. Why have I not known this before?"

"You were not ready before. You have come to the end of your struggle. Now I can give you a true gift . . . the gift of love."

She caught the tears in the apron of her garment . . . it was laced with gold thread! She stared at it . . . blinking through the mist in her eyes. With his hand, he brushed a tear from her eye. It glistened, jewellike, on his palm.

"None of these are wasted. Not one! My Father who sent me will cast them into a crown of joy for you!"

He was gone as suddenly as he appeared.

Sarakabel's head was spinning again, this time with the strange experience. She put her hand to her temple. It felt very hot, and her fingertip brushed something hard—a circular band was on her head. She took it down and made her way very carefully to the altar, where the taper glowed. In the soft light, she found herself in possession of a golden crown gleaming with teardrop shafts of light. Gasping, she held it to her breast. Were this a dream, she would certainly not be cradling this treasure, though its quality, admittedly, was not of *this* world. The greatest reality of all had been the Christ. And now . . . this token of his promise. She wept as she had never wept before. Joy came in a flood! At last, she slept.

A new weaver was at the loom. In the days that followed, Sarakabel was the focus of many unbelieving eyes. Her step was swift and sure and her fingers flew. She was sparkling in her wit and more measured in her negative answers. Even her appearance had changed. With the return of her smile, she looked younger, softer.

Fringes. She could see the finish work coming before her eyes in the course of a few hours on the tapestry she was working. The yarn was packing in firmly and smoothly, the way she liked it.

"I never tire of watching you put those tiny gold threads in place," Abahlia sighed, looking over her shoulder one morning. "One goes in, and it looks like an error . . . then two or three, and the outline of the cherub builds right before my eyes!" Abahlia shifted the water kad from one shoulder to the other. It was empty, and she was on her way to the well to fill it.

She caught Sarakabel's eye, and a smile passed between them. Turning on her heel, she pushed through the striped curtain of the front entrance. "I'll make you some cassia bark tea when I return," she called over her shoulder.

A shadow on the wall duplicated Sarakabel's deft movements. She turned to pull the spindle closer—a knot had formed in the thread as it flipped about on the floor. It would be so much simpler if the spindle rotated on its own. She would think about that and see if an easier way could be found. A child could sit beside her during the weaving and hold the spindle horizontally and release the thread as the weaver needed it. For her it was easier to work without the nuisance piece except when long strands made it necessary! Her shadow . . . Sarakabel caught sight of it and angled to view the dark lone figure on the wall. *Alone.* She had spent her life alone at this loom—no child's hands to help her . . . no babbling voices about her . . . even Ardon away. Her heart quickened suddenly as she plucked the knot from the dark yard, for now she had someone . . . someone who knew her and loved her . . . even more than Aridatha had! She shrugged the shadow away, a singing in her heart, its energy coursing through her very veins.

Drawing the thread through securely, she flicked it into place with the long teeth of the shuttle, wiping her oily fingers on a rag at her side.

But what of Ardon? a voice deep within her probed.

"What *of* Ardon?" she heard herself respond. "He does what he wants. I do not interfere. He loves the sea and his nets . . . and the clamor of the bazaars. He is tied to me only by an old promise . . . it means nothing." The explanation didn't satisfy her inner churning. An inward tug continued, and she felt a searing heat at the core of her being. Her eyes stung with it, and so did her throat. Tears! More tears. Hadn't she confessed her neglect once? Was the guilt endless then? On the night of the golden tears she had felt so free of it. What now? *What are you going to do about Ardon?* What *could* she do that would undo all the hostile years? She dabbed at her eyes with a clean end of the cloth. The tears were falling more profusely now. Once more she was forced to catch them in her apron. *What was it the Lord said? Not one would be wasted? Yes, that was it.* She would find a way. Just as a knotted spindle could be untangled, so could this knot of guilt! A flash of gold caught her eye in the sunlight, but it was not on the tapestry. She knew where to start. Reaching down, she unclasped the gold chain about her ankle. She held it to her face, and her lips pressed the leaves. No . . . she couldn't face being rid of it forever—it was her only link with Aridatha. But she knew she could not be to Ardon what he needed as long as a shred of inconstancy remained. Stroking the chain links in her palm, she resolved that as she had given Yahweh her heart, so could she give him this! Another gold cherub was due to appear in the piece before the fringes went on. Wiping her eyes again, she peered at the work before her, crumpling the damp apron in her fist. Yes . . . yes . . . it would all come together. She reached out to finish the head and trumpet . . . now . . . now was the time. Rubbing the oil from her fingers, she picked up the chain from her skirt and threaded it into place. Lovingly, she wove the gold threads about it, stabilizing it, yet letting its gold shine through. Two leaves became the cherub's wings, the chain the golden cord that held the trumpet. A warm glow of satisfaction and release rewarded her effort.

"Tea?" Abahlia held out the wooden tankard.

Sarakabel turned to take it, her left hand remaining, lovingly, on the final cherubim. Her face glowed up at her cousin. A sip . . . a smile. Eagerly, she resumed her weaving. Abahlia had never seen her so at peace. *How that woman loves her work!* Abahlia stepped away, contemplatively, glancing over her shoulder. There was something else . . . it was almost . . . yes . . . as if Sarakabel *were in love.* Abahlia smiled to herself. She, of all people, knew how to recognize *that!*

CHAPTER 11

"Hurry along, Elnah!" Abahlia guided her younger sister between two posts, narrowly preventing Elnah's collision with one while she ogled Seth, who was stringing fish for his father inside the stall. Seth smiled, showing his large, pearly teeth and his unabashed admiration of Abahlia's black-haired younger sister. Abahlia thought she had circumvented the string of admirers that impeded their progress by choosing a path that did not go by the well, where several of them lolled about every morning to see Elnah draw water. Seth was a new one!

Elnah dropped her empty basket and bent very slowly to retrieve it. In a twinkling, Seth had bolted from the stall and swung it onto her arm. He stood, hands on hips, looking sheepish.

"Why . . . thank you," Elnah murmured, as if taken by surprise, a saucy grin on her round rose-amber face. With a coy tug of her shawl, she gave the gangly boy a long parting look over her shoulder as Abahlia reclaimed her hand and pulled her around the corner out of sight.

"I wish you would not *ask* for attention. You get quite enough as it is!" Abahlia declared. Just the week before, their father, Jeremiah, had chased four different lads from their front steps where they loitered about in the early evening on one pretext and another, never quite satisfied until Elnah peeked out the door.

"You are just jealous," the young sibling remonstrated, "because you do not have *anyone!*"

"Do not need anyone. I am quite happy just now without someone hanging about!" The taller girl shook her kerchiefed head and, releasing her sister's hand, traded grips on her basket, shrugging the coarsely woven shawl around her neck. She glanced at her baby sister, the family's youngest, with a clutch of boys between the two in age. She was all rounds, was Elnah. A ripe apple polish to her face, fully rounded breasts and hips, little dimpled hands, and plump sausage feet that showed creases from the sandal straps. Such a contrast was she to the linear, well-proportioned Abahlia that the older girl felt gauche beside her. Yet, if the truth were known, Abahlia was the prettier, with a slightly muscular look that would serve her well when she had borne her babies, whereas Elnah would be all lumps in a few years. But Elnah had something called "allure," and she had already become expert at using it.

Abahlia had just turned her head from studying the ringlets framing Elnah's beguiling cheek when her eyes locked, in that mysterious way of profound relationships, with Nebak's eyes as he entered the street from a doorway. She had not expected to see him this morning. She was taking Elnah to pick herbs for temple and household needs. Instead of looking away, he pushed through the crowd and stopped in front of them. Abahlia had never taken her eyes from his, and her heart was pounding.

"Ah, this must be your sister." Nebak patted her head scarf, and with that gesture, Elnah made the leap back from womanhood to childhood. She wrinkled her nose, distastefully, but managed a smile of sorts.

"Elnah . . . my sister's name is Elnah, Nebak." Abahlia might have been reciting numbers backward for all the words meant to the two of them. Unaccustomed to being ignored, Elnah squirmed restlessly.

His eyes looked as if they wished to speak of deeper things, but his lips merely said, "Your baskets are empty."

"We are just now going to the hill outside the gate . . . to pick bay leaves, hyssop, and capers," Abahlia acknowledged with a nod of her kerchief.

"Sounds appealing to hear you tell it. If I did not have a sickly council member to see, I would join you for the fresh air and company!" His eyes were teasing, but a note of sincerity hung behind the words.

"Abahlia—let's *go!*" It was Elnah's turn to be impatient.

Clouds rode the hilltop in the distance. If they were to finish ahead of the misty messengers, a fleet foot was in order.

Leaving Nebak gazing after them with a mix of humor and longing on his face, the girls hastened toward Chad's gate.

"Ah-hah-hah!" Elnah's little-girl chant sprang unwelcome into Abahlia's ear. "I saw the look that passed between you. Why didn't you tell me you had a lover, Abahlia?"

"Shush! Someone might overhear you! I do not *have a lover,* as you put it." Abahlia quickened her step and glanced back to see a hole in the landscape where Nebak had been. Her heart was still drumming strangely, like the reverberations of a once struck brass gong.

"*Really* . . . Abahlia," Elnah persisted. "And him a priest too!"

"That is precisely why you must keep quiet—it could hurt his name in the village." Abahlia's little tug on Elnah's hand was not altogether due to haste.

"Well . . . if there is nothing going on between you . . . why worry?" An impish smile played around the young girl's lips. She was entirely too worldly-minded for her own good, Abahlia thought, and reveled in an opportunity to goad her older sister.

"Elnah!" The gleaning spot was in sight, and Abahlia dropped her sister's hand and ran into the field, curtailing the conversation.

She bent to the plentiful caper blossoms and plucked a handful, dumping them back into the basket. The plants were heavy with the buds, now drying. She could already smell the pickling jar that would brim with the dark delicacies. "Get some bay from the branches you can reach. I will finish up on that while you get hyssop," she called.

"You do not have to shout," Elnah said, right at her elbow. "I am going to gather capers with you." She yanked Abahlia's sash for emphasis. "Nebak is certainly pleasant looking." The tease was back in her voice. "But he is only a poor priest, after all. You will end by mopping temple floors . . . and teaching poor widows how to pray for their bread." She shook her head in mock consternation.

"What do you think I am doing now, but mopping temple floors? The one thing has nothing to do with the other, sister."

"But I am disappointed," Elnah sulked. "I always thought you would marry a city official or something."

"Who said anything about marrying? No one has asked for my hand." Abahlia yanked on the branch and capers scattered in all directions. "But there are days, I must confess, when I would take him on any terms," she added more to herself than aloud.

"Abahlia! What are you saying?" Elnah's hand flew to her cheek. "Oh . . . oh . . . if Father could hear you now!" Elnah, recently the center of much fatherly advice regarding the young men of the village, was pleased to catch her sister in this little confession.

A surly rumble of thunder echoed Abahlia's feelings on the subject. "Please get some hyssop in your basket before it rains." She sought to separate herself from her sister before she became angry with her, for which she would also be called to account.

She was so weary of never being able to have an honest emotion or commit a single misstep without someone in the family rising up to cry "foul." *When—just when—did I become the standard-bearer of this family?* she wondered. It must have happened when her mother was pregnant with Elnah and very ill for months. Abahlia had taken over the household so her mother could bring the baby to term, and after the dark little bundle began to rend the night with cries, everyone, even her father, still thought Abahlia was in charge. Her brothers had continually looked to her since that point, and even her mother relied on her judgment in many things. She supposed it was a tribute to her capability, but mostly it just seemed a burden. Like now. She had no desire to be everyone's strength. Since going to work in the temple, her family had relinquished their hold on her for practical help, and Elnah was learning the finer household points in her absence. But now . . . they looked to her as some sort of spiritual purveyor who would keep them in line with temple practices, of all things! Her brothers were always in some sort of mischief, and her sister was a constant concern. All Abahlia wanted was to be a woman. To feel some good man's arms about her and know she would be protected and loved for herself. Was that too much to ask?

Her yellow brown skirt caught on a snag. She turned to free the hem and saw that Elnah's basket was brimming with hyssop a few paces from her. Swinging her arm above her head, Abahlia hummed to herself as she clutched the fragrant bay leaves from a large bay tree. Burrowing her nose in the cluster, she thought how much more alive the scent was for the rain being on the way. Thunder slapped both her ears at once, and cold spits of water darkened her skirt. "Elnah!" she called. Her little sister was already running toward her, holding her scarf from her face. The spatters were gaining in size and momentum. They would soon be drenched to the skin.

"I will race you to the gate!" Elnah called, dark streaks of liquid on her blue skirt.

They ran for the gate. A figure met them there with a tarp. It was Seth, who had been watching them during their gleaning and anticipating the deluge.

Giggling nervously, the girls sank against him, under the cover. Elnah managed to shift her weight right up under one arm so she was resting against his chest, her round little mouth snickering against his flesh like a crawly thing, trying to gain his pocket. It tickled, but he chose not to pull away. Since Abahlia had also taken advantage of his hospitality, she had no words to scold her sister. Sometimes it wasn't so bad having a winsome baby sister!

One morning, Sarakabel came tripping in breathlessly as Nebak and Eshed sat down to breakfast. She was late at her loom, and her tapestry bag was missing.

"Forgive me . . . eat your meal while it is hot!" She lit beside Eshed. "Could I remain at home for a few days?" Her words rushed at him. "Ardon is in from the sea. I need to mend and cook for him. He has been away many months!"

"Go with our blessing, Sarakabel. If everyone worked as diligently as you, we would be finished with our tasks. You deserve some time away!"

"Ah, you are so kind. Thank you, thank you both!" She squeezed the forearm of each.

The two priests beheld each other over the rims of large mugs of hot brew. A changed woman flew out the door without further comment.

Swallowing, Nebak presented a wry smile. "I hope Ardon is as strong as his reputation. The shock could do him in!"

Days later, Sarakabel returned to the temple to weave, Ardon with her. They found Nebak and Eshed positioning a new support post in one corner, fastening it in place with long spikes. The sound was deafening, and sawdust flew.

Ardon, wreathed in a smile, wore a quizzical look as he faced the two men Sarakabel had told him so much about. She hurried away to her loom, drawing his eyes after her. Facing him when seated, a long look passed between them. Sunlight that played on the weaving seemed to reflect on her face. Rainbow-wrapped, she smiled at her burly mate. And he smiled back. Turning to Eshed, he spoke.

"Had Sarakabel asked me if she could come here to weave, I would surely have said no. I am glad I was away. What has happened to her in this place? I do not understand." He had lowered his voice, yet it seemed to echo off the walls. Truth, after all, can never be contained.

The trio silently watched the weaving in process. This too, was an old taboo. According to custom, men were not permitted to watch a woman expose her arms in spinning and weaving. Therefore, all such craft took place at home. Here, in this instant, however, it was not Sarakabel's arms they were viewing; it was the transformation of her soul!

Warmed by this latest fruit of a new age, Eshed inquired, "Why don't you ask Sarakabel?"

CHAPTER 12

Eshed rose from the prayer stone. It was so good to have that familiar ritual again . . . so good to have Loana again . . . so good to be home. He breathed in the freshness of his native air and allowed himself the luxury of a stroll through the trees, stopping to examine the leaves and checking the bark for healthy signs. Fingering the dew-flecked greenery, he wondered what the Lord had in store for him next . . . another trip, another mountain to climb?

Jarad had found an assistant and returned forthwith to Saramhat. Occasionally, Loana expressed a little disappointment over the development, but otherwise she seemed to be accepting her role in Kerielan well, for which Eshed was grateful. He had many issues to ponder, and a restless spouse was a distraction, to say the very least.

Foraging in the corner of the arbor, he scraped a large clay pot from beneath the seat and poured newly fetched well water from the kad into the gaping dry chamber. Sitting cross-legged on the ground, he put in loose soil from the garden with his hands and pressed it into the fluid at the bottom. Carefully, he unwrapped a flowering tree that he had found along the trail and planted it in the pot, pouring on more water. After rinsing his hands in fresh water, he carried the jar to the front step. When the plant bloomed again, its riotous purple flowers would be seen from the road.

"Loana!" He knelt beside it, fingering the dark leaves and pulling them into shape where they had lain against the coarse wrap.

When she pushed aside the door, a boyish looking Eshed beamed at her, his dusky eyes dancing. "Yes . . . *Eshed!* What is it called?" She stooped down beside him and kissed his cheek.

Blushing and stammering, he replied, "I knew you would ask. The names of things are important to you. But I gathered it from beside the path. I have no idea what it is called. You will have to name it. I brought it for you."

"Then," she said, laying her index finger against her cheek thoughtfully, "I shall call it Shalom-alekhem! It will greet everyone who comes through our door!"

Surging with joy at her apparent pleasure and his own sense of blessedness, he stood quickly and, grabbing Loana's waist as she stood up, tossed her into the air and negotiated a circle with their bodies as she came down in his arms. Laughing, they pushed back the inner curtain to the scent of warm bread and had breakfast.

Daily tasks of the priesthood moved life forward quietly. No messages came. Weddings, burials, and blessings of homes and new babies were performed. It was a secure and happy time for Eshed. When he prayed for future assignment from the Lord, he was given one word, invariably: "Wait!"

Loana was driving her tent peg deeper every day with the acquisition of new friends and the strengthening of existing bonds. Tamar was sharing household duties with her as often as time would permit, and the two had grown close. Eshed would find them giggling over some new commonality they had discovered when he returned for a meal at midday. Tamar would scamper off, unready to break away but respecting the couple's time together.

One evening, on his return, Tamar heard his footfall on the tile entry and popped playfully into view through the hanging tapestry that separated the sun porch from the living quarters.

"See what Loana gave me," she whispered, her eyes shining. She fingered a gold chain about her neck and held the gold piece dangling from it to the light. At first, he perceived it to be a free form metal sculpture of some sort, but on closer inspection, he made out the outline of a dog's head. It was an ancient civilization's amulet of death and had been used to mark the burial place of royalty. It was thought to provide a continuing link with the spirit world after death and *had been worshiped as an idol!* He could think of nothing to say, which was fortunate, since there was no way to express what he really thought.

He feigned an interest in the chain.

"Tamar . . . I believe this chain has a weak link. I know Loana would not want you to lose it. May I take it and repair it for you? I will have to secure a little gold and a torch, so it may take a few days."

To his utter relief, she agreed, and he lifted the chain carefully over her head and placed it in the inner fold of his sash.

He felt totally justified in the little deception as there was no way to correct the situation except through Loana. He decided not to mention it until later that evening. He waved to Tamar as she took the path toward home. "Greet Simonus . . . my brother . . . with love!"

Loana was scurrying about the room, turning bits of meat on sticks on a little brazier and arranging the cushions near the food so that they might have a brief time together before the evening meal. The fragrance of the newly polished cedar floor greeted their nostrils as Eshed placed himself on the floor beside her and planted a kiss on the back of her neck where the little ringlets parted. It was a particularly delicious thing to do, and she squirmed and giggled, shrugging him away as she poured the goat's milk from a leather pouch into earthen cups set before him.

Her cheeks were flushed from her time in the garden, harvesting root vegetables and pulling the thorny brush that threatened to choke out the good growth. She had put on a fresh muslin apron, and the blue of the dress set off her eyes in a special way. It would be hard for Eshed to broach the subject of the amulet tonight . . . when his greatest desire was to take her in his arms, but his priestly duty and his duty as head of the household made his position clear—there could be no softness in that.

"I saw Tamar as she left."

"Um-hum." She smiled, fondly remembering the garden work they had shared.

"I asked her to return this." He held the necklace to the light. Firelight in the corner of the room caught the gold. His greatest impulse was to toss the thing into the fire, but he maintained control.

A hurt look came into Loana's eyes. This was going to be harder than he had thought.

"Why?" she whispered. "Don't you want her to have it?"

"I do not want anyone in Kerielan to have it—including you!" Unable now to keep the edge from his voice, he caught Loana's puzzled look. *Dare I hope it is just a mistake?* he thought. *No, no, she has to know what it means.*

"Loana . . . this is the ancient god of the underworld. We do not have such things. We serve the one true God, and he would not have us wearing these things about our throats." Eshed's heavy brows formed a solid line, hooding his eyes in a scowl.

"But it is only a—a—*thing*. What harm can it do?" She grabbed for the chain, and the head fell into the folds of her garment. She fished it out and clasped it tightly in her hand.

"Give it to me, Loana!" Eshed's voice was commanding now. His eyes shot fiery glints.

Tears streamed down her face as she quietly handed it back to his keeping. She had never seen him like this. "I have had it ever since I can remember. It has never hurt *anything.*"

"You cannot be sure about that. In a priestly household, we certainly do not need the influence of such an amulet. What if Tamar had worn it among the other women? Soon they would have made an idol of the thing!" Eshed shuddered to think of it.

Placing it in his robe, he resolved to take it the next morning and place it in the altar fire of the worship chambers. For tonight it would be safe enough.

His face softened slightly, and he reached to hold Loana. She sprang away from him. Running into their sleeping room, she pulled the curtains, shutting him out. Shaking, Eshed arranged the cushions near the fire, secured a heavy throw from a large basket in the corner, and settled down for the night, granting her the privacy of their room for her tears, which flowed profusely and much longer than he had hoped. Still, any further comment on his part would appear a compromise, so he must keep silence.

Somehow, Eshed slept . . . and dreamt. He was in a room full of howling jackals. Their eyes gleamed in the firelight as they closed in on him, sharp teeth bared. One small one moved in unnoticed and pierced his chest with stinging strength, shaking her head wildly and howling. He woke with a start and was grateful to see in the wavering peaks of light that his fears were unjustified. The room in which he slept was empty.

Rolling over with his back to the fire, he prepared to sleep again, but his scalp began to crawl, sending splintery shocks down his neck. A sudden chill went through him, and he drew the covers close. There was some unseen presence in the room. His fingers pulled at the amulet, and its touch blistered his fingertips. The skin on his chest felt prickly, and he sat up suddenly and parted his tunic. There on his chest where the amulet had rested was the outline of a jackal . . . seared into his flesh! He jumped to his feet. Sliding into his sandals, he determined to go to the temple immediately and be rid of the thing. Loana parted the bedchamber tapestries, eyes red and puffed with crying and sleeplessness.

"Eshed? Where are you going?" she whispered hoarsely.

He clasped her in his arms and stroked her hair. "I will be back before sunup. I must go to the temple."

She sprang from his grasp, her eyes wild.

"No! No! Give me the amulet!" She thrust her hand forward, fingers taut.

He was beginning to see, to his horror, the effect of this idol on her. *Can she have been saying prayers to it?*

She struggled with him, and for a moment, he felt compelled by his love for her to return it, but he pushed that thought aside with a much more powerful impulse to be rid of it, forever. Wrenching himself from her, he ran from the house. Loana fell sobbing onto the cushion, the tangle of her dark hair glistening in the firelight.

Zerubabel's hooves moved effortlessly through the moonlight, as though they were winged. He was hardly out of breath when they reached the temple. Eshed composed himself and walked inside, lest someone see the priest in such an unholy state. After a brief prayer for his protection and that of his household, he flung it, chain and all, into the flames of the brazen altar. With a sudden gust, the flames shot upward, and he saw a large jackal's face mirrored in the light. Opening its mouth with an unearthly howl, it disappeared. He shielded his face from the flames, and when his arm came down, he saw the blue tassel of his mantle fall into place. A symbol of the commandments, he was never without it. In this instant, it reminded him of the commandment, "Thou shalt have no other gods before me."

A brief rest was all that was left to him before the dawn, and he returned home. Loana snuggled to him as he fell limply into bed. They slept like babes.

Thereafter followed some of the gentlest days their marriage knew. A barrier that they had not even known was there had gone down. Their days flowed in a sweet interplay of tender regard for one another.

Eshed was sorting through some old papers on a shelf in the main room of his home one morning and came across a gift from Jarad's friend, Nebow. It was the tastefully bound book marked *Kerielan. Such a fine volume should not collect dust,* he thought.

Blowing the dust particles from the page edges, he took a quill down from the shelf. After sharpening it with a metal blade, he went outside and plucked a handful of berries for ink. As he crushed their blackness into stain in a mortar Loana used for herbs, he made plans for the book. *This will be my log. Missions for the Lord will be recorded here.*

Loana had ridden into the marketplace with Tamar to make some purchases. Eshed took the opportunity to sit quietly under the fig tree where his lessons for the priesthood had been recorded, rehearsed, and memorized. It was a good thinking spot for him, and he welcomed a time of reflection.

Iysh

Sarakabel

Ardon

He formed the names at the top of three pages. The pages would record their transfer from darkness to light with the Lord.

Lost in recollection, he had written for some time beneath the murmuring tree when he was startled by a voice at his elbow.

"Love?"

Leaning his head against the tree trunk, he felt Loana's full-skirted leg beside him. Swiftly, without warning, he circled her legs with his arm and she toppled into his lap, spilling a basket of brass bells, wooden ladles, and colorful head scarves on the grass. He caught her in his waiting arms and nibbled her neck.

"You made me spill everything!" Giggling and squirming, she reached for the basket, resting sideways on his forgotten log book.

"Leave it!" he ordered, grabbing her wrist gently and kissing her mouth, half opened with mirth. The deep green skirt had pulled up onto her thighs, and he put his hand inside the cloth and eased her hips onto a grassy spot in the shade of the tree, obscured by shrubbery.

"Eshed!" she admonished, feeling his warm mouth engulfing her breast. "Not now. We are invited," she gasped, "to supper at Naveh and Martseah's."

"Shhhh," he crooned, his fingers stroking her flesh pleadingly. "Use your beautiful lips on me . . . not on talk."

Needing little urging, she placed her arms around his neck. She kissed his eyelids and cheekbones, then his feverish mouth, interrupted only by a sigh of release as she gave herself fully to his pleasure against the hard coolness of the grass.

A throb of bees purred among the clover blossoms behind Martseah's house. Honeycomb, a trophy from Eshed's wanderings, dripped its tangerine essence on the window sill.

Baby Ariel's chubby fingers were locked around his mother's long, rust-colored hair strands as he rode about the room on her hip. Naveh stirred the huge soup pot and tested the liquid with her tongue.

"Let me hold him for you!" Loana held out her hands. Naveh, smiling, placed the titian-haired baby on her lap and turned to tend the supper Loana and Eshed had been invited to share.

Ariel examined the fastenings on Loana's fluted tortoise shell collar. Turning them about with practiced fingers, he glanced up from time to time for her approval. She entertained him with clucking and crooning sounds as his mother clattered about the work board, chopping and dishing a spicy rice dish to go with the broth. Naveh paused to tuck her hair back under the deep green tie that bound it. Somehow the baby always managed to find a strand and pull out the mass of it. She scattered cumin seeds over the rice and stirred them in for seasoning.

Loana interrupted her cluckings with, "Where did you get lemons? I miss them so. We always had them in Saramhat!" She breathed in the clean scent as Naveh sliced them.

"A treat my father brought from one of the sheep markets! A little village called Sukon, south of here. They are also noted for delicious figs in that valley."

"Umm . . . yes." Loana clapped little Ariel's hands together in agreement. "Fathers can be counted on for such things. Father Jarad brought some choice spices on his last visit. I will be happy to share them with you."

"Agreed!" Naveh's soft eyes shone. "If you will carry home some lemons with you!"

Their husbands were in a huddle, discussing the trade areas Eshed had recently visited. Martseah was continually on the lookout for new areas to market his leather goods, and his boyhood friend was giving him several intriguing suggestions.

Leaning into the wooden work table beside the reclining

bench, Martseah gouged a splinter from the rough surface, heavily scarred by blade marks. Eshed took the awl from his hand and traced a map sketch on the tabletop. "Ohad would be a good stop, but the best trade takes place to the north, in Spatale, on the coastline above Ohad." Eshed directed his gaze to a wooden peg inset in the table surface to indicate his destination, tapping it with the awl for emphasis.

"And how far is Ohad from here?" Martseah queried, eyes bright with anticipation.

"Four days by horse . . . six with a pack mule. The terrain is not too difficult, the way I go. Spatale is two days farther by boat."

"Can't I pack in from Ohad?" Martseah had not considered a sea voyage.

Eshed wagged his head. "Much easier by boat. The terrain between is mountainous. Many traders have lost their lives to thieves in those mountain passes, not to mention the ones who have tumbled into canyons. No . . . the merchants I know go by boat—and for good reason!"

Martseah turned down the oil wick on the table and stood, stretching his arms upward, pulling his back muscles into a more restful position. Little Ariel saw his opportunity. Wriggling from Loana's lap, he crawled quickly to his father. Chortling, he pulled himself to a stand by holding onto Martseah's legs. The baby's chubby feet were wrapped in soft leather drawstring boots, fashioned by Martseah. His father looked down, hands on his hips. Naveh turned from her pots to gaze proudly at her son.

"Well, my man . . . you are getting rather good at that . . . eh?" Martseah asked.

Ariel craned up at him. Pawing the floor with one foot and resting his weight on the other, he shrieked agreement. The room rang with laughter.

• • •

Seated in a sun-drenched corner, Eshed carefully arranged the tattered and yellowed papyrus—the temple records. He poured over the history of this temple site and the families that inhabited Etser and the surrounding countryside. Always interesting reading, the legacies had gone from father to son, generation to generation. Some bountiful, some meager, but always something. And the most significant ones could not be recorded . . . training, love, discipline, sharing.

Watching Martseah with his son had briefly unearthed Eshed's buried pain of rootlessness . . . his constant seeking for a place and a harbor in life. To read what others had done was reassuring somehow. It restored a sense of continuity, and he could be grateful once more for the tending of good folk such as Checed and Pala.

Footsteps echoed through the chamber, startling him from his reverie. Members of two old Etser families were paying a call—Martseah and Namath.

Rising, he closed the dusty covers. "Hello, my brothers. What brings you here?"

Namath, in his dusty work clothes, unwound his head covering. Shaking the earth from it, he observed his bare feet. "My sandals are off, but I am not in a fit condition to be in the temple just now. You tell him, Martseah . . . while I wash." He went to the laver, prayed briefly, and began cleansing the visible portions of his body. His dark beard glistened from the droplets pouring off his balding head.

"Namath has brought someone to see you. They rode in together to my place. We told him we are the council, but he will only speak with you." He gestured toward the open doorway where a man stood profiled against the light. As Eshed approached from the dark recesses of the room, he could see only the stranger's back.

"I am the priest here. May I be of some assistance?"

The man turned to face him. A turban bound his head, and he wore travel clothing. His face was somber. Slowly he smiled and extended his hand.

It was Iysh.

After an animated greeting, they retired to Eshed's study, and Iysh told him of the Lord's commission. "I am to go to Spatale by way of Protos. You are to go with me."

Before the two elders went their way, travel plans were made to include Martseah, who agreed to make passage with Eshed and find new markets for his leather goods.

When they had gone, Eshed turned to Iysh. "What a delight! The Lord has trained you in my tongue, so we do not have the speech barrier . . . just as he let me know in our first meeting what *you* needed. So tell me—if you are free to—what has happened since I last saw you?"

"Many things. Adonai has been training me in many ways. I must return to my people soon and do a work there, but first, he gave me *this* assignment." Iysh's most expressive feature, his mouth, formed a thoughtful pucker.

"And exactly what *is* this assignment?" Eshed probed.

"I know no more than you do. We are simply to *go*, trusting, and it will be revealed. That is all."

Stroking his chin, Eshed replied, "This could pose a problem for us. Martseah, as I am sure you know, is an elder in our council, but he is not one of us." He gestured from Iysh to himself and back again. "If he is to go, we will just have to trust that he will be kept out of the way when questions might present themselves. He will, of course, be very busy in the marketplace. As for an explanation of our journey, he knows our business is somehow official . . . perhaps he will not ask more. And now, my friend," he said, clapping Iysh on the shoulder, "come home with me. You must meet Loana!"

• • •

They were on their way the next day—three men on horseback and Martseah towing a pack mule of goods. They traveled pleasantly for a time, discussing the terrain and good watering holes for their horses. Loana and Naveh had prepared a large quantity of food, and the men made each meal a feast to lighten their pack. It was a cheerful camaraderie that developed. With the exception of his honeymoon, Eshed could not remember when he had enjoyed a trip more.

CHAPTER 13

Early in the second day, after a refreshing night's sleep under the stars, Eshed noted that they were coming into an elevation where lilies grew profusely. The perfume met their nostrils before the cloud of blossoms appeared. He slowed Zerubabel.

"It is in this part," he said, "that we will come to the road fork that leads to Protos."

"Where does the other road go?—the one that breaks away?" Martseah asked.

"To Ohad," Eshed replied.

"Why aren't we going to Ohad instead of Protos? I remember your saying it is closer to Spatale," Martseah probed.

Eshed shot a sidewise glance at Iysh, whose eyebrows implied a question.

"Our instructions are to go to Protos first," Eshed hedged.

"They are both seaports, and Ohad is closer. It might save us valuable time, don't you think?" Martseah persisted.

The young priest was really stuck for an answer. Iysh wisely maintained silence. Perhaps it wouldn't matter if they took the shorter route, Eshed thought. It was more logical, after all. How could he justify such a decision to his councilman if he went on to Protos as planned?

Just then they came to the fork.

"Then to Ohad, it is." Eshed led the way, urging his horse onto the new pathway.

Lilies rippled in the light breeze as they cantered along, a soft hum of bees prickling their ears, a thick perfume about their faces. They were so caught up in the enchantment of the countryside and their own compatibility, they didn't notice the thickening cloud approaching them. The first drops of rain took them by surprise. Still it was spring, and spring rains were common enough in this region, otherwise there would not be such proliferation of flowers.

It didn't sprinkle for long. It began to pour! Great gulps of water rained down on them, making the earth slippery for their horses. They strained their eyes for a glimpse of shelter and spied a chasm lined with a rocky outcropping large enough to shelter the three of them with their horses and pack mule. They rested in preparation for the rain's end.

"If it keeps up like this," Eshed roared above the rain, "we will have to make for Rhantismos between showers." Water dripped off his chin as he spoke. "There is a small inn there . . . not much else, but it would shelter us and our animals for the night."

As if in answer the rain abated. They headed out as quickly as prudence would allow. It was rock bed underfoot now, which kept them from the slick mud. They traveled in silence, concentrating upon retaining a firm footing. Suddenly Eshed's horse reared up in front of the others, halting progress. The men stared ahead. The chasm was filled with huge boulders—there had been a landslide in the rain! It was impassable. They looked to the steep hills on each side which were slick with mud and lacked good undergrowth for safefooting. It was the shape of circumstance in which riders lost their mounts and frequently their lives, as well.

They wheeled.

Only one course was open to them—Protos!

Eshed and Iysh exchanged glances. Ohad had never *been* an option. What they did not know was that a band of Circan soldiers were camped just beyond that rock slide!

Protos was a diminutive version of Spatale. It was, as it turned out, a preview of things to come. Restless natives of Spatale resided there for a part of the year. It was not a bustling trade center, as Spatale was, but emanated leisure and repose that the wealthy Spatale merchants enjoyed. It had become their hideaway. Some brought their families to sail and fish and shop at the bazaars. Many of them did not. For them, it became a place for riotous living far from watchful eyes at home. The charming village was built for comfort and novelty, with the ocean fully in view to all residents.

Slowing their horses to a trot, the three rode in, whiffing the breads of Protos' ovens, their appetites stirred by the open air spits roasting a variety of meats unknown to them. Excellent fruits and vegetables tumbled from bins on all sides, and slotted stalls tinkled with jeweled offerings, hung from the walls and stirred by soft winds off the water.

Much cedar and colorful stone carried in by merchant ships from distant ports had gone into the buildings. The water sparkled, backing the rooftops, a freshness for eye and lung.

Tying up their mounts, they entered an inn. Heavy tables, candled, were framed against an open window to the sea. The men selected places in the corner, eyes probing the strange new surroundings.

"May I serve you?" A female voice stirred Eshed from his focus on the sea, which he could see through a heavily draped window at his elbow.

A platter of fruit held bosom height and a black ripple of cloth displayed the curve of her breast in a most arresting way. A mass of red-brown ringlets brushed her shoulder and green eyes sent off little sparks as she turned her gaze on Eshed. A full, sensuous mouth broke the smooth complacency of an oval-shaped face. Martseah and Iysh, observing, sensed that Eshed was being offered more than supper. As she leaned to place the tray upon the table, the scooped neckline eased forward and revealed a charm dangling between her breasts. Iysh recognized it as the goddess of fertility. For the unattached female, it was a love charm. A female figure had been gouged from the gold, flowers nudging her breasts and rivers emerging between her thighs as a symbol of procreation. Eshed riveted his eyes upon her face as she placed the fruit servings in front of his companions.

Shifting in his seat, Eshed cleared his throat. "We will have supper. . . . What sort of drink do you have?"

"We have a hot brew, a coffee of sorts, and an ale made with apples."

Ale was agreed upon, and she swept away.

Viewing one another uneasily in the candlelight, they were beginning to feel like dogs in a manger. Eshed's scalp crawled with the presentment of trouble. Hunger made his restlessness more acute, and a leaden fatigue from riding all day caused his mind to rumble as well as his stomach. What could happen, after all? His mind went through the check points of reason. This was only a stopping place. Still, there was a creeping evil amid the opulence of Protos, and as a couple sat down at the next table, he began to feel its intrusion even more. The couple was laughing boisterously, obviously under the influence of strong drink—and it was barely sunset. The woman whispered in the man's ear and he hooted gleefully, placing his hand at the nape of her bare neck. Hair tumbled in a cascade from the top of her head, where it was held by a jeweled clasp. Her heavy brocade dress with balloon sleeves was worn off the shoulder. Embroidered vertical slits along the neckline opened revealingly as she moved, and her heavily-painted face wore a masklike smile.

"Um . . . where do we book passage for Spatale tomorrow?" Martseah drummed his fingertips on the tabletop, wrestling their attention to the business at hand.

"This is my first time in Protos." Eshed shrugged self-consciously.

"Will we be staying at this inn tonight?" Iysh wanted to know, his wide mouth suppressing a mischievous grin.

"Let us ask the innkeeper about the boat when we book lodging," Eshed assented.

A platter of crackling roasted meat and steaming fishes arrived at their table. A cream soup dipped from a large pot warmed them, soothing the restless spirit engendered by their surroundings. Between satisfied bites, they mumbled agreeably, trying to blot out the noise of the place.

Beckoning for the innkeeper, who was moving around the room, greeting the guests, Eshed made arrangements for three small, separate rooms.

"Rest at your table awhile. . . . I will send more ale. We have musicians coming," the innkeeper confided with a wink. The men pulled leather pouches from their girdles, rattling coins on the table for his collection. Stuffing a coin into his own bulging girdle, their host signaled the serving girl to bring them another round of ale and hastened toward the sound of drum and horns making an entrance through a billowing curtain at the rear.

A quick, rippling tune met the ears of the travelers. They were beginning to enjoy the sounds coming from the three tunesmen who waggled their heads and performed a shuffling dance to accompany them when, without signal, the tempo changed. Sipping fresh ale, they heard a slow, undulating rhythm. The melody contained a girl, entering the platform in a sideways movement through the curtain, hips gyrating, her back to the audience. Long green ribbons of cloth flowed over her legs to the floor, revealing her limbs as she danced, confining her waist in a tight wrap. Intertwining snake figures, striped green and black, sprang from a band on her forehead. Whirling suddenly to face her audience, she paused with the slowed tempo. Torches lit the dancing area, and antimony burnished her eyelids. Her breasts were totally bared and pushed high by the wrap like two great eyes surveying the crowd. She used glittering strands of cord encircling her fingers to create serpentine shadow patterns described by their gestures.

Blushing to his hair roots, Eshed signaled to leave. Iysh was already on his feet. A grasp of the collar turned Martseah from the gape-mouthed position he'd assumed toward the doorway. Once in the open air, Eshed spoke.

"I am sorry. . . . It is my fault. I should have found out about this place. Usually such displays are identified in some way."

"You could not have known . . . any more than we did. The girl's costume was somewhat surprising," Iysh commented.

"My thought exactly," Martseah concurred, smirking.

"No . . . what I mean is . . . her costume is a replica of the costume worn by goddess of fertility dancers centuries ago in Arcan palaces. My mother, my real mother . . . had an old jug with such carvings on it." His hand described the height and shape of it. "The snakes symbolize earth, and the goddess the taming of the elements to bring forth new life. . . . This place is surely full of idol worship."

"Perhaps that is why we are here," Eshed offered, his eyes somber.

Martseah shot him an odd look. Since when was this

foreign culture Eshed's business? The circumstances were most puzzling.

Shut away in his room, Eshed filled the copper basin with water and rid his hair of road dust. Elegant towels with loops of gold thread on the bottom swung from a brass ring of brass near the basin.

A quick tap came at the door.

Such a useless display of gold thread. Flinging the towel aside after extricating his large knuckles from its fluff, he pulled an outer coat over his tunic on the way to the door.

The door swung open.

"I am Tasia." The girl who had served them earlier managed a small curtsy. An inviting platter of delicacies rested on her arms: dried apricots glazed with honey, dates with almonds wrapped inside. Her lips parted slightly as she held the tray out to him, arms bangled with love charms.

"No . . . thank you very much." His words came rapidly, impelled by his survival instinct.

"It will cost you nothing." Her lips formed a pout. "The innkeeper wishes your stay to be pleasant." She pushed the tray toward him again and this time turned her body to slip past him through the door.

He caught her wrist. "No—I do not wish . . . anything!" His firm tone made a hollow echo against the door panel.

A stifled gasp escaped her lips. Retreating hastily, she lost her grip on the tray. It clattered onto the stone entry. Tears sprang quickly to her eyes and streamed onto her cheeks.

Eshed knelt and piled the delicacies onto the flat copper receptacle.

Catching her skirt, she knelt on the cold floor and began rearranging the food on the tray. "I will be beaten now." Her voice shook, and accusation spilt from her eyes with the salt water. "I have failed—and these are ruined!" Her fingers tried to brush the dust particles from the sticky fruit.

"Very few will be lost. . . . We have been careful with them." His voice was strangely soothing, not at all defensive. "Who will beat you?"

"The innkeeper . . . Please . . ." she implored, sensing out his soft side. "May I stay in your room for awhile . . . so he will not think I have failed?" Her eyes, damp and luminous against the night, tugged at his heart.

"Go back to the kitchen." Eshed swallowed. "Do not speak to the innkeeper unless he speaks to you. I will pray for you. I am a priest."

Tasia's fingers pressed her lips. Her eyes grew even wider. "But what will that do?" she stammered. "He will find me tomorrow, if not tonight. . . ."

"If he troubles you, come to me. I will intercede for you." His large hand pressed her shoulder.

Nodding, and taking the tray, she trailed into the darkness, turning to look at him twice, smiling tremulously. He nodded. Her curls shook, disbelieving.

Early rays of sunlight found Eshed on his knees again—this time in prayer. After a considerable time he left his room for the dining hall, where he breakfasted alone, watching the sea gulls pick their morning's catch along the patch of shore by the inn.

Ruddy from a morning trek to the boat landing, Iysh and Martseah joined him at the table and ordered a tankard of hot brew and a hunk of bread.

Sharing his basket of fruit with them, he inquired, "What time do we sail?"

"Midday tomorrow." Iysh broke a pomegranate in two and handed half to Martseah.

"Why is that?" The news rankled Eshed. "I do not understand why we had to come so soon if we cannot leave

until tomorrow." Irritation was overcoming logic, it seemed
to Iysh and Martseah. Only Eshed was plagued with the
sense of troublesome possibilities of which Protos reeked.
Moving on was the best defense.

"There are no boats bound for Spatale until tomorrow."
Iysh stretched out his hands imploringly. He, for one, was
glad the matter was settled. Grabbing a chunk of hot bread,
he spit the pomegranate seeds on the tabletop.

"I am *glad* we have another day here," Martseah concurred, lips reddened with juice. "I may be able to sell some
things and have less to carry on the boat. Good information
has come my way for marketing leather in Spatale by talking to the tradespeople here." The leathersmith was elated.
Sipping the hot brew, he gazed at the foam of water coming
onshore. He felt good. The morning air was invigorating.
His blood pulsed in his veins. His cheeks were flushed.
That was what Eshed needed . . . a brisk stroll outside. He
was getting sour from so much time spent at the prayer
books, Martseah reflected.

The beaten, smooth-stoned paths of Protos opened a
new world of commerce for Martseah. He would be discussing some matter from home with Eshed and Iysh one
moment, and the next they would address empty air, finding him plying his wares at a stall instead. Villagers and
tourists were enthusiastic about his designs and tool work,
while merchants stood by with jaded expressions designed
to cost them the least in a bargain with the leathersmith.
Eshed and Iysh were finding it profitable, also, to observe
the colorfully arrayed patrons wandering among the stalls.
They were learning much about what to expect at their
final destination.

"Sir! Wait up!" A tubby, bewhiskered gentleman, paisley-
robed, trailed behind Martseah, who had just been showing
his nodahs to a merchant.

Martseah's head turned in the direction of the voice.

Eshed and Iysh, selecting some fruit from a bin for their journey, heard the man say, "Six . . . I want six of them. I have six sons. And leather wall maps—do you have those . . . of Protos?"

A few minutes of bargaining brought Martseah forward with the man to speak to Eshed. "Here is a gentleman of Protos who is a stabler. He will care for our mounts while we are in Spatale in return for six nodahs and a promise of maps!" The leathersmith was elated. The bargain was sealed with a handshake all around and Martseah arranged to drop off the nodahs with the animals the next morning.

"What an idea he gave me! Wall maps!" Martseah exclaimed when the man had left. "I may make some for Spatale as well. If people want them here, surely Spatalians would buy them. The people in these markets will buy all sorts of things that Kerielanians would have very little use for. Who would think our areas would be so different?"

"Money . . . my friend. It is a matter of money. There is much of it in these port cities," Eshed replied. "They cater to a different breed of man than in our little villages."

"Well, that is surely working to my advantage. I must pay particular attention to the way Protos is laid out, today, and make a sketch of it tonight!" Martseah's eyes swept the comely village with new purpose.

Returning to the torchlit inn late, they had partaken of seafood at a stall along the way, and eaten the remains of it by the glistening shore at sunset.

Mellowed by the sea air and good food, Eshed was preparing for rest when a familiar tap sounded on the doorpost. The door opening revealed a trembling Tasia, wrapped in a dark blue hooded cape.

"Please . . . it is Boris. . . . He is looking for me!" she whispered, urgency in every syllable.

"Come in—quickly!" Eshed pulled her inside, closing the door softly.

Hardly daring to breath, she sank against the wall, listening for footsteps. A heavy gait passed the doorway, paused, then disappeared out the back way.

Tasia slid to the floor, still trembling, her back against the wall.

"May I stay here awhile . . . to rest?" She eyed Eshed nervously.

"Yes . . . of course." He sat on a cushion and handed one to her.

Her eyes widened, the pupils large. "I cannot think why you are so nice to me . . . unless—" Suspicion sought a hold between them. "Unless you have changed your mind and . . ." She fastened her gaze on the tanned collarbone showing beneath his loosened tunic. Until now she had not admitted, even to herself, that she had longed for his touch since she first saw his Davidic profile at her table.

Eshed's smile was kind.

"I have not changed my mind. I am willing to protect you. . . . That is no more than any man would do." He shifted on the cushion, folding his arms over his chest.

"Ha!" She threw back the blue hood from her hair, arranging the ringlets behind her ear. Huge gold loops jangled from the lobes. The circumference of a cephel, Eshed gauged. "For a priest, you do not know much about people. Some would give me over after a good time just to watch Boris beat me. Liars! All of them!" Her lip curled in derision.

"Why do you wear those loops in your ears? You are beautiful without such adornments," Eshed remarked.

"Boris makes me wear them. He thinks they attract attention. He knows how the men look at me. They hurt, too." She pulled them from her ears, dropping them on the floor, rubbing her earlobes next to her flushing face.

Reaching suddenly for her love goddess amulet, Eshed pulled it from her throat with one swift, painless yank. Her hand flew to her collarbone.

"You do not belong to the worship of this thing . . . anymore than you belong to Boris. You are a child of God. . . . Do not let anyone tell you otherwise!"

Her expression was at first inscrutable; then her whole face softened. "You are so kind . . . you do care about me . . . I feel it. Yet . . . it is not like the others. You care about *me* . . . not what I can do for you." Trying to shake back the tears, she swallowed, her face contorted with surprise at his gentleness. After a moment, she began to cry softly.

A firm knock resounded against the door.

"Oh—no! It is Boris. Tell him I have pleased you. . . . Tell him anything!" Fear emerged behind the glass pane of tears in her eyes.

Eshed held his finger to his lips and opened the door slightly. She moaned as he swung it wide for a man to enter. Cringing behind the door, she refused to open her eyes.

"Tasia, do you trust me?" Eshed asked in a whisper.

"Y-yes . . ."

"Then come from behind the door. I want you to meet someone," Eshed replied.

She crawled around the door, and Eshed's strong arms lifted her to her feet.

"Iysh, this is Tasia, our serving girl." Eshed urged the aborigine inside and closed the door.

"Yes . . . I remember," Iysh smiled, reflectively.

"Tell her," Eshed urged, "about the bondage of your early life."

Tasia looked from one man to the other, her hand resting self-consciously on her throat where the charm had lain, lips parted in anticipation.

". . . and how you were delivered from it." He gave Iysh a meaningful look.

A slow, arresting smile took over Iysh's mouth and a space of eternity was well used to unlock a heart shriveled by abuse.

CHAPTER 14

Full sailed, they headed for Spatale.

Myriad sun glints frosted the water, a bright assault on the eye. Two boyhood friends leaned on a rail of the aft deck, watching a swirl of water spew from the ship's belly. The prow was lifting majestically toward the northeastern horizon.

Iysh was below, keeping an eye on Martseah's leather craft. It had created such a sensation in Protos that Martseah had taken to sleeping on top of it to insure its safety.

Martseah had never been on a ship before and was thrilling to the lift and roll of the watery ride, the swoop of the gulls, and the creak and whip of lines as the sails went up. For Eshed, it was a return to old haunts. He had spent much time on the sea as a child. Orphaned early, he had spent several years on his Uncle Josiah's fishing boat. One day that was indelibly engraved in his memory, they hit a squall, and the boat broke up on some rocks. Eshed was washed up on shore. Josiah, the crew, and the entire ship were lost in the storm. It was at that point that Eshed began to feel the touch of God upon his life. He was taken in by his rescuers and there remained until he learned stone masonry from his surrogate father. Once the skill was mastered, he hired out and had been on his own since.

"I will go now . . . and spell Iysh," Martseah shouted above the roar of the wind and water. Eshed thought he detected a greenish cast to Martseah's face. If so, Martseah would be back topside very soon. He disappeared into the hold, and soon Iysh was leaning on the rail with Eshed. They were still in sight of the coastline and probably would remain so, though at times the coves threatened to disappear. Large, fishlike creatures resided in this warmer water that hugged the coastline, and occasionally they viewed one leaping from the foam. Iysh pointed excitedly, childlike in his appreciation of nature.

The supper the ship's captain served was of a crude sort. Only the fish was edible. This was just as well as Martseah had no appetite and spent the night running between the rail and his stash. Iysh was mildly uncomfortable when the ship rolled around excessively. Eshed alone, due to his early life on the water, rode its restless swells with equanimity.

The young priest was plying Martseah with dry bread and ale, hoping to find something to soothe his stomach, when he overheard one of the crew talking with Iysh. He was a small, dark, rough-looking man who seemed to stay to himself most of the time, only showing up to alter the sail. Iysh was asking how he maneuvered the sails to best utilize the winds off the coast. The sailor explained, pointing and gesticulating, the motions of each sail as the sun set and the importance of the sailsman in keeping ropes mounted and sails loosed properly. Suddenly he stopped and said to Iysh, "What are you two fellas and that priest doing here, anyway?"

"We are summoned to Spatale on a special mission," Iysh replied.

"Who summoned you? What is the job?" Raphel, the sailsman asked.

"Adonai summoned us. We will not know what the task is until we get to it." Only Iysh could be so candid . . . and with such a straight face! Eshed reflected.

"What sort of job is that . . . that you do not know what it is . . . and you have to come clear out here to do it? Sounds crazy to me."

"Nevertheless," Iysh replied with dignity, "it *is* important. In fact, when it appears most useless, that is when it is most important." He nodded for emphasis. Clasping his hands behind his back, Iysh began to walk the deck, fore and aft, in the dwindling light.

Shaking his head, Raphel returned to sorting and arranging the lines.

For the rest of the trip, Raphel watched them closely. He dogged Iysh's footsteps when he saw him, asking silly questions and making derogatory comments. If Iysh was annoyed, he did not show it but simply focused his attention on the changing colors in the water or on Martseah, who was continually in need of something.

Martseah awakened with a start, in the middle of the night, to find Raphel pawing through some nodahs that had slipped from under his body. Very uncomfortable to sleep on because of their roundness, they rolled from the pallet with the lift of the boat. Shaking himself awake, he made out the outline of Raphel against the moonlight streaming through the hold. Catching his movement in the semi-darkness, Raphel dropped the nodah and made for the deck.

"Wait!" Martseah called, moving as quickly as his wobbly legs would allow. This sleep was the first reprieve the sea had given him. Raphel was faster, but Martseah followed him, blonde hair signaling his approach in the moonlight. The seaman held up empty hands—he had only been curious about their stash since he could make no sense of what Iysh had told him!

"Come!" Martseah beckoned him toward the hold.

Whites of his eyes showing, Raphel shook his head vigorously and turned away, lifting a rope and coiling it on deck.

Martseah disappeared inside the hold alone. He reappeared, shortly, and placed the nodah strap over Raphel's shoulder.

Startled, Raphel turned and felt the object in the darkness. Facing Martseah, he parted his lips in a crooked smile. Martseah clasped him on the shoulder and struggled back into the hold to get such rest as he might.

As he sank into a queasy sleep, he chided himself. Now everyone on board would want a nodah . . . for nothing, too. Odd . . . he felt peaceful at the thought. Smiling at the prospect of a dozen seamen parading through Spatale with his nodahs on their flanks, he drowsed into a deep sleep.

"Haul the mainsail!" Raphel bellowed.

Scrambling, the crew pulled down the sails one by one as they made for port.

To the left, a stand of trees followed a sandbar as far as possible into the water. As they passed the small peninsula, the cove for which they were headed burst into view. Turquoise, emerald, amethyst, and foamy white rolled in layers onto the pale sand of a perfect beach. Outcroppings of white rock fastened tree growth to the shore at distant points.

The anchorman leaned over the edge with the plummet, detecting the depths. When they had come to the proper level, the captain charged four grunting, sweating men to heave the massive anchor overboard. Amid a babble of instructions, rowboats were lowered, and groups of men began departing the mother craft for shore.

Spatale was gloriously attired with white, stone buildings, boasting spires of gold and inlaid mosaic underfoot between its major edifices. As a trade center, it was unsurpassed. Virtually anything purchasable could be found in Spatale.

Solid ground. It felt good to be done with pitching and retching for awhile, Martseah allowed. That his work would bring a good price here, the leathersmith had no doubt. Eshed observed his friend eyeing the bazaars excitedly and wished fervently that his own mission were so clear-cut. Iysh did not appear to be troubled by these thoughts, pausing to talk along the way with strangers in the stalls, asking the names of items he had never seen before. The young priest's concentration was on a suitable place to stay. Pausing at a stall, he selected some fruit for them as the day was warming and they were all thirsty. As the young daughter of the proprietor placed oranges in a mesh bag for him, he inquired, "Where might we find a good inn?" She pointed down the cobbled path to a place with a large fish carving over the doorpost. Eshed nodded his thanks.

After the mule was stabled and they had assisted Martseah to their room with the pallet of goods, Eshed stepped to latch the door so that a little repose could be found before he assaulted the marketplace. It was an interesting latch, a miniature wooden fish that slid through a metal loop. He examined the intricacy of it and noted that it was duplicated on the outside of the door, for latching on leaving. Just then, a man stepped from the next room into the hallway. Nodding and smiling to Eshed, he walked past their room. He wore a short grey toga with a stole flung over one shoulder. The opposite arm carried a bag that was clearly visible and had a special symbol on the side. Two snakes intertwined on a winged pole. He was a physician. Olive-skinned with thick, wavy salt-and-pepper hair, he had a sturdy muscular build and an ageless quality about him. Eshed was captured by the thought that this man moved beyond the routine practice of cuttings, unguents, and potions. He felt an odd compulsion to know more about him. Closing the door, he tossed each of his friends an orange from the mesh bag and sat down to peel his when he saw Iysh watching him intently.

"What is it, my friend?" Eshed asked.

Iysh gave the orange a little toss, caught it, and, pursing his lips, watched Eshed as he continued to pull the wrapping from the soft fruit. That was it! Iysh had never seen an orange and didn't know how to peel and eat it.

Martseah was eager to be off and had finished his fruit when he beckoned Iysh to join him, leaving Eshed to his prayer time. Iysh followed the leathersmith out the door, still pulling little bits of peeling off the orange and sucking the juice, smiling and shaking his head in delight.

Eshed knelt. A weight was on his heart. A vagrant breeze carried the scent of blossoms to his face from the outside where the dogwood offered white flowers at the fringe of his window. Flower petals in a dish . . . Loana's fingers crushing the petals into water for his cleansing. The image sprang rich and clear before his eyes, closed against the waning light of the room. *Home!* He wished this were all over and he were home. Being away from the one he loved was painful.

Missing someone was new to him. He felt the need of her arms, the rapturous scent of her hair. Nothing was going to be easy on this mission. He felt it in his bones.

Putting aside clerical vernacular, he said simply: "Lord . . . quiet my heart. Make me receptive to our mission in Spatale." He remained quiet for some time. Then a sense of assurance, a strong undergirding, entered his being.

When he raised his face and opened his eyes, he was looking outside through a slitted opening in the wall, designed to let in air but prevent entry from the street. He noticed something odd. A young boy was running from one set of doorposts to another on a building directly across from the inn. There—there he went again. Over and over he ran. And there was something else. He couldn't see from this angle, but someone was watching. The boy cast his head up and spoke to someone near the first lintel every few minutes. "Watch this. I will go faster!" Eshed heard him say. The boy ran in a straight line and began in a sprinting position as though racing. *He will certainly get no speed running in that manner,* Eshed mused. By moving his face down the wall slit a bit and angling to his left, he could see that the boy, who was about eight years old, was speaking to a baby who was lashed by a thong to the post to keep him from wandering off. Where was the mother? Why would she allow such an arrangement to continue?

Watching for several moments, he saw no one approach or speak to the children. Perhaps she was in one of the stalls nearby, and the boy was amusing his younger sibling for her. The baby clapped his hands, and the boy ran some more.

Interrupted by the sound of his two friends at the door, Eshed moved to open the inner latch.

"I am buying supper tonight!" Martseah declared as he entered gleefully, holding a stuffed money pouch. "My leather mezachs are the latest gossip in Spatale!"

Iysh had helped him make contacts, and between the two of them, Martseah had been totally relieved of the girdles he had carried with him that day. For safety's sake, he was carrying only a few items at a time into the marketplace.

They left their room eagerly in search of food. It had been a long time since the last stale meal on shipboard.

The evening air was mellow with the scent of open-air offerings—spiced meats, cakes bubbling in oil, and fresh flowers in front of the inns all contributed a special quality to the evening.

The piercing tone of an oboe drew their attention to a knot of bystanders. Gyrating, big balls of hot pink fringe at her waist, was a dancer. Her bare feet, fashioned with toe rings on the largest toes and bells on the ankles, flung circles in the air, interspersed with swiveling hips. She held a large red scarf which she draped about her face and then her body as she made a forward foray into the crowd and squatted upon her heels, the cloth in front of her like a ship's sail. She flung it aside, and, taking a sword from its sheath that lay on the ground, she balanced it on her head. Resuming her standing position slowly in measure with the pulsating drum, she pivoted in all directions from her turn, balancing it without a hitch. The crowd sang its approval. Removing the sword, she made little hitching steps around the circle, purple sheer balloon trousers and long sleeved, deeply cut midriff fluttering in the breeze. Legs apart, as the drum increased its tempo, she described the curve of the sword with a backward thrust of her body, hands and feet grasping the earth, head flung back, hair trailing the ground. The oboe resumed for a flourishing finale as she rose to a headstand. Assarions and denarions stamped with absurd deities clanked around her ears.

Martseah and Iysh seated themselves on the ground under a cluster of trees and watched Eshed bargain at the stalls. He held up meat and vegetables laced on a stick and called, "Would you like these? They smell good!" Every tooth presented itself in his smile. The two nodded agreement. "How about these too?" He gestured to a stand serving spicy lebibah, hot from the oil.

Martseah, true to his bargain, insisted on paying for them and tossed his leather pouch into Eshed's hand. They were talking and laughing their way to a good digestion when Eshed sensed a pair of eyes on them. Turning in the direction of the sensation, he saw an outstretched hand, a tiny outstretched hand.

"Please, sir, have you something for my brother?" It was the little boy who had been running in front of the inn. Eshed looked into his hollowed eyes. Iysh and Martseah stopped chewing, their eyes riveted on the boy's outstretched hand.

"Where *is* your brother?" Eshed inquired, placing a piece of meat from his stick and cakes into the boy's palm.

Martseah thought immediately of Ariel and felt a stab of longing for home. "Bring him over . . . eat with us," Martseah instructed him. The boy smiled shyly and ran to untie his brother. He plopped him in Martseah's lap and sat down by Eshed, eyeing his food hungrily but asking nothing for himself. The baby, pale and thin, chewed on the bread and ogled the three men, beginning with a long appraisal of Martseah. An impromptu juggling act of three oranges plus Martseah brought a smile to the urchin's face.

Eshed and Iysh shared their food with the boy.

They did not speak for several moments, allowing time for the boy to eat. He, too, was thin, but had a bright eye and an air of determination about him.

"How are you called?" Eshed inquired, smiling down at the boy.

"I am Heli. My brother is called Zetema." He rubbed his foot beneath the ragged sandal.

"I saw you running today in front of the inn," Eshed interjected.

"Yah . . . I am in the race in a few days!"

"What race?"

"The boys in Spatale . . . every spring they have a race." Heli chewed hungrily on the meat.

The men looked at the spindly legs and eyed each other in wonder.

"Do your parents know you are racing?" Iysh wanted to know.

"We have no parents. They were killed by robbers along the road when we came to Spatale." At this, Eshed and Martseah exchanged knowing glances. "They hid us in the bushes, so we were safe. A caravan passing through brought us this far."

"Where do you and your brother . . . ah . . . Zetema stay at night? Where do you sleep?" Eshed handed Heli an orange he had peeled and sectioned for him. His very soul strove with the boy, whose beginnings seemed much like his own, the difference being that Eshed had only himself to care for while this child—a mere baby himself—had an infant!

"At the inn where you are staying. There is a room in the back where they keep sleeping mats and baskets. We are quite comfortable there." Heli seemed almost unaware of the gravity of the task of raising a baby alone.

Martseah was feeding the baby an orange. "Why do you race in a few days?" he asked.

"There is a money pouch for the prize. I am going to win it for Zetema!" He thumped himself on the chest and beamed at his brother, who smiled back, his chin streaked with orange juice.

The four of them walked together to the inn. The baby rode on Martseah's shoulders. "What do you think? Should they sleep in our room?" Martseah asked the others.

The night was warm and the storage area appeared clean. It was obvious to Eshed that much more remained to be done for these two, but what that should be was not yet apparent. "They might be more comfortable where they are accustomed to sleeping. It looks safe enough." Who would think to look for them among the rugs and baskets? It had probably been the innkeeper's thought as well. Stray children ran the risk of being sold into Circan slavery . . . or worse. In his travels, Eshed had heard reports of their being used for pagan sacrifices!

As the children snuggled into the cracks between the rolled mats, Eshed found a loose cover and tucked it over them, saying, "I will come for you in the morning. I know a place just outside Spatale. We will go there to practice your running. Perhaps I can give you a little training."

Heli nodded agreement. It was like a dream. Except for the innkeeper, no one had paid much attention to them since they were left by the caravan.

"Head up and chest out," Eshed barked. Somehow, he had to get some air in Heli's lungs. Most children ran naturally in the manner he was prescribing for Heli, but due to his physical condition and the heavy load of responsibility he carried, Heli ran with his head down, suppressing lung capacity. "Stretch your legs out longer as you get speed!" He was going to need all the reach and pacing he could manage, Eshed thought. Heli had pointed out his competitors as they left Spatale together. Every boy was larger and older than Heli by a season or two!

Eshed dangled Zetema on his arm. As they watched Heli churning up dust, Zetema clapped his approval. He was so spindly that Eshed hardly had a sense of holding a child. It was more like holding a house cat—and a small one at that!

Zetema waved both arms at Heli. The boy was learning fast. Eshed understood that Heli had a pressing reason to earn his own way. The tenuous arrangements of his own childhood had made him more determined than most to carve out and maintain his independence early. After Checed's training, he had hired out to a learned man to do stonework in his home in exchange for reading lessons. Eshed had shown such promise he'd been taken to the temple for further education. Thus his present vocation had evolved.

To avoid overdoing a good thing, Eshed called a halt to the practice. They had eaten a light breakfast before the run to make movement easier for Heli. He now appeared to be weakening.

Heli ran to Eshed's side. "Time for a good meal. You have run well!" Eshed rumpled the boy's curly hair, which was badly in need of a washing.

Heli skipped along beside him, gazing happily into his face on the return to Eshed's room.

The priest got out a basin and some towels. His sense of order would not allow the boys to carry dirt about any longer. Stripping to his tunic, he filled a crockery pitcher from the full kad of water he had hauled from the well that morning. Water service to the rooms was an extra he could not afford from a temple purse.

"I thought we were going to eat," Heli reminded him, eyeing the basin distastefully. His stomach, getting used to having food again, was kicking up fiercely.

"You will wash first. Then you can help me bathe the baby." Eshed smiled, ignoring the plea in Heli's eyes. "Take this jug of water and heat it by a fire. I will stay with Zetema." It was time to teach Heli the rudiments of personal care, as well as running!

Heli soon scrambled back with a warm jug, heated by a fire where roasting meat had only increased his pangs.

The boy washed quickly. A little *too* quickly, Eshed decided.

"Your ears get dirt in them too!" he admonished the youngster, taking a cloth and probing the inner surfaces which Heli had skipped in his haste.

"Ouch!" Heli grimaced and pulled away.

"See!" Eshed held the cloth out for his inspection. A great clot of grime was smeared into it. "I'm surprised you can hear me when I call you!" *This must be what it is like being a father. A lot of homely tasks no one likes or remembers, but necessary nonetheless.*

While Eshed was performing the rite of ablution, the baby saw his chance. Crawling over to Eshed's travel tote, he found a bit of stray cloth poking from the heavy woven reed parcel and pulled at it insistently till it was on the floor. It was a pale blue tunic that Eshed favored and one that he had recently washed. Zetema, unnoticed by the picking Eshed and the complaining Heli, crawled with it to a puddle of dirty water dripping onto the floor from Heli's elbows. The baby pushed the cloth about in the puddle, gleefully noting its color change.

Heli dried off but remained stripped to help wash Zetema. Eshed scowled as he scooped the baby from the floor and separated him from the newly grimed tunic. Zetema gurgled in delight at his accomplishment, eliciting spontaneous hoots of laughter from the others. Bathing the baby was fun, the lad decided, not at all like washing oneself!

Eshed rubbed the baby's head gently with a towel, fluffing the sparse hair. "What would you like to eat?" he asked Heli as the boy slipped into his grimy clothes. The boy's mouth watered as he thought of the aroma of the meat at the fire where he had heated water.

"Roast pork . . . at the sign of the Sea Urchin!"

Tossing the clean baby aloft, Eshed threw back his head and laughed at Heli's quick response. Fastening the soiled garment back on the baby, using a clean towel for a diaper, he made a decision to find proper clothing for him. "I cannot eat pork, but you may, if you like. I am certain there will be fish there for me."

Waiting for food service by the spit that rotated a succulent boar, Eshed caught sight of Iysh, heading toward the stall with a gentleman.

"Eshed!" Iysh raised his hand in signal. "This is Appelles, a fine physician."

Appelles was the man he had seen in the hallway the day before. They clasped hands and shoulders in greeting. The physician inclined his head toward Eshed. He had a high forehead and patrician features. In the warm, friendly grasp of his hand, Eshed once again sensed an incredible strength emanating from the man. He moved his sturdy body as one who handled timber or stone, not human flesh. He was tall, his legs like great tree trunks, slightly bowed at the base but powerfully muscled.

"Would you join us in a meal?" Eshed asked. Appelles nodded, his eyes on the youngsters. The food was carried to the tree area where they had met the children, and they scattered about on the green carpet, parcels of food sizzling among the leaves.

After the food had been blessed, Eshed portioned some out for the boys.

"You should see what Appelles did this morning." Iysh, too, was in awe of the man. "A girl with sores on her arm—very red—he placed something on it, an unguent. Immediately the swelling went away. Then a man on a crutch with a bad swelling of the joints . . . he took him to an icy spring and bathed him, and he was walking so much better when he left us!"

Appelles did not speak but continued to watch the children, especially the baby. After eating, they tumbled off to play under the trees. He leaned forward and asked, "Eshed, how did the baby get the small bruises on his feet?"

"I do not know," Eshed replied between bites. "We only found the children yesterday . . . I noticed them when I bathed him today. They are in an odd place, considering that he does not walk yet—or even wear shoes."

"Are you the one who is buying their food?" Appelles inquired.

"We are all helping with them while we are here," Eshed demurred.

Appelles shook his head. "What I mean is . . . there are certain things the baby should eat just now. If you could see to it, I will make a list."

"They are both very thin. Mostly, we are trying to put some meat on their bones," Eshed replied.

"I know, but beyond that . . . there is a problem," the doctor confided, his eyes serious.

"What is that?" Eshed asked, pulling the spine of bones from his fish with practiced fingers.

"I am not certain yet." Appelles averted his eyes. "I will keep watch on the child and let you know." Scribbling some things on a papyrus, he handed it to Eshed, along with a bottle of dark brown liquid. "A tonic." He tapped it with his finger. "Give him a spoonful with his meals."

Eshed took his coin pouch and offered a fee for Appelles' service, but he waved it away.

"Let me do this." Appelles smiled. "It gives me pleasure." The doctor's eye had been softened by the witness of much suffering.

After the meal, Iysh continued to make rounds with Appelles, and Eshed took the children to fit them with new tunics. He caught up with Martseah, who was bobbing in and out of stalls, selling his wares at a rapid rate.

"Have you any sandals in Heli's size?" he whispered in Martseah's ear.

Without hesitation, Martseah turned back into the booth from which he had just made a sale. He pulled a pair of sandals from a hook. "Sorry," he told the proprietor. "Can't sell this pair to you. They are promised." He dove into his pack just as the man opened his mouth to protest and came up with an intricately tooled mezach, of considerably more value than the shoes. "Take this instead?"

The man's scowl was replaced by a smile. He nodded, his eyes gleaming. The tooled portion had been rubbed with pomegranate juice, and the red etching contrasted smartly with the pale brown leather. He took it and placed it about his own waist, shifting it to fit above his paunch. Fastening it in place, he gave it a slap. The bargain was made.

Heli experimented with his sandals all afternoon. Putting them on and taking them off, lacing and unlacing them. They fastened about his ankle, which kept the straps out of his way for running. Skipping and hopping about, he practiced running in them. The shoes did everything well, he decided. His new tunic was beige with a green band at the throat and wrists. Smoothing the front of it, he pranced about in his new trappings. Heli's old tunic had been beyond soap and needle and had been discarded.

It was a thoroughly spent Heli who tumbled into slumber that night. For once, he was asleep before Zetema. His brother gurgled and jabbered, trying to get his attention. The baby tugged at his hair and patted his face. When Heli made no motion, Zetema settled back into the mats, wide-eyed, and chewed on the fringe of the throw covering them. Finally, for lack of something better to do, he went to sleep.

Iysh and Eshed met back at the room that evening after Eshed had settled the children. The young priest was full of reports on Heli's pleasure over the sandals and was eager to see Martseah.

Seeing Iysh alone, he said, "Where is Martseah? I thought he would come with you."

"I supposed he was with you," Iysh countered. "I have not seen him since sunup."

A worried look crossed Eshed's face. "I last saw him in the stalls, after noon—when he gave me some sandals for Heli."

They discussed going to look for him but agreed that he would be along soon. Settling into their prayer books, neither spoke for awhile. Eshed was feeling restive. He tried to pray, but he couldn't concentrate. He was about to take leave of Iysh and go looking for Martseah when they heard a shuffling sound at the door.

"Iysh! Eshed! Let us in!" A frantic knocking set both men on their feet.

Eshed flung wide the door. Raphel, the sailsman, was half carrying, half dragging a man covered with blood gushing from a wound in his side. With the two men's help, he was lowered gently onto a mat. The light from the taper on the wall crossed his ashen face.

Martseah!

CHAPTER 15

Appelles burst through the door. Bag in hand, he knelt by the bleeding Martseah.

Struggling to mask his shock at the sight of so much fresh blood, he grabbed a clean cloth from his bag and began to mop the blonde forehead. "Cloths . . . bring more clean cloths!" he barked. Eshed and Iysh, rooted to the spot with fear, were galvanized into action. They tore up cloaks and tunics, anything at hand. Raphel stood to one side, babbling.

"Get hold of yourself, man!" Appelles fixed a stern eye on the oarsman. "We will need some hot broth—bring it!" The doctor dove into his bag and pulled out a needle. Raphel left the room. Stringing a metal object, he began to suture the wound. Iysh and Eshed, both fascinated and repelled, watched his hands at work. Appelles was reputed to be the finest physician in the province. *Thank God*, Eshed thought to himself. But just as Appelles was about to close the wound, it began to spurt violently.

"An artery!" he exclaimed, shaking his head. The rupture was wider than he had thought and much deeper. "Stanch the flow—apply pressure!" Eshed took the first shift while Iysh sat by, ashen-faced, wringing his hands. Eshed's cloth was quickly soaked, and he flung it to one side. Iysh moved quickly into place with a fresh compress.

Appelles checked Martseah's eyes, lifting the lids. "No . . . no . . ." the patient moaned, pushing the air with weak arms.

"The flow of blood . . . it's stopping," Iysh remarked, pulling a partly soaked cloth from the gaping hole.

The physician grasped Martseah's wrist, his heart pounding hopefully. Holding his own breath, he listened apprehensively for Martseah's short gasps of air and moved in closer over his patient's face, ready for any sign of change. His other hand felt for a pulse at the neck.

Martseah's head rolled to one side, the taper on the wall flickering ominously on his pallid features.

"He is gone."

Appelles staggered into the hall and leaned against a wall. Ghastly! It was beyond comprehension. Death had come so quickly.

Eshed's blood-soaked hands clawed his face. "My God . . . why?" He flung himself across the still form, his voice swallowed in the mute cloak of Martseah's departure.

Raphel entered the hall with a cup of broth. He stopped short at the sight of Appelles slouched against the wall. The silence of that room was a high and slippery bank he could not risk. He sought Appelles' eyes and received a negative head shake in confirmation. Backing away as quickly as his trembling joints would permit, he dropped the cup and ran from the building.

Appelles felt some need to reassure the two remaining inside. When he leaned into the door frame, he was startled to see both men kneeling in prayer. Puzzling, he returned to his room. What did those two expect to perform in that position? Some sort of absolution for Martseah's soul? Crumpling on the mat in exhaustion, he dreamed the whole sequence over again and awoke, sweating profusely. He bumped along the wall to see to his friends and peeked into the room at the kneeling figures.

Martseah's lips, still parted, moved.

"Eshed . . ." he whispered. The word seemed to echo off every wall.

At the sound, his friend's head swung round, and he hastened to Martseah's side, weeping. "My friend . . . my dear brother." Eshed clasped the white hand. The color was flowing back into Martseah's face as he smiled up at Eshed. Iysh pulled himself up and knelt at his other side, wiping tears on his tunic sleeve and laughing.

Wet-faced, Appelles entered and knelt, placing his hand on Iysh's shoulder. "My friends," he said, his eyes fixed on the recovering leathersmith. A tear trickled down his face and fell from his jaw onto Martseah's chest, now heaving with life.

"My friends . . ." was all he could say.

With morning's light, Eshed took Heli and Zetema for Heli's practice. Appelles looked in on Martseah as he and Iysh breakfasted in their room. "I have come to dress your wound, my friend!" He knelt by Martseah, who was sitting propped against a wall, eating a piece of fruit. The doctor opened his pouch and brought out some bandages and a bottle of solution to swab the wound.

"I saw Elohim last night!" Martseah's face shone. He pulled aside his tunic.

"I know. . . . So did I," Appelles nodded. It was indescribable, the way he felt today because of it.

Martseah felt his side with his hand and then opened the tunic on the other side. "Which side was the stab wound?" he asked, his sparkling eyes puzzled.

"The left," Appelles replied, folding a fresh bandage.

Iysh sat smiling at them from across the room, sporting a fresh headband, a cup of hot brew between his palms.

The physician examined his patient with his eyes, probing about with his fingers. "There is nothing here," he gasped. "Just a small scar where the wound was. I don't even see the suture marks."

The question Eshed had been dreading came on their return that morning.

"You will be leaving soon for . . ." Heli probed.

"Etser," Eshed replied.

"Will we go with you?"

Eshed placed the baby on his shoulders to rise, and said, "Not yet." Zetema latched on to Eshed's thick hair with his fingers.

"Why not . . . yet?" the young lad insisted.

"I am praying about it, but I have no answer yet." Eshed averted his eyes. He knew it sounded like a dodge.

"What is . . . praying?" Heli responded.

Eshed wondered why most of what young children said ended in question marks. Yet, these were good questions! His hand rested on the boy's head, and his other supported the baby as they walked.

"It means asking the Father what should be done about such matters."

"My father?" Heli asked excitedly. He had often felt his father was somehow looking after him since he died.

"Our Father in heaven, yours and mine."

"You must mean God."

"Yes."

"I've heard about God."

Their shoes shuffled in silence for a space.

"But how does he hear us?" Heli wanted to know.

"We speak to him through the Holy Spirit who is always with us."

"*All* the time?" Heli's face lit up.

"Unless we choose otherwise. . . . Then he waits for us to ask him in."

"I see." Heli was thoughtful. Eshed sensed that he really did comprehend. Would that grown men were so open to the truth!

"Then can I ask him to help me win the race?"

"By all means," Eshed agreed. "But remember . . . he will choose what is best for you. If you do not win, that is best!"

"Then why are we practicing?"

"Because we both believe you will win!"

Their laughter was joined by Zetema's giggle.

The path for the race was marked by colored flags, a red one to start and a blue one for the finish line.

The route approximated the area where Heli had practiced running, with one exception. A little hill had been thrown in for good measure. The blue flag was mounted on top of that hill. It was the hill for the final lap. Seeing it made Eshed wish they had practiced some hill running!

It was a fine, clear day, and the townspeople had assembled for the event, cheering their favorites as they gathered at the starting line.

The runners were jogging in place to warm up and kicking up lots of dust in the process. Heli was hopping about excitedly. Eshed took him aside. "Remember . . . head up, chest out . . . long strides . . . and *most* important, the Lord goes with you!" He gave the boy a firm hug and sent him to the starting line. There was some tittering at the sight of his build alongside the bigger boys. Heli glanced up at Eshed for reassurance. He nodded to the boy and gave him a "thumbs up" victory symbol. *All things are possible with the Lord,* Eshed thought. He hoped he had conveyed that to Heli . . . the odds against him were heavy.

"On your mark!" The boys toed the line drawn in the dirt.

"Get ready," the starter intoned.

"Get set." The contestants leaned forward, hand to right knee in the starting stance.

The starter held the red flag aloft. The only sound was the cloth flapping in the breeze. The flag came down—"*Go!*"

They were off, running evenly at first. Soon the stronger boys began to pull ahead. Heli was moving somewhere in the middle. One tall boy, rumored to be the favorite, moved confidently into the lead. The crowd was shouting its approval. Eshed shifted his feet and handed the baby to Appelles. Cupping his hands, he yelled encouragement to Heli. The boy turned his head slightly to hear Eshed's voice above the noise of the crowd. As he did, his foot hit a hole—and he went down.

"Keep going! It is all right!" Eshed shouted. Heli picked himself up and continued. He was now out of earshot. He would have to make it on his own. The runners rounded a curve and were out of sight. The crowd surged to the hill where the blue flag waited.

The starter waved the crowd back against the trees at the hill's crest. The runners would need a clear view of the flag as they made their final lunge up the hill.

The runners were coming! The crowd murmured excitedly.

Eshed angled for a glimpse of Heli.

"Can you see him?" he asked Appelles and Iysh in turn. They strained forward but the boy was not in view.

Eshed's heart was in his throat. *What if one of the big boys has tripped him?* It was an old trick, usually perpetrated on the strongest contender and sometimes, cruelly, on the weakest.

Suddenly, as they started up the hill, the runners slowed. The crowd had a clear view of the runner moving from the back through the center.

It was Heli!

He spurted ahead and began to gain on the tall boy in the lead.

The cheering increased. It would not be a shoo-in, after all!

The other runners, a dozen or so in all, observed Heli passing and struggled to retain position. The leader, misinterpreting the crowd's roar as his easy victory, slowed a little on the toughest part of the incline.

Heli's spindly legs churned up and down. His head was back and his strides were long. He had reached the reprieve point on the incline, and it gave his speed a boost. He covered the gap between himself and the leader and burst past the blue flag, his arms thrown high!

Eshed was at his side in a flash, lifting him for all to see.

The crowd cheered. "The winner!" Eshed cried.

Heli panted, his small chest gulping in air. He hugged Eshed. The two wooly heads appeared as one. "I never could have . . . made it . . . if you had not been at the hilltop waving me toward you," he gasped.

"But I wasn't. . . . I was with the crowd at the side of the hill," Eshed explained. "We moved back so you could aim for the blue flag."

"Never saw the flag . . . I saw a man waving me toward him. . . . I kept my eyes on him!"

"It was the Lord Jesus, lad . . . not me!"

The starter held up his hand and asked the crowd for quiet. Eshed set Heli on the ground beside him. Appelles and Iysh crowded in behind to slap the boy's shoulder and offer congratulations.

"And what is your name, sir?" the starter asked the winner.

"Heli." The boy smiled up at Eshed, his eyes shining.

The starter took Heli's hand and held it up . . . holding the money pouch aloft with the other.

"This is Heli! To the victor . . . go the spoils!" He dropped the purse into Heli's waiting hands. The crowd became one affirmative voice, cheering the spindly youngster.

Heli placed the pouch in the baby's hands. Zetema jiggled the pouch awkwardly, listening to the coins jingle inside it. The pouch was too heavy for him and Appelles handed it back to Heli, taking note of a new bruise on the infant's forehead. His remedy was not working. He must tell Eshed.

After a joyous victory supper, during which Heli recounted every step of the race, it was decided the boys would move in with the men to protect Heli's winnings. He sat on their floor, surrounded by coins. "Twenty-nine . . ." the boy counted. "What comes next?" he asked Eshed.

"Thirty." The priest showed him how to stack the ones he'd already counted in sets of ten. "Now, when you check your counting, just add up the stacks. Do you know how to count by tens?"

Heli looked at him uncertainly and dropped his head.

"Never mind," Eshed told him. "A man who can earn this kind of money will learn to count it very quickly! I will help you tomorrow!"

Heli grinned, trickling the leptons he had counted back into the pouch on top of the larger denarions. "Just tell me now," Heli implored. "Do I have enough to buy a small cart for Zetema to ride in so I can pull him about in the village? Then I wouldn't have to tie him to a tree." A pained look crossed the boy's face.

"You have *more* than enough. . . . Now, get ready for bed. You have had a big day!"

Eshed tucked the boys in bed and snuffed out the wall candle. The men sought their own resting spots. Appelles, heading for his room, called to Eshed from the hallway. "Eshed . . ."

Moving silently across the floor, he joined the older man in the dim light of the vestibule. "Yes?"

"I do not know how to say it. . . . There is no easy way." Appelles fumbled for the words, his eyes serious. Eshed leaned closer to catch his whispered words, a line creasing his brow.

"The baby . . . the bruises . . . he has a rare blood disease—I cannot help him."

Eshed squared his shoulders against the frame of the doorway. "It is a hard thing—" A tear glistened in the corner of his eye. "But we are not without a resource."

He motioned Appelles back into the room with a twist of his head. Calling to Iysh and Martseah, he shared the news in hushed tones. They knelt about the sleeping baby and began to pray silently. This they would continue to do, every night, as the child lay sleeping.

The marketplace was abuzz with Heli's triumph.

Eshed was examining some mesh hair coverings in a booth when the proprietor said to him, "You, Sir. . . . You know the boy who won the race. . . . Tell me, how did he manage against such odds?" His eyebrows arched.

The young stranger from Kerielan lifted his eyes, head still inclined toward the merchandise. "You have heard," he said, "about the spirit of determination."

The merchant wagged his head. He was having none of it. Still, it did not seem like an appropriate moment to tell the real story.

"Where do these mesh hair coverings come from? I see many women wearing them here." His eyes followed a girl, probably in her fifteenth year, as she passed close to him at the stall front. Her plump cheeks were pink and her eyes sparkled. She saw Eshed looking at the blue netting that held her dark curls from her face and mistook his intention.

Turning her face toward him as she passed, she smiled provocatively. "I was thinking to get one for my wife," he stammered, flustered.

"For your *wife?*" The proprietor leered at him mischievously.

"Yes. For my *wife*," the young priest insisted, frowning.

"Ah, yes." The merchant slipped immediately into his "selling" voice. "They are exquisite . . . from the bargaining of Ardon of Ohad." His inflection was syrupy as he fingered the fine handiwork, holding it to the sunlight.

Of course! Why hadn't he thought of it—they were Sarakabel's handiwork!

"A blue one, please!" Eshed remembered the one the girl wore. "And this pearl as well." He held up a single delicate pearl on a gold chain. He wanted to buy it for his love. It was extravagant, he knew, but soon he would be heading homeward, and his pouch was not yet empty.

As he pocketed his purchases, a scuffle behind him caused him to turn.

Heli was on the ground with a tall boy standing over him, fists clenched. The larger boy had a bullish head and a sour look on his face. Eshed recognized him as the runner who lost the race to Heli.

Quickly Eshed stepped between the two boys, pulling Heli to his feet and dusting him off. The larger boy jerked his fist back menacingly, and with one eye on Eshed, slunk away, bent on revenge at a later opportunity.

Heli wiped his dusty cheek with his hand. Everyone, it appeared, was not in a congratulatory mood. Observers of the skirmish began pressing about him as they walked through the crowd, telling him what a fine show the race had been.

Martseah, observing from a booth nearby, was holding Zetema and feeding him an orange. He feared the press of the crowd for Heli. Since his own harrowing experience at the hand of a stranger, he was cautious in the marketplace. He strode over and, handing Eshed the baby, squatted down and directed Heli to climb on his shoulders. Then he stood, lifting Heli into the air. Now strangers could question him all they wanted. Heli would be safe.

A short, swarthy man elbowed his way through the crowd and spoke to Heli, squinting upward against the sun's rays. "You there—I placed a wager on the race . . . but not on *you!* Now it is empty." He patted his pouch. "You must race again and help me win it back." He glanced at Martseah and the twisted smile on his face disappeared. His face went white and he backed away, stuttering. He turned and quickly pushed his way through the crowd.

Martseah recognized him. It was his assailant, the man who had left him for dead!

He grasped Heli's arms. "Slide down my back—quickly!" He turned Heli back to Eshed's keeping and sped off through the crowd, grabbing the murderer in a corner between the stalls. He tried to shake himself off, but Martseah hung on. Fists were flying from both directions as they shoved one another against the stalls. Martseah seized the man's tunic at the throat and drew back to bloody his face with his fist when he suddenly let go. Some inner working would not let him harm the man.

The stranger slid down the stall side to the ground, trembling. Martseah stood over him, his chest heaving, his legs weak. "What is your name?" he wheezed, looking hard at the man.

"Tabeel. I do not understand . . . I thought you were dead." Great beads of perspiration crested the smaller man's brow.

Martseah was still struggling to comprehend why he had let the man go when he put out his hand and drew the flinching man to his feet and uttered words that seemed to be coming from other than his own lips.

"Tabeel, I forgive you."

Tabeel backed away, confused. Then he turned and ran, throwing Martseah's partially empty money pouch at his feet as he went.

Tucking the reclaimed pouch into his girdle, Martseah rejoined his friends.

Tabeel wandered brokenly about the marketplace, having forgotten why he had come. To his surprise, he arrived shortly thereafter at his own doorstep. He greeted his wife in a state of confusion.

"What is it, Tabeel? What has happened to you?" She brought the lamp to his face and smelled his breath, thinking he had been too long with his drinking cronies. His clothes were in disarray and he smelled sweaty from the warm day—nothing more.

His eyes rolled about strangely in his head. "I saw a man dying yesterday . . . covered with blood," he blubbered.

"Yes, yes . . . go on!"

"Today . . . he walks in the marketplace . . . *whole!*" he whined.

"Tabeel, you must be mistaken. It was not the same man! You have been too long in the sun, my husband." She put down the lamp and wrung a cloth in cool water. Helping him to a resting mat, she had him stretch out and began to bathe his face.

"No, no." He revived a little. "I talked to him. . . . He was the one, all right. He is a stranger to Spatale—tall . . . blonde. Doesn't look like our people, hard to forget." Tabeel dozed into a fitful sleep.

CHAPTER 16

The marketplace of Spatale was abuzz with a new story.

Women, merchants' wives mostly, attired in elegantly draped gowns and with gold ornaments dripping from their ears and wrists, whispered and pointed at Martseah as he and his companions strolled by.

If Martseah's good fortune held, he would have nothing to carry home but his pouch. While he was selling the few items that remained, the merchant purchasing them studied him closely.

Suddenly, a woman who had been watching him from the shadows exploded into the foreground. She was of the lower class and spoke shrilly, not in the cultured tones of Spatale. "This man—" she jabbed a finger in Martseah's direction. "He was dead—and now he walks."

A hush fell over the bystanders. Their eyes turned to Martseah. Disbelief, awe, and curiosity reigned on their faces.

The commotion, followed by stillness, then whisperings, reached Appelles and Iysh's ears and they hurried to a spot where they could see Martseah's tall blonde head gleaming in the sunlight. In that instant, they saw what the crowd saw: He looked like a young god. He stood silent, wreathed in a glow.

The two boys were occupied under the trees. Heli was making flower chains. Zetema, his baby hands poking at flower stems, was trying to imitate his brother's movements.

Eshed sensed this was the turning point ⟨. . in the Lord's favor. He stepped forward into a circle cleared for him by the murmuring crowd.

"Friends of Spatale . . ." Heel-wheeling a half circle, his dark eyes scanned the gathering. He could see Tabeel weaving in and out of the backdrop, trying not to be noticed. "We are men . . . as you are. We are not purveyors of fraud or magic, as some of you believe, but followers of the one true God—Elohim . . . of old." He observed several women clutching amulets around their necks and could see the men, whose stalls showed emblems of foreign gods on their posts, scowling. ". . . And of his Son, Jesus Christ, who walked the earth as you do and by whose death and resurrection we all may live. . . . Acknowledge the God who made you . . . and no other! He loves you. . . . Each of you." Eshed's eyes settled like a firebrand on the man who would have taken Martseah's life. "Come to him, and you will have life . . . evermore."

The tradesman from whom he had made his purchases for Loana called out, "How do you know this? Who told you?"

Eshed's voice rose above the increased mumbling of the crowd. "We have his promise . . . and we have witnessed his power." His outstretched arm called the crowd's attention to Martseah. ". . . As you have!"

"It is a trick," the merchant called. "How do we know this man was dead?" The crowd muttered ominously and moved closer.

Tabeel, propelled forward by some impulse he could not understand, fell on his knees inside the circle.

"Because I killed him! I stabbed him and left him to bleed to death. . . . May God forgive me!"

The man was under no threat from the leaders of Spatale. Foreigners were considered fair game, and there were no laws to protect them from exploitation. Still, only the power of Christ could have wrung the admission from Tabeel's lips. Of that, Martseah was certain. Tabeel hung his head, tears streaming down his weathered face.

Eshed caught sight of Iysh standing at the edge of the crowd alone. That brief glimpse told him something of the changing nature of the Spatale mission. His own participation was coming rapidly to a close. He had done what he was sent to do.

That evening, in their room, the four men held a prayer council. After an hour or so of silent communion, it was resolved: Eshed, needed in Etser where Namath and Simonus had been in service since his absence, would return home. Appelles, a new brother in the faith still awaiting his commission from the Lord, would travel as far as Protos with the group. There he would confer with Tobias, an old friend in medicine, who had certain information he wished to include in a biblios he was developing that would aid students in the art of healing. Martseah, Heli, and Zetema would remain in Protos with him so that he might keep watch on Zetema. (Martseah would tool wall maps!) Daily the bruises were diminishing. It was a result, the men felt, of the nightly prayer for the baby. Iysh would remain in Spatale for a time, ministering to Tabeel and other new converts who were sure to follow in the wake of the day's experience.

Spatale's spires pierced a shroud of morning mist. A light fog persisted, seeping into their clothing as they packed and impressing on Eshed the suffocating reality of leaving a man behind alone. It was the Lord's choice and must be obeyed, but it did not ease his heart to think of the trauma of ministering alone in a pagan community such as Spatale.

The parting brought a fresh realization to Appelles as well.

"I have a confession to make." His hand rested on Iysh's shoulder as he faced him eye to eye. "When first we met, I thought you a fool. You were so simple and childlike in your ways. I could not understand why you were determined to follow me about, engrossed as you were in my work. I want to thank you now for knowing what was important. For persisting, for loving me when I did not care for you!"

Iysh interrupted the doctor with an embrace. "Think no more of it. We are brothers in the Lord now." He beamed at the new friend Adonai had chosen for him.

The lone missionary to Spatale accompanied his companions to the shore where a rowboat was crossing the water to take them to their ship. He spent the last few moments enjoying the company of the children. Pulling a little cloth sack filled with honey-glazed apricots and pistachios from his tunic, he tucked it in Heli's hand for the trip to Protos.

The rowboat cut a v in the damp sand behind the footsteps of the oarsman who towed it in. Filmy pockets of fog were lifting off the water, and as he neared they could see that Raphel had been sent to carry them across the light blue crust of the fog laden cove. Raphel smiled his recognition of them, but as one face swam at him through the mists, he gave a yelp of recognition and fell backward into the boat.

"He's fainted," declared Appelles, bending over the boat. "I think the sight of Martseah was too much for him." Climbing in next to the oarsman, he began immediately to massage his hands and pat his face with cold sea water. When he came around, Martseah told him what had happened. Only when it came from Martseah's own lips would he believe that he was not dreaming.

Eshed found the parting too painful for proper expression; he smothered Iysh in a tight embrace and stepped wordlessly into the boat. Iysh lifted the children up and kissed them, handing them to Eshed in the boat. After everyone had said their good-byes, Raphel, dazed and robotlike, dipped the oars into the crystalline bay, moving the boat shipward. The white blanket of fog had swept upward from the water, leaving a long, clear view of Iysh waving from the shore. The aborigine's figure grew steadily smaller. Then it was gone.

Once aboard the ship, Eshed turned to speak to Raphel and saw that he had remained behind in the rowboat. He was gazing out over the water, but he was not alone. Eshed felt sure of that. Raphel was lingering in some new dimension of his soul, lifting his sails to something much deeper and much safer than the sea.

The captain hurried to the prow and leaned out over the edge. "That lazy rascal! What is he staring at out there? Doesn't he know it is time to shove off?" He glared at Eshed, suspecting some connection with Raphel's insubordination. The young priest, leaning on the rail with his eye fixed on the empty shoreline, was praying silently for Iysh's ministry to the Spatalians. He looked at the captain, returning a smile for his scowling.

They had settled in the hold for the night, and Appelles was recording in his log by the dim light of an oil lantern. "One thing I do not understand . . ." he whispered to Eshed, who joined him sitting cross-legged on the plank floor.

"Yes?" The boys had just been bedded on a pallet nearby and Eshed's attention was still on the wriggling baby who had to be propped with stowage to keep from rolling away from his brother as the ship rocked.

"I am recording the effect of diet on Zetema's blood disease. How do I know which part I affected with diet and which part is the Lord's healing?"

Eshed considered his answer. "It is *all* his work. But we are partners with him in healing, just as we are in all other areas of his caring for his people. He has made us partners."

Appelles reflected on the partnership idea. Perhaps it would be more clear to him when he received his special commission from the Lord as Eshed and Iysh had.

"We pray to the Father for healing . . . just as he did," Eshed continued. "And sometimes we are required to do some concrete things that implement that healing—as the baby's diet does. I think it is a sign of our obedience to him, our partnership with him, and the link with our earth home which is provided for our physical sustenance while we are here. Someday, when we dwell with him in glory, we will not need any of these things." Eshed smiled as he thought of it.

"But how do I know that my diet is the right thing for the baby? It is, after all, only my own idea," Appelles countered. Eshed marveled at the change of attitude in Appelles, who only recently had been more than willing to take credit for healings. "He will show you what is right in each instance. The Lord, himself, when he healed on earth as a man, used different methods. Sometimes a touch . . . sometimes a word . . . and when healing a man blind from birth, he mixed his spittle with dust and applied the paste to the man's eyelids. He did whatever was required at the moment. Sometimes he passed by deliberately so that his followers might perform the healing later, when empowered by his Holy Spirit."

"Which brings up my next question." Appelles' eyes glistened in the lantern light. "If he has all power available to him through God the Father . . . why does he need us?"

Eshed smiled. He enjoyed most remembering who God

was and why he bothered with man, especially when he had a perfect Son in Jesus Christ.

"The old scrolls tell us that God made us for fellowship with himself. When we choose him, he presents us . . . in fact already has presented us . . . to his Son. We were given to him for his own at the dawn of time, and he chose us then as channels of his love and power to the world around us. He could, of course, do it all without us—make stick dolls of us, if you will—but he chose our partnership and us, with all our humanness. So you see, no one is really fatherless or brotherless, without kin. We have him and he has us!" It comforted Eshed to speak of these things, thinking of Iysh on that foreign shore!

Appelles nodded. He could see he would have to become an acute listener if he was to heal as the Lord intended. He planned to do just that!

Only a few more miles.

The hour was late. Eshed had no hope that Loana would be awake. Still it would be good to know that she was there beside him, at rest, to be greeted in the morning.

Eshed had left Appelles, Martseah, and the boys with Tobias in Protos. Martseah had agreed to look up Tasia and see how she was faring since leaving the employ of Boris. They would remain in Protos till given further instruction. Eshed's commission was clear: *Home*, and the sooner, the better. He felt compelled to lose no time in returning.

Expecting the glimmer of a candle lamp or two as was Loana's custom in the event of his return, he was unprepared for the sight that met him—candle lamps all through the house and harp strains pouring from within. Laughter met his ears as he stabled his mount and entered the house stealthily, his scalp prickling uncomfortably.

His first glimpse was of Loana's arms glowing amber in

the lamplight as she stroked a harp against the shadowed backdrop of rapt faces.

"And she gave him her heart," she sang. It was a ballad he had heard in Protos—in Protos! "That was not the best part." She shared a conspiratorial wink with her audience. They responded with laughter and murmurings. One of the men sitting in front grabbed playfully at her foot in an elaborate high, tilted shoe extended from the stool on which she sat to play. Her leg was bare— and she was wearing the forbidden white dress!

For the first time, she sensed Eshed's presence, standing just inside the curtain. Her eye caught his. "Eshed!" She tossed aside the harp and flew to him, kissing him deeply. An aura of wine and strange perfume surrounded her. The guests applauded the embrace amid murmurings of "Aahhhh!" Later, Eshed recalled being pulled into the dimly lit room to greet the Nebows, who had supplied the infamous dress. Among them Telles lounged on the cushions. An insolent smile played on his lips and Eshed identified him as the footgrabber. Jarad was there, too, laughing lustily with some of Nebow's distant relatives.

A mixture of rage and betrayal surged in Eshed's weary breast. He was grateful that all departed speedily for Kamar's inn—or at least as quickly as their mismanaged mounts would carry them. As he saw them away into the night, he checked the wine vat in the shed. One thump told him it was empty. It was little wonder that the sodden Nebow left resting heavily on his horse's withers. Loana had not cut the wine! He smashed his fist into the cask, sprawling its splintered staves across the shed. His tongue was in check, but it threatened to break loose at any moment!

The house was a shambles of half-eaten food and empty wine flasks. In addition to the dress, shoes, and perfume, Loana had a smear of blue-black kohl about her eyes that gave her the appearance of an enchantress. He stroked her hair and said nothing until she was fast asleep. Eshed could not bring himself to make love to her, much as he wanted to. When he heard the even breathing that signaled deep sleep, he slid from the covers and knelt upon the bare floor, praying for the wisdom and patience he would surely need to restore order to his home. Only the Lord could restore his trampled heart. . . .

The ritual at the prayer stone gave Loana time to clean away the incense pots, wine flasks, and dirty crockery before preparing their breakfast. As he approached the sitting room for their meal together, Eshed wondered how much of the night Loana remembered. He had asked the Lord's wisdom and the right opening to talk about it.

Loana bent over the mat, filling their bowls. Eshed slipped the chained pearl he had brought from Spatale around her throat.

"My love . . . thank you!" She kissed his cheek, averting her eyes, apparently engrossed in arranging fruit segments on his plate. He knew the wine had not erased the memory of last night completely.

The room was cleared of debris, and a mound of cushions tossed in one corner served as a mute reminder of the large group she had entertained. In another corner was an assortment of choice vases, bolts of cloth, and metallic trivia hauled in, undoubtedly, from Jarad's travels.

"How do you like my face this morning?" She tipped her chin so the light from the window bathed her face. Her eyes were puffy from wine and heavy sleep.

"Your face always looks beautiful to me." He cringed inwardly at his own words—last night had certainly been an exception!

"Proustia sent some of the herb cream she used to prepare for me. My skin feels so much better—I have been without it for so long," she sighed.

He found himself staring at the single pearl at her throat and thought how insignificant it must be, compared to all the things her father seemed able to provide for her. Feeling self-conscious, he offered her the other present, the net hair covering. She took it and arranged her long, loose hair in it. The weave framed her face and made her look much more respectable. She pulled at the mesh with her fingers. "The design is very intricate," she commented, "and it fits so well."

He was glad he had gotten it for her. "They are made by Sarakabel of the temple in Ohad." He smiled in remembrance of the testy weaver. "You know, she is the one who wove the tapestries and mended the vestments."

"You went again to Ohad, then?" she asked, lifting a long strand of honey into the air from a cephel and twirling it on a spoon.

"No. We went to Protos and Spatale. The road to Ohad was blocked by a rockslide and it was very muddy. Sarakabel's wares are marketed in Spatale by her husband, Ardon." Eshed reached out and touched the blue net, his eyes full of memories. "She told me once that these sprang bonnets are made from horse's tails. They are usually brown, white, or black. But Sarakabel is a clever woman. She developed a special dyeing process that turned a white one into this blue one for you."

"Good morning, children!" a voice called from the doorway. It was Jarad.

Loana kissed her father good morning and went to fill another bowl.

Jarad seated himself across from Eshed. "How were your travels, my boy?"

Father Jarad had only intended to make conversation,

but Eshed detected a note of condescension tucked among the words.

"Longer than I had hoped . . . this last journey . . . but we accomplished a great deal, I think," Eshed responded.

"Where is Iysh?" Loana asked, placing a bowl of hot grain before her father. "I thought he would be returning with you, love." All her movements and even her tone sounded self-conscious this morning.

Jarad looked puzzled at mention of the stranger's name.

"Oh, Father Jarad—Iysh is a man Eshed met on one of his other trips. I like him!" Loana explained.

Yes . . . Iysh is a good brother in . . ." Eshed hesitated. ". . . in our work." It was so difficult, not being able to share their real mission together, but the time was not right. "He remained in Spatale on assignment, and Martseah is staying a short time in Protos with a new friend of ours, a physician. Appelles is his name."

"I believe I have heard of him," Jarad responded. "He has a fine reputation in healing circles! He worked for a time with another physician in Eshkolia . . . which brings up another subject . . ." He glanced at his daughter across the table, clearing his throat. "Nebow and his family are being amused by Kamar in my absence today, but knowing Nebow, he will soon be pawing the ground. Can't stay too long in one post, you know! Eshkolia is our next visiting place, and I would like to take Loana along. There are many good shops and restful spas there." Jarad arched his brows. "I thought, since you are away much of the time . . ."

Eshed's heart plummeted. What would these two think of next? Eshkolia was a Circan holding. Surely Jarad was not serious! He had left Loana behind only to protect her from worldly interests and dangers. Now it appeared her father would undo his good intentions!

"Eshkolia! Father Jarad, that would not be wise. . . . The Circans!"

Jarad laughed.

Has his brain gone soft? Eshed was steaming!

"We would be quite safe, I assure you. The villa we are going to is actually outside of Eshkolia and well guarded. We would be looked after like babes."

Loana pretended interest in her food, tipping the blue bowl at an angle to get the last spoonful. Jarad detected a twitching muscle in Eshed's jaw and a lingering silence. He concluded that a change of subject might be in order.

"It appears that Nebow's youngest, Samantha, has found favor in Kamar's eyes. What can you tell me about him? Nebow was asking . . ." He cocked his head to one side, watching Eshed's jaw.

So! Kamar's sybaritic nature was gaining ground again, swamping his promises to the council.

Loana and Eshed exchanged glances. Her head went down once more, and she gathered the dishes from the mat.

Eshed leveled his gaze at Jarad. "He is betrothed to the widow Sernas," Eshed replied, his voice edgy.

Had everything gone to rack and ruin in his absence, Eshed wondered? Surely now the council must speak to Kamar. More gossip on his behavior could not be tolerated! And when it was discovered that the latest source of trouble came from Eshed's own household, well, there could be repercussions.

"Come." Eshed addressed the older man, remembering his role as host. "Let us take the morning air." Inwardly rankled, he stood stiffly and motioned toward the door. "A brisk walk over the hill to fetch some water will do us both good!"

Jarad, hopeful for a reprieve from the tension of Eshed's household, agreed.

The day was given over to entertaining Jarad, after which he returned to the inn for supper where he and his party were regaled by Kamar's travel stories. The innkeeper could be witty and urbane. With the sloe-eyed Samantha simpering her appreciation, he was in his element.

The sun had been hidden behind a heavy cloud all day, spindle-shaped in its webbing, but now, just at sunset, it broke free and slipped, disclike and golden into the hills. Eshed took it as a good sign. He could finally tell his bride the gloomy preoccupation of his thoughts.

Loana, fingers jeweled with an assortment of rings her father had brought, rubbed garlic and herbs across a hot swirl of fried bread and handed it to Eshed. "A new taste . . . Father told me about its preparation. He sampled it in Eshkolia. It fits in well with our prescribed diet, don't you think?" She handed him a basket of goat's cheese and some olives and poured two mugs of hot pear juice.

"Loana . . . about Eshkolia. I cannot permit you to go, you know . . ." It was now or never, he felt. He sighed heavily.

Her eyes glinted darkly in the light and her chin held a defensive angle. "And why is that? Do you plan to be *here* awhile? Or is Etser only a resting place for you?"

"You know my journeys are not predictable! I should be here for a time . . . yes . . . but one never knows what tomorrow will bring. I do not *choose* to be away from you. It would please me greatly to take you along!" His brow was ridged with little furrows, and he shifted the hot bread from one hand to the other as he spoke.

"Then why don't you?" Loana flared. Plopping an olive in her mouth, she chewed it sullenly.

"I consider it unsafe . . . just as I consider it unsafe for you to go to Eshkolia." The candle flickered with his pronunciation of the last word.

"Then you are questioning my father's word?" Her back stiffened. She swept a shank of hair behind her shoulder with her hand. She had removed the sprang net. His eye detected a corner of it hanging off the chopping board where she had flung it during dinner preparation.

Eshed recognized a snare when he saw one. Loana's choice of words was deftly designed to throw him off balance so she could have her way. He chose his next words very carefully. Rumor had been saying ugly things about Jarad, but he had chosen not to listen or believe them for Loana's sake. Since taking an associate, Jarad had spent very little time ministering to his flock but had taken a series of sabbaticals with Nebow and his worldly consorts. It was a delicate situation, clerically and personally.

"My love." He reached for her hand and gave it a squeeze. "Do not feel that I wish to deny you any pleasure or valuable experience that the trip might bring . . . but there are things taking place with Nebow's people that are not proper for me and you. The party last night . . . it is not in keeping with a priestly household in Kerielan."

She drew back her hand from his grasp. "Are you telling me that I am not free to entertain my friends when they come to see me?" The color rose from her throat to her hairline. Eshed met her blush with a gasp and a toss of his hand. "Entertain . . . yes—but not in *that* way!" He rested on his arm, trying to appear relaxed though his stomach was churning. He jostled the harp, propped against a stool. It toppled to the cedar floor beside him. Eshed picked it up and laced his big fingers into two of the strings. It gave a resounding twang which softened the two scowling faces, smiles teasing the corners of their mouths.

The young husband decided to use this mood change to advantage. "Where did you get this instrument? It is a fine one!" It was small and gold leafed and fit well into Loana's shapely hands.

"Father brought it from Eshkolia for me. It is lovely." She took it from his hand and played an old shepherd's tune that stirred childhood memories for Eshed. "That song, I like." Eshed's eyes crinkled in the waning light. "Play another?"

Loana chuckled softly at his innuendo and played a lull-aby. A rosy ray of sunset reflected off the gold of the harp. Her eyes were dreamy as the last soothing tones died away. "My mother played that for me when I was very small."

"You have never spoken to me of your mother," Eshed coaxed.

"It was a long time ago. There is nothing much to tell. . . . I was very young." A look of pain crossed her face.

Eshed took both her hands in his and kissed them. Her eyes brimmed with tears.

"If you want to go to Eshkolia, I will not stop you." He could hardly believe what he was saying.

There was a pause. The candle flickered ominously as if weighing the balance.

"No, Eshed. I want to be here . . . for *you*."

CHAPTER 17

Asleep, entwined in each other's arms, they were unaware of a rap on the lentil. Eshed rubbed his eyes and blinked back darkness. That inky shadow that precedes dawn wrapped the room. *Rap! Rap!* More insistently the knock came. Startled, he slid from the covers and grabbed a tunic. Pulling it about him, he fastened the girth as he went. Parting the curtains, he jerked open the outer door, lifting the lit oil lamp against the darkness. Two weary sets of eyes blinked at him.

Nebak and Abahlia!

Eshed shepherded them inside, bidding them sit down. They sank wearily into place, dropping their totes where they were. He set the oil lamp down beside them.

"What . . ." he began, finding his voice.

"Ohad has fallen to the Circans. We got out just in time!" Nebak reported wearily.

Eshed looked from one to the other of the exhausted faces before him. He had seen no sign of a mount when he admitted them. Had they walked all the way? The tattered sandals and dried blood on their feet answered his question. Wordless, he put his head between theirs and drew them close in a three-way embrace. His body felt strong against their weakened limbs. Abahlia was shivering. Recovering his wits, Eshed put some sticks on the fire. A crackling flame rewarded him.

Loana, sensing his absence, reached out to the empty

spot beside her. She pulled the caftan about her and followed the glow of the oil lamp to the sitting room.

"Loana . . . it is Nebak and Abahlia," Eshed explained. "Ohad has fallen to the Circans."

Groggily, she grasped the scene before her. Eshed's words spurred her to action. Murmuring her sympathy, she arranged cushions and urged them to rest back against the wall. Tucking a warm shawl about Abhalia's shoulders, she said, "Some hot soup will chase those chills!" Sloshing the remains of yesterday's prepared vegetables into a pot of broth, she hung it on the fire. A drop of broth made its way down the huge pot and met the fire with a sizzle.

"The temple?" Eshed almost feared to form the words.

"Burned to the ground." Nebak, who had spoken firmly till now, began to weep softly, his hand to his eyes.

"We were warned shortly before they came. Sarakabel and Ardon took his boat to Protos, where he has family. Nebak and I were to go with them, but we were cut off by troops and had to come this way. We tried to save some things from the temple, but there was not much time. Mostly it is gone, I fear." Abahlia spoke for both of them. "I lost track of my family."

Nebak began to sob.

"Temples can be rebuilt," Eshed offered, holding Nebak's shoulder.

"But my people," Nebak sputtered. "What happened to them? I wonder . . . I should have seen to them!" He continued to weep, his face contorted, like a child in deep distress.

"Nebak, you know we were the last to receive warning. Almost everyone got out before we did. I am sure they made it to safety," Abahlia insisted, her face close to his.

Nebak refused to be comforted. "I wish I could be sure. We had to hide from the soldiers a whole day's journey after we left. Who knows how many were caught outside of Ohad and—" Aware of Abahlia's concern for her family, he caught himself before adding the word *butchered*. "We hid the temple scrolls and a few small altar items—incense boxes and the like—in a passing donkey cart. We rode with them for a while . . . never would have made it over the pass if we hadn't. It was blocked by a landslide."

"I know . . . Martseah and I passed that way recently . . . or tried to!" Eshed concurred.

"We left the cart when we came to a road fork. They set up camp there, waiting for other members of their family to join them. We waited a day for sign of Abahlia's family, but they never came. Abahlia and I—" His eyes sought her face lovingly. "We walked the rest of the way." He put his arm around her. "And here we are."

"Ardon and Sarakabel are in Protos, I am sure," Abahlia added. "I saw their boat sail."

"You said they have family there?" Loana, the firelight playing mysteriously in her loosened hair, handed them hot mugs of broth. Grimy fingers grasped the mugs—washing seemed extraneous for the moment.

"Ardon has an uncle there . . . Tobias," Abhalia murmured, her voice lost in the mug's rim.

"Tobias . . . the physician?" Eshed asked.

"Um . . . yes," Abahlia answered, swallowing the soothing liquid.

"Loana, that is where Martseah is staying with the good doctor Appelles that I told you about, and the boys, Heli and Zetema." Eshed felt a strange excitement. It appeared to be another of the Lord's appointments!

The women settled for a rest in the sleeping room, and Eshed and Nebak reclined against the cushions in the sitting room and conferred further into the night.

"Couldn't talk about it in front of the women," Nebak

confided, "but there is a rumor that Etser is on the Circan map for conquest!"

Eshed thought of the inconsequential village that had been his home for so long. Being mainly a coming together spot for farmers and sheepherders, it had grown very little in these years. "But why?" he asked. "What could we possibly have that they want?"

"Access to the seaports—just as in Ohad. You have the major roadway and easiest approach to Protos, once they leave Eshkolia," Nebak countered.

They were still talking when the rising sun spilled yellow on the greenery outside the window and invaded the opening to bless their drowsy heads. As its early warmth permeated their skulls, sleep stored their secret in an inner chamber.

Eshed tethered the little white donkey and climbed the hill, pulling a dray made of limbs in which he would carry stones from the hilltop. Loana had been requesting a small room added to the back of their house for visitors. If he could lay in a supply of stone every morning before going to the temple, he soon would have enough to begin laying a foundation.

When he returned for breakfast, the women were bustling about the kitchen together, Abahlia in a rosy caftan borrowed from Loana, her face scrubbed and a glow of peace about her.

"Last night I dreamed my family made it to cousin Nathaniel's house in Tsalah. I am sure it is true!" she confessed.

"Of course! It *must* be!" Loana inclined her head, sprinkling sesame seeds on the flat bread before she thrust it onto the steaming stones of the oven.

Nebak, pen in hand, was recording some thoughts in his

log. "Eshed . . . I have taken your suggestion." He indicated
the log, lifting the pen with a flourish. They had been in the
Kerielan household two days now, and he was sounding
much more like the old Nebak this morning.

Nebak's mentor, barely older than himself, stood for a
long moment reading over the shoulder of the young priest.

> Am I, the Father's crowning creation, a proper clay for
> molding? Shall I withstand the fires? Shall I yield an urn
> graceful enough to hold the baptismal waters with which
> he has entrusted me? Shall rivers of life flow from its spout
> to bless the hot and dusty souls he sends along my space
> of belonging? And if so, will I be fitted to grace his temple
> someday when he reigns in peace and joy?

Nebak lifted his head inquiringly.

A long look passed between the two men. "The true
meaning of this has only been partly revealed," Eshed said
at last. "I believe you have written something inspired in
your groaning." He placed a firm hand on Nebak's shoulder.

As they broke rocks together on the hillside, Eshed
asked suddenly, "What arrangements have you made for
your wedding?"

Nebak shot a quick look at him through narrowed lids.
"Ah . . . in all that happened, I quite forgot. We were awaiting your return so you could do the honors." He smiled
shyly, concentrating on turning a rock.

"Here I *am!*" Eshed threw up his hands in answer, a quizzical smile on his face.

"Ah . . . um . . . nuh!" Nebak grunted as he dug a stone
out of its lodging between two others. He rearranged his
sweatband to pick up the beads on his forehead and blew
out a gust of air for emphasis. "Ah . . . uh," he panted. "I
don't know, Eshed. What can I offer her now? The temple

is gone . . . the town is gone. I am without appointment."
His shoulders slumped.

"Nebak, stop hedging. You have everything Abahlia
wants!"

"And what is that?" Nebak asked, concern in his eyes.

Eshed rubbed his gritty palms on his tunic front and
placed his hands on his hips. "It is true that a man is always
the last to know." He grinned, his eyes twinkling. "Such a
heart you have . . . such a sense of what is right and beautiful. I have seen it in few men, Nebak. She wants *you!* That
is all. Just *you.*" He faced Nebak, emphasizing each word.
"Anyone with one eye and half a mind could see it . . . and
still you wait!"

"Then," Nebak reflected, a tear softening his eye, "I will
tell her tonight!"

The day was fresh with the last vestiges of dew drying
from the grass when Simonus and Tamar, bearing an acacia
wood platter of pomegranates, arrived to witness the wedding.

The arbor formed a canopy as Eshed spoke the rights of
matrimony for Nebak and Abahlia.

A yellow lupine against the poor and wintry soil of circumstance, the bride lit the landscape in a flowing, elegant
gown Loana had been saving for a special occasion.
Creamy in color with tiny saffron rose buds needled at the
waist and neckline, it was striking against the dusty peach
of Abahlia's throat. But she would gladly have worn her
travel rags, such happiness was in her eyes! Fragrant, yellow
camphor blossoms had been twined into her silky hair,
which was bound atop her head like a crown. As a final
touch, Loana had hung around her neck a golden flask of
myrrh, a gift from the priestly house of Kerielan.

Nebak wore a white and blue priestly vestment borrowed from the temple at Etser. He stood with a sureness he had not exhibited since their arrival. As his eyes met Nebak's in the recital of vows, Eshed knew that this marriage, now, would give new purpose to Nebak's life.

Kerielan's priest, replete with ephod and a turban wrap headdress, concluded the ceremony with a prayer book selection taken from the old scrolls. "But he knoweth the way that I take; when he hath tried me, I will come forth as gold."

A celebration followed. They gathered figs and breakfasted on jujube berries, millet, apricot cakes, and wine while Loana, her dark hair tucked behind her ear with a white anemone, strummed the harp. Discarding the gold ephod and headdress, Eshed grabbed Simonus and Nebak's shoulders and initiated the traditional wedding dance while the women watched. The three men moved horizontally to one side, then the other, kicking their legs high, then breaking while the two of them, with arms upthrown, twirled in place, holding sides and facing one another. They switched to the opposite side, repeated the circle, and broke to accommodate a new partner, their feet beating a staccato rhythm against the turf, matched by the clapping of the women's hands.

Moonrise.

The Kerielan household was peaceful.

Eshed and Loana had sequestered the newlyweds in their sleeping room, which Loana had fitted with new linens and fresh flowers in abundance. The two of them retired to the sitting room and lit an oil lamp near the window. Loana stood, absorbing the enchantment of a starry night through the portal. She turned from the opening to Eshed at his prayer book. He laid it aside and picked up his log and pen. Dipping the quill in berry juice, he began writing a page marked *Appelles*. The oil lamp behind him caught the nobility of his profile. His lashes were lowered, his eyes intent upon the page. In that instant Loana sensed something fathomless . . . an instinct to reach out and touch some unknown part of him. It was passion, but in a higher sense. It was tenderness, but beyond the tenderness a mother feels for her babe. She could not explain it but it was there—some eternal binding . . . some whispered promise.

From the crest of the hill, Eshed and Nebak could view much of the Etser valley. They were climbing up in search of chunks of stone in myriad colors that Eshed had seen there before. Pushing in among the grasses with the toes of their sandals, they probed about for the right ones.

"Here is a good one—look at the purple and red in that, will you?" Nebak asked.

"And look what is growing next to it!" Eshed gave a tug and produced a long, greenish white object, soil crusted. "Spring leeks—look for more!"

The two foraged about until they had a meal's worth of leeks, stuffing them in their tunic fronts to carry home. Casting about for some long sticks with which to pry the big stones loose, Eshed's foot hit something metallic in the grass. Reaching down into the dampness, he pulled out a helmet, brass with a greenish-blue iridescent visor. "What . . . ?"

"A Circan helmet," Nebak explained. "Belonged to a scout, most likely. Probably got surprised and left without it!"

"It has not been here long," Eshed observed. A pair of footprints cleaved the grass. He followed a short way and pointed to a treed area, heavy with oak growth. "He mounted his horse here." Hoof prints led down the other side of the hill toward the road to Ohad.

"This helmet has given us warning," Eshed remarked, turning it over in his hands. "We will be watchful."

They heaved the purplish stone onto the dray and tied the helmet to the handle. "Hey!" Eshed gouged the little white donkey into a forward movement, and they made their way back. They hid the helmet in the donkey's stall. It had caused *them* alarm. That was enough.

The women fell on the leeks gleefully. Abahlia washed some and added them to the soup for the midday meal. Loana chopped one finely in a wooden bowl, then mashed it with the pestle. Taking a soft cloth, she began polishing the gold leaf on her harp with it.

Eshed and Nebak paused to take in what she was doing. Shaking their heads, they returned to digging the foundation for the new room.

"It will shine like new. You'll see!" Loana sang after them. She was in high spirits these days. The longed-for room was being prepared, and with her father off to Eshkolia, it was good to have Abahlia for company and help with daily chores. Often, in the evening, Abahlia stitched new clothing for her and Nebak from the cloth bolts Jarad had left while Loana practiced new songs on her harp.

As the two priests labored for the addition, they shared insights on the priestly function. The council had not yet decided on a new appointment for Nebak, so he was at Eshed's disposal for the time being.

Shared labor always speeds things along, and in a very short while the stones were mortared into place halfway up the L-shaped addition. Standing away from the structure, Eshed and Nebak were identifying the stones they had personally selected and admiring the way each contributed to the whole, when they heard a voice behind them. "Eshed, Nebak, take pause to see what I brought!" Simonus, his ruddy beard glinting in the sun, was dragging two good-sized stones, tied on each end of a rope loop. "May I contribute these to your new room? I have been saving them for a back shed, but I think they should be used now!"

They untied the rocks and marvelled at the way they fit into the row they were composing, perfect in size and color!

Simonus helped to secure them in place. Breathing heavily from the task, he turned to Nebak. "My friend, I have a message to you from Namath. He has a small cottage that you may use until we have decided on your new appointment. It used to be occupied by the flock overseer, but he is old and has gone to live with a son and help tend his flocks. It is yours for as long as you want it!"

Nebak smiled broadly. It had been very pleasant staying with Loana and Eshed, but . . . a place of their own— Abahlia would be overjoyed!

"I will go with you when you are ready and help you get settled," Eshed offered.

The little white donkey was laden with food, brass cooking pots, seed bags, resting mats, and quilts when Eshed accompanied the young couple to their first home.

It was a small cottage and badly in need of cleaning. Nebak fashioned a broom from a stick and dried grasses, and Abahlia set about giving the room a woman's touch, singing as she went.

Eshed hauled in water and a supply of wood for cooking. Nebak cleaned out the cistern, full of mud from lack of use. "You may not have a well nearby," he called to Abahlia, scrubbing the stone with a thistle implement and fresh water, "but you have a supply of fresh water from the hills right by your door!"

Nebak was pulling cobwebs from the rafters with sticks while Abahlia cheered Eshed from the doorway as he and the white donkey pulled a wooden plow through the soil, loosening it for her vegetable garden. The furrows were beginning to appear on his third time around the plot when she heard scuffling and exclaiming behind her, punctuated with bird sounds.

"Oh, drat! Oh, folly!" Nebak tumbled onto the floor from his kneeling stance in the fireplace. Beneath the soot on his face, his chagrin was apparent. A finely woven bonnet of bird nest, feathered, strawed, and lacquered with broken eggs, sat on his crown. A black starling shrilled in his ear, swooping past his head again and again. Numbly, he held the stick that had caused his debacle in the air. When the bird knocked it from his fingers, Abahlia could contain herself no longer and fell in a heap on the floor, convulsing with laughter, as the irate mother found the door and chattered away.

"Too bad!" He took the nest down from his head and inspected it. "If I had not broken the eggs, we could have had supper!"

Abahlia grabbed her husband, and they rolled in the soot together, laughing till their sides ached.

They took supper at Namath's house the first evening. Naveh and her red-haired Ariel were visiting in Martseah's absence. She carried a huge, steaming bowl of bulgur laced with herbs and lemon to the table. "Eshed, when is my runaway husband returning, do you think?" Her large, luminous eyes were merry at the mention of him.

"Soon, Naveh . . . it will not be much longer, certainly!" he replied, dipping a polished gourd into the bowl and serving plates for the others. When a priest was in the house of a friend, it was considered a special blessing for him to serve the plates as well as give thanks.

Abahlia's contribution to the table was a brass cooking pot, its hanging handle laced with vines and a full complement of spring flowers crowding its mouth. A candle lamp was at each guest's place on the well-provided board.

Naveh and Abahlia chattered together while they served the steaming vegetable platters and freshly baked tsuwl that came from Serena's kitchen. Naveh's mother was short and stout like her father, with silvered hair and a tooth missing in the front of what had once been a very comely mouth. She tottered about in a long green apron appliqued with daisies that stretched tight over her bulging waist. When she called the women to carry in food, her voice rang out over their merriment: "Naaaaa-vuuuh!" She sang a high note on the end of her daughter's name. Serena had always considered Naveh, the youngest of her three daughters and two sons, to be something of a dreamer. Indeed, it was Naveh's soft manner, as well as Namath's money, that had made her so popular in the village.

"Soon," Serena confided to Abahlia, handing her a tray of corn ears, "we will have melons to share with you!" The *s* sound sang through the tooth gap.

Abahlia's face broke into a big smile. Serena must have read her thought! The days were growing hot now, and melon was one of her favorite refreshments.

"Just help yourself, child. The melon patch is over near the sheepfold. Take them as they ripen!"

Abahlia remembered the stone sheep fold. It was not far from their cottage!

"Naveh," Serena said as she turned to her youngest, "I forgot the mint sprigs for the pilaf. Chop some, will you? And hurry!" She managed two whistles on the word *sprigs*. How she wished Naveh had Abahlia's quick step!

While talking temple business with Eshed and Nebak, Grandfather Namath bounced Ariel on his knee. Ariel reached up and took hold of the woolly black beard. The next knee pump caused a firm yank. "Ah! Oh!" his grandfather exclaimed, disengaging the chubby fingers from his chin.

Nebak and Eshed laughed. Namath rolled his eyes, smiling indulgently.

Sobering, Eshed leaned forward. "While the women are occupied, may I suggest that you not allow Naveh to go home just yet?"

"Go home . . . does she wish to go home?" Namath asked, puzzled.

Eshed nodded. "She wants to be there for Martseah, but we have seen evidence that the Circans are scouting the area! We do not want to alarm anyone, but I think each merchant and landowner should be told. I plan to ride through the fringes of Etser tomorrow, telling everyone to be watchful. Simonus has been warned. If you could tell your people . . ." His voice had fallen barely above a whisper.

"Of course . . . of course . . ." Namath nodded, his eyes serious. He held Ariel close and gave him a squeeze.

CHAPTER 18

Two days' travel through Ke-rielan assured Eshed that his message had reached everyone. As he spoke to farmers in the area, one or two reported hearing troop movements at night! One had seen the helmets of a small contingent gleaming in the moonlight near his flock. A count the next morning, however, revealed that none had been lost.

Loana saw Eshed at a distance and ran to meet him, her blue skirt billowing and the vivid splash of color that was her apron threatening to engulf her face. Throwing herself at him, she kissed him playfully. Laughing, they held each other very close. It had been good to have the company of Abahlia and Nebak but it would be good to be alone again too.

The aroma of dinner met him outside the entry and he threw aside his travel garments and washed quickly, eager to partake of the meal and Loana's good company. She had become such a good listener and had much to impart. She passed a pewter plate of garden vegetables and lentils and turned to offer a spicy shank of meat.

Eshed selected a piece and bit into it hungrily. Only as he began to swallow, did he realize that according to their calendar, a meat meal was forbidden! One other thing dawned. Only the disreputable would sell meat at such times for they were all governed by the same law. He spat it out and ran quickly from the room, emptying the remains of the meat in the basin. Loana was right behind him. "My love—are you ill?"

Eshed mopped his face with a wet towel and tried to keep his voice even. "Loana, where did you get this meat?"

"Why . . . ?" Her sea eyes grew wide with the realization that something was terribly wrong.

Speaking softly, he looked at her steadily "Answer me, Loana . . ."

Her hand teased a curl from her temple and she stroked it self-consciously. "A man on the road sold it to me when I was working the garden."

"And you bought it from someone you did not even know?" His voice was beginning to rise in spite of his efforts.

"It . . . it . . . looked all right." Her eyes dropped, and she tugged her apron.

"Darling . . ." He rested his hands on her arms. "It was strangled in its own blood."

She gasped in sudden horror at what she had done. "But how do you know?"

"It was undoubtedly caught in a fence by a wild animal and the man knew he could not sell it in the market. It would have been foul by meat-purchasing time. This is a time of restriction."

Loana knew they ate nothing strangled in its own blood—only animals properly killed and dressed according to Mosaic law were acceptable to them and then only at a time of meat feasts.

Eshed returned to the table to eat his vegetables. Loana swept the meat to the sideboard. As she did, he observed a sudden stiffening of the shoulders. She stayed at the sideboard several seconds longer than seemed necessary, and he called over his shoulder, "Loana?"

Turning, he observed a muscle pulling in her neck, and

he bounded to the board, wrenching the shank from her hand. She was eating it. Pressing her jaw on both sides, he forced her to spit out the meat. She grabbed her apron and covered her face to restrain him, but the meat had already fallen to the sideboard.

She confronted him, eyes blazing. "It is *my* feast day!" she screamed. "Have you no respect for that?"

"The meat . . . it is not fit to eat."

She smiled a slight, knowing smile. "Perhaps not for you," she taunted and picked up the shank again as if to take a bite.

Eshed grabbed the platter, meat and all, and threw it into the yard, slamming the door. "The jackals may have it—but *not my wife!*" he roared. It was all too clear. After acquiring it, she had offered it in sacrifice to idols and according to pagan belief, that made it right!

He sat down, dazed, stunned, to think that they had made no more progress than that. At this rate he could never be sure of what was placed before him. A little mumbo jumbo would make anything right! *Will the enemy ever release us to the total caring of the Lord?* The Lord. Yes. He had been away doing the Lord's work and this had happened. Just the sort of bait the enemy grabbed for—Eshed couldn't be everywhere at once . . . but the Lord could . . . and was—then, why?

Loana was still at the board, her back to him in frozen rage. He stepped up behind her. "Love . . . ?" He placed his fingers lightly on her shoulder. She stiffened against him. "We have definite rules to follow. . . . It is not as if you did not know." His voice was soft against her ear.

"*Why?*" She wheeled abruptly, her eyes blazing. "To satisfy some long-bearded patriarchs who are no longer living? Why follow rules that have no meaning to us now?" The pitch of her voice was rising with each sentence.

"To protect us from bad things—such as poisoned meat!" he spat back.

"And I suppose this—" She gave the blue tassel on the end of the blue ribbon he wore about his neck a vicious yank. "—protects you in some way!"

Cheeks ablaze, he replied, "It reminds us of the commandments."

"Superstition! All of it!" Her knuckles were white against the cutting board surface as she leaned into it.

A festering boil made its way to the surface and spewed out on Eshed's tongue. "And what of the Sun-god buckle your father wears and the amulets you clasp to your breast when you think I am not looking?"

Her face flushed crimson.

"Oh, yes—you think I do not know. You are an idol worshipper—and that is older than the patriarchs and the commandments . . . and as wrong as night is dark!"

Loana looked as if she had been slapped. Limp against the chopping board, she whispered hoarsely, "I am sick to death of your stiff-necked proclamations. If you serve a living God . . . as you say . . . why do you need them?"

Not trusting himself, Eshed left the room while Loana sullenly put away the food and washed the plates. He made his way to the prayer stone in the back corner of the garden. He could not go to the temple tonight, much as he needed to. He could not approach the Lord as priest . . . he was too ashamed and confused. He must simply appeal to the Lord as a man, a husband, who somehow was not succeeding in either role.

His foot struck the prayer stone in the gathering darkness. As he folded himself to it, gratefully, her words echoed in his head. "If you serve a living God, why do you need them?" The words grew louder in his ears.

Loana brushed the amulet with her fingertips and held it

against the light of the candle. Was it true what Eshed said . . . these little tokens of providence were older than the patriarchal line? They served as a reminder when she prayed that the earth and everything in it was God's. That much was true . . . but she did not need them to pray . . . did she? Her fingers stroked the metal—the shape was satisfying to her touch, a vestal virgin holding a basket of grain aloft. She had used this one for prayer of late to insure a good harvest for everyone from the spring planting. And this one, she pulled another from the pouch in her lap. The beautifully sculpted face smiled back at her. . . . It was the head of a legendary beauty. It insured the wearer of everlasting enchantment—a swarm of admirers or husbandly devotion, or both, if one were so inclined. And a third . . . she smiled as she thought of the implications of this one. Apparently she needed it right now. She held it to her bosom and breathed a sighing plea that her husband's anger would be overcome. Her heart ached with a sudden longing to be held by Eshed as her eyes took in the detail of the burnished couple she held in her fingers. They were merged in an embrace, the woman's long hair completely enveloping the man so that only his head and a portion of his foot could be seen. Loana's throat burned with tears. She wished she could call back her biting words. If only she could touch Eshed . . . surely she could overcome his anger.

Eshed felt a touch on his shoulder.

He looked up into the compelling countenance of the Lord. His heart leapt with joy! The Lord Christ would handle this matter for him. Reassurance flooded his heart as he felt the pressure on his shoulder. He watched the Christ turn up the path to the house. A beam of lamplight widened and filtered through the trees to the spot where Eshed stood as the Lord pushed the door

open, tentatively, then called softly, but imperatively,
"Loana . . . may I come in?"

After a time, the Lord returned, alone, to where Eshed
waited in the darkness.

"Make your mount ready my son. You must go to Ohad. Ne-
bak and Abahlia will go with you." His eyes seemed to take in
Eshed's shaken condition at once, yet his words pointed past
that.

"But . . ." Eshed looked pleadingly into his eyes, unwilling
to depart just yet.

"She has rejected the instruction of the Church . . . and—"
his eyes softened—"yours as priest and her husband." The words
went through Eshed like a knife. He sank wearily on the rock for
support. Only the voice of the Lord could compel him to listen
further.

"Remember, Eshed. This is my struggle, not yours. It is the
product of the work of my old enemy—the prince of the air. I will
finish my task. You are free to go."

As minds so often do in moments of great stress, Eshed's
turned suddenly from this matter of deep concern to his next
priority, his priestly function. "I am to lead the Festival of
Lamps through the village tomorrow evening." He was uncon-
sciously grasping at any excuse to stay. He so wanted to see
Loana safely into the Kingdom!

"I have summoned Martseah to lead the all-night vigil.
Even now he is on the road. Eshed, do you trust me to complete
what I have begun?"

It was an important question. Eshed knew he must answer it
honestly. Yet letting go now went against everything he felt as
husband and lover . . . and yes, even as priest. Eshed swal-
lowed perceptibly, sighing deeply. There was no one he loved
and trusted like the Lord, but he still had no idea what the Lord
planned for Loana. Eshed knew that she was in some danger
from the prince of the air at this very moment, for the evil one

did not relinquish his holdings easily and she was in a prime position to thwart the work in Kerielan. He also knew that the Lord loved her more than he did, as impossible as that seemed, and that he would be the victor, come what may.

"Yes, Lord. . . . I know this is your mission and you have trusted me for a little while to help, even as you have before. Yes, yes . . . I have no claim on her. I trust your mercy and your love." Eshed was weeping now. It was the only sound he heard. The house was so quiet, he wondered if Loana was already gone.

Through the blur of his tears, he saw something glisten in the soft light. The Lord had extended both hands and in his palms were broken gold amulets and images—Loana's! He looked searchingly into the Lord's face for further explanation.

"We exchanged trophies," he said, simply. He had received the trinkets from her hand. The shattered fragments fell at his feet. The Lord's hands were still extended, palms up. Glistening red against the amber of his skin at the wrists were his offering—roughly gouged nail prints.

Three sets of hoof beats pulsated through the night.

Eshed had roused Nebak from sleep. He struggled to the door, holding a candle against the night, his face slack from dreaming.

"It is time," Eshed said simply, "to return to Ohad."

Nebak, eager to see to his people, kissed Abahlia awake. She struggled to her feet and began to dress for the journey while Nebak stuffed some provisions in a bag.

Swiftly Eshed procured two promised horses from Namath's stable, and the three were away. Timing was everything. They were entering enemy territory and would need to travel by night.

They made the first lap of the journey almost totally in silence. They rode past the fork in the road that led to

Protos and over the hill to Rhantismos. The pass was still blocked. There was some question of Rhantismos' occupation, so they avoided the stopover and rested in a cave during the day.

While Nebak and Abahlia slept on the totes they carried, Eshed took advantage of a little light entering the cave's mouth and pulled his log from the saddle grip.

He sat mutely for several moments, his heart aching for Loana. Tears streamed down his face as they had frequently during the night's ride. The circumstances in which he traveled had provided privacy at least for his grief. Pulling a charcoal stick from a forgotten fireside near his foot, he began to scratch in the log.

He paused. The word *Tasia* swam before his eyes. He needed Martseah's report from Protos to fulfill her portion of the log, but for now he would simply record what had happened on his journey to Spatale.

Leaning into the light, he stroked the paper. Writing would keep his mind off Loana momentarily. The knife in his heart caused him to cry out suddenly, "Oh, Lord. What is it all for?" Casting the charcoal aside, he knew he had not felt such despair since he had washed up on the beach to an empty world years ago. Fresh tears brimmed his eyes and fell on the paper, blurring the charcoal. *Is my destiny to always be a wanderer, to have no place, no one to call my own? When will it be clear to me why I have been commissioned to leave my wife, my priesthood, and my home to serve the Lord when I have been doing a perfectly adequate job of serving in Kerielan?*

Physical fatigue and mental exhaustion were taking their toll, and he found his thought process drifting, putting together parts that didn't fit. He leaned against the cave wall and put his head back for a moment.

A bee hummed softly above his head. When he opened his

eyes, his nostrils were filled with the clean sweet scent of lilies and his head was cradled in a cluster of white. As he rose to a sitting position, he was afloat in a sea of them, all white with a blue blaze of sky above. They must be nearing Ohad. Where had Rhantismos gone and the others? He was alone and it was the wrong time of year for lilies. Burying his nose in one fragrant shape of petals, he thought: It is true; lilies do have faces. He had never noticed before that they had individual markings. Soaking in their freshness, he turned a little and saw a crushed one that he had lain upon. Shifting, he pulled it back into standing position. The stem would not support the blossom, so he pulled it off and rubbed its coolness on his cheek. Within the golden throat were black images. They swam before his eyes, and he thought the warm afternoon was having its effect on him. Then he saw Loana's face within the damaged pistil. Her tears became the dewdrops on the petals. A passing breeze whispered in his ear: "See . . . the tender shoot is damaged. She is only a young sprout, after all. Sometimes you ask too much, Eshed. Sometimes you ask too much."

Another voice spoke. He was back in the murky bowel of the cave. Nebak was mumbling in his sleep. A jab of Eshed's elbow brought him around. Darkness was pressing in on them, coming on fast, and they must be away. The trio moved stealthily from the cave and mounted their horses. They filed silently down the hillside, picking their way in the velvet drape of night.

They had watched the Circans make an encampment just below the cave as they stole into its recesses and had been concerned about how they would get out. After discussing several possibilities, they concluded that all paths would lead past the scattered contingent. They would stay as far from the firelight as they could manage. That was the best they could hope for. The risk of having their horses spotted in the daylight made remaining in the cave another day unwise.

Suddenly, they heard a rock break loose and topple down the hillside. They froze. Listening, hardly breathing, a little voice whispered to one side of Eshed. He strained to catch the words.

"It . . . it was me! My horse did it," Abahlia confessed.

"Stay still!" Eshed hissed, displaying his annoyance. Why had the Lord sent a woman along! They were nothing but trouble on such a mission. And that annoying dream — if only those voices would go away.

Continuing down the hill as softly as their horses could travel, Eshed hoped the noise of the soldiers would cover any sound they made. He took hold of Abahlia's reins and led her horse behind his. *If Nebak can't manage his woman, I will have to!* Disgusted, he turned. In a fleeting patch of light, he saw Nebak bringing up the rear.

Midway down the hill, the moon came from behind a cloud, allowing a glimpse of the horse train. Eshed used the brief light to check behind him. Abahlia was following closely but Nebak had fallen behind! He paused briefly till he saw the white muzzle of Nebak's animal nodding down the path. He was in sight anyway. Eshed sighed, relieved.

The moon slipped under a gauzy cloud as Eshed gave his mount a gentle kick and edged forward. His horse jumped a little and nickered softly. The Circans' loud laughter coincided with a slap on Zerubabel's flank by his master. They were passing very close now as they neared the bottom of the hill. If only they could reach the ravine without being detected!

A thicket separated them from the warriors. The smell of meat roasting over the soldiers' fire made concentration difficult. They had already consumed the scanty provisions they'd brought with them. A small amount of water sloshed in Eshed's nodah, all the more reason to travel as swiftly as possible past enemy lines!

Abahlia's hands were beginning to chafe against the rope

on her horse's neck. Since Eshed insisted on holding her reins, she had nothing else to hold onto. Being very careful, she took one hand away and blew on it to relieve the pain. Just at that moment, two arms encircled her waist and, clasping a gloved hand harshly over her mouth, pulled her abruptly from her mount! She wriggled desperately but to no avail. In this blackness, she would not even be missed! Terror screamed within her. She kicked her strong legs fiercely but was being held with her back to a man's chest like a plundered fowl. Her feet were flailing air. Still in his armor, he did not even feel the jab of her elbows. Somehow she must warn Nebak and Eshed—they must not all be taken prisoner! If they could escape and return for her later . . . or if she could escape . . . Her head spun with speculation.

Any moment now her captor would call out for aid, and other ruffians would grab the two priests. She listened for his voice or the voices of Nebak and Eshed. But they were all silent. The only sound she heard was the rustling of bushes and grass.

Panting, the brute dragged her into a clump of bushes and forced her to the ground. He leaned his back against her so that she could not move until the horses were all past. She dared not cry out. She would not alert his accomplices to the passage of the priests!

Smelling of smoke, grease, and ale, the abductor breathed into her face, his gloved hand over her mouth to prevent her screams. Using his teeth, he tore the glove from his other hand and grabbed the neck of her garment, ripping it from her body with one wrenching tear. She was paralyzed with fear as his fingers clutched at her body and ripped away his own tunic. The metal of his breast plate crushed the breath from her as he forced himself on her. She couldn't breathe and she couldn't move. A rock tore into her hip. Even though she was choking, she managed to bite his hand. He slapped her mouth and moved his fingers around her throat, making sound impossible. She felt faint. She longed to cry out for help before he crushed the life from her.

Eshed's concentration on the warriors around their fire was distracted by a change in the gait of Abahlia's horse. He reached out for her thinking she might have fallen asleep. "Abahlia," he whispered, risking everything. "Abahlia!"

Terrified, he stopped both animals and waited for Nebak. Maybe when they stopped in the moonlight, she had slipped unnoticed from her mount and climbed on with Nebak. The white muzzle came into view and he saw, to his horror, that Nebak was alone!

"Please, Father," Abahlia prayed, "do not let me die like this!" The drunken warrior grabbed her wrists in a vice-like grip above her head and ravished her face and breasts. His hands squeezed into her rib cage and he forced his body between her legs with a brutal thrust. Her head spinning, she tried to pull away. She was losing consciousness. As he drew back for another lunge, she heard a sickening crack and the brute pitched backward in the darkness. She was gathered, gasping and whimpering, into her husband's arms.

"Beloved. . . . Are you injured?" Nebak held her tightly.

Grateful he had found her, she whispered, "No. . . . Thank God you came when you did! I thought I would die."

"Hurry!" Eshed urged them to the horses. "We have broken the scoundrel's neck!"

They picked their way to where the horses stood, stepping over the body as they went. Abahlia shuddered as her foot brushed the head of her attacker. Nebak helped her climb onto his horse and she leaned against him as they rode away. He clutched her tightly and crooned reassurance in her ear.

Later, when they were safely hidden, Eshed and Nebak wondered how they managed to find Abahlia in that dark terror-filled place and they acknowledged they had murdered a man. Everything had happened so quickly. It seemed they had had help. Still, they knelt and asked the Lord's forgiveness for taking a life.

Circan troops were moving all over the area. They constantly patrolled and guarded their new territories. Each time the travelers thought they could make some time during the day, they were driven back into hiding—a thicket of trees here, a ravine there. Four days and three nights were required to cover the distance ordinarily managed in two days. They drank water from streams and foraged for food.

Eshed was amazed at how little he cared to know the source when Nebak pilfered a shank of meat from a Circan campfire and brought it to share. As they tore hungrily into the flesh, he remembered the incident with Loana. *And to boot, this meat is probably wild boar,* he thought.

"How is it no one was tending this morsel?" Eshed asked, wiping grease on his tunic, streaking charcoal into the dusty cloth.

"They were busy . . . gambling and drinking ale. They were only a few paces away, but they did not notice me."

During the final part of the journey, they led the horses through thick, low brush. The trees were not high enough to cover their movements and they dared not mount and ride.

"We will have to move into Ohad a little ahead of the sun," Eshed confided. Riding back out in daylight would be risky, but it was the only way they could scout the area. He had never dreamed he could be so fond of the dark. As a boy, he had been frightened of the nighttime. But now it provided escape from the Circans. It also relieved him and Nebak both of the pain they felt when they looked at Abahlia's scratched and saddened face. Eshed rebuked himself for being so headstrong. Perhaps if he hadn't been annoyed with her and had allowed her the rein . . .

Nebak, also, was in pain. He told himself he should have followed closer and been more attentive to his new responsibility. But Abahlia was so able. He never thought of her needing help with anything!

Abahlia blamed herself for the attack. Letting go of the rope at such a time was a careless thing to do, even though Eshed did have the bridle. Her safety had cost a man's life, and they would not soon forget it, even if he was a violator of women—a rapist.

Pale light was turning the hills surrounding Ohad into grey and blurred gold as they struggled to a place where they could survey the valley for signs of life. They waited in a nearby cave for morning and, exhausted, fell into deep sleep. A lone rooster, straying into their hide-a-way, announced the dawn as usual and they jumped at the interruption of the quiet. They marveled that he had escaped the Circan cooking pots. All the livestock had been cleared from the area along with the people.

They looked down into the valley where Ohad had nestled. A few singed black, scraggly poplars remained. A large, irregularly shaped gouge of ash was all that marked where the town had been.

They viewed the travesty in silence.

Slowly they mounted their horses and picked their way down to the valley and wandered through the rubble. There was nothing recognizable. Ohad had been looted and totally burned. It was destroyed. The Circans had made certain no one would try to return to live there.

They groped their way to the spot where the temple had stood. At least they thought it had stood there. With the ash everywhere, it was difficult to be sure of anything.

What do a bunch of dead patriarchs have to do with NOW!
Loana's words haunted Eshed.

Abahlia pulled her torn garment closer about her and
tried to comprehend the enormity of the scene. To the
priests, the temple mattered most, but Ohad had been her
home. She had lived there all her life. These squares of
black were homes where living, breathing people—her
people—had lived out their days. A tear found its way down
her bruised jaw. Then a fleck of color caught her eye. She
slid from her mount and picked up a fragment from the ash.
She held it in her hand for a long moment. The men's eyes
were fastened to her. They saw a smile play at the corners
of her lips and exchanged glances. It was her first smile
since encountering the Circan.

She moved to Nebak's side and offered the scrap to him.
He leaned from his mount and carefully took it. When he
saw it, he too smiled and passed it to Eshed.

It was a scrap of Sarakabel's tapestry—a cherub holding
a trumpet aloft against a purple backdrop. A golden chain
and leaves were intermingled with the thread to form wings
and the trumpet cord. Amazement sprang from face to face
in the emerging sunlight.

The storm clouds were gathering and a sudden, stiff
breeze whipped ash into their eyes, making them cough.
Eshed placed the salvaged treasure in his tunic pocket and
turned to go. Abahlia mounted and gave her horse a gentle
kick. The ashes flew thickly in their faces. They moved
briskly from the darkened blotch of ground.

As they reached the peak of the hill, sun came out between the clouds. They felt their strength returning. The
air was easier to breathe.

Nebak and Abahlia spurred their mounts and came even
with Eshed. Fresh, golden-green grass, untouched by the
carnage below, wrapped the hillside in wind-kissed ripples.

They looked like long fingers beckoning them around the side of the hill. Overhead, webbed plumes of cloud cover drifted silently across the summit, separated by blue sky from the sharply formed bank of gray above. The clouds appeared to be within a hand's reach.

Nebak and Abahlia didn't know where Eshed was going, but they wanted to be there with him.

PART 3

REFLECTIONS IN STONE

CHAPTER 19

"Proustia!" The dark head lifted from close scrutiny of the stitching in progress as she saw a skirt hem flick by the doorway.

"Yes, ma'am!" The servant's hawklike face poked around the doorjamb. Her mistress was sitting at the window, a hoop and cloth in her hands, a dark tumble of hair over one shoulder. Her long, robin's-egg-blue gown rippled with deep blue beads. Loana was every inch the mistress of Saramhat. It was almost as if she'd never left, her maidservant reflected fondly.

"I am hungry. Is anything prepared?" Loana's sea-blue eyes left the needlework, briefly.

"I will bring you some tsuwl, curds, and a dish of currants if you like. Master Jarad will not be back till evening for a meal." Proustia's black eyes snapped.

"Almonds, too, dear! And a cup of lemon wine!" The moment's lapse at her work brought a painful jab to her finger, and she thrust it between her lips with a little whimper.

Proustia was out of the door in a flash. By nature quick of step, she hurried more these days with the mistress at home.

As Loana bent once again to her task, she held the cloth from her, momentarily, to admire the emerging red pomegranates. She was needling a border of them, interspersed with green leaves on a muslin shawl. It was for her good friend Tamar, in Kerielan. She supposed she would have to send it by courier as it would soon be completed and she had no plans to return. She had heard nothing from Eshed in these months. *Eshed!* A stab of pain went through her heart. She would never have believed he could stay away from her so long. Every night she tossed upon her mat, dreaming he had come to beg her to return, and every morning was the same as the day before. No word. No letter. Nothing. It was unbearable, but bear it she would. She would continue to behave as though she were on extended vacation . . . for as long as she could!

Such an inner wrestling had been hers since the night of the broken amulets. Within she knew she was being called to put aside her old ways, but here, in Saramhat again, it had been so comfortable to go along with the customs. Father Jarad had catered to her every wish. It had been like the old days at home.

And the women of the village had been delighted to see her. She shopped the bazaars with Drusilla and was invited to Artemis' splendid new home to visit his bride and sup with them. Father Jarad had claimed that her very presence had saved the social season from doldrums. Everyone had tried to outdo one another with parties for her in this village where the mix of customs and trade opportunities had developed a buzzing cosmopolitan lifestyle. Yes, in the beginning it had been exciting.

She turned the hoop to work another part, and in her mind she could see Tamar coming through the gate with the shawl about her, fringes fluttering in the wind! A sudden tear blurred her view of the hoop. She was homesick! But how could that be? Saramhat was her home . . . always had been, always would be! Blinking, she saw the red thread emerge once more as she pulled its glossy fibers through the coarse cloth.

Feeling eyes upon her, she turned, expecting Proustia and a tray. The doorway was filled instead with the muscular frame of . . . Eshed!

Their eyes met and held. Loana dropped the needlework into her lap, her voice blocked by a lump in her throat.

Eshed presented a formal posture. It was not the priest she saw framed in the light of the doorway, nor was it her husband. It was Eshed's "little man" that emerged before her eyes . . . a pose he had developed early in life as a defense against insecurity.

Unsmiling, he said softly, "How are you, Loana?"

Her eyes widened, and her hand flew to her constricted throat. Words would not form in her mouth. She swallowed. Her face felt hot. "H-How are *you?*" she managed at last.

He shifted his weight from one foot to the other. His head cloth dangled from one hand and his tunic was dusty from the road.

"Well enough . . ." His eyes took in the lavish tapestries of the room and the richness of her gown. ". . . as you seem to be."

He made no move toward her but leaned instead against the doorjamb, his eyes drinking her in noncommittally. She felt the urge to go to him, but pride rooted her to the cushion. The sarcasm of his last remark still stung. *Where did he expect me to be, holed up in a cave somewhere?* If their life together wasn't working, surely he could see that the blame was his!

She resumed her work, and as she leaned into the light a gleam of it caught her marvelous eyes. She sucked in her cheeks, thinking how best to answer him. She regarded him, head cocked to one side. "Would you like something to eat?"

Eshed struggled, boyishly, almost shyly, to a seat by her side, stroking his newly acquired chin whiskers. He had rehearsed so many things to say. Why could he not think of a single one of them?

Proustia entered with a tray and was startled by the sight of Eshed. "Oh, sir! I did not know you were here!" She put the tray down hastily. Eshed nodded to her.

"Bring another tray for him, please, Proustia!" Loana's voice was strained. She tugged at the corners of the cloth, tightening it in the hoop.

"Yes, ma'am!" Birdlike, the servant fluttered out of the room. In an instant she was back with a basin and towels for his refreshment. He took them from her with a smile and loosed his sandal straps.

Eshed trickled water over his arms, rubbing his hands together. "What are you making, Loana?" he inquired.

"A shawl . . . for Tamar." Her hands shook as she worked. He was so close, and his eyes were upon her constantly! "Perhaps you would take it to her for me?" She glanced up briefly.

"You could take it to her . . . in person!" He ventured a little smile. There . . . it was out . . . the reason for his journey!

"And how long will your temple business detain you in Saramhat?" Loana asked stiffly. If he thought she was going to fall into his arms at first appeal, he was wrong!

Proustia interrupted with Eshed's tray. She glanced nervously from one to the other, shoved the tray at Eshed, and excused herself.

Loana put aside her work and placed her tray at a table by her side. Eshed broke the bread on his tray, blessed it, and handed half to Loana. It was automatic, and he did not realize how comfortable it was until his eyes met Loana's as she took it from his grasp. Her gaze mirrored what he felt . . . great pain and longing. A weed of dissatisfaction had grown up between them, choking out the good growth of their life together—and he would have it torn out and done with! "I have not come on temple business. I have come to take you home," he said simply.

Her reserve was broken. A tear seeped from one eye and made its way slowly down her cheek. Eshed reached out and took her hand in his, stroking it softly.

"My children!" Father Jarad ambled through the doorway, pulling his priestly mantle from his shoulders. It was as if he had seen Eshed only yesterday, so casual was his tone.

Eshed jumped at the sound of his voice. Upon seeing him, he rose, and the two priests embraced.

The sun-god belt ornament that Eshed recalled from the day of his wedding glistened on Jarad's person as he bent and kissed Loana's forehead. She brushed the tear from her cheek self-consciously, and regarded Eshed coolly.

Her look prodded Eshed into his "take command" stance, and he decided to forgo the amenities. "Father Jarad, I've come to take Loana home with me."

The elder priest eyed first one and then the other, trying to assess the situation. "Well . . . ahem . . . of course . . . she may go anytime she wishes!" *How like him to agree*, Eshed thought, *with me standing in the room*. Yet while they were apart, he was sure Jarad had made staying in Saramhat as attractive to Loana as he could. And Loana, for her part, had someone to cater to her every whim again. It was that very warm and loving side of her character that made Eshed miss her that also attracted whatever she needed in any given situation. It was a mixed blessing to have so ingratiating a spouse!

Jarad's long fingers fluttered. "I had plans to take her to Kerielan soon . . . soon!" he said, placatingly.

"It is just as well you did not. The Circan contingent has

moved on, now, but for a time they were at our very borders . . . as you know!" Eshed leveled his gaze at the older man.

"Oh, we have been moving about with very little interference, here!" Jarad replied. "I think their influence has been greatly exaggerated!" He nodded, patting Loana's head.

"Then you have not witnessed the devastation in Ohad . . . as I have. Surely Loana told you what happened there!" Eshed shifted his eyes to Loana as Jarad pulled up a chair.

"We really never discuss such issues. We have been busy with other concerns since she has been here!"

"Father Jarad!" Eshed's face flushed as he thought of Loana crossing that dangerous country to Saramhat. "The Circans are an evil we can no longer ignore. Must the devil camp on your doorstep for you to notice?" His eye was drawn to the sun-god Jarad was wearing, and Eshed reflected to himself, *In fact, he already has!*

"It is very simple," Jarad intoned. "We simply do not acknowledge a devil!"

Eshed could no longer conceal his anger and frustration. "He is the father of deception! The Lord Jesus Christ has made his doom sure in his death and resurrection, but do not discount Satan's present influence. That, sir, is the greatest lie of all!" Red-faced, he shifted his gaze from the ashen countenance of Jarad to Loana. "Are you coming with me while you have safe passage?"

"No . . . no, I am not," she said softly, her hands in her lap and her face down. She shot a sidewise glance at Jarad for support. She loved Eshed . . . some part of her still belonged to him. But she could not leave her father under these strained circumstances.

"You made a vow to me! I have waited patiently for your return!" Eshed knew he was not handling things well. His "little man" seemed to be in control despite his best efforts. Did she want him to have their marriage dissolved? He pushed the thought from his mind. There must be some way to get this girl to do what she was supposed to! He paced the floor, leveling meaningful looks at Loana, who twisted the folds of her skirt in her fingers, tears escaping the end of her nose, her face still lowered.

"Very well, then—as you wish!" With one distraught, piercing look at Jarad, Eshed's "little man" stomped from the room.

Jarad stroked her neck and crooned comfort into her ear. She stood suddenly and flung herself into her father's arms and sobbed.

"Child . . . perhaps you should go . . . while you have escort. It may be some time before you can travel again!"

"Kamar will take me back when I choose. I have only to write him!" She drew a deep breath to ease the tension in her lungs.

"Little Loana . . . I did not want to tell you this, now." His ominous tone caused her to cease crying and look up into his face.

"What is it, Father?" Her wet eyes searched his.

"Kamar . . . is not coming back!"

"Oh, Father—I know Eshed disapproves. I know I should not have asked Kamar to bring me here. It would not seem proper to those in Kerielan, but there was no other way. I am a married woman. Nothing improper happened!"

Her father stroked her hair, and she nestled her head against his chest. "I was not referring to that, my dear. Kamar . . . is dead!"

A gasp escaped her lips, and she strained for a look at his face. "I do not understand. What . . .? How?"

Her father looked at her, ruefully. "When he was returning to Kerielan from bringing you here, he was caught by the Circan horde . . . and killed!"

"No! No! Why has no one told me of this? Oh, Father . . ." She began to cry again and struggle against his chest. He tried to hold her and soothe away her hysteria.

It came to her vividly as she wailed and flung herself about the room. *If only I had been where I belong . . . with Eshed—and if only Kamar had been where he belonged . . . in Kerielan . . . then Kamar would still be alive!*

Eshed urged his horse onto the green pathway that led from Jarad's land. The sooner he left Saramhat behind, the better! His heart burned sore within him. He berated himself inwardly for handling the situation so poorly. If only her father had not come in. For one instant, he knew, she had been willing to come with him. He had prayed and felt the time was right for them to try again. Why had it ended so badly? His horse stumbled on a downed tree branch. He must be more careful. No use in losing a good animal because he couldn't keep his mind on the road!

Zerubabel was moving strangely. He seemed to be favoring a front hoof . . . the right one. Eshed reined him up, climbed down, and folded the hoof backward for inspection, resting it on his knee as he crouched in the roadway. He probed gently in the pads and drew out a splintered piece of wood. Pulling his nodah from the horse's flank, he poured a little water on it to check for other particles and wash away any small pieces that might remain. He made ready to remount and just then heard a sound. It was familiar somehow . . . but out of context with the situation. A speck of color caught his eye. Something was moving toward him on the roadway, partially obscured by the trees dipping into the opening. He held his hand to his eyes and strained for a clear look. The sound came again. It was a voice, a woman's voice. *It was Loana!* He could just make out a faint "Eshed! Wait!"

She was on horseback, but he didn't wait for her arrival. He mounted his horse and spun about, urging him toward the meeting point. Soon he was close enough to see her face and her waving arm. He heard his own laughter, and dismounting he pulled a breathless Loana to the ground and held her close. They were laughing and crying together. He kissed her cheeks and pressed her to him again. It was some moments before they drew apart. Only then did he notice the change in her appearance. She had been seated in the house, and his thoughts had been only to bring her back with him. He had not noticed the bulging waistline. He placed his hand gently on the spot and sought her eyes. "My love . . . why didn't you tell me?"

She looked shyly into his eyes. "I thought it deserved a better moment than we had."

He held her very close, then lifted her gently onto her horse. To think! They would be a family. He had come not a moment too soon. It would not be good for her to travel later on. He thanked the Lord for the blessing of her return and the good timing of it all!

Loana clasped her hands, fingers pointing up before her face. "It is just right . . . perfect! I'm so pleased, my love!" She was standing in the middle of the new room Eshed had completed in her absence.

Eshed beamed his pleasure at her approval. "See!" he exclaimed, excitement mounting in his voice. "The walls are very strong. I hauled thick clay from the river bottom to grout the stones." The stones had all been turned with the texture to the outside and the flat surfaces to the inside for the inner wall. The heavy grout surface blended in any imperfections between the stones. The inner wall was practically as smooth as if it had been mortared, and the outer wall sparkled as little discs of sunlight reflected off the mica deposits in the many colored rocks. "Will it be a good room for visitors, do you think? Father Jarad . . . Abahlia and Nebak, when he comes in for council meetings?"

"For now." Loana's eyes were spinning webs in the future.

"For now? Why not later as well?" Eshed was inspecting the air shaft he had placed in the top corner of the L-shaped room to circulate air in both directions from the bend.

"In a couple of years, it will become the weaning room," she confided, patting the bulge in her middle.

"Ah!" His eyes shone with anticipation. It had never occurred to him as he laid the stone that this room would house a son. And why *not?* His thoughts had been so filled with Loana and the issues at hand that he had given little time to anything else. His whole life, till now, had been a matter of doors slammed abruptly on the past and the unknown rushing in to meet him. He had learned never to look back and rarely to look forward. Loana had been a different matter. Through all the hurt, his heart had managed to keep the door ajar for her returning. It was the grace of the Lord resting on him that had allowed it to come to pass!

He folded her into his arms gratefully and held her very close for a long time. A quick jab in his midsection brought him back to the moment.

"It is Aaron!" she giggled, using the name they had chosen together. "He likes his room!"

"He packs a wallop like a mule!" Eshed chortled, rubbing the spot with his fingers. "We must remember to enter him in the foot races at Spatale!"

CHAPTER 20

Soft slices of wood under the chisel peaked and fell away like small bits of goat cheese. Eshed hummed and whistled as he labored the corner pieces of the cradle into a perfect fit. Loana was perched on a stool near him, her tiny feet braced on the rungs and a colorful mat in her hands. She was needling the corners into place and hopped down to fit it once again to the bottom segment of the long basket that formed the cradle's interior.

"This will certainly be the envy of all the mothers in Etser! I have never seen such a stable resting place," she remarked, smoothing the rust-colored cloth into the basket's oval interior. "Most cradles are simply slung by a rope from a beam, but this one has its own strong stand so I can move it around. You are a marvel with a chisel, Eshed!"

When not in his mother's arms, it was necessary to keep a sleeping baby free from drafts and crawling insects on the floor. This device of Eshed's would keep him safely at eye level while Loana went about her tasks.

A smile of pride and contentment slowly took over Eshed's mouth at her words. He watched her pull the mat from the basket and—struggling a bit with her bulbous waistline—remount the stool. *To belong . . . to have someone young bear my name . . . to have Loana so close to me again— this must be considered a forerunner of the heavenlies men are promised!*

• • •

Dark clay oozed between Tamar's fingers. She daubed big handfuls onto a weathered wooden tray. The morning was cool, the air fresh after a rain the evening before. Her fingertips unearthed some small stones, and she examined them, washing the soil from the surface with the brisk water that coursed through the stream bed. Unusual shapes . . . she selected two and tossed the others aside. These would stamp a fine design on the pot lip she was teasing from the mound of grit at the oben, the potter's wheel Simonus had given her. Resting the board on a cluster of large stone, she took a small square of cloth from her waistband and scraped a soft stone into powder with a sharp implement, catching the grains in the square of cloth. She would combine this powder with other elements and paint a fine film of it over the pot before baking it in her outdoor cook oven, where the oxidation would bring forth a cobalt blue streak in this pot. Wouldn't Loana be surprised when Tamar delivered her goat's milk in such a vessel! It would be her welcoming home present, a remembrance of the long months Tamar had spent at the streamside, refining her skills with pots as a solace against the gaping hole Loana's absence left in her days.

Tamar had made a reputation for herself in Etser with the clay work she sold. She had labored with hand-formed models for some time when Simonus proposed an oben, which helped her get the leverage she needed for slender objects. Her wares grew from rough, thick jars to well-formed designs of her own making. In the process, she had made several important discoveries about the clay and about herself. That one must be in rhythm with oneself and the Creator had come first with her solitary mud daubing. That one must be in harmony with the element at hand was a second thought. She could sew and cook and tend house all day and never feel quite as at home as she was with her pots. Those other tasks . . . they were all expected, things she must do anyway. But this was something she *chose* and, more important, that chose *her*. Just building household pots had its place, of course, but a real craft . . . that had to be chosen. Yes, she had made some important discoveries. The potter had a rare opportunity to pull from that meanest of elements, earth, a treasure of grit and grace. Her whimsy could pull a candle stand from the circling of the wheel or a hollowed vessel for flowers. She shaped each piece gently, with a plan. Occasionally, the earth would not take direction and had to be taken from the wheel and rewedged to take the puffiness out and produce a smooth texture for teasing upward and outward into a particular bloom. If a bubble formed as the pot was being born, it had to be pricked or it would crack when subjected to the heat of the oven. The glazes, too, were always surprising. The potter might expect a glaze to color a certain way but find a different looking, more glorious pot when the doors were opened and the pot had cooled. Some clays were intrinsically softer, more delicate than others, but all would form rock-ribbed, water-retaining shells of equal strength after being well wrought and put through the fires.

"Tamar!" A frenzied call pulled her from her reverie. She scrambled to her feet and looked about, wiping her wet fingers on her apron. Martseah was approaching at a full gallop. His horse skittered down the muddy stream bank to her side. "Where is Simonus?" he panted, grief in his face. "We need him—*now!*" The horse, in a lather, flung his head about, breathing hard. Martseah's chest was heaving as well.

"Eshed!" There was an urgent pitch to Simonus' voice as he pounded the front door with his fist. Dropping his tools in place, Eshed hurried to the door, eyes changing suddenly from a dreamlike state to a sharp intensity.

His face was two inches from that of his friend as he opened the door to Simonus, who leaned, panting, against the lintel. "It's Namath—he's missing. Come quickly— Serena is fainting with fear!"

The young husband's first thought was for his own wife. His head swung in her direction. Anticipating his thought, Simonus jerked his head toward the approaching figure of Tamar, scurrying through the gate, pulling her skirt above her ankles, the fringes of the scarf Loana had given her fluttering uselessly about her jaw. "Tamar will stay with Loana. We must go. Now!" Simonus spoke with such urgency that it was hard for Eshed to think.

"But . . . Loana . . . the child could come at any hour," he said more to himself than to Simonus. A small sound behind him caused him to turn. Loana was crowding her girth against him at the doorway, her eyes large.

"What is wrong, love?" She snuggled against him, and he put his arm about her shoulder.

"I must go and help search for Namath." His gaze probed Simonus' face, reluctant to voice what they suspected. Namath's sheep had been disappearing nightly, and he had sped away three days ago to urge his herdsmen to gather the animals into the sheepfold each night, a practice they usually ignored during the balmy weather. It was feared that along the way he had met with Circans who had been pilfering from his flock.

Reading his thought, Loana placed her hand on his cheek. "Then go—quickly—so you can come back to me sooner!" She smiled at the distraught faces of the men.

"You," he said, his eyes on the bulge just under her heart, "will be all right?" The last thing he wanted was to be away *now*.

Loana rested her hand on her abdomen. "There are no pains . . . yet!" she explained. She drew Tamar in through the door with her free hand as Eshed turned from kissing her forehead to join Simonus and the horses.

The young priest's eyes never left the plump little figure in the doorway as he galloped away, trailing Simonus. She watched him till he was out of sight. Difficult as it was to see him go, she felt that she would be provided for.

As Martseah met them at the door, a loud shriek ripped their eardrums. His usual calm demeanor was shattered, and his eyes had a distracted look. Wordlessly, he led them to the sitting room where the crisp morning air and sunlight from the curtained aperture belied the depressed state within.

Serena was seated on cushions against one wall, rocking to and fro, holding Naveh tightly to her breast. Her scrawny fingers interlocked the buoyant auburn locks of her daughter, and she bawled loudly in her grief.

Baby Ariel toddled about the room, picking objects from the floor and grabbing at lint pieces floating in a shaft of sunlight. He wore the same distracted look as his father.

"Eshed . . . oh, Eshed!" Serena spluttered. Releasing Naveh, she held out her arms to the favored young man who had been so close to their family. Eshed took her in his arms and reassured her. Simonus embraced Naveh, whose face was tear-streaked.

After a brief conference, the men agreed that Martseah would stay with the women while Eshed and Simonus searched.

Serena was crying more softly now, her apron held to her eyes. She resumed her rocking. Naveh, stroking the gray head, reached the other hand toward Eshed as he made for the door. "Do be careful—oh, please be watchful of yourselves!" she implored. Simonus' eyes met hers, and with a quick, solemn nod, he grabbed Martseah and pulled him toward the doorway.

"We will return and report at sunset . . . even if we must go out again!" he confided to Martseah, his head inclined slightly toward the women. Martseah grasped his meaning.

Smiling slightly, Martseah clasped both men's shoulders before closing the door. "Godspeed!" he exclaimed, looking into their faces and then watching them move from the shade of the step into the sunlight.

The trees seemed full of eerie shadows as they rode through Namath's property, cautiously at first, searching every spot where a lone horse—or worse—might be sequestered. On such a large property they scarcely knew where to begin, but they were determined to cover every inch of it if necessary. They had ridden about five miles when they came to a clearing. A scattering of sheep— possibly four hand counts—were grazing there. Nothing seemed amiss except that there should have been a larger number and an overseer visible in the area. Glancing at one another briefly, the men moved on by silent agreement. A few minutes' ride brought them to another clearing and a few more sheep. Namath's herd had been systematically divided into small caches for easy retrieval. They became cautious again, knowing their movements might be observed. Someone obviously intended to move these sheep to other quarters.

They reined up under the trees and rested their horses for a moment, contemplating their next movements. Eshed's horse snorted and shook his head, clearing from it the flies that the sheep had attracted. Another snort answered his from nearby. The two men looked at each other, their eyes narrowing. Slowly and cautiously, Eshed dismounted. Signaling for Simonus to remain in place, he pushed quietly through the leaves on foot. He had gone only a short distance when he came to the source of the snorting. A sheepherder's mount, reins drooping to the ground, was nibbling grass.

The animal started at his approach. "Whoa, there . . . take it easy," Eshed murmured, patting the horse's neck. A half empty nodah swung from a strap on the harness. The big *N* tooled on the nodah left no question. This was Namath's horse. But where was Namath? Eshed refused to pursue his fears. He led the horse back to where Simonus waited and showed him the nodah.

Simonus shook his head, forehead furrowed. "Where do you think he is, Eshed?"

Eshed sighed deeply and scanned the area. "That," he said, replacing the nodah onto the harness, "is a very good question." He rubbed his jaw with his fingers and re-mounted his horse, leading Namath's horse along behind.

They chose the direction in which Eshed had found the horse and followed a small herdsman's trail through the trees. Speaking softly, they tried to piece together the known parts of the puzzle. Namath . . . gone three days . . . horse had not returned without him . . . probably because he was trained to stay with the herd . . . or perhaps Namath was still in the area.

A strange patch of color caught Simonus' eye, and he gestured toward a spot just off the trail ahead. It was a striped coat . . . and someone appeared to be in it! The figure was sitting propped against a tree with his back to them. They hurried toward him. A strange excitement overtook them as they recognized the frazzled hair and dark beard that rested against the tree trunk. Reining up the horses and tying them to a tree, they made their way to him on foot. As they saw him full face, he did not move but stared straight ahead. Fearful, they moved forward. He was so *still*.

Their bodies cast a shadow over his face. Each waited for the other to touch him. Then they saw him blink. Relief swept over them. Slowly, he responded to the shadow . . . to their presence. He looked up at them. His eyes took them both in, but without recognition.

Eshed stretched out his hand to touch Namath's shoulder, and he jerked back, fear filling his eyes. Then they saw the deep cut on his forehead and the bruise on his temple. He was sun- and windburned with berry stains on his chin, beard, and fingers. The berry bush that had provided them was beside him. He appeared dehydrated, though clearly the nodah was not empty.

"Namath . . . my friend . . . can you hear me?" Simonus asked.

The sheepherder gazed straight ahead, as if they were no longer there.

Carefully, and with great tenderness, they set him on his horse for the trip home. He struggled against them briefly when they lifted him in place, snarling and slapping at them like an animal. Too weak to resist for long, he slumped into place on the horse's back.

Saddened at his condition, Eshed could only think of his jolly, loyal friend who now rode behind them like a piece of baggage. He had seen the tears in the eyes of his burly companion as he lifted the small man in place and knew that neither of them would forget this day.

Namath had slipped behind a veil that shut them out. Only his body remained in their world.

CHAPTER 21

Eshed's shoulders sagged. He leaned heavily against Zerubabel during the last stretch of the journey from Namath's house. It had been a sad homecoming for his old friend. And Namath had not known his family. They clustered about him, trying to help. Even the tear-streaked faces of Serena and baby Ariel tugging at his knee had not unlocked his memory. Serena, in the way women seem to have of sensing truth, had been sadly right. She had known that Namath was lost to them. In a very real sense, he was.

The lone rider rubbed his eyes, trying to clear his thoughts. Lassitude was claiming him, after the gargantuan energy output of the search was over. Eshed thought he should try to reach Appelles by messenger. Appelles had extended his stay in Protos since troop movements were intruding daily into people's lives at unexpected times and places. But no, it would be too risky. Appelles would be needed where he was, no doubt, for incidents such as Namath's.

They might never know the whole story. Simonus had stayed behind to help make Namath as comfortable as possible. In undressing and bathing his body, they had found more lacerations and bruises and they understood he had been attacked and left for dead. Simonus kept hoping for a word, any word, from Namath's lips to describe the experience or to signal a return to his surroundings. But none came.

Eshed drew his lightweight coat about him. No time had been taken for provisions all day. He was cold in the clear, starry night. His stomach gnawing, he shook the nodah. It was empty. He would welcome a drink of something, perhaps a little warm broth when he got home. Loana would have prepared something for him. She always did, even when there was no sign of his approach. The hour was growing late and Simonus had insisted he go home for Loana's sake. He nodded off for a brief moment, leaning forward toward the horse's neck. Suddenly, in his mind there was a snap, like the clapping of two hands together.

Loana!

He jerked upright. Very much awake, he was receiving an urgent signal. *Go home!* Urging Zerubabel forward, he galloped past the turn toward Etser, round the big curve, over the hill, down the roadway, and into his yard.

Flickers of light and women's voices drifted through the window and he could hear soft movements within. Leaving Zerubabel, he ran into the house. Tamar met him at the sleeping room door—wide-eyed. "Oh, Eshed—I have been praying you would come!" A moan and a stifled scream from the rest chamber drew him through the curtain, brushing past Tamar. Loana, her knees bent and her body soaked with perspiration, was leaning into a stack of pillows. Resting for the moment, she gratefully acknowledged his presence.

At the sight of her, Eshed's knees went weak. The midwife, who Tamar had summoned from Etser, was bending over Loana, giving her an herbal drink. A large woman from the house of Unger, she had delivered Ariel and many other Etser babies. Her head was covered with a clean muslin wrap, and her apron was spotless. She had a certain reputation to maintain, and when she saw Eshed enter the room, she greeted him with her standard statement, "You cannot stay."

Eshed knelt by Loana, took her hand, and kissed it. He was so dirty and disheveled, it seemed wrong to touch her, but he couldn't help himself. Their eyes locked, and he smiled tenderly at her.

The gruff midwife turned to him, her hands on her hips. "You know it is forbidden for men to see this!"

As he started to form a reply, Loana gave a sudden lurch. Her back arched, and she grabbed his hand tightly, pushing her feet against the floor for leverage as the pain gripped her. Instinctively he put his arm around her back for support. The mound of flesh that encased their baby hardened and took a more definitive shape. As the long pain released her, she slowly rested her head on his shoulder. Her hands had let go of him and were gripping the outer edge of her thighs under the leg to assist in the pushing.

"Splendid, my darling. You are the best of mothers already!" he whispered, his lips close to her hair and his eye on the midwife.

"Now, Loana—" The midwife's gravelly voice pulled her from the cool, floating moment nature provides between the searing pains. "When the next pain comes, I want you to push with everything you have!"

Loana's legs were still trembling from the force of the last contraction, and her fingers wrapped them tightly as she felt the next one beginning.

"Are you leaving *now* or not?" The woman's voice was growing indignant as she watched Eshed arrange his body behind Loana to help her. Most men would know their place! They usually got out of earshot completely at a time like this. But this one—

"Can't," he retorted somberly over Loana's shoulder.

Then with a touch of the imp in his eye, he said, "I am this woman's priest!" The midwife opened her mouth to respond, and he interrupted, "and yours as well!"

A great whoop issued from Loana's throat as the bag of waters broke. "Push!" yelled the midwife. "Push like your donkey was stuck in the mud!" Eshed heaved against her back and Loana, her face puffed and red, gave a final releasing groan. A soft, round shape with black ripples of soaked hair appeared.

"One more push, quickly!"

Loana summoned her waning strength and gave a final thrust that rode the coattails of the last contraction. The infant's shoulders gave a little twist and fishlike, it plopped onto the toweling. The midwife seized it immediately and put it on Loana's abdomen, as Loana sank back wearily against Eshed. Her eyes never left the round pink face. The babe's first cry brought Tamar running into the room with hot broth. The baby squirmed a little, hiccupped, and began to suck its fingers.

"You have a son!" Tamar cried.

Eshed kissed Loana's wet face and neck. Tears streamed down his face as he took the baby and placed it in her arms. Loana, so pained and disheveled a moment before, crooned to the baby, "I am your mama and this is your papa." Eshed had never seen her look so beautiful. A fresh wonder of their love and life together flooded him.

The baby whimpered and thrashed his little arms from under his wrappings. A whitish roll of skin tissue appeared on one cheek and Loana tried to brush it away. Noticing the gesture, the midwife said, "He will peel for a few days. Rub 'im down with olive oil and that 'angel skin' will come off sooner."

"Is it supposed to?" Loana asked, checking his tiny fingers.

"Um . . . yas . . ." The midwife bent, grunting, to pick up

her cutting and tying tools. "They all come wrapped like that!"

Holding the baby in one arm, Loana sipped the broth from the mug. "Is he hungry, do you think?" she asked Eshed and handed the mug to him. "You must be . . ." He shared her drink and thought how his own weariness and hunger had suddenly vanished.

"If he doesn't eat the first day, it won't hurt him!" the midwife declared, "but if you let him nurse now, it will help your milk come in."

"Aaron. Oh, Aaron . . ." Tamar clapped her hands excitedly, speaking the baby's name for the first time.

Loana smiled at her friend. "I am so glad you could share this with us. You were the very first friend I had when I came here . . . and still the closest!"

Tamar, radiant at Loana's words, wiped away a tear and hurried off to fetch a more substantial supper for the new parents.

A bunch of purple calumnies nestled in Loana's arms. Eshed had arrived home at midday, having pulled them from beside the stream. She held the blossoms to her face, absorbing their fresh wonder. Aaron slept in his cradle nearby.

Eshed was just removing his outer coat and preparing to wash when they heard a quick step at the door.

"Halloo . . . May we come in?" Without waiting for an answer, Abahlia bustled through the door. Having once lived with Loana and Eshed, it seemed like her second home. Seeing Loana with flowers, she remarked, "The star thistle by your door is growing abundantly!"

"Is that what it is? Eshed brought it to me last year. We've just been calling it our welcoming plant—it sees our guests before we do!"

Abahlia handed Loana a basket of blessed thistle, her

favorite herb for developing good breast milk, gathered from near her home on Namath's property. "Now . . . Loana, you make up a brew of this . . ." Her instructions were all but drowned out by Nebak's greeting to Eshed.

"I see you have finally grown up! A baby . . . and a beard!" He gave Eshed's dark bristly chin whiskers a tug.

"An example you might well follow." Eshed chuckled and playfully slapped at Nebak's smooth jaw.

Nebak proudly produced a scroll. He had penned a poem for the baby and set it to music. Bending over the cradle, he unrolled the scroll with a flourish and recited the words. The baby did not move. "No taste for beautiful words, eh?" he replied in mock consternation. He hummed a little of the music. The plump babe wriggled slightly, gave a sigh and slept. "No taste for music, either? Esh! What have you begotten?"

"He is beautiful!" Abahlia crooned, bending over the cradle.

Grinning at their friends, Eshed slipped his arm around Loana.

Loana pulled a purple flower from her bouquet and handed it to Abahlia, who sniffed its fragrance and tucked it into the cord at her waist. "I think these people look hungry, Eshed. Why don't you and Nebak watch Aaron while Abahlia and I serve the food?"

"Sounds like a plan I could agree with!" Nebak's eyes twinkled. He gave the cradle a tap to set it in motion.

"Nebak," Eshed observed, lounging contentedly on a cushion near the serving mat, "I do not believe you will be satisfied till you wake the child!"

"But I want to see his eyes. . . . He does have some, doesn't he?" Nebak continued to stare into the cradle. Abahlia also took a peek each time she brought food to the mat.

"Blue . . . if you must know." Eshed perpetuated the teasing.

"Ah, good. Good! They must be Loana's. How very fortunate!" Nebak rocked on his heels and toes, hands clasped behind his back, still bent over the child.

Loana chuckled. "You haven't long to wait, Nebak. As soon as we begin to eat, Aaron will wake and demand his share!"

"Really! What does he eat?" Nebak turned and watched her place a large tray of millet on the table.

"Nebak!" Abahlia scolded, embarrassed by his chatter.

Loana poured a steaming mint tea into their cups. Her breasts were aching and oozing milk. She would welcome the feeding time. "Mother's best," she retorted calmly. She had always been able to put the clowning priest in his place.

Eshed and Abahlia hooted appreciatively. Nebak blushed and claimed his place at the mat, a puckish grin on his face.

"Did Loana show you the tooled leather harness Martseah brought?" Eshed asked Abahlia, indicating an object on a wall peg near her.

"Why . . . no." Abahlia fingered the straps, lined with a padding sewn by Naveh and designed to hold Aaron on his mother's back when she gardened or went to the village for provisions. "What a clever thing!" She smiled at Loana as she placed a tray of persimmon loaves on the table.

The sideboard was laden with the offerings of the village women, hearty lentil soups, citron and pistachio cakes, artichokes, and other provender that had supported the household during the early days of Eshed's baby.

Eshed gave the blessing, broke a loaf, and distributed it to the others.

Nebak, sobering suddenly, took his share from Eshed's hand and said, "We went by to see about Namath . . ." His voice trailed off, his eyes somber.

"And . . . ?" Eshed looked up from his plate.

"No change." Nebak shook his head, sadly.

"I had hoped we could get a message through to Appelles, but with the border so closely guarded, it seems unlikely," Eshed reflected.

"In truth, I do not know that Appelles, skilled as he is, would be any match for Namath's head injury. His other wounds are nearly recovered." Nebak sampled a dried fig.

"It is so hard to see him like that." Abahlia pulled at the flower on her smock, her eyes filling with tears. "He just stares out the window but seems to see nothing."

"Dear Namath . . ." Loana sighed. "I have grown quite fond of him!" Lifting a wooden platter of carp, she passed it to Nebak. "Eshed caught these this morning," she said.

As Nebak passed the platter to Eshed, he reminded his friends, "Prayer is all that is left to us." His eye fell on Eshed's hand grasping the platter's edge. The glassy eyes of the fish reminded him vividly of Namath's vacant stare. He watched Eshed's big brown hands serve the fish. "Eshed! Have you touched him and prayed?"

"Why, no, no I have not." Eshed's face wore a stricken look as he handed the platter to Abahlia. "With all that has happened . . . I had not thought. I mean . . . it had not occurred to me! I have prayed constantly for him, but . . ." Prayer for healing was so new to him, he rarely thought of what the Lord had vested in him—in them all! He suddenly felt very ashamed.

"Perhaps this is one of those times when a touch is required," Nebak said quietly. "Especially from you . . . Namath loves you."

"Of course!" a light broke over Eshed's face.

Abahlia smiled broadly and tipped her little head to one side, grasping Loana's hand and squeezing it.

Loana, nibbling a citron cake with her tea, looked puzzled. "I do not understand, Nebak."

Nebak regarded her over his cup. "Oh—of course—this happened in Ohad. And you were not there! Is it possible that your husband is too modest to tell you how his baptism healed the baby's birthmark?"

Eshed shifted, uncomfortably, avoiding Loana's open-mouthed scrutiny. "Please, Nebak, it happened also in Spatale to Martseah and to Zetema. . . . Our brothers Iysh and Appelles prayed as well!"

"But Appelles is a doctor. Did he not apply his skills?" Loana was having trouble taking it in.

"He did. But the bleeding and wounding of Martseah was beyond his methods. And he told me that he could do nothing for Zetema but recommend a diet. His was a rare blood disease. There is no cure for it." Eshed rested his eyes on hers.

"And . . . ?" she prodded.

Eshed smiled. "The last I heard, Zetema was running circles around all of them!"

Loana's head was spinning. What did it all mean? For the moment, she was speechless.

Feeling an inner prodding, Eshed knew to whom he must give the glory. It would probably only serve to confuse Loana further, but a witness must be made. *It will be easier now in the presence of others,* he decided. "It is all the work of the Lord . . . and his Holy Spirit!" His face shone.

Thoughtfully Loana put her cup down and considered a response.

"Wahhhhhh!" The babe had given her a little repose for food. Now it was his turn.

She hurried to his cradle in the corner and lifted him out. "And how is Aaron?" She clutched him to her and giggled softly. "He is wet—of course. I should have known." Excusing herself, she went to the sleeping room and made him presentable. Abahlia was clearing away the food scraps and pouring more tea when she returned.

Nebak insisted on holding the baby.

"I warn you. He is hungry." Loana handed him the wriggling bundle. Seating herself, she prepared to nurse.

"Does he bite?" Nebak grinned at Eshed. Perusing the rosy, round face and sparkling eyes, he held the babe close. "Ahh. I am safe—no teeth." He stroked the tiny chin tenderly.

"Bawww!" Aaron was unhappy. Quickly, Nebak returned him to Loana's arms where he snuggled into the breast. Loud sucking sounds replaced the wailing. She sat cross-legged on the mat and sipped her tea contentedly, her dark cloud of hair brushing the top of the infant's head.

Abahlia sat very close to Nebak and watched. Nebak, for all his jesting, had all the earmarks of a doting father. She could hardly wait to be a mother!

CHAPTER 22

Nebak and Eshed were seated in the sun streams of the room Namath occupied. He spent most of his day in a corner, propped against one wall and unwilling to move. Simonus and Martseah had been summoned from tasks in Etser, and their voices now mingled with those of Serena and Naveh, who had lingered to help care for her father.

The two pairs of men nodded to each other and knelt around Namath to pray. He sat like a piece of furniture in the middle of the room where Serena and Naveh were supporting him in a sitting position, one on each side. Baby Ariel was taking a rest in another room, and the house was very quiet.

Someone looking on would have likened them to an arrangement of statuary, so intense was their concentration on the immobile Namath.

They remained that way for some time. Simonus' curiosity got the better of him, and he peered from under his eyelids at one point to see what the effect might be on Namath. *Nothing!* Much as he wanted to do this for his friend and fellow elder, he was personally doubtful that there would be a change. After all, the man had lost his wits! It was a strange and complex affair. How could their praying supply what wasn't there—namely, Namath's mind?

Martseah, sensing his friend's restlessness, opened his eyes, too, and nodded reassuringly to Simonus, who shifted on his knees and resumed concentration.

The air had been stifling. Now a sudden breeze poured through the open window, pulling at the hair of the bowed heads. Their tunics wrapped about their legs and the tiebands on their foreheads fluttered loose ends against their brows.

As if to signal their departure, Eshed stood suddenly and left the room, touching Namath's head briefly as he went. Leaning against the front lintel, he stroked his bearded jaw, wondering what the next step should be. He heard a stirring behind him. Simonus touched his shoulder. "Come!" he said, hoarsely.

Simonus' firm hold on his arm caused Eshed to turn quickly.

A tone change had come into Serena's voice. "Praise Yahweh!" Serena declared, using his name without hesitation. Naveh was sobbing ecstatically. Namath's head had miraculously broken loose from its post-like configuration and was turning from one to the other of his family and friends. He was as one awakened suddenly from a dream and was unable to take in what the fuss was about. A slow smile tickled the corners of his mouth, and the twinkle could be seen reasserting itself in his eye.

A tear made its way down Eshed's jaw, losing itself in his chin whiskers. Holding his arms out, he gathered the group about Namath and gave a brief prayer of thanks, after which the elder was nearly engulfed by hugs and tears. His distinctive laugh, a little weaker than usual, gurgled from his barrel chest. Infectious as ever, it made others laugh, too, amid much knee slapping and tear wiping.

On the eighth day, Simonus presented himself to assist Eshed in the circumcision. As he entered, harp strains greeted his ears.

"The lambs are on the hill . . . I hear their voices still . . .

baa . . . baa . . . baa." Loana sang by Aaron's cradle with the familiar little harp in her hands.

Seeing Simonus, she rose from her place with a pained expression. Laying the harp aside, she handed him a basin with a towel folded inside to cleanse his hands.

He set his tools on the sideboard. The knife metal gleamed ominously from the corner of the chamois pouch by the basin.

"Eshed!" Loana called loudly. She jumped when he responded close behind her, the babe in his arms.

"Yes, my love!"

"Do be gentle with him . . . please." She knew it was necessary, but the anticipation of cutting his pink flesh in so sensitive an area was abhorrent to her.

"Now, now," Simonus responded, wiping his big arms with the towel, "we both lived through it—Eshed and I— and I heard the midwife tell Tamar they do not even feel it."

"How would *she* know?" Loana's jaw jutted toward them. "She has never been . . . cut like that, and you two cannot possibly remember what it was like!"

"Maybe Simonus cannot be trusted," Eshed said winking at him behind Loana's stiffly turned shoulder, "but I am the child's father and would never do anything to hurt him!" He held Aaron close and nuzzled the fuzzy head.

Loana wrapped her head in a blue shawl that matched her eyes and, tossing one end of it over her shoulder, hastily retreated to Tamar's house. Women were not permitted to watch the operation, which was just as well. Her church law required it, but just for today, she wished Aaron were an Abigail!

The two men bent over the child in prayer. Eshed passed the instrument through a candle flame. The metal reflected a small pool of light that fell on the baby's abdomen. He moved to lift the child into Simonus' arms, then, changing his mind, handed the tool to his friend and arranged the child for cutting.

A small nick, expertly supplied by Simonus, brought two drops of blood onto Aaron's blanket and a little whimpering complaint. Eshed murmured soft words into Aaron's ear as the baby wriggled his round little head uncomfortably and kicked his bowed legs.

"Taken like a man . . . I must say!" Simonus wiped the knife blade on a cloth from the pouch and cocked his head at the child. His father's eyes warmed toward his friend. "Thank you." Eshed smiled.

Tamar opened her door.

Loana stood there with one hand on her hip and the other arm around a cephel of preserved olives. She brushed a tear from her cheek with the flat of her free hand. "May I sit with you while you work?" she asked, observing the pot of steam on Tamar's hearth.

"Come right in!" Tamar was always glad for company when she was preserving condiments. The room reeked of vinegar and spices, and a mound of sliced cucumbers rested on the board.

The large cephel of olives changed hands. It seemed like a meager exchange for all the pears, milk, and other bounty Tamar had shared, but since those were taken as partial payment for priestly services, she supposed it came out even. Tamar's friendship was by far the thing she valued most in her neighbor.

Loana sat cross-legged on the cushions and arranged her skirt.

"Loana." Tamar drew a heavy curtain aside to let the vinegar fumes escape into the fresh air. "What do you hear from Father Jarad?" She handed her guest a cup of pomegranate juice and some seed pods to crack. Taking a quantity of pods in her apron, she sat down in front of her and broke one between two stones.

"Oh . . . a messenger came and said he will be here soon to see Aaron. I can hardly wait!" She broke a shell on the rock and probed within for the seed.

"Where is he coming *from?*" Tamar's voice had a funny note in it. Hers was an easy voice to read because of its unique timbre, and Loana looked up quickly.

"Eshkolia! Why aren't you looking at me, Tamar?"

"I do believe this pod has an insect inside it!" Tamar hedged, brushing her palms together.

"Tamar!"

Her friend turned to face Loana. "Yes . . . what is it?"

"I know you too well . . . and trust you too much!" Loana pleaded. "Tell me what you are keeping from me!"

"It's nothing, Loana . . . only a rumor I heard in Etser. You know how women talk!"

"What?" Loana smashed a seed beyond use. "He is my father. I have a right to know!"

"When I was calling on Naveh the other day with the embroidered tunic I made for Ariel, I heard Sheila, Laban's wife, telling his mother in the shop that she had heard about Father Jarad's 'goings on' in Eshkolia . . . that is all."

"What sort of *goings on?*" Loana's face was a study in angry disbelief.

"He is there with Nebow, is that correct?" Tamar was beginning to feel like an executioner.

"Yes." Loana clutched the cup to drink from it. She felt steadied, somehow, with it in her hand.

"Well?" Tamar's uplifted palm said it all. Nebow had become known for his carousing, drinking, casting lots for money, and bedding low women.

Loana's cheeks were redder than the pomegranate juice on her lips. She gulped hard, trying to suppress a sob. "But my father is a priest. He would never live like that!"

"What can I say?" Tamar placed her square palm on Loana's shoulder. "Can one cavort with donkeys and not learn to bray?"

"He is probably there to try to keep Nebow out of trouble. Yes, that's it!" Her blue eyes and quivering lips made an attempt at recovery. She squared her shoulders.

Tamar resumed cracking the pods. "If what Sheila said is true . . . it is not working!"

Loana put the cup down with a thud and covered her ears. "I don't want to hear any more!" She began to cry, covering her mouth with her crossed hands.

"I am sorry, Loana, truly I am." Tamar's eyes teared for her friend, and she reached again for her shoulder. "But I thought you should know. It may be some time before he gets here."

"Please," Loana sobbed, "promise me you will not tell Eshed!"

"Never! It was difficult enough telling you!" Tamar handed Loana the muslin scarf from around her neck to wipe her tears.

Aaron snuggled against Namath's arm, snoozing peacefully. A little ripple of anticipation ran through the curious gathering of villagers. They had been looking forward to the fortieth day and the rite of purification and blessing to be bestowed on the babe from the priestly household. Watching for the moment, they had come as if by signal to the temple, when Eshed and Loana had ridden in with the new bundle in their arms. Now the infant rested against Namath's ample proportions. It was a special honor granted to him as friend, elder, and surrogate grandfather.

Nebak, officiating with Eshed, lifted the lid of the laver, while Loana and Abahlia stood by, heads wrapped in muslin shawls. The mother's face had been scrubbed to a glow in her own ritual purification. Her hair clung damply in little ringlets against her brow, the shawl obscuring most of it.

Tapers flickered in the background. The smell of incense was heavy in her nostrils. Loana viewed the sleeping babe dipped fully in the water. Aaron came up struggling and screaming in Nebak's hands. He relinquished the dripping baby to his father. Turning, the father-priest lifted the babe to the altar and held him at head-height before his eyes, pronouncing the benediction of offering his life back to God.

"In the name of the Father, Son, and Holy Spirit," he proclaimed. Pivoting, he placed the child in the waiting arms of his mother. She received him in a heavy green wrap, bound him, and pulled him close to warm him. With this, his fussing subsided.

Eshed, every inch the new father, beamed at the waiting faces of his flock. "We have just presented to you Aaron, of the house of Eshed!"

The new family descended the platform and greeted those who had come to the rite of purification. As Loana passed Tamar, a little stab of self-pity overtook her. Tamar had been right. Her father had not come for the rite of purification as she had expected. By now, he surely had received the message if he was in Eshkolia as he'd led her to believe. She kept her eyes down upon the infant. A touch on her arm caused her to look up. Tamar's eyes met hers. Hesitating, she smiled weakly. Tamar hugged her shoulder, a pleading look in her eye. Love edged out resentment as Loana returned her embrace and smiled. After all, it was not Tamar's fault. It was her father's shortcoming that embittered her special moment.

• • •

The officiating party and the elders had been invited to Martseah's home for refreshments, and he moved ahead of the crowd to signal their approach. Naveh had remained at home to cook and was spreading a lunch of goat cheese, pastries, olives, and fresh fruit when Martseah bustled in.

Ariel had a strong grip on his mother's leg and was getting a ride with each stride she made as she dished up the meal. Already slow of pace by nature, Naveh was finding it difficult to get things done with her adventurous son at her heels all day. Martseah, sensing her nervousness over feeding the approaching crowd, whisked Ariel into his arms and tossed him a little to distract him. "Are we having your carob cakes, then?" Martseah inspected the offerings, dangling the wriggling boy under one arm.

"Oh!" Naveh exclaimed, whirling suddenly through the drape. "I almost forgot!" She pulled a rack of delicacies from the steam of the oven outside and plopped them quickly on the sideboard, curtain swaying with her entry. The cakes were heavily browned on top, and she pressed one with her finger. "I hope they are not ruined!" she confided.

"Nonsense!" Martseah fingered one from the rack and dropped the hot object on his tongue. Chewing quickly with his mouth partly open to let out the heat, he declared, "Delicious! Never better!"

Ariel reached toward the rack from his swinging position. "Ah . . . chew . . . chew," he suggested, his mouth already rimmed with fruit stains from earlier samplings.

"No, my boy . . . hot . . . hot!" Naveh responded, wiping her hands on her apron and gingerly lifting the bite-sized cakes onto a platter. "Your father could eat a flaming lamb shank . . . but not you and me!"

"Will he always say 'chew' when he wants food?" Martseah wondered aloud, holding another cake to his lips.

"Silly!" Naveh remonstrated, "I say 'chew' to him so he will not take such big bites and will use his teeth more. That is why he says 'chew.'" She smiled at her tall, gangly husband and whisked the last cake from the sideboard before it, too, found its way into his mouth.

The group swept in, ruddy from the coolness of the day, chattering and laughing.

"How is Ariel?" Loana asked, pinching his cheek.

"Busy—*very* busy!" Naveh replied. "Tell Aaron to grow up fast. Ariel needs a playmate!" She brushed a stray red lock from her eyes and smiled at Loana, peeking into the bundle she carried. Eshed's child had a mass of dark hair and cherubic features. "I'd say he looks just like you." Naveh cocked her head and peered at Loana appraisingly. "But I see a stubborn little Eshed wriggling in that blanket too!" She laughed.

Martseah set Ariel down and moved about the room arranging cushions and seating their guests in comfortable clusters. Ariel tiptoed over and gave Loana a big-eyed stare, curious to see inside her bundle. She stooped down and pulled the green wrap aside. Ariel, with that sense that all babies have about others of their kind, rocked a little on his toes and smiled a slobbery smile, poking one forefinger inside the blanket on the baby's cheek. Just then, Aaron hiccoughed and Ariel jumped back fearfully, shaking his red curls and searching Loana's eyes for reassurance. "It's all right," she said, sensing his discomfort. Hanging on her side, he continued to watch in wide-eyed wonder as she arranged the green wrap discreetly and breast-fed the baby, cross-legged on a cushion beside him. Though he no longer nursed, the sucking noises struck a familiar chord in him. He pulled at the cover and peeked behind when Loana had her head turned, talking to Naveh. Glancing down, she saw the rapt expression on Ariel's face as he watched the baby eat. Abahlia, sitting across the room, also viewed the exchange. She caught Loana's eye, and they traded smiles. Abahlia was glad Loana's milk had come in strong and felt her contribution had helped. A pang of envy shot through her middle. She rested her strong fingers on her waist in an unconscious gesture of longing.

Namath's robust laughter rang out above the group noise. It was his first outing since his harrowing experience, and he was enjoying it immensely. Serena was chattering animatedly in her familiar lisping tongue, and her husband was punctuating the tale with little guffaws. "Never heard tell of a friendship between a chicken and a mule before . . . but that's what we've got. Old Sadie will not go anywhere— not even for a drop of water—without that setting hen on her back! How that chicken keeps from getting stepped on, I will never know. The mule has bruised my toes more than once. *Naveh!* Sit down and eat. If we need more food, I will dish it!"

Eshed and Loana sought one another's eyes across the room. It was so good to see Namath restored and enjoying himself. Loana basked in the new found sense of family she enjoyed with these people. Had she had any presentment of the terror that was on their doorstep, she would have hugged the moment even closer than she did.

CHAPTER 23

Above the roar of the small waterfall, Eshed called, "Let's haul it in—we have a few!" He pulled at the net, pitting his muscle against the rush of water. Strong hands on the opposite side of the stream managed the other end of the heavy netting. Two more silver bellies flopped into it where the falls broke. With care and sureness, they drew the catch into a big bundle and joined each other at the stream's edge.

Flashing small knives in the sunlight, they slit the wriggling creatures, spilling the entrails on a rock for the carrion to gather.

"This one has a mind of its own!" giggled Iysh, groping after it on a rock. With one expert flip of its shiny tail, it slithered to the side and dropped back into the water, disappearing through the foam, not even nicked.

Eshed wiped his forehead on his tunic sleeve and smiled broadly at Iysh's amused response to the creature's getaway. No one he knew laughed as Iysh did, without any sort of restraint—it was the giggle of a girl having an advanced attack of hysteria. The sound of it, following their lengthy separation, did his heart good.

They were scrambling home with their catch through brush on the side of the hill when Eshed caught sight of an opening in the rocks. "Hello—come and see this!" he directed. They turned sideways through a thicket of limbs, bending at the waist to enter a hole in the rock.

"What?" Iysh's voice resounded off the dark walls in end-less echoes down the chasm.

"I used to play here as a boy. It was my favorite hiding place from Martseah. He still reminds me of the day he found it—and ruined my game!" Eshed's voice tumbled off the walls in confusion, leaving "game . . . game . . . game" trailing the air. "It is an old sluice. Heavy rains used to enter the streambed at this point, but we have not had that much water for some time now," Eshed recounted, holding the dripping fishnet in one hand and fingering the rock with the other. His hair caught a halo of sunbeams as he departed the opening, and Iysh thought he detected a momentary glimpse of the child who used to play there in place of the bold young man who had once saved his life.

The lamp's afterglow caught the young mother's back and the splendid shape of the babe's head as Loana ex-cused herself and took Aaron to nurse before bedtime. Iysh and Eshed sat together at the mat's edge, warmed by the sight and nurtured by Loana's cooking and their own good fellowship. Eshed watched the softening of Iysh's expres-sion in the lamplight. It was a refreshment to be with Iysh because in the reworking of his docile resolve, the Lord had given Iysh a compliant and tender regard for time and his associates. Eshed had every hope that in their limited time together some of it was rubbing off on him. Still given to taking his leadership role more seriously than he ought, he found himself wanting to direct everything that happened around him, even when it was being performed without his assistance. He had been curbing his tongue, however, since the night his anger and ego bluster had almost caused the loss of Abahlia in the Circan camp. He was learning what it meant to let the Lord take charge . . . what it meant to be a worthy vessel.

A little flat stone in Iysh's hand drew his attention. His expressive mouth worked in rhythm with the sound of the knife blade he was sharpening. The fish knife glinted in the lamplight to the accompaniment of a pursing of lips in the swarthy face. Presently, he laid the knife aside and looked into Eshed's eyes. Softening his voice, he leaned over the mat. The metal of a crudely made cross rotated on its chain around the young man's neck, picking up the candle gleam at intervals.

"Choikos, for all its rudeness and inhumanity, is showing real signs of following the Christ!" He smiled, studying his open palms in the interim. *A servant's hands,* thought Eshed warmly.

Eshed beamed encouragement. Iysh continued, "The innkeeper is meeting with the faithful in my absence. Several of the merchants have joined with us, one a traveling tradesman . . . and even a magistrate!" he said with a wink.

"It would be interesting to know," Eshed interrupted, "how that humble little village will be used in the Lord's plan." He tugged at his chin, elbow on knee, and added, "But that is his business. Ours is to do the work. Right?" How very simple it was, the young priest thought, and how very hard to do!

The night about them was dark and deep. The stillness held only the muted singing of Loana to Aaron in the next room. A swift intake of breath caused Iysh to glance up from his reverie. "What is it?" he asked.

"I don't know . . ." A look of pain leaped from Eshed's hazel eyes as he stared into the candle. "Something," he said, his neck prickling uncomfortably, "is coming . . . as surely as the dawn." He turned his head toward the window briefly, as if expecting a visitor. When Eshed fastened his eyes again on Iysh, his mind amplified the cross on Iysh's neck, and it appeared to have taken over, replacing the head and shoulders of his associate. It was a fleeting moment, but its impact lingered long after he had taken Iysh to the new room to rest.

Iysh's final whisper accompanied it in his mind: "We will be ready."

Eshed awakened later with his muscular calf wrapped about Loana's still form and his cheek nuzzled into her full breasts. It was still dark, but Aaron was restive. Feeding time again. He struggled to his feet and brought the child from the cradle and placed him in the warm, comforting spot next to his mother. He shook his head groggily and yawned as the child clasped the breast with his tiny fingers. Loana stirred a little, moaned and placed her hand about the baby's shoulders, pulling him in closer to the breast. It was too dark to watch, so Eshed stretched out on his side by them, taking in the sweet infant smell of Aaron's neck. Feeling a sudden chill, he reached for the quilt. He covered the three of them, leaving a good air pocket for the child. Loana wriggled. "No . . . no," she said, casting the cover aside from herself and the softly sucking babe. The night *was* warm. It was the foreboding that caused his chill.

His priestly vestments had been hung by the window to air. He pulled on the coat, neck vestment, and cap, arranging the blue riband about his neck and picking the brass menorah from its place on the shelf, and hurried to the altar to light tapers and present a special prayer to El Shaddai, God of all power. He had been unable to shrug away the lingering sense of evil from the evening prior. If anything, it was more pronounced as he entered the temple that morning. Martseah's report that some of his best pelts had been stolen virtually from under his nose during the night did not help.

"Master Eshed! Oh, there you are!" Haman tottered into the altar place, squinting against the light from the window.

"Yes . . . Haman. What is it?" The young priest extinguished the taper and turned to greet him. Incense spiced the warm morning air, sending little rivers of smoke high into the drape overhead.

"At the inn . . . I went there for a bite of millet and a cup of broth. They only charge me for the second cup, y'know . . . on account of my work here at the temple. I saw some strange folk there, I tell you, not the usual passers-through. I know they were not there yesterday—I go every morning. They don't charge me for the third cup, y'know. The millet bowl is big . . ."

"And?" Eshed frequently had to prompt Haman, who would ramble on all day, rubbing his bony hands together for emphasis.

"Oh! Er, well . . . these strangers are there . . . no uniforms you understand . . . but people from Circan country if ever I saw it. Strange, they are . . . crafty of eye."

Eshed shrugged his shoulders. The prickly feeling was back. He considered a reply, then dismissed Haman with a wave of the hand. "It is good that you report to me each morning. Thank you, Haman." There was no point in sharing his fears with Haman, who would panic and carry tales through the village, only to forget within an hour what he had reported.

He sank to his knees as the old man shuffled out and began to examine his heart before initiating formal prayer. A chill pressed his neck, and he turned to see if the outer curtain was left blowing in the wind by Haman's exit. Only a few feet behind him was a figure, hooded and robed with a pack under one arm.

"I am sorry . . . you may not come in during the priestly function!" Eshed got to his feet and waited for a response.

He attempted to cover his annoyance with a smile, but chagrin won the day. The figure stepped backward.

"I . . . will come back." It was a woman's voice, somewhat hollow sounding. She turned slowly to go.

"Wait!" Eshed knew he should offer something . . . if only a moment's time. "What can I do for you?" He dropped his hands in front of his vestment and folded them, waiting quietly.

"I am looking for work." Her face was half turned, and the hood prevented a good look at her.

"What do you do?" Eshed asked, his brows arched politely.

"I have always worked in temples . . . like this." She gave a slight movement with her hand toward the altar.

Odd. What sort of employment did she want? Everyone knew the temple at Etser had a council of elders whose wives, along with Haman, maintained the work. He knew she had not been long in the village. She moved closer. She had a wild look about her mouth and a brazen, challenging gleam in her eye, though her smile and manner were respectful. She shifted the bundle to the other arm, and her foot wriggled impatiently in her sandal.

He could not continue the interview till he had completed his prayers.

"Come," he said, "you may wait in this room. I will speak to you after prayers!" He smiled and indicated a small cubicle used for interviews. Pulling aside the rich curtain, he stepped to one side for her to enter. Slowly she moved through the opening with her head bent. As she passed him, she turned slightly and touched his vestment with her fingertips. He took it for a thankful gesture. "You're welcome!" he intoned softly.

How long he spent in prayer, he did not know. His foreboding had given way to assurance of victory, even in the face of Haman's assertions following on the tail of Ohad, Kamar's grisly death, and the maiming of Namath in the space of a few months' time. He knew who was in charge, and he would have to remember that.

Iysh was making the rounds with Martseah, and Haman had returned to the market for supplies. It provided a lengthy period in his study.

Completing his supplication, he bowed his forehead to the floor and kissed the altar steps. Rising, he moved slowly in his heavy robes toward his study chapel.

The building was quiet.

A small cough caused him to turn. *The young woman.* He'd almost forgotten.

Carrying the brass candle cephel with its tiny flicker of flame, he drew aside the heavy drape and entered the small room. In the next instant, the lamp almost tumbled to the floor. He sucked in his breath. There, gazing up at him with eyes of serpentine intensity, painted with long lines to the scalp and a reddened mouth, was the woman, reclining on an animal pelt. Her head was shaved except for four braids tied in large loops like a hat about her face. Little gold spikes jangled about her waist on a chain and were echoed on her ankles. She appeared to be clothed in some transparent garment with finely etched design, but Eshed suddenly realized that her body was tattooed. He took a step backward. She wore nothing! Her breasts were circled with a design of lotus petals, forming around the nipple as the stamen of the flower. Her long legs were arched invitingly, as was her back. She leaned on her elbow and leered up at him, vines inscribed on all her limbs and a hideously coiled cockatrice etched below her stomach.

She took hold of his leg with a slow pressure of her fingertips. Very slowly, she undulated her hips on the fur pelt, jangling the small metal spikes. "Come," she breathed, "enter my garden of delights . . . an offering that only you may enjoy . . . a gloriously handsome priest you are!" Stroking his calf, her head tipped back, she opened her mouth lustfully and encircled his leg with her ankles to pull him to the floor.

He yanked himself free from her suffocating insinuation. Such revulsion overcame him that his legs nearly failed to carry him to his study where he vomited in a basin, head pounding with the pressure of blood in his temples as his eyes tried to forget the horror of the seduction prepared for him by his enemy.

Wiping his mouth with the back of his hand, he shuddered.

A temple prostitute!

He had heard of them but had never seen one till today. They were a pagan carryover employed in areas riddled with idol worship. But how did she come here? She must have known Etser's practices were different. Why would she risk such a thing? Was she displaced by battle and desperate in her wanderings? No, she did not appear to be starving or needy. What then? Had she been planted for his downfall? He had no enemies in Etser that he knew of. There was only one explanation—she was planted by someone, someone from outside. But why? To what purpose?

Squaring his shoulders, he returned to the cubicle intending to evict her speedily from the premises. The curtain, however, was flung back, and she had taken herself elsewhere. He mopped the perspiration beads from his face with the flat of his hand. Breath still coming in short gasps, he was pacing about, praying sporadically, when Nebak came into view.

"Esh! How goes it? I am in Etser to have some harvesting tools made for Abahlia's first crop and thought I might give you a hand with something!" The short priest spun in, smiling infectiously, the perfect picture of good humor. He stopped short when he saw Eshed's shaken condition. "My friend . . . by the stars and moon together, what is wrong?"

Eshed grinned slightly on hearing another of Nebak's many little sayings. He took off his cap, shook his head, and began trembling again. Nebak grasped both arms to steady him, and he haltingly related the horrifying sight he had seen, concluding with "Never doubt that God has an adversary in our realm. There is an enemy, Nebak. There *is!*"

Nebak, ever the theorist, responded, "Are you sure it was not an apparition? It *was* a flesh and blood being?"

"Ah, she was *real*, all right. She even touched my leg. It was like a burning brand where her hand rested."

"Come . . . we must talk." Nebak looked about them and led the shaken Eshed to the study. He plucked a little flask of wine from the cupboard and poured two mugs. They faced one another across the roughly hewn writing table. "There is more . . . much more to this, I am afraid, than one temple prostitute and a chance encounter." He spoke in hoarse whispers as Eshed sipped the wine with unsteady fingers wrapped about the mug.

Eshed nodded, leaning back against the wall to steady himself.

Nebak, bathed in light from the window, continued. "In the stalls today, they are reporting losses . . . unexplained theft of their goods . . ."

"I know. Martseah lost several pelts last night," Eshed said. A fresh realization flashed across his face. "And . . . I think I know where one of them went!" He swallowed perceptibly. "That . . . that temptress was reclining on one when I found her in the cubicle."

"Did she have any other stolen goods on her . . . new

sandals . . . or cat's eye stone settings around her neck . . . do you remember?" Nebak prodded.

"No . . . I would remember *that!*" Eshed gave a wry smile. "She was wearing only tattoos . . . in significant places . . . and some gold-spiked charms about her waist which I suspect have some meaning tied up with her . . . calling."

"We should pray for her release . . . from such bondage!" Nebak placed his hand on Eshed's shoulder and looked into his eyes for a long moment.

"Yes . . . yes. Let's do that."

Bowing their heads, Nebak led out in prayer for the deliverance of this vessel of evil.

"One more thing," Nebak said in a hushed tone. "Did you hear that there is a young woman missing from the inn?"

"No!"

"Mala . . . the serving girl . . ."

"She comes to service here. Loana knows her well!"

"Disappeared . . . during the busiest part of the serving this morning. She was sent to the storage shed out back for millet . . . and never returned. Very unlike her to just up and leave, I understand!" Nebak shook his head.

"Nebak . . . what does it all mean?" Eshed threw a hand in the air in consternation and began pacing the small quarters.

"What we have here, my friend, is the same thing we saw in Ohad before the Circan invasion. It is part of their advance strategy. They operate by disrupting the town, setting people at odds with one another, creating a climate of fear and distrust. It makes it easier to take over without having to destroy the things they want to keep, such as buildings for hosteling troops, foodstuffs, and other spoils."

"So what do we do . . . arm ourselves and our families

with clubs and knives . . . and wait for the onslaught?" Eshed, calm once again, clenched a fist and gave the table a *thwack* on passing.

Nebak was silent for a moment. "I can tell you this . . . you would be no match for them in battle. We resisted to keep them from carrying off our women, livestock, and fishing boats, and you see what happened to little Ohad—a cinder!"

Eshed swung his head sideways and looked down at Nebak in his seat for a long moment. "Then . . . I think I have a plan," he said.

CHAPTER 24

Tamar slowed the slanted wheel of her obed with toe pressure, trickling water from one of her jars onto the wooden disc that held a half-formed pot. Her hands firmly about its base, she kicked the wheel into revolution again and coaxed the brown blob upward as the wheel reached top speed. The clay was cool against her fingers, and the morning air freshened her face in the early light of the courtyard. A shelf of pots waited near her elbow, some drying, some in need of carved design before entering the oven.

"Ble-ah-ah-ah!"

Nanny had been milked. What did she want? The goat's voice was closer in range than Tamar remembered.

"Ble-ah-ah-ah-ah-ah!" Her baby sounded distressed in answer. *Probably caught in the fence again.*

Simonus was in Etser on temple business. Tamar stopped the wheel reluctantly. It was a crucial moment in pot building, but never mind. The livestock came first. She hurried to the corner of the building, and holding her hand to her eyes against the sun, saw what Nanny saw. A squinty eyed, gimpy footed, scruffy man was dragging the kid through a forced opening in the goat yard fence!

"You, there!" Tamar called, pulling her short figure erect.

At her outcry, a moment's lapse of concentration caused the man to lose his grip on the scrambling animal. At the same time Nanny charged the fence and he fell backward into the dust. Tamar surveyed the ground at her feet and picked up a long piece of firewood. Swiftly she was upon him, pounding the dust from his rags and shouting indignation.

"If you want food, ask for it—but keep your hands off our young!"

Grabbing a fence-post, he hauled himself up again, shielding his face from her blows with his arms. Muttering indecipherably, he ran down the beaten path and disappeared into the trees.

Shaking with rage, she handed the kid, big-eyed and trembling, over the fence to her mother who nuzzled her and cleaned her face, amid soft complaints. Tamar used her weapon for a temporary fence mend and struggled, weak-kneed, to her work bench. Re-wetting the pot, she used a shard to scrape unwanted clay from its base and set about finishing it. *It is unthinkable . . . stealing in broad daylight. A practiced thief would not be so careless. He appeared too energetic to be starving . . . So why?*

There was no time to lose.

According to Nebak's account, there had been a scant ten days between the entry of the Circan puppets into town and the invasion itself. The next two days, Iysh and Nebak and Eshed carried on a quiet word-of-mouth campaign among the villagers.

It was extremely important that no Circan ears hear their plan, and many individuals were brought to Eshed, by night, for conference. Even the temple was being watched, and Iysh was the only stranger to the area who could be trusted to bring the villagers together. He became the escort since Nebak and Eshed had families and should not risk being seen abroad too much at night.

Eshed was receiving hourly confirmation that his plan

was the right one. Not only did the villagers trust him as their priest, but no one disagreed with the strategy he had laid out. Recent events had helped firm their resolve to take action, but most of them would have clung to their property no matter what. Such unity was unheard of, even in the close-knit community of Etser. Was this little hamlet being spared for some greater purpose? Speculation was forming in Eshed's mind as he saw how readily they agreed to his plans.

One by one the tradesmen of Etser took all but a token amount of goods and crept out of town with their loved ones, staying with relatives at remote farms or taking extended journeys in the direction opposite the roadways favored by the Circans. Some piled their families into boats and took their summer holiday on the water. Everything was prearranged, so that no mass exodus would be noted. Goods still hung in the front of shops, and one individual was left behind to tend the selling and keep up appearances until the last possible moment. Those on outlying farms, such as Namath and Simonus, would remain in place till the final hour to pass along the word of troop advance. Then, when the time was upon them, they too had places to go and hidden canyons that only local folk knew about picked out for secluding their livestock.

"I cannot help being grateful that Etser has not grown much in all these years," Eshed confided to Loana. "It makes evacuation that much simpler."

Aaron hiccoughed.

Loana was holding him on her shoulder, following his feeding. "Another bubble," she confided, sitting cross-legged on the floor, watching tender movements of Eshed's hands lining a portable basket cradle for Aaron with grasses. Iysh had woven it of river reeds. It was a fine rendering of his craft.

They were startled by a rap on the lintel.

Eshed rose and stepped noiselessly to the door. The faces of Simonus and Tamar caught the light from a taper as he opened the door. Wordlessly he beckoned them in.

Tamar kissed the top of Aaron's fuzzy head and draped a little quilt she was carrying into the newly woven pannier. "I was making it for his two-month birthday," she whispered in her little girl voice, "but I thought you might need it more now." Her stubby fingers stuffed the soft blue into corners. "It just fits!" she announced.

"You're as silly as I am, Tamar, celebrating his birthday every month!" Loana grinned. "And right now—when we have so many other things to think of!" Her face clouded, and she bit her lip as she shifted the bundled baby to the other shoulder.

"A fresh skin of goat's milk is tied to a tree near the streamcrossing we use. It will be cool in the water tonight. Take it with you when you leave!" Simonus instructed. "And when are you going?" Eshed wanted to know, scowling at Simonus.

"I will still stay on a bit. The goats must be milked. There are two fresh ones—*two*, not *one*, thanks to Tamar."

"How is that?" Eshed asked, taking the sleeping babe from Loana. She picked a resting mat from a roll in the corner and began arranging a sleeping place for Tamar, who would go with them.

"I have not seen Eshed to tell him . . ." Tamar's eyes shyly met her husband's.

Simonus related the story of the attempted theft, concluding with, "and we think what he really wanted was the fresh nanny. He knew, by taking the kid, she would follow, making his departure simpler."

"And the kid, of course, would have ended up in a Circan stewpot!" Eshed said, shaking his head.

"Tomorrow I will move the other goats to a secluded pasture. My dog will protect them there . . ." Simonus added.

"That is fortunate!" Eshed placed the sleeping babe in his new cradle, "since Tamar will be with *us*." His eyes twinkled as he turned toward his friends.

"Esh!" Tamar stomped her foot at his teasing.

"I am very proud of what Tamar did. I am not sure I could have acted that fast!" Loana said, rolling a quilt to pillow her head.

"And I am proud!" Simonus gathered his tiny wife in his arms and kissed her.

"Take care!" she whispered. "Come soon . . . our land is not worth anything to me . . . without you." Tamar's voice broke, and he rubbed his beard against her round cheek, stroking her freckled nose as if she were a child.

Just before dawn, Eshed woke Loana and Tamar. Loana swaddled Aaron and tucked the corners of his shawl in the pannier. Taking her blue scarf from the peg, she wrapped her head and gathered a tote of foodstuffs she had prepared. Handing it to Eshed, she strapped on her heavy sandals. They would have to go on foot, since a horse or donkey would be hard to conceal. Tamar put away the sleeping gear, grateful that her shaking hands did not show in the dark room. If only Simonus could come now, too, she would feel a lot better.

Eshed quaffed the candle, and they stole from the house. In the emerging light, a lone horseman passed through the gate. It was Iysh. He dismounted and took the rope from his horse's foamy mouth, sending him with a slap to join the other livestock. There was grass a plenty and a stream nearby. They would survive. He swung into step beside Eshed.

"They are two days away, at most," he whispered. Iysh

had gone alone to the Rhantismos fork and had seen the force of troops breaking camp and heading for Etser. He had returned at top speed and would assist Eshed in protecting the women and providing lookout.

"Pull that skin from the stream," Eshed directed Iysh as they prepared to cross the water. Iysh complied and returned to the group. Loana and Tamar huddled close together in the faint light and took turns carrying Aaron. So close were their signals that when Loana stepped in a hole and went down, Tamar quickly caught the pannier without missing a step, and Aaron was none the wiser. Eshed drew Loana to her feet and brushed off her skirt.

"Are you all right?" Iysh asked, touching her shoulder.

"Yes . . . thank you." Loana squeezed his arm and leaned on him for support. Iysh had become the brother she never had.

"Hurry!" Eshed admonished. "We must get to cover before the sun is up. I don't want *anyone* to see where we are going." He had made no mention of it to Loana, but he was well aware that the spiritual leader of Etser would come into focus sometime during the occupation. He wanted to spare her that concern as long as possible. The elders had urged him repeatedly to stay out of sight, and though his personal inclination was to be at the forefront of what was happening, he had to agree that he could do them very little good hanging from a Circan gibbet!

Pushing through the brush on the hillside, they bent low to enter the opening Eshed indicated. It would be cramped but safe—for the time being at least.

"Ah-ha! I thought this was where we were coming!" Iysh whispered in Loana's ear, deflecting some small stones to make a sitting spot for her. "Did you know this is your husband's hideout?"

"No!" she replied with a giggle. "The next time I miss

him, I will look here!" The comic relief was welcome to all but Eshed.

"Shhhh!" he admonished. "You must get accustomed to talking very little. In the silence of these hills, everything carries, especially at dawn."

"But we are safe here, don't you think?" Tamar rocked the cradle on her knees, sitting cross-legged on the chasm floor.

"If there is one thing I know about Circans, it is that there is really no way of knowing where they will crop up next. We must behave as if they were camped right outside!" Eshed vividly recalled the Circan helmet he and Nebak had found on this very hill scarcely more than a year ago!

Nebak! Eshed hoped fervently that he and Abhalia had made it to their destination safely. They had gone with Martseah, Naveh, Namath, Serena, and Ariel to a similar place in the hills.

Footsteps.

The following morning at dawn, Iysh was taking his turn as lookout, posted part way down the hill from the hideout, when he heard a stirring in the brush below. Crouching low, he waited to see which way the sound would take. Hardly daring to breathe, he hoped fervently that Aaron would not choose this moment to cry. The baby had done so well, one would think he was accustomed to living out of doors. But he supposed anything could be borne when one's mother and a fresh supply of milk were at hand. The brush crackled under foot. The steps were coming toward the hideout! Heavy steps . . . armored steps? Iysh felt a chill at the thought of the weapon he might encounter when he tried to bring the man down.

Wait! There are other feet, too. The intruder was so close now, Iysh would hear him breathing.

Suddenly, from behind a bush, Iysh jumped the intruder. "Aa-argh!" the culprit exclaimed in surprise. Iysh bounced off his big chest like an ant off an elephant's belly! Iysh picked himself up from the dust and prepared for another lunge. From within the dust cloud he heard, "Ho . . . my man. It's me, Simonus!"

Through the dust Iysh saw the barrel chest of Simonus, the two small she-goats that trailed him, and the baby goat he carried under one arm. The two men collapsed against each other in relief, laughing quietly in spite of the danger.

Reaching the chasm, Simonus placed a tote of fresh fruit and vegetables next to Tamar and kissed her forehead. "Your fresh milk delivery is here. . . . Where is your cup?" he asked her.

Tamar offered a mug from her tote, sliding under his arm in a graceful embrace. Eshed and Loana exchanged glances. With Simonus accounted for, they could relax a little.

The closest nanny was pulled through the chasm opening by expert hands and the teats milked into the cup. "Anyone else?" Simonus looked at the watching faces.

"Here is mine!" Loana gave him her mug. "I am glad you are here." She squeezed his arm and smiled up at him.

Simonus crouched next to Eshed, supporting himself against the rough stone with one hand. "A dust cloud and the rumble of many horses were on the main road into Etser as I left home," he said. Simonus had been right to stay, though all had been concerned about him.

"Thank you . . ." Eshed clasped his friend's shoulder. Now he had the report he needed.

CHAPTER 25

Aragon halted the contingent a few yards from Etser and wheeled his horse to face the troops. He had brought seventy-five of his best men—more than enough to put down this small village.

The sun was just nuzzling the horizon, and a pink gold bounced off the breastplates of his men. It was a pretty sight in the eyes of a man who witnessed so much ugliness. He was squat and beefy, his visage that of a stunted bullock. Crusty and squarely formed, his features proclaimed the rough cruelty and ruthlessness of his trade. Watching him ride, his aide, Sulao, often thought of the battering ram itself—a solid piece of junk aimed at barrier after barrier, breaking through, despoiling, pillaging and moving on to repeat the terror. Sulao had the sort of respect for Aragon that one accords mad-dogs. He could deal with it only if he remembered where the teeth were.

"Presss-ent swords!" Aragon barked with a voice-crackle that came from eating a lot of dust.

A rattle of blades preceded a formation of silver tips glittering upright in the hovering daylight. A twisted smile creased the solidly formed patina of his face. This ceremony was what he enjoyed the most. The sight of blood had long ago ceased to move him. But moving on an unsuspecting village before dawn! That was like taking a woman by force—all the more pleasurable for the use of cunning and muscle!

Dismayed that the light was coming on so fast, he urged

his troops forward at a trot. They must not enter too hastily. A certain amount of stealth suited his nature. Then, when the shock value had done its job, they could rid Etser of its inhabitants.

The village's main path was unoccupied except for a chicken squawking and winging to a perch out of hooves' reach. An eerie quiet hung around the stalls. Produce and leather goods dangled in the door openings, but no one seemed to be stirring. *Strange.* By this time, someone should be abroad. Babies crying for milk and livestock braying to be relieved of it usually accompanied their forays into villages. But here every hoof beat seemed to echo through stillness. Something was stirring in the temple doorway, though. Calling a halt with an upward thrust of his hand, he moved stealthily forward, his horse at a walk, and his eyes riveted to the spot.

A figure raised her hand in greeting and pulled back her hood, her stiff braids arched against the door frame. A wise smile creased her lips. "How do you like the way we take a village for you?" she asked. Half a dozen wastrels crowded the lintel, sleepily acknowledging the commander's presence. The men scratched themselves and yawned, their hair tousled and their dirty clothing stinking of strong brew and assorted food stains.

As Aragon leaned forward in his saddle, his metal breastplate clanged stiffly against the brass saddle horn. "Where . . ." his arm swept the shops and homes, "is everyone?"

"Don't know . . ." She yawned. "Do you suppose it is something I said?"

Aragon grunted his impatience at her little joke. "Is that all you can tell me?" he growled. He felt cheated. A little bloodshed would have spiked up his morning. Without resistance, there could be no fight!

"There were people here yesterday. We stole from them. We should know . . . huh, fellas?" She jabbed a toothless vagrant next to her, and he giggled foolishly.

"Sulao!" Aragon shouted. "Take the men into the buildings. See what you can find. I'll attend to the temple."

Aragon's nostrils flared. He could still make his invasion brutally worthwhile. Dismounting, he poked the rabble out of the doorway with his sword. "Get off, will you! Go find my men some breakfast," he growled. Replacing the sword in the scabbard, he took the girl into the temple. Their voices echoed in the chamber. "No one in here either?"

"I did as you said," she smirked, "but the priest has not come in for *services* today." Her twisted meaning would throw him off. She was not about to let Aragon know that the handsome young priest had escaped her clutches. One would never knowingly court the displeasure of so brutal a man as Aragon.

Aragon's loins had begun to trouble him viciously. One thing he loved was physical comfort and he had had precious little of that as commander of the Emperor's army. With a swift motion, he tore the heavy scarlet curtain from the side of the altar and threw it on the floor. Its softness and sheen soothed him momentarily. Wrenching the cape from the prostitute's shoulders, he seized her braids and without bothering to remove his metal breastplate, yanked her to the floor and repeatedly took her.

Sulao strapped the beautifully tooled mezach about his waist, stroking the smooth leather. It was well designed and suited his brawny frame. He was virile and well-shaped in his skirted uniform and gleaming breastplate, and he knew it.

"Sir?" One under his command dangled a pair of leather

sandals in front of his face. "Are you taking these for your-self?" The young warrior knew Sualo's penchant for leather goods.

"You may have them." Sulao chuckled as the youngster romped off with the sandals.

It was true, leather was one of the spoils of war Sulao welcomed. He earned too small a wage to buy it for himself. The bags of salt that were his salary, valuable as they were, did not cover personal extravagances. A small plot of land, inherited from his father, had to be worked and maintained in his absence. Therefore, his share of salt was sent directly to his overseer in Eshkolia. Someday, if he settled down, he would build a house on it. For now, it was the only place he could call home, an anchor in a rootless existence.

The inn was next door, and he helped himself to a platter of bread and cheese and a tankard of ale. The room was teeming with soldiers serving themselves no end of delicacies.

"Mutton, sir?" One of them passed his table and offered a shank to him.

"No, you enjoy it!" Sulao nodded. For two days they had come to him with requests because Aragon was rarely available. Sulao was beginning to enjoy his assumed position of authority and to feel the command was rightfully his. After all, wasn't he making all the decisions, monitoring disagreements between the soldiers over booty, ale, and the like? He would be separating fights over women too, if there were any, but Aragon had posted himself somewhat permanently at the temple, it seemed, staking his claim to the only one available.

The girl had first been taken as a spoil of war from the temple in Balamia. Out on the trail she had been passed among the men as any other trinket might be. But here

Aragon had used his prerogative as commander to reserve her to himself and was satiating his cravings, making up for all those comfortless years he had spent at war.

For her part, the girl felt important that she was now aiding the emperor's cause in much the same way that she had helped countless men worship in the pagan temple at Balamia. She was good at what she did. After an hour with her, the men would take hold of the golden bullhorns on the altar and, in a state of euphoria, commit themselves anew to the idol, drinking the heady wine from its skull and chanting rhythmically while she caressed their bodies with sweet unguents. She was accustomed to being at the call of men and yielding herself at any hour for their refreshment. And now all of that was Aragon's.

Sulao had maintained discipline while Aragon indulged himself many times in the past, and he was glad, personally, not to share the commander's vice. He felt that eventually it would be the officer's undoing.

Haman crept down the steps.

Hiding for days on the rooftop of the temple, he had gone undetected by the activity below. Relieved he had not been discovered, he couldn't forget he was there against Eshed's orders. But he reasoned that he had been at the temple longer than Eshed and it was his responsibility to defend the sacred edifice, if need be. Haman was not just the keeper of the keys. The temple had been his whole life. And probably he would die there. There was no place he would rather be.

Unexpectedly, he heard a sound below, near the altar. He drew back into the shadows and froze on the step. Two voices, a man's and a woman's, were drifting toward the ceiling. His old ears could not make out what they were saying. He leaned forward slightly to get a view of who they were. Perhaps Eshed had returned!

Sprawled on the curtain was a stocky, hairy ape of a man. A young bald creature hovered over him. Haman thought it was a boy until, squinting, he noticed the braids and as she turned slightly, he could see naked breasts. The rounded hips were rotating over the man, and his head and arms were thrown back in a total yielding. She was stroking his chest and neck with a liquid and the strong musk scent of it was noticeable even at this height. She sat back suddenly and wiped the remainder of the liquid on her posterior, flinching a little where he had bitten her flanks in his frenzy.

It is good that I am here. The temple does need protecting! In all its years, it had never been desecrated like this! The horror of it made his throat dry.

Haman began to form a plan in his mind. He saw the warrior's helmet nearby and his cape thrown over a cushion and concluded that he must soon go on duty and leave the temple vacant. But Haman had to make several more trips from the roof before the lurching and moaning ceased and both slept on the floor.

The shadows were deepening. The girl wriggled slightly, her waist ornament tinkling against the floor. Slowly she reached for Aragon and tugged his ear. He tossed his head and groaned but did not awaken. She took hold of his thigh and gave his leg a playful yank. He rolled toward her, still asleep but willing to be wakened if properly motivated. She smelled the unguent on his chest. Strong! She began to cough. Her eyes were smarting. Something was wrong!

Slowly, she pulled herself to a sitting position. It couldn't be late, but the room seemed dark. She coughed again. *Smoke.* She smelled smoke!

"Aragon—wake up! Wake up, I tell you!" She shook him hard. "The temple is on fire!"

CHAPTER 26

I simply cannot bear another minute in this cramped, airless hold. I am getting out of here. . . . If I am caught, I am caught!"

Loana struggled out, leaving Aaron behind, asleep in his grass nest. The very odor of the river reeds that formed it made her long for freshness and movement.

Eshed glimpsed the baby sleeping peacefully. A quick look at Tamar assured him that Aaron would be looked after. He smiled gratefully at her and stepped outside to walk with Loana. It was growing dark and their chances of being seen were lessened. He put his arm about her waist and helped her negotiate the steepest part of the hill. "Some fresh air will do you good," he whispered.

Every bone in Loana's body ached, partly from sitting so much and partly from tension. "Dearest . . ." she began.

"Yes?"

"How do we . . . how do *you* know we are doing the right thing, staying holed up here like ground squirrels? Are we really in any danger this far from Etser?" Her lovely features swam at him oddly in the diminishing light.

Shades of Father Jarad, Eshed thought. Neither of them had the foggiest notion of how to protect themselves. Had they been house cats, they would have been trodden under foot long ago! Actually, the plan had not been Eshed's, at least not altogether. "I don't . . . but I am trusting the inner peace I have that we are acting out of obedience . . . and will be looked after," he replied.

"Then, why do I only have misgivings right now?" Loana wanted to know.

"Probably because you hurt!"

There was much more to it than that. As they strolled about in the shadowy twilight, he kept a sharp eye for any unusual movements about them, thinking to himself that Loana was really not suited to this kind of intrigue. She didn't bear discomforts well and being away from their little house was hard for her, especially with a nursing baby draining her strength. He wished they could spend the night at home, at least, but that would certainly occasion a Circan strike—if their previous tactics were any guide.

Loana pushed her fingertips against her lower spine as she walked. The back muscles so recently taxed by the weight of her pregnancy pulled at her bones painfully. She longed for one of Proustia's massages! Her mind wandered to other inhabitants of this valley. *Mala.* Pretty little Mala with the great eyes, soft voice, and brilliant smile, what had become of her? Eshed still had no word on her whereabouts. *Abahlia.* Dear Abahlia, so strong, why, she could take anything! She had come in bleeding and bone weary from the trail and been singing among the pots the next morning, polishing all of Loana's copper. And *Tamar.* A tiny little thing, Tamar was just about as fragile as a cockroach! Her endurance frequently outlasted even that of her husky husband. Of course, neither had a baby to care for night and day. But *Naveh.* Naveh would understand. She was not terribly rugged either. But Martseah seemed to know that and was always looking for ways to make things easier for her, whereas Eshed . . .

"What are you thinking about, my love?" Eshed whispered in her ear, the scent of her hair against his face.

His voice gave her a start. "Nothing! Oh, not much really." She grinned sheepishly.

"Look! The sky! Over Etser!" Iysh, on lookout duty, pushed past them and pointed through the trees. Smoke was rising from a red-gold glow. "It is on fire!"

Iysh tore down the hill toward Eshed's place. He was going for his mount.

"Wait!" Eshed stumbled after him. "My friend," he called hoarsely, "don't go. Wait—*don't go!*"

The aborigine was swifter on foot than Eshed and was soon raising a small cloud of dust on the road toward the village.

Long faced, Eshed returned to his wife. "I cannot help it if the whole village burns. He should not go near there just now!" His voice cracked and his eyes were moist. He loved Iysh and was afraid for him. Sorely tempted to ride after him and bring him back, he was being torn asunder by his loyalties. He shook his head with disbelief.

"I am sure he will be careful," Loana stroked his cheek, trying to erase the worry lines that were forming. "He only means to report what is happening!"

"I know what is happening." He turned to look at the smudge against the darkening horizon. "We saw what happened at Ohad!" Eshed trembled with a mix of rage and powerlessness. Still his orders had been to evacuate and not to return till further notice. Iysh's failure to understand the second part could cost his life!

Aragon fled the temple, the girl trailing behind. His troops, gathered outside to watch the flames shoot upward, cheered his departure. Coughing and choking, he pulled the vestment about his nakedness only to discover that the cape on his shoulders was the prostitute's, not his own! He saw her emerge from the smoke wearing his cape and clutching his breastplate and helmet in her arms. He yanked the helmet from her, dropping it in the dust, and pulled his cape from her shoulders, leaving her naked in the light of the flames.

For one fleeting moment she seemed to accept his callousness. Then, with her eye fixed on Aragon, she stooped slowly to retrieve the helmet, turned its chin strap down in the dirt, and spat on it! Turning it over with her foot, she spat inside it. The men fell silent, their eyes on Aragon.

The warrior, fixing one bulging eye upon her as he fastened the breastplate over his perfumed and reeking body, struck her viciously with the back of his hand. A murmur of camaraderie ran through the crowd. It served her right—defiling the Circan uniform! The crackling timbers of the building became only a backdrop for the drama being played out by Aragon and his wench, now sprawling in the dirt.

"Commander!" A voice broke through the gathering, and Sulao pushed through to the front of the men, tugging the collar of a man out of uniform.

Aragon shifted his weight, turning slowly from the woman struggling out of the dust. The fire glinted strangely in his wild hair.

"Here he is—the men brought in the priest!" Sulao crowed.

Amber flickered off the metal object around the man's neck and his face showed pale in the temple's shimmer. He was silent. Aragon stepped close, riveting his eyes on the man's face. He stared for a long moment. "So! You're the runaway fanatic, are you?" he snarled.

The girl was wiping blood from her mouth and standing uncertainly behind Aragon. Through the smoke, her watering eyes made out the form of the accused man. She blinked. He certainly did not resemble the priest she'd met. He was too slight, too dark.

Aragon swaggered about, enjoying the power of the moment in front of his men. His eye fixed on the prisoner, he rasped, "Here is the plaything you left behind." One booted kick lifted the girl from the ground, and she fell back into the dust like a broken branch, spewing oaths under her breath.

Sulao released his hold on the prisoner and made a move to help her up. Then he checked himself. He did not approve of Aragon's treatment of her, even if she were a mere trollop, but speaking out could threaten his aspirations to be commander of his own brigade.

"No!" the girl objected. She had never seen this man before. He was not the priest. The stranger was watching her with compassion on his face. She had witnessed it so rarely, it was like a shock of cold water to her spirit. "*No,*" she repeated, stunned by his composure.

"We will hear no more from you!" Aragon exploded over her head. Shrugging his shoulders into a taller stance, he faced his aide. "What is the story here?" His bulldog eyes bulged.

"He was spying on the village, sir. Two of the men brought him in."

The accused man lowered his gaze to look directly at the commander who was several inches shorter than he. His expressive mouth was set in a firm line. A cross glittered against his dusty tunic. His fists were clenched, but he made no move toward the little despot or to retreat from him.

"Can't you say something?" Aragon bellowed. "Something . . . anything," he waved his hand toward the cluster of men watching, ". . . for the crowd that has gathered to hear you?" He was at his caustic best, and a snicker of acknowledgment festered among the men.

Watching Aragon's arrogant disregard for the colorfully

disfigured young woman only strengthened Iysh's resolve that no harm befall Eshed or the people of the village. Everything the aborigine had done to this point had been toward that aim and he would not relax his effort now!

"If there is one thing I know about Iysh, it is that he has always reached for the best, in himself, in others," Eshed reflected. Crouched by the stream of water in the pallid grip of evening, he was rinsing his face. As Loana watched him, her eye caught the faint glow of a solitary star against the gauzy retreat of the sun. The sky was darkening quickly now, and the star would soon have its moment to light the sky. Musing on this, her mind went again to Iysh who had brought so much light into her life . . . and Eshed's. She still wondered about their meeting. Eshed never spoke of it.

Eshed leaned back on the rock next to Loana. The dark blot that signaled the razing of the village was waning. It could not have affected the entire village. Such a fire would still be blazing.

"You have never told me about your meeting with Iysh." Loana placed her hand on his arm and stroked it lovingly. "Do you want to tell me now?" She combed through her damp hair with her fingers. It had felt good to let the stream water rush through it, cooling and soothing her.

Eshed cleared his throat. "He . . . I . . . met him under strange circumstances," he faltered. "I had just ridden into Choikos for the first time and learned that a man was being whipped in the public square, supposedly for stealing from a city official. . . ." A tear rose in his eye and he blinked it away. "The man being whipped was Iysh."

"Oh, no. Iysh would never steal. I know it!"

"No . . . no he didn't do it, but I didn't know it then."

"What happened to him?" Loana persisted.

"I had some coin with me. I paid his fine, and he was released." He scratched in the streambed with a stick and rinsed the muddy end in the water.

"But, how did you know he was innocent?" She brushed her hair from her face where it had fallen from the knot she had made on her crown to keep her neck cool.

"I didn't. I felt led of the Spirit to take care of him. . . . I do not understand these things." He turned and faced her. Her eyes glistened, and she was silent against the aphotic backdrop of evening.

For an interval, only the gurgling of water could be heard.

"Why did you go to Choikos in the first place?"

"That was strange, too. . . . I was looking for a man named Barak, who had some old scrolls for a festival we were planning. The council sent me to find them . . ."

"And . . ."

"I never found him. But I met Iysh. And soon after, Iysh found himself in Christ!" It was no time to hold back. It was time Loana knew what his journeys had been about. Keeping secrets from her built fences between them.

"Oh . . ." She beheld her empty hands resting in her lap and thought suddenly of Aaron and that he must soon be fed. She stirred to leave, but something prevented her. Eshed sat, very still, listening to the water slip over the rocks.

"Call it the lure of God," he continued, "I could not resist doing what I did, though fear was in my heart, competing for the instant to snatch away our freedom." Eshed rubbed his jaw thoughtfully. "And Iysh responded to God with great joy, having expressed his longing for him many times before. Yes, he is a man who wants only the highest for himself and others, and some part of him knew that to be possible only through Yahweh."

"We all believe. What is different about Iysh's belief?" Loana smoothed her skirt, trying hard to keep her tone casual.

"For Iysh it was no longer just 'knowing' or 'knowing about' God. It became a partnership through the Spirit that Jesus Christ bestowed through his death and resurrection!"

Loana was getting a strange feeling inside. But her confusion did not disturb her as it once had when Eshed talked of things beyond her understanding. Tonight a spark of illumination was kindling in her mind and heart. She felt compelled to follow its light although her heart was still rebelling.

"Then do you believe Jesus was the Messiah?" The words struck a note of clarity against the night.

"I can believe nothing else," Eshed assured her. "Only the true son of God could have left behind such a gift as his Spirit."

Loana fell silent again. Her arms were about her knees and she hugged them to herself. Deep in thought, she watched the water ripple past.

Eshed tossed a pebble in the water and they heard the "plop" though they could hardly see in the darkness. Soon the moon would light their way to the cave, and the glassy shimmer of the water would be visible.

"What does the Spirit do . . . that Yahweh cannot?" Loana inquired.

"He—the Spirit—is the mover of all things for God, the Creator. Jesus, God's son, came so that man could see God in the flesh and understand his purpose for man. He made God real in our lives in a way that no messages from heaven, like those the patriarchs received, could do. He was, and is, the true hand of God. We, being persons, needed to behold him in his personhood. And we still need him, and have him, in the person of his Spirit. And the

Spirit honors Jesus continually by doing his work in the
world through us, those who believe. Ages from now people will still know God and his Son through his Spirit—long
after we are gone and there is no one left to tell them about
the Son who walked these very hills!" Eshed could not re-
late himself completely to the flow of words going out to
Loana. It was as if the dam had finally burst and all that he
had kept carefully hidden was being revealed.

Loana was listening with her whole being. She felt as if
her body had just become an ear and she was straining forward for the next sounds.

Eshed dipped his hand in the water and let it trickle off
his palm. A deep silence wrapped them both. He looked
intently at the water droplets on his open hand, lit by heav-
enly lights. Moonlight was forming between the trees and
the first silvery threads of it reflected on the stream.

His voice had a rich yearning as he spoke again. "The
waters tumble from the snowy mountain peaks, through
rocky crevices, over moss covered stones in trickles and in
great bursts of dancing liquid. They fall into quiet pools and
darkened eddies and brash showy waterfalls that can be
viewed from afar, and they become minuscule droplets that
traverse the length of a fern leaf." He fingered a giant leaf
that drank at the water's edge. "And they plunge into the
anonymity of a rock-hollowed pool, a blessing, a comfort, a
life force for all they touch. The Spirit, like the waters, em-
braces every moment of life in a quiet, steady, moving, resting, churning, mighty, frequently surprising yielding of his
own, not unlike that of water gurgling over stones. Water is,
at the same time, one thing and many, both one source and
many tributaries. It is a bonding of several life-giving elements. The Spirit is also many things to us. Just as water is
water wherever it touches and blesses, the Spirit is himself
in all circumstances. As water splits to share space with a

rock," he pointed to a moon drenched boulder in the middle of the stream, "and rejoins with no loss of rhythm, the Spirit is displaced but never limited. Onward, ever onward, even at its final destination in the sea, water finds no rest but moves about in great peaks and pulls and pushes the shoreline in some wondrous and mysterious affirmation of itself. The Spirit admits no limit and no boundary save the shoreline of our hearts. . . ."

CHAPTER 27

Sulao struggled out of sleep. It was just before dawn.

Leaving the comfortable furnishings of the best room in the inn, the one reserved for dignitaries, he strapped on his metal and stepped furtively to the stable.

His horse snorted a welcome between munches of fodder Sulao had left the night before. After securing the saddle, he led another horse, Iysh's horse, from the next stall. A long wrapped bundle lay across its back. As quietly as hooves would allow, he left the village of Etser and headed out into the foothills.

There was a spot he knew of. It was not far from Etser. He had been there once, as an underling, scouting the area. From that hill the temple could be seen in the distance. He would now have to choose a different landmark, but no matter. He was sure he could find the area again. There was a stream nearby. It was a singular spot in the surrounding terrain and he felt he owed it to his mission.

The two animals trotted a gentle cadence on the hard soil of the roadway. Sulao found himself enjoying the ride alone in the emerging light. It didn't usually fall his lot to dispose of the dead but he had chosen this one. Routinely, carcasses were taken by the newest in the ranks and left, downwind, for the carrion to find. But this man, Sulao decided, deserved a decent burial. He had received the death sentence reserved for spies and was dragged to a bloody end between two horses. He had died without a whimper, without a word to recall the sentence. His dignity made Sulao ashamed of the casualness with which outsiders lives were treated. He resolved to do the one thing he could to show that humanity still coursed in his veins in spite of his evil associations.

"Wh-a-a!" Aaron demanded his breakfast. Loana sat up slowly from the hollow of Eshed's arm where she had slept, and lifted the babe from his grass cradle.

"Sh . . . sh . . . sh," she soothed, stretching the full tunic Eshed had loaned her over one shoulder. She sighed as he sucked her milk. It was a relief, even in this cramped position. Eshed moved slightly. One eye opened and he made out her outline against the cave front where the first rays of sun were slanting in. He rolled his head to one side. Simonus and Tamar were still asleep on the rolls of fabric and bundles of grass she had used to improvise a bed. He could hear the young nannies and the unweaned kid cropping small plants outside the door where they had been tethered to keep them from wandering off in the night. They would soon need to be relieved of milk as well, although the kid was undoubtedly taking care of part of it.

Groping for the nodah behind him, he opened it and drank in an attempt to wash the taste of sleep from his mouth. He held it up and nodded to Loana. She assented and he wriggled over to her and held it to her lips. She took a long drink, and as he replaced the stopper, he bent his head and kissed her breast and the baby's head. His hand cradled the back of her neck. He kissed her softly on the lips, and lingering with it a moment, she sensed his desire for more. He put his arms about the two of them and held them close.

"I am going now . . . to see if there is any sign of Iysh," he whispered in her ear. Simonus moaned and rolled over. He would soon be awake. Eshed knew he must hurry if he was to go alone. It was better that he did. Loana nodded solemnly and kissed his cheek. As he left, he heard only the suckling of the baby.

Fitting his sandals expertly into the rock niches and small tufts of greenery, he made his way up the back side of the hill. From that vantage, he could see a long way. Taking hold of a large stone near the top, he heaved himself up over it in time to see the tip of a Circan visor approaching the summit on the other side. Panting from effort, he quickly hid himself behind the rock and clung to the precipice. The soldier was on foot but with the sound of hooves behind. He was leading his horse up the steepest part. With effort, Eshed inched to one side of the rock and peeked around it. The warrior was tying his horse to a tree. At the horse's flank, Eshed could see another horse's head and carefully shifted until he could see that it carried only a parcel.

He held his breath, considering his next move. Climbing down would be noisy at best and perhaps alert the officer to the whereabouts of his family and friends. That was out. The only course seemed to be to remain where he was for as long as possible.

The Circan groped among the knots on the horse bearing the parcel and brought something out. At first Eshed could not see it. Then the man turned slightly, and Eshed saw the gleam of a short-handled digging implement. He found himself praying that Iysh would not return just now. All would be in danger if he did. But there was no sign of Iysh.

Eshed could see the whole of Etser valley and the common route. No one was approaching. As he watched the soldier assemble his tools, it gradually came to him that the horse with the parcel looked much like Iysh's. It had a white muzzle and black hooves and a sturdy brown coat. Squinting from another crevice in the rock, he was almost certain of it. A cold fear began clawing at him. *Where is Iysh?* What was the soldier doing with his horse?

As the mind is wont to do in stress, he did not proceed to the next step and ask himself what the bundle on the horse's back might be, but watched, dry-mouthed as the man began to dig the earth. What was he looking for? Eshed had been here countless times and there was nothing of any real value among the rocks that he knew of. The greatest treasure he had ever acquired here were spring leeks. *Spring leeks!* He recalled with a jolt that this was the spot where he and Nebak had found the Circan helmet some months before! Could this be the man who left the helmet? Had he buried something there to return for it later? Eshed thought about that. He did not recall having seen any freshly turned earth.

His musing made him a trifle careless and one foot slipped a bit into some loose rock. He caught himself from the fall but the sound of the pebbles tumbling down the hillside was enough in the still morning air to alert the officer. With a grunt, the man threw down his tool. Eshed followed his footsteps with his ear so that he might go around the rock on the opposite side and surprise the man. It would not do for him to look over the edge. If nothing else did, the tied goats would give away their hiding place.

Sulao's investigation of the sounds turned out to be totally predictable. When he came around the rock, Eshed was waiting for him and lunged. They rolled together on the open ground, kicking and jabbing fiercely. Sulao's metal breastplate was harsh against Eshed's body. Eshed had no weapon, but Sulao had a dagger under his belt. Wielding it, he slashed at Eshed's head and neck, aiming for an eye or a vein. They rolled about locked in combat for some moments. It seemed like an eternity to Eshed, who watched the knife blade descend repeatedly near his eye and, on one pass, graze his temple. He felt a trickle of blood begin. He was strong but Sulao was stronger and Eshed had been unable to disarm him. At last, in a frantic effort, he was able to put a knee between them and then a foot. Planting his foot against the breastplate, Eshed kicked fiercely and Sulao fell backward, panting and coughing.

Eshed grabbed the dropped knife and leaped to his feet, half crouching in readiness. Sulao, quite spent for a few seconds, recovered himself. He sat forward and pulled the helmet from his head. He wiped his brow. "Enough!" he bellowed, rolling his big head back and forth on his neck as if he had sustained some injury. He glowered at Eshed. "Don't you know this is now occupied country . . . under Circan command? I could have you killed for attacking me. And I may!" Sulao struggled to his feet and adjusted his visor.

Eshed slipped the knife under his own belt for safekeeping. "You are still on my property—until I am told otherwise!" he declared.

"I just got through telling you!" Sulao barked. "Officially, you are under arrest. Is that what you want to hear?" He pushed Eshed by the shoulder, who lost his footing on the uneven ground Sulao had dug and went down hard.

Shaking his full head of hair, he asked Sulao, "What are you digging here for, anyway?"

"If you must know, a decent burial for Etser's priest. I may not respect your property as you would choose, but I do have some respect for . . ." He gestured toward the bundle on the horse's back.

Eshed had ceased to hear the droning of Sulao's voice. Chilled to the core, he pulled his heavy limbs to a standing position. Slowly, and with a sodden weight on his heart, he strode over to Iysh's horse and pulled back the wrapping. A great mass of straight, black hair, matted with blood, tumbled from under the canvas. Tangled within was the cross Iysh had worn since the day of his meeting with the Christ. His horse pushed at Eshed in an attempt to nudge him away, then as if recognizing him as a friend, nickered sorrowfully, fixing a great dark eye on his stricken face.

It came from his throat but seemed to have no part of him. A profound shrieking "No-o-o-o-!" Loss, guilt, frustration, and sorrow filled his breast as he clawed the wrapping that bound the still form. He flung them all aside, still unbelieving, and in the next moment, wished that he had not. Iysh's arms hung at a strange angle, all but torn from his body. But the feet—those marvelous swift feet. Eshed would remember the feet with haunting sadness. *Gone!* The legs were worn to the shinbone. Iysh had bled to death long before, of course, but the horror remained as Eshed saw the stumps hanging uselessly against the horse's flank. The awful sight swam before his eyes and he backed against a tree. He began weeping violently. Through his tears Sulao's white, mute face swam before him. Then everything went black.

CHAPTER 28

The sun was at its zenith and the day had grown warm. Eshed forced his eyes open against the startling light. He started to rise and found himself unable to do so. He was bound hand and foot. Rolling to his side, he saw the officer placing the last shovelful of dirt on the grave. The canvas gaped on the horse's back, and Eshed fought a great wave of nausea as the horror rushed in on him again.

Sulao heard him retching and turned from packing the loose soil. Wiping his brow he announced, "We will be going, now." Then, as if in afterthought, he touched the water flask on his hip. "Would you like a drink of water?" It seemed the least he could do. Keeping an eye on Eshed, he satisfied his own thirst. The dark tousled head shook negatively, and an involuntary shudder ran through Eshed's body.

The Circan tore the canvas from the horse and helped Eshed into place. Untying his feet and retying them by a lash under the horse's belly, he removed the temptation to jump from the horse at some unguarded moment. The ropes behind his back were switched to the front, his wrists looped securely so that he could balance himself while riding. Much too numb to offer any resistance, Eshed did not give thought to Simonus, a good stone's throw away, who could have handled this brute and another like him, if need be.

"Your . . . ah . . . priest . . . must have been a good friend. I want you to know . . . I never saw a man die more bravely. It is too bad he came spying on us. Such a key person in your community should have sent someone else." Sulao's words pierced Eshed, heart and soul. *Will he never shut up!*

As if ashamed of his softness, Sulao shrugged at the passive figure sitting on the horse so forlornly, and testing the strength of the ropes, leaned over the hind flank of his own horse and pulled at the lead rope on Iysh's pony.

Descent was slow with loose rock underhoof. Sulao anticipated no trouble from his captive, putting his thoughts instead on the wavering command of Aragon. That little despot was turning into a paper tiger right before his eyes! He had wasted valuable time in the Circan campaign, wenching. By now Sulao would have deputized an occupational force and sent the rest to capture Rimza beyond the hills. Once it was secured, Protos and all access to the sea would be theirs!

Perhaps he would employ a line of questioning with Aragon, he mused, if he could get him alone long enough. Freeing him from that weird little spider of a girl had become like shaking a true arachnid . . . and a black widow at that. She clung to him like road dust, weaving an erotic web of well being that bound his loins and paralyzed him for decision, let alone action.

But Sulao must try. If he could make Aragon believe the idea was his own, perhaps he would commission Sulao to head the foray into the hills, leaving Aragon to maintain Etser for the time being. It was a long shot but sensible, Sulao thought, to send out a man who still had a heart for action. If Aragon chose to pursue this vulgarity, let him do it in the obscurity of Etser rather than in the more cosmopolitan Protos where all the world could see. Aragon would certainly be relieved of his command if headquarters found out. Yes . . . Sulao was seeing more and more ways that he could head the battalion himself and be rid of this puny community and that lascivious pair!

Sitting spraddled-legged on a rock by the stream, the girl dangled her bare feet in the cool water and giggled. She pitched forward and swam a few rounds in the deepest part of the pool. Aragon was dozing against a tree, his shield and helmet resting beside him. He stirred slightly, hearing the splash. His eyes drifted to the water just as she bobbed to the surface.

"Come on!" He waved her in his direction. She flung the water from her eyes and made for shore, then turned, laughing, and swam away again. Aragon, drowsing in the noonday sun, opened one eye. "Hey!" he called, stirring. She dove under, legs kicking air, then disappeared. She explored under water until her breath ran out. When she came to the top, Aragon was wading into the water with a long vine in his hand. He plunged into the deep part where she was and she felt his hands grasping her buttocks. Playfully she slipped away from him. He grasped the chain around her waist, halting her swim and taking the breath from her body. Looping the strong vine through the chain, he began towing her to shore as she pulled away, kicking and pushing at his chest with her fists. The challenge only made him more determined to pull her from the water. He laughed, a sound that would have been hideous to any but his playmate. She stopped her pummeling and relaxed in the water, enjoying the lazy motion of being eased through the pool by another's energy. They fell like sodden puppies onto the mossy ground, laughing and choking on stream water.

He lay back, breathing heavily. His strength did not seem to be what it once was. As an aide he had been able to ride horseback all day, swim heavy water, battle hand to hand for hours, and still bed a woman any time. Pushing up on his elbow, he toyed with the vine at her waist, watching the rise and fall of her breasts as she regained her breath. Matching the vine tattoos, he spiraled the vine about her bent thigh, tying it at her ankle and picking a flower to place in the knot as a decoration. She raised her head and lifted her foot to see what he had done. The vine was twisted, snakelike, down one side of her body from the waist chain.

"You!" She gave his chest a nudge with her knee. Aroused, he flung himself atop her. A pleasurable squeal rewarded him.

His horse, tied to a tree close by, bolted at a painful sensation in his thigh. A scream tore from the warrior's lips as the heavy hooves crushed his skull and backbone with two blows and glanced off, then came down upon the girl's esophagus, smashing her wind pipe and breaking her neck.

"What? Ho!" Sulao was startled by the sight of an oncoming horse, running erratically through the trees in front of them, trailing a torn rope. As he came closer, Sulao grabbed at the binding and noted the distraught appearance of the horse. He missed the lash, and momentarily leaving Eshed behind, he urged his horse ahead and made another pass. He looped the rope through his fingers for stability as the animal reared, wild-eyed. When he could see the muzzle, he recognized it immediately. It was *Aragon's* mount. The animal trembled violently for a few confused seconds, then his eyes glazed over and he dropped to the ground. Sulao slid from his horse and carefully inspected the dead creature. At first, he saw nothing unusual. A little foam drying on the lips caused him to investigate more fully. He ran his hand over the silky coat, the scent of hot fur in his nostrils. There, on the flank, low and into the leg muscle of the hind quarter was his answer. Snakebite!

Signaling, he urged Eshed forward where he took hold of

the tow lash again. Eshed still locked in shock, seemed barely to notice the proceedings. Somewhere nearby Aragon was afoot and probably furious, Sulao thought, and he felt constrained to get to him with provision hastily. "Where could I find another horse around here? Hey . . ." His brow furrowed as he turned his horse halfway round to confront Eshed.

They rode on, searching for Aragon.

Nearing the stream again, Sulao paused to refresh the horses. Idly sitting his animal till the drink was finished, he began to speculate Aragon's whereabouts. *Somewhere in the bush with that girl*, his wager! A glint of bronze near a tree to his right caught his eye momentarily and he turned his head, never expecting to see the propped shield so close at hand. A short distance from it, was the wasted form of his commander, sprawled, facedown, on the girl. Slowly and with a mixture of revulsion and sadness, he moved toward the lifeless pair, leaving the horse behind, drinking. A dazed Eshed stared blankly after him.

It is the old "eye for an eye and tooth for a tooth," though no one lifted a hand against Aragon, Eshed reflected, as he helped Sulao tie Aragon's body on Sulao's horse. Releasing Eshed's hands and feet, Sulao had allowed him to assist in the second burial of the day. Eshed led Iysh's pony to pick up the girl. Her head fell back like a broken doll when they lifted her from the ground. Sulao paused and looked away, choking back emotion as he picked up Aragon's shield and helmet. He didn't approve of the pair, but this—this was gruesome.

If the first shock of seeing Iysh after his execution had silenced Eshed, the second one—seeing Iysh's executioner—had loosed his lips and limbs again. "It is surely a sad day for you, too," Eshed said.

"He—Aragon—will have military honors from his men." Sulao squinted against the light falling in shafts through the trees. "Where might we bury the girl?" Without the commander, he suddenly felt unwilling to command. A temporary condition, but very real.

"She may be buried on my hill," Eshed offered, forgetting the previous conversation about ownership.

Soon they had placed her in the ground not far from Iysh. Eshed threw down the shovel. With fresh tears trickling down his cheek, he said, "May I perform the burial service for my friend, and then for her?"

Sulao nodded, solemnly.

Eshed took his prayer book from his tunic and placed the cowl with the blue ribband over his head. The two men, so opposed in their views of the world and the dead before them, stood on opposing sides of the grave with heads bowed as Eshed intoned the last rites. His voice spoke each phrase richly and with meaning. He closed the book, and they crossed to the girl's grave. He inquired, "What is the girl's name?"

Sulao looked at him, blankly, his steel gray eyes shifting across his face and coming to rest on the blue ribband of his neck drape. "I do not know. We just called her 'the girl.'" He blushed suddenly, at the thought. Not even to be honored with a name, she was better off dead!

The services concluded among the slanting rays of the afternoon. They were both dripping from effort in the warm temperature when Eshed removed his cowl and submitted to being bound, again, on his own horse, to go into Etser. He wished fervently that he could tell Loana and Simonus of his departure but to do so would endanger everyone.

Sulao's hand rested on the horse's neck momentarily as

he knotted the tow rope. "You . . ." he said, "you are Etser's priest, aren't you?" He looked Eshed in the eye.

"Yes . . ." Eshed took a deep breath. "I am."

"And the spy, the one we killed?"

"A dear friend, not even a resident of Etser—a co-worker for the Lord," Eshed choked on the last words. Iysh had been the first man he had known who had received Christ. Now he was gone.

The torches were yellow holes in the black night sky.

Eshed stood, bound, between two soldiers. All the unit was assembled, and he could hear the thud, thud, thud of sandaled feet on the hard earth as a group of shieldbearers marched to the center of the gathering. On their shoulders he recognized the upturned shield of Aragon with the shrunken form of the commander in full military dress arranged carefully upon it. His face had the appearance of lying in a shallow plate, so flattened was the back of his skull. Not a pretty sight. Thankfully, it would soon be over.

"Helmets forward!" Sulao barked the command, and each warrior in the cortege removed his helmet with his free hand and placed it over his heart. The men in the unit removed their helmets as well, except for Sulao, who was in command.

"Surrender shield!" he called. They placed the burden carefully on the ground and returned and stood at attention.

"Torchbearer forward!" A soldier at the rear of the group strode forward, torch in hand.

"Light Commander Aragon's way!" The torch went down and the body burst into flames.

"Cortege retreat!" The shieldbearers marched in two columns from the flaming shield.

The smell of burning flesh fouled the night air. Eshed

watched Sulao's face throughout the ceremony. The light from the funeral pyre and the standing torches played upon his face. Eshed was sure that Sulao was proud to have Aragon's command, but from the little he knew of the man, he knew also Sulao would have preferred to earn it. The circumstances of Aragon's death sickened and infuriated the new commander. The ashes would have to be returned to Circan headquarters for entombment there, according to rule, but Sulao had the tasteless job of having to tell them why his commander had died. Full military honors could not be accorded a man who had not fallen in battle but had disgraced himself and his unit. It was doubtful that he could be interred there at all. Yet if Sulao didn't tell, someone surely would. Headquarters would extract it from the honor guard bearing his ashes, if nothing else. Aragon had made many enemies in his years of command and it would discredit Sulao if he were not the first to tell that Aragon had not died in the fiery heat of battle but with his head kicked in like a papier mâché bauble while in the searing embrace of a whore!

"Company dismissed!" Sulao released the group from duty. One lone trumpet sorrowfully blew the retreat theme while torchbearers carried the yellow plumes to light the unit's way to their quarters. Sulao strode quickly to Eshed's side. *Now. Now,* Eshed thought, *it is my turn to suffer!*

"Respect for Aragon prevents any action toward this man tonight!" he growled to the soldiers holding Eshed. "Until the ashes are cold, we are to initiate nothing new in the name of conquest." He looked Eshed full in the face as a torch swept by. "Release him to me."

The two soldiers untied the thongs that bound him to them. Tipping their visors in salute, they left him with Sulao. Sulao took hold of the cords and led his prisoner away.

"Tomorrow," he spoke in low tones, "we ride out for our next engagement. I am leaving a small deputation here as a symbol of our authority over Etser, but they will not interfere with the life of the village. I will see to that!"

Eshed was puzzled. They seemed to be headed for the stable where Iysh's pony was tethered.

"I will come back from time to time to enforce our occupation, but such a peaceful village as Etser should have no trouble meeting our demands."

The warrior led Eshed to his horse and, releasing his bonds, spoke urgently. "Go! Do not look back. Hurry! I will watch here until you are safely out of town."

Eshed managed to speak.

"But . . . why?" He groped his way onto the horse in the dark, feeling the warm flank under his leg.

Sulao handed him the reins. "Ride! . . . before we are seen and I must lash you with this rope!"

CHAPTER 29

Iysh's horse trotted out of the stable, slowly at first, hooves whispering on the sod. Eshed turned to look at the blackened earth where the temple had stood. The smell of burnt timbers and ruined cloth drifted up to him. As he gathered speed by Martseah's place, he wondered again at the burning of the edifice. What had happened to Haman? Had he left as he was told? The loss of the building would be a shock to everyone, but most of all to Haman, for whom it had been home.

Glancing over his shoulder, he saw the raw glint of Sul-ao's helmet as he watched him from the stable door. Eshed slipped the animal between Martseah's home and another small building and disappeared into the trees, rather than be seen on the road this night. His heart pumped fiercely, and as he rose to meet the speed of the horse, they encountered a clearing that would open onto a section of road farther out, a safe distance from Etser.

He was grateful that this stretch was familiar to him, for the night was dark with incumbent clouds. Taking no time to look behind, even on the roadway, he plunged on. The moon scattered flickering patches of light along the way when the clouds separated. A dreamlike quality rode with him. So much had happened in twenty-four hours, and images sprang, undigested within his breast—hurting, soothing, horrifying, infuriating, sorrowing, frightening, assuring images—kaleidoscoping in his mind and tearing at it as surely as the rope lash from which he was spared would have torn his flesh. His lungs and back ached with unexpressed emotion. Iysh . . . gone! The temple . . . decimated! Haman . . . unaccounted for. Behind him a roll of thunder echoed the turmoil within him. What began as small flecks of water on his face soon turned into a deluge. By the time they reached shelter in the stall by his house, both rider and animal were soaked. There could be no stopping now, not for Eshed. He must get up to the hideout and tell the others he was safe. Grabbing a blanket, he flung it over the wet animal. Water splashed from the horse's mane onto Eshed's face as it shook the streams of dampness from its eyes. "Whoa, there. I will be back and rub you down soon." He stroked the damp fur.

At the sound of his voice, there was a stirring in the corner of the stall.

"Who goes there?" he asked with a start, a heartbeat staccato against his ribs.

"Me . . . Master Eshed . . . it's Haman!" The quavery voice came from the corner. The raindrops beat against the roof of the shed. The old key keeper tottered into Eshed's arms, weeping against his cold, wet tunic.

They sat down together in dry straw, and Haman poured out his tale of the temple's destruction, sobbing and wiping his face with the singed corner of his robe. When he had finished, he gulped and began to shiver.

"Temples are made by hand, Haman. They can be rebuilt," Eshed assured him, his arm around his shoulder. "The true temple . . ." He tapped Haman's chest with his forefinger. "You, my friend," Eshed continued, "have shown the true temple by doing what you did!"

At Eshed's insistence, Haman was taken into the house and sat down with cheese and fruit before a cephel's beam. A few dried crusts of tsuwl were wrapped in a cloth on the ledge of the stone oven, and these Eshed handed to the old man with the words, "I will be back soon with the others. Loana will make a place for you to sleep then."

Taking no time to change from his wet clothing, Eshed hurried into the night. The rain had stopped, and the moon was once again his companion as he climbed the hill eagerly. The air still felt heavy, and his breathing was labored by the time he reached the cavern. At the sound of his breathing, a body blocked the doorway. He halted. The moon had shifted behind a cloud, and he could not be sure who was in that opening! A peek of moon lit Simonus' tunic front.

"It is Eshed!" he whispered hoarsely.

"My love . . . my own!" Loana pushed past Simonus with her baby in her arms and fell weeping against Eshed. "We did not know," she gulped, "what to think!"

Eshed held the two of them in his arms, trembling in mute response. Aaron squirmed against his damp chest, snuffling for sustenance.

Simonus tugged the back of Eshed's neck affectionately. Tamar had joined Loana, who was weeping softly. The goat trio nudged their legs as they stood clustered together in the dark cavern, interjecting a "ble-ah" here and there. Aaron whimpered in his sleep.

Eshed had taken to wandering the house at night when Loana and Aaron were asleep. He would discover himself sitting by a window, looking out at the stars, weeping in his heart for all that was lost to him—Iysh, Ohad, the temple, his parents, Uncle Josiah, Checed and Pala, Kamar, the old ways, the boyish idea that everything could be made simple if given enough thought and application of body heat. Could he have been wrong about all these things, about their importance in his life? Oh, but that was petty of him . . . as if it all existed for him. Was he wrong to develop attachments beyond his kin? He could not imagine not loving Loana or little Aaron . . . but could too much be invested even in these so as to finally leave nothing behind when they were gone? Was he being given away, piece by piece, never to be recovered?

One morning, he chanced to glance out the same window in time to see a strange bird sitting in a puddle of new rain. Small and butter-yellow, the bird was of a type he had never seen. Rapturously, it was brushing its wings and feathers in the cool liquid. It looked, in that instant, like the only bird that had ever discovered bathing. Silent at first, it began to chirp as it performed its cleansing. Eshed's soul rested within him as he watched. How like God to provide that pristine spot of rainwater for one little bird! Even with no one else in view, certainly *he* could trust for such provision also. It was a hopeful sign— and one that he never forgot.

The rough wooden cross, two sturdy limbs of a sycamore tree, sank into the soft soil under the weight of the sledge. As Eshed completed its positioning, Loana and Tamar cast purple calumnus and white water lilies on Iysh's grave. Loana gathered her skirts and sat down at the grave side to arrange the blossoms. Tamar touched her sleeve and signaled her departure to see to Aaron—and the cook pot simmering in Loana's kitchen. Loana nodded, fingering the creamy pearl of the white lotus buds. Eshed threw down his tools and sat beside her. Silence enveloped them as he watched her slim fingers at work on the cool freshness of the blossoms.

Eshed's eyes were circled and grave. He had known more of grief and terror in the past few days than in all of his life before. Sitting in the sunlight with Loana on this fragrant morning had an unreal quality. There had been times when he had feared he would never see her—or anyone—again. He thought of Aaron asleep in his cradle and a stab of pain went through his chest. To have missed watching him grow up and take his place in the community . . . not to have shared with Loana in the pain and pleasure of a son . . . and not to have known the ripening and softening of his wife's character, now showing so vividly in her love and grief for the dead aborigine. The tears ran down his face in gratitude to Christ . . . and—yes—to Iysh!

Eshed laid his head against her neck, his arm propping the two of them from behind. She rested against him, surveying the mound of earth and flowers fronting the cross that marked Iysh's resting place. "He did it for us, you know . . . you and me." Eshed's voice caught. He swallowed. "And all the others . . ."

Loana closed her hand over his. "Dearest . . ." she began.

"Let me finish," he whispered. "He let them think that he was me. *He took my place!* Sulao told me—the new commandant. They knew if they killed the leader, they would have control of the flock—and they thought Iysh was the priest. He *let them kill him!*" Eshed could not bring himself to tell her of the mutilation, but instead added, "And he never said a word!"

"Is that why they let you go—they did not know who you were?" Loana asked, her wet face glistening in the morning light.

"Sulao knew who I was. I do not think he revealed that to his men. Why did he release me? I am not sure . . . but I think it had something to do with the way Iysh died . . . so peacefully in spite of . . ."

"In spite of what?" Suddenly Loana's blood ran cold as she thought of the torture he might have endured.

Eshed shook his head. "Sulao may have thought one death was enough for the same offense. They saw Iysh as a spy. Sulao saw me as a captive of war. It must have made the difference." It was a weak explanation but the best he could muster for the moment. He knew that he had been spared for further work . . . again! But he did not know how to tell Loana that without sounding pompous. He resolved not to do that anymore. It was a hindrance to his witness before her.

She closed her eyes, still leaning back against him. The whole of what Eshed had said washed over her. Iysh had been so much more to them than a friend. He had been a brother—but *more* than a brother. What was it she was reaching for? He had been a lamb, a sacrificial lamb. He had carried away with him all the hate and fear of God that Eshed's priesthood represented to those bloodthirsty pagans! Of course! He had stood in Eshed's place just as . . . just as Jesus—if he was messiah—was supposed to have stood in mankind's place. To have taken man's wrongdoing on himself so that man could go free—wasn't that the story? It crowded into her brain with frightening clarity. A subtle reassurance began to take shape in her breast. She felt the same way now, in the wake of her grief, that she had felt long ago the night her amulets broke and Eshed rode away, leaving her to seek her solace with Jarad in Saramhat for months . . . and again the night she and Eshed had sat by the stream. Such a short time ago, but it seemed long in light of recent events. She had been stirred by Eshed's words . . . or was it more than mere words . . . of Christ's provision for his beloved in his Holy Spirit. Why at that very moment, Iysh was probably no longer among the living . . . or *was* he? Eshed had told her that Jesus had promised life evermore to those who believed. Was that what his own resurrection was about? Would she see Iysh some day and touch him as the disciples had touched the risen Lord? Might she even see the Lord as well?

She felt a great sense of peace within. A security of warmth enveloped her that seemed unrelated to Eshed's presence. Loana opened her eyes. The cross reflected the sun more brightly than it had. She closed her eyes against its glare. But what had been behind it? She opened her eyes again and perceived the form of a man. Eshed was still right beside her. It was not the form of Simonus, nor of Iysh. Her mind, in its grief, was playing tricks on her. She closed her eyes again. Somewhere, from deep inside her, a voice seemed to call, "Loana . . ." Suddenly, in her mind, she took the form of a woolly lamb and scampered in the direction of that voice.

A place to sleep, with a fresh suit of clothes laid beside, had been prepared for Haman in the new L-shaped room of their home. He had protested that the new room should not be his, but Eshed had insisted that it was where he should stay until other provision was made.

Haman busied himself with looking after the garden, the animals, and the olive trees. Loana was grateful for him since her days were brimming over with things to be done with the young master in the house. This Haman knew, and he ceased to feel "in the way" very quickly. He had tended the temple for so long that he had forgotten the simple joys of family life. Though he missed the temple, it was good to stay with Eshed!

A few days restored the people of Etser to their homes again, following a tour of the surrounding hills by Eshed and Simonus. Slowly, the little village breathed life again. Under the watchful eye of twelve of Sulao's best men, citizens quietly pulled the barred latchings from shop windows and put all of their merchandise in plain view. Once or twice a week, a Circan would barge in and demand some trinket or service without pay, but other than the continual obligation to feed and bivouac the occupation, the people of Etser moved about unmolested. The Circans seemed inclined to rule peaceably.

Loana took fresh flowers to the grave each morning. Soon the fall wind would whip the petals from their moorings and scatter the seeds for next season's wildflowers, and the bulbs would sleep in the earth till spring summoned them forth again. She would keep flowers there, while she could, and evergreen boughs after. Often she climbed the hill with Aaron strapped to her back in the heavy sling Martseah had made. Today he was sleeping. She came alone. Eshed and Haman were about, and she could savor the peaceful surroundings, undisturbed.

It seemed a space in which to pray. The hilltop was becoming a retreat for her. It was not only Iysh's resting place but, in a sense, hers as well. For hadn't she met the Christ here? She was still seeking a way to tell Eshed. To let him know that since Iysh's death she had come to understand, in a unique way, all that he had been sharing with her for so long.

Silently, head bowed, she sat little-girl fashion before Iysh's grave and gave thanks . . . for him, for Eshed, for Aaron, for knowing the Lord of her life. The air seemed incredibly fresh and alive, and every tree sighed agreement that life was good and hope eternal.

Standing, she carried a handful of apricot and crimson shaded anemones, the last of the season, and placed them on the grave of "the girl." No one, it seemed, had cared for her in life. Perhaps she could do something for her in death. How strange it was . . . that she felt a bond with this poor wretch. When Eshed had first told her of the encounter in the temple, she would have gladly torn her eyes out! Now . . . now . . . it was all different. Not because the girl was dead. It was because she had never really lived!

Loana turned her eyes again to the abundant offering on Iysh's grave. The thought struck her suddenly that in these two cuts of earth, she saw herself. The old self was much like the girl, attracted to earth and its lures, bound by the misbegotten concept that she served the living God by serving in the temple and sacrificing all that she was, in her flesh, to that end. She shuddered as the similarity struck her full force.

In the new self emerging, Loana was Iysh—openhearted and openhanded toward the living God. Receiving and giving only that which he desired. A vessel—wasn't that what Eshed had called it? A vessel for the Holy Spirit's habitation. Just as Jesus had died in his body . . . wasn't there much dying of self in this faith . . . to be resurrected in Spirit with him? And one day in the body as well?

CHAPTER 30

Olives plopped into the basket, thick green ovals against brown netting.

Eshed pulled himself through a fork in the tree and stretched for the highest branches, plucking the fruit that Haman could not reach. He wiped his forehead on his sleeve. Thirsty. Just a few more clusters and he would come down for a drink.

Haman would soon need feeding—and Aaron, too. *Why is Loana gone so long?* He wasn't hungry, as the others would be, but he felt a great need of her all the same.

Everywhere he looked, he saw Iysh. In the marketplace he had been startled, just yesterday, by a look-alike buying wares at Martseah's stall. Even one of the Circans, unhelmeted, washing his face at the watering trough, had looked like the aborigine! He supposed it was normal, they had been together so much of late. Emotionally, he had not relinquished his joyful comrade. And Loana was so preoccupied these days—was she grieving, too? He had found himself looking at her more than usual. There seemed a great peace—almost a joy—about her. Yet the mention of Iysh brought tears to her eyes as well.

He stowed the basket and trudged up the hill to get her. Life seemed so difficult of late. With the temple gone, a whole new order had to be established to accommodate the Circan occupation. He had hardly found time to be grateful for the sparing of Etser—its dwellers and buildings intact, for the most part—or to make the myriad decisions that each day brought. Trifling matters, it was true, but all demanding to be honored equally. Disruption of order had always troubled him. Its cumulative effect was a sense of powerlessness. Yet, his mind chided him for the untruth of that. Hadn't his Lord given grace for every situation?

Coming upon the grave site, he heard the twittering of a small clutch of birds in the top of a tree. The clear sparkle of the morning was having its effect on them. *Am I so different?* The next thing that cut into the gloom he was carrying about his ears was the sight of Loana. She was bent low near the cross at the head of the grave. No . . . she was praying! He had never seen her pray before. Not like this. He paused, not wishing to disturb her. Shortly she sensed his presence and lifted her head until she was half-facing him.

He smiled a long, slow smile—the first she had seen since Iysh. She flashed one in return. Uprooted, he strode to her side. She stood, raising her eyes to his, and put her arms about his neck. Eyes shining, she formed the words, "I know . . . I *know*." His impulse was to shout—to toss her in the air as he had before in moments of pure elation. Instead, they clung to each other for a space, tears in their eyes. He felt transported beyond any joy earth could hold. And so did she. He buried his face in her hair, then, gazing at some nameless point over the low hills of Etser Valley, he said simply, "Thank you, Lord. Oh, how can I ever thank you, Lord?

Bargaining continued unabated in the shops and stalls of Etser. Abahlia plunged her hands into a bin of wheat burrs and let the individual grains trickle through her fingers thoughtfully. She hoped her garden grains would be more abundant next season. For now, she would purchase some for grinding and some for planting.

"I want a measure of this." She held a gourd scoop of it

aloft. The tradesman nodded and began scooping it into a cloth sack. Hanging a metal weight on one side of the scale, he lifted the partially filled sack onto the other disc.

Loana knotted a small sack of seeds onto the leather thong of her belt. "Shall we see Martseah, now?" she asked, giving the seed sack a tiny thump. "I do not see how he can refuse your thong belts. I really like mine! When did you make them?" Loana shifted the baby sling on her back to a more comfortable position—Aaron was getting heavier.

Abahlia carried her seed sack, of a good weight, to the horse tied outside and roped it about the animal's neck, resting it on its shoulders. "While we were hidden away in a small sheep tender's shelter in the hills," she whispered. "Sarakabel gave me the idea in Ohad, and I had been wanting to try it ever since." She pulled a cloth wrap of them from a pouch the animal was carrying.

Loana shook her head. "You are amazing. You can get things done under the most trying conditions!"

"Waiting day after day in those cramped quarters made me fidgety. I had to do *something!* There were some odd scraps of leather in the shack, and Nebak got the thistles for me by night. After working with it awhile, I talked Martseah out of some good leather to make these. He said if they fit well he would sell them for me. Did you know these thistles color beautifully with berry stains? If these sell well, colored belts should do even better . . ." Abahlia turned quickly on her slender ankle to head into Martseah's and stopped short, her face draining of color.

"What is it?" Loana asked, touching her friend's arm. Abahlia's eyes were wide, and she was struggling to find her voice. Loana turned slightly and saw a Circan soldier regarding them a few steps away. Lounging against a stall post, he was whittling a piece of wood with his knife. His shaggy brows only partly hooded his eyes, which were

shifting now from Abahlia to Loana. "Do you know him?"
Loana said under her breath. Abahlia shook her head negatively, her eyes fastened to his hands and the knife in them.
He nodded in their direction with more than passing interest, his attention still riveted on Loana's profile.

"Come—step inside!" Loana urged her. Abahlia seemed
to be rooted to the spot. Aaron began to wriggle, his face in
the sun. Loana grabbed Abahlia by the shoulders and, spinning her around, ushered her into the first doorway she
found open. She took both Abahlia's icy hands in her own.
"Abahlia—you look like you have seen a ghost!" she hissed,
trying to bring some response from her normally ebullient
friend.

"I . . . I . . ." she mumbled, and she began to sob softly.
Loana perused the room for a place to sit and saw some
cushions in the corner. It was not a shop they had planned
to visit, but no matter. Women were milling about, pulling
at cloth bolts and small items of brass—household things—
and no one seemed to notice the two of them huddled on
the cushions. "Did he—the Circan—make you remember
the attack you suffered?" Loana asked gently.

Abahlia nodded, numbly.

"I am sorry." Loana thumbed a tear from Abahlia's
cheek. "It is all over . . . you know that . . . no one is going
to hurt you . . ."

"I am not afraid . . . it is just that I have tried so hard to
forget . . . and it seems I really haven't," she said. She had
just become comfortable again at night, warm once more to
Nebak's touch. She didn't want anything to threaten that.
She wanted a child, more than anything. And she wanted to
please her husband. How could she when this paralysis of
fear was descending upon her again?

Loana, as if reading her thoughts, said, "Right now . . .
let's pray!" They bowed together in silent agreement. No

one seemed aware of their conversation. The buzz of the stall droned on, weaving in and out of their silence. In a few moments, Loana was able to coax Abahlia out of the stall and on to Martseah's. The centurion, as luck would have it, was gone.

"I am so grateful that you were with me today," Abhalia told Loana while they were waiting for a word with Martseah, pressed in among the customers in his stall.

Smiling sweetly, Loana squeezed her arm.

The crisp fall air had invested a chill in the L-shaped room. It could well serve as a cooling room for milk and fish. Loana shivered as she arranged brightly-colored cushions near a sun-filled window. She made a note to sit near that window. She had never acclimated completely to the cool air currents that frequently invaded them from Protos.

A hum of voices was rising outside the front stoop, and she knew it signaled Abahlia and Nebak's arrival—and probably that of Martseah, Naveh, and red-haired Ariel as well. The polished cedar floor gleamed under her sandal steps as she crossed to meet them through her kitchen entrance.

She was in for a surprise.

Abahlia's head tilted as she eyed the tall, stocky frame of a man Loana did not know. A slender woman, older than Abahlia but somehow like her, held his arm, and three young boys, one of them Ariel, scampered among the bushes about the doorway. Another gentleman, with the arm-draped toga of an aristocrat and bowed legs like a sturdy tree trunk shaped in the wind, chatted with Nebak and the effervescent Namath. Martseah was helping a young woman from her horse. When she touched ground, her sun-spotted curls showed a few shades lighter in deep red beside Naveh's as they spoke together. She showed

Naveh the contents of her travel bag. "Do you think she will like it?" she asked, and Naveh nodded, her eyes shining and her lips parted in a mysterious smile.

"Ah . . . here is the mistress of Kerielan now!" Martseah's tongue stumbled over the term. With the invasion of the Circans, a new regime was taking over their lives, and the old order was passing rapidly away. Titles were becoming meaningless. The Circans, however, seemed only a tool in the leveling, not the real cause. Eshed peered through the curtain of the front stoop, pulling the blue-edged cowl in place about his neck. Martseah's voice repeated the names for Loana: "Ardon . . . his wife, Sarakabel . . . this is Tasia . . . Heli—settle down, Zetema! You and Ariel keep one another going too long! The noted physician who failed to save my life, Appelles." A ripple of laughter ran through the group as Appelles made a courtly bow before Loana.

Striding quickly to the L-shaped room, Eshed was fussing with some scrolls when the group entered. This was the first "official meeting" in their home, and he was having trouble getting into the mood. With no incense, no candles, and only the cowl remaining of his vestments, he felt somehow unprepared.

Tasia and Loana lingered behind the others, poking at the contents of Tasia's travel bag. Tasia pulled a string of freshwater pearls from the bag and placed them about Loana's neck.

"Thank you! But why?" Loana flushed, overwhelmed by the gift from someone known only through Eshed's scanty accounts.

"Someday . . . soon . . . I will tell you how meeting Eshed changed my life," Tasia whispered, her eye on the profile of the young priest. The two women seated themselves by the window and gave him their attention.

Where was Simonus? Eshed watched the doorway for

his entry, uncertain of how to open this meeting. He was torn between offering the old liturgy and simply welcoming all his friends with an embrace. It was a long interval since having seen Sarakabel, Ardon, and Tasia. He smiled at her red-gold head in the sunlight and Loana, who sat beside her fingering her new necklace. Tamar sat down by them, a tiger-striped kitten in her hands.

"Ble-ah! Ble-ah!" One of Simonus' nannies skittered onto the polished floor with Simonus in hot pursuit. Unaccustomed to the slick floor, the big man slipped and fell sprawling while the little goat pattered aimlessly about the room, her eyes wide and her nostrils flaring. The gathering exploded in laughter. Eshed scooped the goat into his arms and held her up for all to see, a twinkle in his dark eye.

"Friends," he exclaimed as the noise trickled to a stop, "meet Nan. She became a close companion when we hid out in the hills." The goat's ears dangled humorously as she gazed, somberly, upon the crowd. "She has opened the meeting for us today." She turned her fuzzy head and nibbled at Eshed's hair. "Need I say more?"

Simonus smiled broadly and brushed himself off as he strode forward to collect the animal. Nebak and Tamar were laughing convulsively on the back row where Tamar was retrieving her startled kitten. The fluff ball scrambled up her shoulder, big-eyed, hackles raised. Haman, nestled in the corner, roused momentarily from his dozing and smiled foolishly. This room seemed always to inspire him to naps. Serena hissed loudly in his deafened ear, "Ever seen anything like that?" Haman wagged his head and drowsed off again.

The goat was thrust outside to find her way home. Eshed greeted Sarakabel and Ardon with an embrace and exchanged a few words with Heli, tousling his curly head. Zetema and Ariel were too busy scuffling to notice much else. As Eshed returned to the front to speak, Ardon seized Zetema with a big hand round his middle and dropped him into his lap, puppy style.

Eshed held up his hands for silence. "I had prepared a special message for you today . . ." No need for candles— the light on their faces would emblazon the darkest room. "But instead, I am going to talk to you about love and acceptance." His eyes roamed the room and rested momentarily on Tasia. "The sort of love that needs no reason . . ." He cleared his throat. He caught the glow of pride on Loana's face as she watched his every move. "It is love for love's sake."

A clang of metal interrupted his speaking. All heads turned toward the door. Sulao entered, armored, chin flap on his helmet dangling. Faces paled. Sarakabel leaned instinctively into the hollow of Ardon's shoulder, and his arm surrounded her protectively. Zetema's big eyes ogled Sulao over Ardon's spare shoulder.

"Welcome!" Eshed addressed the centurion. He alone did not seem startled by this interruption. He had not thought their meeting would go unrecognized as Sulao made it his business to know everything that went on in the village. Still . . . he had not expected him so soon. Eshed's eyes swept the assemblage with reassurance. They turned to listen to him.

Sulao nodded and beckoned two aides to stand by the door. They clanked into place and fixed their eyes straight ahead. Sulao sat on a bench near the rear, removing his headgear. The metal of his breastplate sent little arcs of light about the room as the sunlight from the window bathed it. His eyes made an appraisal of the room and its guests. *Strange.* In this room an air of levity and warmth prevailed. Such things, if present at all, were usually erased by his entry. One of the things he disliked about his job was the effect of fear he had on any gathering. Some men thrived on it . . . to Sulao it was a necessary evil.

Eshed had been speaking for several minutes when Sulao's ear tuned in. "Love, as we share in it, should bear any load put upon it and shoulder responsibilities not rightfully ours, as we have witnessed in our dear brother . . . Iysh." Eshed paused, a catch in his voice. Sulao's head went down at the mention of Iysh's name. When it lifted again, a strange light was in his eye, and a softening of the heavy-boned brow was noticeable.

"I have no more words today." Eshed surveyed the faces of his friends. "Would anyone else care to share some thoughts with us?"

The group sat silent. Chained to the old liturgy, they felt a barrier to participating. Only the reading of the old scrolls by the elders had been an acceptable departure in the past. Men shuffled shoe leather and women rearranged the colored weave of their skirts, their eyes avoiding Eshed.

"I do! I have something to say!" Abahlia jumped to her feet. Her cheeks blazed. Women had not been permitted to speak in the temple, and she was unsure of her reception.

Eshed was taken aback momentarily. He recovered quickly amid whisperings in the group. "Of course, Abahlia. What is it?" Only Nebak looked at ease with the new wrinkle Abahlia had presented. He smiled broadly—as though a great honor had just been conferred upon him.

"It is about freedom . . . the way we have become free." Her eye caught Sulao's face, which revealed a strange mix of amusement and consternation.

"Free? What is she talking about?" Whispers went about the room.

"Oh, I know we are a captive nation." Her fingers fluttered nervously in front of her. "But in Christ, we are free—

indeed. Let me explain." She shook her head at the continued exchange between Sarakabel and Serena.

"She never has known her place, you know!" Serena babbled her amazement. Sarakabel shrugged.

Her cheeks two red splotches that could be seen throughout the room, Abahlia continued. "Before we were captured, I had . . . a bad experience . . . at the hands of one of the Circans." She choked as she recalled that time. "And when the Circans came here, it was especially frightening to me." Her eyes probed Sulao's face. She was saying dangerous things, she knew, but there was no other way! "But Loana . . ." Her eyes warmed as she turned to face her friend. "Loana gave me assurance that in faith I could overcome my feelings and fears . . . and . . ." She smiled at Nebak, her hand unconsciously resting on her slightly bulging waist. "I have, praise Yahweh! I *have!*" Tears trickled down her face now, becoming a stream. Loana moved swiftly to her side and embraced her, exultant over her participation and the news she expressed.

The murmuring group moved out the doorway past the Circans—as if they were not there. Abahlia's speech had made overcomers of them all in that brief instance. *The young woman has courage . . . and they must have courage, too, for all that lies ahead,* Eshed reflected, sharing in the embrace Loana was extending to Abahlia.

The intimacy of the moment with the two women crowded from his awareness the lone figure who had remained behind in the room. Everyone else had moved out into the sunlight. The Circan guards had been dismissed. Even Haman had roused himself from the corner and stumbled outside, his crackly voice greeting the others as though they had just arrived.

"Sulao!" Eshed noticed him at last.

The physical tower of strength that was Sulao seemed

smaller somehow. His shoulders drooped, and his aura of assurance had departed with his men.

"I would like to talk with you . . ." He hesitated. Loana's protective instinct went up, but one glance at Sulao's face told her that her husband had nothing to fear from this man—not any more. She urged Abahlia outside, leaving the men alone.

In a hushed, young boy's voice, the warrior faced Eshed. "Can you explain something to me?"

"I will try . . ." Eshed removed the cowl from around his neck and, folding it carefully, tucked it under one arm.

"What is going on here? I mean . . . my eyes tell me what is going on—but what is *really* happening to these people," he asked, "that is *not* happening to *me?*"

Eshed took him by the arm, and they walked together toward a sunbathed corner. "Let me begin by telling you about Choikos . . . and the man Iysh . . ."

APPENDIX
Cast of Characters

Names have been contrived to express something about the characters' personality, character, or lifestyle and, in many instances, have been derived from two or more root words from the Hebrew, Greek, or Latin languages. Since originally all names began this way, and biblical names are based on this tradition, the interpretations may be of interest to the reader.

HEBREW CHARACTERS

Aaron (air'un) *gathering*

Abahlia (u bawl yuh) *willing*

Ardon (arr'dun) *roaming*

Aridatha (air i daw' thuh) *Son of Haman*
  (not related to Etser's Haman)

Ariel (air'ee uhl) *lion of God*

Barak (bair'ak) *to bless God*

Beryth (bair'ith) *a Schemetich deity*

Boris (bore'is) *tiresome*

Checed (ched'said) *mercy*

Cheselia (chez sell'yuh) *beautiful oak*

Daman (day'mun) *to refuse to consider*

Elidad (ell' i dad) *God has loved*

Elnah (ell'nuh) *these pleasant places*

Eshed (esh'ed) *an outpouring*

Haman (hay'mun) *to destroy; be faithful*

Iysh (ee'sh) *to show oneself a man*

Jacel (jay'sul) *goodly patriarch*
Jarad (jair'ad) *an antediluvian man*
Jeremiah (jair eh my'hyuh) *trodden hundreds;
    of goodly weight*
Jessia (jess' ee uh) *a female Hebrew*
Josiah (jo sigh'uh) *Jehovah supports*
Kamar (kuh mar') *to be deeply affected
    with passion; to yearn*
Laban (lay'ben) *white maker of brick*
Loana (lo wahn'uh) *praying throat*
Mala (mowl'uh) *trespass*
Marissa (muh riss'uh) *bitterly sown*
Martseah (mart say'uh) *an awl*
Namath (nay'muth) *great oracle; friends*
Naveh (nah'vuh) *comely*
Nebak (nay back') *to burst forth*
Nebow (nee'bow) *a Babylonian deity*
Pala (pah'luh) *to accomplish miracles*
Raphel (ruh fell') *God has cured*
Ria (ree'yuh) *to look on*
Samantha (suh man'thuh) *merriment*
Sarakabel of Arag (suh raka'bell of air'ag)
    interlace; meadow; weaver
Serena (sair een'uh) *harsh axle*
Seth (sehth) *appointed*
Sheila (shee'luh) *to be secure*
Simon (sigh'mun) *weak-willed*
Simonus (si mo'nus) *empowering*
Tabeel (tuh beel') *pleasing to God*
Tamar (tu mar') *city of palms*
Tasia (tas' ee uh) *adversity; bait*
Tobias (toh by'us) *a goodly man*
Zerach (sair'ack) *an Ethiopian prince*
Zerubabel (zer oo baw bel') *born in Babylon*

GREEK CHARACTERS
Appelles   (uh pell'us)   *a Christian*
Drusilla   (drew sill'uh)   *a member of the Herodian family*
Heli   (hell'ee)   *my God*
Proustia   (prow'stee yuh)   *meek*
Sophia   (so fee'yuh)   *worldly wisdom*
Sulao   (soo lay'oh)   *to despoil*
Telles   (tell'us)   *conclusion; telling act*
Zetema   (zuh tee'muh)   *search; question*

LATIN CHARACTERS
Aragon   (air'uh gawn)   *arrogant; from the province of Aragon*

PROVINCES
Kerielan   (car ry'ay lawn)   *tree of the Palestinian mountain*
Saramhat   (sa i ram'hat)   *deliver from power*

CITIES
Choikos   (choy'kos)   *dusty; earthy*
Eshkolia   (esh coal'ya)   *utter hollowness*
Protos   (pro'toz)   *before; foremost*
Spatale   (spuh taw'lee)   *to be wanton*
Trenz   (trenz)   *trend*

TOWNS AND VILLAGES
Balamia   (buh laim'yuh)   *a false piety; wrongdoing for gain*
Etser   (ett'set)   *treasure*   (Eshed's village)
Megev   (may'give)   *a measure of precious fruit*
Mezmerah   (mehz mair'uh)   *pruning hook*
Ohad   (o'had)   *united*
Rhantismos   (ran tis'mos)   *sprinkling*
Rimza   (rim'za)   *beyond the hills; over the rim*
Sukon   (soo'kawn)   *fig*

Tsalah (tsah'lah)   *timber*
Zebed (zay'bed)   *gift; dowry* (Loana's village)
Zerces (zur'sees)   *king's battle*

ABOUT THE AUTHOR

Kay Stewart is marketing director for Cooperating Authors Marketing Service and president of the Seattle chapter of the National League of American Pen Women. She has been both teacher and administrator in the area of early childhood education and was the first woman named district manager of multimedia sales for a major U.S. corporation.

She is a Bible study teacher, professional storyteller, puppeteer, composer, and vocal and Celtic harp soloist. She has published numerous articles and stories for children and teens as well as several on foods.

She lives in the Pacific Northwest with her husband, Don. She is the parent of two grown daughters and has two grandchildren.

Chariots of Dawn is her first novel.